LEGACY OF THE RUNES

Christina Courtenay

First published in 2024
by HEADLINE REVIEW
An imprint of HEADLINE PUBLISHING GROUP

2

Cataloguing in Publication Data is available from the British Library

ISBN 978 1 4722 9325 1

Typeset in 11/14 pt Minion Pro by Jouve (UK), Milton Keynes

Printed and bound in Great Britain by Clays Ltd, Elcograf S.p.A.

Headline's policy is to use papers that are natural, renewable and recyclable products and made from wood grown in well-managed forests and other controlled sources. The logging and manufacturing processes are expected to conform to the environmental regulations of the country of origin.

HEADLINE PUBLISHING GROUP
An Hachette UK Company
Carmelite House
50 Victoria Embankment
London EC4Y 0DZ

www.headline.co.uk
www.hachette.co.uk

To the lovely Word Wenches,
Mary Jo Putney, Patricia Rice, Susan Fraser King,
Anne Gracie, Andrea Penrose and Nicola Cornick,
with huge thanks
for your support and friendship!

VIKING RUNES SERIES – FAMILY TREE

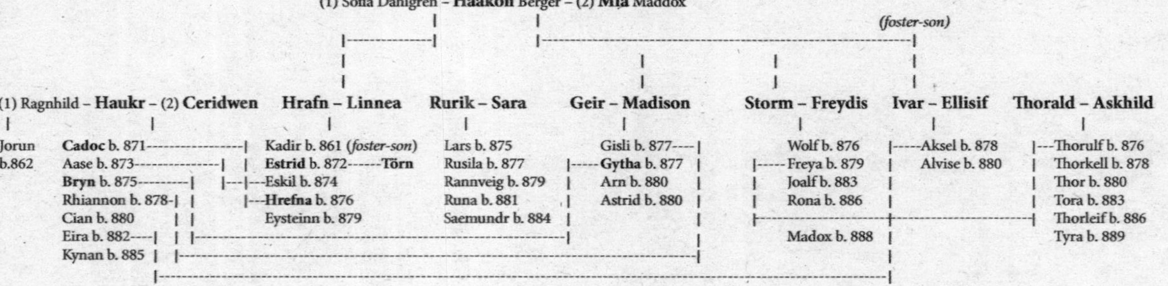

**** Couples marked in **bold** have had a published story*

**** Couples with lines connecting them are married*

Prologue

Langnes, Sogn (Western Norway)
Heyannir (August) AD *867*

'Why do I have to go? I don't *want* to leave!'

Freydis Úlfsdóttir stared at her mother, Dagrun, while trying desperately to hold her tears at bay. Her father had taught her to be strong and never cry. Having seen ten winters, she was old enough to use her emotions to fuel her actions instead. But it was so much harder to follow his advice when he was no longer there to support and encourage her. How was she supposed to cope without him?

'I told you why.' Dagrun sighed impatiently and propelled her daughter towards the ship that waited by the small jetty. 'My new husband doesn't want to look at a reminder of my previous marriage every day. This is his domain now. I'm sending your portion with you to be used as a dowry eventually. You have no further claim, you know that.'

'I never wish to marry! Father taught me to fight. Why can't I stay here and do that? You can keep the dowry.'

'Ridiculous! You are a girl and should behave as one. I don't know what he was thinking, filling your head with such nonsense,'

Dagrun grumbled, huffing slightly from the effort of having to push her recalcitrant child along the path. 'It's all very well being able to defend yourself if necessary, but you'll never be a warrior. Your place will be at home, looking after your future husband's household and your children.'

'But—'

'*Enough*, child! You cannot stay here. Bjarni is not a patient man and I fear he might do you harm. He has a temper on him, have you not noticed? With you out of the way, I can concentrate on soothing him as a wife ought. Otherwise he might turn on me as well. Is that what you want?'

Her new stepfather had always seemed even-tempered to Freydis, although he'd thrashed her once for not doing as she was told. She didn't blame him for that, though, as she had brought it on herself by disobeying. And she had never seen him raise his hand to her mother, but perhaps it was only a question of time. If it kept Dagrun safe, could she really refuse to do this? Her father would have wanted her to protect her mother as much as possible. It was her duty.

'Very well.' She swallowed down the misery.

'You should think yourself fortunate that my cousin is willing to take you in and raise you as his own,' Dagrun continued. 'Be grateful. Assur is a good man. If you're obedient and work hard, you'll thrive. Mind your manners and listen to your elders.'

'I will, but when can I come back?'

This farm near a small fjord was her home. The place where she had grown up and spent her happiest moments with a father who had treated her like the son he'd never had, teaching her to fight, hunt, fish and look after their domains. They'd done everything together from as far back as she could remember. She had thought she would inherit the farm and live here with a husband her father would choose for her. Now it all belonged to Bjarni through his marriage to Dagrun.

'I don't know. I will send word when it is safe. Now go, Freydis. My cousin's kinsman is waiting.'

They had reached the end of the jetty, where a big bear of a man stood. Wild, unkempt red hair and a huge beard made him look fearsome, but he bent to greet her with a smile and a twinkle in his eyes. That put her at ease somewhat.

'Greetings, little one. I am Joalf, and I will have the pleasure of escorting you to the Orkneyjar. Come on board, do.'

Freydis jumped over the gunwale easily and sat down on her chest of belongings, which must have been loaded earlier. She knew it was hers because it had her name carved in runes on the lid. Reading and writing was yet another skill her father had taught her, and she was proud of her proficiency. She also knew how to count and haggle for goods to best advantage. Perhaps one day this would come in useful.

She lifted a hand to wave at her mother, schooling her features into an expression of calm acceptance, directly at odds with how she was feeling. 'Farewell, Mother.'

Dagrun nodded. 'May the gods go with you.' Then she turned and walked up the path without waiting for the ship to cast off.

Freydis swallowed hard several times, but turned her head away so that no one would see. It hurt that her mother could dismiss her so easily, but they had never been close. Dagrun had despaired of her unwillingness to learn female tasks, and had often bemoaned the fact that she was allowed to run wild. It was something her parents had never seen eye to eye on, but now it was a moot point.

Her hands were shaking and she buried them in the folds of the *smokkr* her mother had forced her to wear. Underneath, she had on the tunic and trousers she was usually dressed in, which were more practical. As soon as the ship had moved out of sight of the settlement, she pulled the overdress off. She glanced defiantly at Joalf as she began to fold it, then stood up to place it in her kist.

'You have something against women's garments?' the big man asked mildly, one eyebrow quirking up. He looked amused rather than annoyed.

'Yes. My father raised me to be a fighter, not a girl. I cannot do that in skirts.'

Joalf nodded. 'Fair enough.'

With those two words, Freydis knew she had found a friend. Perhaps life with her mother's cousin would not be so bad after all. She would bide her time until she could return. Hopefully that would not be too long.

Chapter One

Dublin
April 2021

Storm Berger smiled and snaked a hand round the waist of the pretty girl who had just plonked herself down on his lap. He was in an Irish pub with some new friends he'd met during the ongoing Clontarf Viking Festival, held in St Anne's Park every year. They'd all taken part as re-enactors, showing off their skills fighting with Viking weapons during carefully staged mock battles. Now it was time to relax, and he was pleasantly buzzed from the strong ale he'd consumed. There was music, laughter and loud voices. The tang of beer and bar food hung in the air, and everyone was having a good time. The girl, whose name he couldn't recall right now, turned to wind her arms around his neck and gave him a sultry glance, then a kiss. She leaned back slightly to look at him, as if gauging his reaction, then smiled when he grinned at her.

Shona. Could that be right? Yes, he thought that was probably her name. They'd been introduced earlier, but he couldn't quite remember. He was about to show her what a real kiss with him would feel like when his mobile vibrated in his pocket. As she was currently sitting on top of it, Shona must have felt it too. She raised her eyebrows at him.

'Do you need to get that?' Her Irish lilt was incredibly alluring, and he almost asked her to repeat her question just so he could listen to her talk. But talking wasn't what either of them had in mind right now, and he shook his head.

'No, it can wait.'

He'd pulled her closer and pressed his mouth to hers, about to dive in properly, when the phone vibrated again. Swearing under his breath, he sighed and made a face. 'Sorry, I guess I'd better check in case it's an emergency.'

'Sure and I'll wait for you.'

Obligingly she lifted her bottom so he could reach his pocket. The caller ID said *Mum*, so Storm hit reply. 'Hello?'

'There you are! Is Maddie with you?' His mother's voice sounded high-pitched and frantic, and his heart gave an uncomfortable flip.

'No. She's at the hotel. Why?' He knew he sounded defensive. His sister, who at nineteen was younger than him by just over a year, had wanted to come with him this evening, but he'd told her he would take her another time. It was a bit lame, dragging your little sis along on a pub crawl with your new mates. She was socially awkward and he would have had to spend the evening keeping an eye on her. Usually he didn't mind, but tonight he'd just needed to let loose without having to worry about her. It still made him feel guilty.

'She's not here. Your dad and I just got back, and when she wasn't in her room, we asked the receptionist. Apparently she went out ages ago and hasn't come back. She's not answering her phone either. I was hoping she was with you.'

A feeling of dread began to build inside Storm's chest, and he stood up, gently pushing Shona off his lap. He mouthed 'sorry' at her, then strode through the pub and outside the door, where he could hear his mother better.

'I'm sure she's just gone for a walk or something. She'll be back soon.'

'Storm, it's after midnight! And as far as we're aware, she doesn't know anyone in Dublin. She should have been back ages ago.'

He tried to breathe slowly to stop the rising panic. His mother was right – this wasn't like Maddie. *Damn it all!* Why couldn't she have stayed put? Normally she'd be happy to just read a book or something. And he'd promised to take her out some other time. Surely she didn't expect to hang out with him every night? But she had been annoyed with him for ditching her, he could tell. Was this her way of taking revenge?

She had been his responsibility while his parents attended some fancy dinner for archaeologists. He should have made sure she was safe. That she didn't do anything stupid. Now he felt like a complete shit, but at the same time supremely irritated to have his fun ruined. If Maddie had done this deliberately, he was going to give her hell.

'Hang on. I'll come back and help you look. Let me just tell my friends I'm leaving.'

The evening was spoiled now in any case, so he might as well head off. He went in search of his new friends and told them something had come up and he had to leave. He promised to keep in touch. Shona sent him a confused look, hurt evident in her eyes, but he didn't have time to deal with her. It wasn't like he'd promised her anything anyway. He wasn't in the market for a girlfriend, just a good time. Clearly that wouldn't be happening tonight.

Their hotel wasn't too far, and he was there in minutes. He and his dad, Haakon, spent the rest of the night searching for

Maddie, but she was nowhere to be found. There was no trace of her or her mobile, which went to voicemail every time they tried calling. She had taken nothing but the clothes she'd been wearing – a Viking outfit she'd brought especially for the festival – and whatever was in the pouch hanging on her belt. As she had spent the day telling fortunes by casting the runes, she must have had those with her, but they wouldn't be much use in an emergency.

'Where the hell can she have gone? And why would she turn off her phone? It makes no sense. She's not that stupid.'

Storm was exhausted, both mentally and physically, from walking around for hours in the dark searching for signs of his sister. He'd accosted random strangers, showing them a recent photo of Maddie and asking if they'd seen her. They'd all shaken their heads, and each time, he'd sunk further into despair. The longer she remained absent, the more the sense of doom built inside him. He was finding it hard to breathe, his lungs squeezed ever tighter by a vice of fear. And the guilt was weighing him down, crushing in its intensity. She was so young, and still a bit naïve. She didn't have much experience with men – if any – and could perhaps have been taken in by some smooth talker. If only Storm had let her tag along, he could have prevented anyone from taking advantage of her. Protected her from predators just by letting everyone know she was his sister.

Damn it! He shouldn't have left her on her own.

'I don't know.' Haakon was pale in the dim glow of a nearby street light. His mouth was set in a grim line. 'Maybe her phone ran out of battery and she didn't have enough money for a taxi? She could be walking back from somewhere, or she's lost. Her sense of direction has never been the best.'

'True.' But they both knew that neither of them believed any of these theories. Storm could feel in his bones that something had happened. Something he could have prevented if only he hadn't been so selfish.

Haakon sighed. 'She usually tells us if she's off somewhere, but she didn't leave a note or a text message. Your mum has searched her room twice. There's nothing else for it – we'll have to report it to the authorities. We need help.'

They contacted the Garda – the Irish police – who helped with the search, but there was no sign of Maddie anywhere. It was as if she'd never existed.

After yet another long look around, helped by some of his new friends, who had called in the morning to ask why he'd left so suddenly, Storm threw himself onto his hotel bed and groaned out loud.

His sister had vanished, and it was all his fault.

Stockholm
September 2021

Storm wasn't massively surprised to receive a phone call from his parents telling him that his foster-brother, Ivar, was gone. That he had decided to try to time-travel to the ninth century, and had just upped and left without any warning. To tell the truth, he'd been expecting it for a while. And now it seemed it had happened.

Well, good for him.

'We found a hand-delivered note in our letter box this morning,' his mum was saying, sounding flustered over the phone. 'For goodness' sake, what was he thinking?'

'What exactly did it say?'

He'd suspected something was up, as Ivar had been acting very suspiciously, both at a recent family dinner and when Storm had visited his house the following day. He wasn't usually cagey about anything – he was a straight-talking kind of guy – so for him to sound vague and evasive had rung alarm bells. And the bear hug he'd given Storm when he'd left had felt final somehow. Extra fierce. But Ivar didn't answer to him, so he had chosen not to say anything. He doubted he could have swayed his brother if his mind was made up.

'Something about wanting to meet his ancestor. Thorald? He said that even though he has us, he's been feeling like he doesn't have any real family. That hurts, you know? I mean, your dad and I consider him our son, although obviously we're not actual blood relatives.'

'I'm sure he didn't mean it that way. He loves you.' Storm had no doubts about that whatsoever.

Ivar had been fourteen when his father had died and Storm's parents, Mia and Haakon, had more or less adopted him. That was the same year Storm was born, but despite the big age gap, the two of them had always been as close as real brothers. They loved each other fiercely. Recently, Ivar had lost his only remaining blood relative, and Storm could see how that would make a man stop and think.

It was understandable that Ivar would be curious. His father had owned a real Viking sword with an inscription that said it had belonged to a man named Thorald, who was apparently his direct ancestor. Strange and unbelievable as it might seem, their sister Linnea had time-travelled a few years ago, met and fallen in love with a Viking and decided to stay in the ninth century. She occasionally visited, and one time she had let slip that she'd met that particular man. Or someone called Thorald, in any case. Of course, Ivar's ears had pricked up. Storm would have been the same in that situation. Curious and excited. He'd want to time-travel too, if he had the chance.

'Yes, well, anyway, he's stolen some artefact from the

museum – a magical one, I assume. That's going to be mega embarrassing for your dad. And he's gone back in time to try and meet this ancestor.' Mia sighed. 'I hope he won't get hurt!'

'Mum, stop worrying. He's a grown man, strong and fit, and he can handle himself. Hell, he could beat the crap out of me any day, even after all the training I've done. And once he's satisfied his curiosity, he'll be back.' Hopefully.

And with any luck, the museum wouldn't hold the theft against him if he returned the magical object. Not that Ivar would be telling them what it could do. He would be wise to keep that to himself. The fact that time travel existed was a secret the entire Berger family guarded closely. They didn't want to end up as experiments in a scientist's lab, or find themselves famous and hounded by the press. Besides, none of them were sure if it was something that worked only for them. The magical items they had found so far appeared to be specific to each person, and didn't always function when used by others.

'I suppose you're right. And maybe he'll come across Maddie somewhere,' Mia added in a hoarse whisper.

And there it was – the guilt trip he'd been expecting any moment. Storm flinched.

It had been nearly five months, and Maddie was still missing. She hadn't been seen or heard from since that trip to Dublin back in the spring. She had simply vanished, as if into thin air, leaving no clues to her whereabouts. Just the thought of that made Storm's stomach muscles clench. He heard the unspoken accusation in his mother's voice. She held him responsible, no doubt about it. Both she and his father had been careful not to say anything outright, but they'd been quiet and withdrawn, and unconsciously tense in his presence. The looks they slanted him on occasion also told him plainly that deep down they blamed him for Maddie's disappearance. So did he, and he wasn't likely to forgive himself until she turned up, but he forced his mind to lock that subject away for now.

'It's just . . . No, never mind,' Mia continued. 'Don't ever become a parent is all I can say! It's the worst job in the world. You worry no matter how old your kids are . . . Wait, your dad wants a word.' There was a muffled noise as she handed the phone to Haakon.

'Storm? Did Ivar say anything when you went to see him yesterday?'

'No, he was just as he always is.' That was a lie, but he wasn't going to tell his parents about the hunch he'd had.

'And he seemed calm and rational?'

'Yes, of course. Ivar is nothing if not rational. Knowing him, he's been planning this for months. He's not like me. I'd go off on a whim and end up in all sorts of trouble.' Although come to think of it, that was probably something he should try to change.

'OK. Thanks.' It was Haakon's turn to sigh. 'Nothing we can do about it. It was Ivar's decision and he's a grown man. Will we see you tomorrow?'

'Yes, I'll be home in time for dinner. Bye, Dad.'

Storm was expected in a meeting within the next five minutes, but after disconnecting the call, he stood where he was for quite a while. His mother had brought up the elephant in the room – Maddie's possible whereabouts. He was sure they had all been thinking the same thing – that she too could have time-travelled – but no one had said it out loud before. They needed to have a serious talk about this, because it was time to do something, and soon. Ivar wasn't the only one who needed to go on a journey. If there was the slightest chance of finding his sister in the past, Storm had to look there. The guilt he'd felt the evening she vanished had only grown bigger for each day of her absence, until it was like a festering wound. He couldn't live with himself if he didn't make an attempt to exhaust every avenue in searching for her. And the ninth century was the only place they hadn't looked.

Although he was tempted to act immediately, he knew he had to be smarter than that. Planning wasn't his forte, but he was definitely getting better at it. He'd been in the Swedish army for two years, which had curbed some of his more impulsive tendencies. And now that he was training to become an officer, he was learning to be more organised and forward-thinking. He'd be damned if he couldn't be as methodical as his brother.

Starting tonight, he'd make a spreadsheet of what he needed to do. Everyone in his family believed him to be immature and not capable of taking anything seriously. Well, they were wrong. He'd show them he had finally grown up and would take responsibility for his actions. And he wouldn't rest until Maddie was safely back home.

'Have you heard anything from the Garda recently?'

Storm was sitting with his parents the following evening sharing a Chinese takeaway. Mia used to always cook for them whenever they had a meal together, but lately she hadn't been in the mood. With only three of them there, he couldn't blame her – the large kitchen table seemed glaringly empty.

'No, not since they sent us that report about Maddie's phone.' Haakon shrugged, his expression bleak.

Her mobile had never been found, and was presumed lost, but police technicians had been able to access the phone records. The last thing Maddie had done was to Google the tidal movements of the Liffey. And the Garda had found some grainy CCTV footage showing her passing one of the bridges over the river. They'd told the family that there were steps leading to the water's edge nearby at low tide, and tentatively suggested she might have gone down there, only to be dragged in and submerged when the water came rushing back.

'So we know she probably went down to the river, and maybe lost her phone there,' Storm said. 'I don't buy the fact that she could have drowned. For one thing, the tide didn't turn until long into the night, by which time we were already out looking for her. And for another, if she did go into the water, her body should have been found by now.'

Mia shuddered visibly. 'It . . . it could have been swept out to sea.'

'Or she was attacked and abducted,' Haakon added quietly.

'Maddie? Never! Come on, Dad, you know she's a black belt in karate, and she's trained in all sorts of other martial arts. Kick-boxing, judo, taekwondo, you name it.' Ivar had had her trying everything to stop her being bullied at school. 'There's no way she would have let herself be captured without a massive fight, and someone would have seen that. Besides, she does tend to stand out in a crowd.'

Maddie wasn't just tall for a woman, but she had striking curly copper-red hair reaching almost down to her waist. It made her hard to miss.

Haakon sighed. 'I guess you're right.'

Storm put down his fork. 'Look, I think we all know what happened to her – she went back in time. She must have done. Although how, I have no idea. She never mentioned having a time-travel device. Where on earth would she have found one?'

'The festival?' Mia toyed with her food, as if she'd lost her appetite. 'Can you remember if anyone there was selling Viking artefacts? There could have been something old among them. You know, stolen or found by metal detectorists.'

'Perhaps. Anyway, it doesn't matter. I'm going to go after her,' Storm announced. 'As soon as I'm done with the officer training, I'll take a leave of absence.'

'What? No! Please don't. Anything could happen to you.' Mia's eyes pleaded with him, the anguish clear. 'I . . . I can't bear to lose you all.' A tear formed and rolled down her cheek.

Storm leaned over and hugged her. 'Mum, I have to. This is all my fault and I need to make it right. If I'm not too late . . .' He didn't want to voice the fears that plagued him nightly. That the things that could have happened to Maddie in the ninth century were potentially much worse than anything that might have occurred in the twenty-first. They all knew it, and had probably imagined it in lurid detail. 'Look, it's the only way, and at least you'll know where I am. And I will do everything in my power to return as soon as possible. Besides, Linnea will come for a visit soon, I'm sure. And Ivar will probably be back before you know it too. I mean, how long does it take to find one ancestor?' He smiled, trying to lighten the mood a little, but his attempt fell flat so he added in a more serious tone, 'I promise I'll be careful.' He looked at Haakon, whose mouth was set in a grim line. 'Dad? Back me up here.'

Haakon shook his head. 'I don't know, Storm. You can be a bit reckless, and . . . your mum and I would worry.'

The fact that they hadn't noticed the changes in him since his sister's disappearance made Storm clench his teeth together, but he refrained from pointing out that he was doing his best to act responsibly. He hadn't done a single reckless thing since that night.

'I'll be fine. We can't afford to wait any longer.' He decided to spell it out for them to make them understand they had no choice. 'She could be suffering somewhere. Kept as a slave. Abused.' He saw his mother shudder. 'I know we don't want to acknowledge this, but we're talking about the Viking age here. Things were different then. There was no such thing as basic human rights if you were a thrall.' He held up a hand. 'I'm not saying that's what's become of her, but if it has, I can do something about it. She's strong, she will have survived this long no matter what, but I have to go now, before it's too late. There might still be a trail to pick up, but if not, I'll come straight back, I swear.'

They both looked shaken and unhappy, but finally nodded their acceptance. Storm was glad, because he'd been planning to go in any case. It was so much better to have their blessing. They had been blaming him for Maddie's disappearance, even though they'd never tell him so to his face, and he had to make things right. He was the one who'd left her alone. It was his fault she'd been angry enough to leave the hotel on her own.

He had to be the one to go after her.

Dublin
October 2021

'Thanks for letting me crash on your sofa for a couple of days.' Storm slapped Cian's shoulder and smiled at him. The guy was a Viking re-enactor, just like himself, and was one of the new friends he'd made back in April when he was in Dublin with his parents and Maddie for the Viking Festival. They'd hit it off big-time, which was one of the reasons he'd been on a pub crawl instead of hanging out with his sister when she had disappeared.

It was something he'd regretted ever since.

'No worries, man, you're welcome any time. We'll go meet up with the others a bit later on, but in the meantime, you said you wanted help with something?'

Storm shrugged out of his jacket and placed his backpack on the floor next to the sofa. 'Yes. Last time I was here, you mentioned that you guys sometimes . . . er, find real Viking artefacts on the internet?'

The Irish re-enactors had shown him a few of their weapons,

and he'd been impressed and appalled in equal measure. As the son of an archaeologist and a museum curator, he knew full well that buying proper antique items on the black market was a despicable practice. Illegal, and one he definitely shouldn't be encouraging or participating in. But he'd drawn a blank at finding a magical object for time travelling any other way, and this was his last hope. So far, the devices used by other family members had all been ancient Viking artefacts either found in a museum or dug out of the ground. Storm didn't have access to anything like that legally, but there had to be one out there somewhere, he just knew it. If this was the only way to find it, so be it.

'Sure, yeah. What are you after?' Cian didn't seem fazed at the question. He clearly saw nothing wrong in this trade, which was lucky for Storm. He'd rather not have anyone question what he was doing.

'I don't know exactly, but some kind of weapon maybe? That would be awesome. I'll know it if I come across it,' he hedged. He needed to check each and every object to see if it had an inscription of any kind. A particular sentence written in runes that acted as some kind of spell or magical formula. All the other time-travel devices had had the same words, so nothing else would do. 'If you could just point me in the right direction, I'll spend some time browsing until it's time to go out.'

'No problem. Here, you can use my laptop. Give me a sec, I'll find the right sites for you. There are a couple of good ones that I use.'

Cian deftly navigated his way into forbidden internet sites. Storm guessed they were somewhere on the dark net, a place he'd never ventured and wouldn't have known how to access. It made him feel vaguely queasy that he was about to do something illegal, but he had no other way of finding what he needed. This was his last resort, and he was becoming desperate, because time was of the essence. It might already be too late, but he refused to acknowledge that.

'There you go. Have at it! I've got some work to do, but I'll come and give you the heads-up when it's time to leave.'

'Thanks, man, that's great.'

He settled down to scroll through the various items on offer. There appeared to be an awful lot of them, and he wondered if they were stolen goods, looted from museums and archaeological sites, or just stuff found by amateur metal detectorists. Either way, he had his work cut out finding what he was looking for among all this.

By dinner time, he'd had no luck, but he made sure he didn't drink too much and was back at the screen once Cian had gone to bed. Towards early morning, his eyes were beginning to hurt and he was squinting badly, but at last he found a promising item: *Inscribed Viking axe head with modern reconstructed wooden handle/shaft. Iron with silver inlay. Good condition. Probably late ninth century.*

Clicking through to the close-up photos, he saw a beautiful axe with intricate patterns picked out in silver. Definitely Viking in style, and hopefully authentic. A tingle of excitement raced through him when he spotted the inscription. He zoomed in and peered at the screen. There were a couple of runes that were too faint to make out, but because he knew what he was expecting it to say, it was possible for him to read the whole sentence. Lately he'd practised both his Old Norse language skills and how to decipher runes.

'*Með blōð skaltu ferðast*,' he whispered, then punched the air with his fist. 'Yessss!'

This was it, his passport to the past, and hopefully to Maddie. She must have found something similar and travelled back in time. There was no other explanation for her disappearance and long absence. At least not one he wanted to acknowledge. He simply couldn't rest until he found her – the guilt was eating him up inside. He should have been looking after her when she'd gone missing. He'd been selfish and left her to her own devices. And then she was gone.

Most people would have assumed she'd been abducted, perhaps by a serial killer, people trafficker or other sick person. That would be the logical conclusion, despite the lack of evidence, and the horror of it had lurked in his mind from time to time. But in the Berger family there was another alternative. One modern authorities would never credit. Well, he wouldn't rest until he could find out for sure. He knew that she was tough and capable, but anything could have happened. She was his little sister and he couldn't leave her to fend for herself among Vikings any longer, if that was where she'd gone. He was going to damn well find her.

Clicking on the 'buy' button, he entered his credit card details and Cian's address. He hissed at the extortionate price, but he'd been prepared for that. He had planned everything meticulously, exactly the way Ivar would have done, and he was proud of himself for that as it was most unlike him. He had taken leave of absence from the army and had no plans to return any time soon.

It was time to go.

Chapter Two

Hrossey, Orkneyjar (Orkney Islands)
Gormánuðr (October) AD *875*

'Freydis, you are wanted in the hall.'

'What, now?' She feinted to the left to avoid the downward arc of Joalf's sword blade and danced away on light feet.

'Good,' the older man murmured. 'You're getting faster.'

The two of them were sparring in a field on the mainland, opposite the sea stack where Assur's hall and associated buildings were situated. Joalf had taken her under his wing from the moment she arrived and had been her pillar of strength. With no wife or children of his own, he had become her protector and mentor, carrying on her weapons training where her father had left off. At no time had he complained about the fact that she was a girl, unlike Assur and his wife Gyrid. They had forced her to wear female garments at all times, but she had compromised by secretly keeping her boyish attire underneath her *smokkr.* Whenever she practised with Joalf, she simply hiked the overdress up and looped it through her belt. That way her legs were free to move.

'Yes, *now*, Freydis.' Assur's son, Asmund, gestured impatiently for her to come with him.

'Very well. Perhaps we can continue later?' She looked at Joalf, who nodded.

'Best hurry. You don't want to keep *bóndi* waiting. Here, give me your sword. I'll clean and sharpen it for you.'

She had brought the sword her father had had made for her. It was smaller than a man's, but just as deadly. And she treasured it because it had been a gift from him. One day she hoped to make him proud while using it.

Following Asmund down a steep path to the rocky shore below, then up another one equally as precipitous on the side of the sea stack, she sighed inwardly. In all the years she'd been here – eight now in total – there had been no word from her mother. Nothing to say it was safe for her to come home or that she was needed. Occasionally Assur had news of Dagrun and her husband, and it sounded as if the man's temper was worsening with age. There were tales of harsh treatment of tenants and thralls alike, and Freydis worried about her mother. What sort of life was she leading? One of constant fear, or did she manage to tame the beast when they were together? She could only hope for the latter, although she couldn't help but wonder why the man had changed so much. The few months she'd spent living with him and Dagrun, she'd never seen any signs of an excess of violence.

She tried to smooth out the creases in her *smokkr* before entering the hall, but it was a vain endeavour. The best she could hope for was that they would think she'd been doing chores, although most likely they knew she had been training with Joalf. They disapproved, but hadn't outright forbidden it. She hoped they weren't about to do so now. It was good for women to know how to defend themselves in an emergency, everyone agreed on that. It was the fact that Freydis wanted to take things much further and learn all the skills of a warrior that was the problem. Just like her mother, Assur and his wife did not consider that necessary, and preferred her to concentrate on domestic matters. Throwing her two heavy plaits over her shoulders, she straightened her spine and stepped inside.

'There she is at last. What took you so long?' Assur groused.

'I'm sorry, *bóndi*. I was on the mainland and I came as quickly as I could.' She stopped in front of the chairs he and Gyrid were occupying. It felt as though she'd done something wrong and was about to be chastised, but for the life of her she couldn't remember any recent transgressions. 'Is something the matter?'

'Yes. No. We need to speak to you, that is all.' Assur scratched his scraggly, uneven beard as if he wasn't sure how to start. 'I'm sorry to have to inform you that the silver your mother sent us for your keep has run out. It is therefore time for you to be married off and the responsibility passed to your husband. We have done our best, but you have already seen eighteen winters. You're more than old enough to be wed.'

'I . . . I see.' Freydis frowned. She hadn't expected this. 'Shouldn't I be sent back to my mother and stepfather for them to decide my future spouse?' Surely it wasn't for Assur to do so?

The man shook his head. 'I sent to enquire and she said it was up to me. You're not to return. Ever.'

That statement was almost like a physical blow, and Freydis took a step back. 'Wh-what? Never? But I thought . . .'

Gyrid sighed, as if she was running out of patience. 'They wanted you out of the way. Why do you think you were sent here in the first place? Use your common sense, girl.'

Freydis clenched her fists and took a deep breath. 'Right. And there is no way I can earn my keep by helping out here?'

She'd thought that was what she had been doing. She worked as hard as everyone else, never shirking any tasks, however unpleasant. She'd even learned how to sew and cook, just to please Gyrid, although she still preferred to be outdoors.

'There's simply no room for you. Now that Asmund is set to marry soon, his wife and future children will be our main concern. And we have found a man willing to take you without a dowry.'

'But I have a dowry.' Freydis frowned. 'Mother said she was sending my portion with me. She must have given it to Joalf.' That wasn't something she was likely to forget, as the day she'd left was etched in her memory.

Assur again shook his head, as if she was deluded. 'That went towards your keep. It's all gone.'

Gone? Shock reverberated through her, but again she managed to keep it inside. It was a blow, no doubt about it, as she'd imagined she would have her pick of suitors, had she wanted to. Marriage had never been high on her list, though, and now she was to settle for someone who'd take her as she was. *Unbearable!*

'Who?' was the only word she managed to get out.

'Ingolf Gunnarsson.'

Freydis gasped. 'No! But he . . . he's been married several times before. And didn't his last wife jump off a cliff to escape him?' She was horrified, her innards frozen with fear. The rumours about Ingolf were everywhere in these parts. No one had a good word to say about the man, apart from the fact that he was handsome to look at and could charm anyone if he set his mind to it. A ruthless jarl whose main ambition was to rule over other landowners here on the islands, he stopped at nothing until he had his way. And his treatment of women was legendary, in the worst possible way. 'You cannot be serious.'

'Don't be ridiculous. It is all malicious gossip. The man is no worse than anyone else, and how is it his fault if he was married to some hysterical female? She was clearly not right in the head.' Assur dismissed her concerns with the flick of a hand, but something in his eyes told her he was bluffing. He'd heard the rumours too and gave them credit.

'Why him?' she ventured to ask.

He cleared his throat, as if he was uncomfortable. 'As you know, he came to our assistance last year after that storm decimated our flock of sheep so badly. We owe him our gratitude, and he said that instead of repayment, he'd be happy to marry you.'

'So in effect you are selling me to him.' She glared at the two of them. People who were supposed to look after her and have her best interests at heart, but who would be using her to escape a debt. She wasn't even their daughter. 'What if I refuse?'

'Then you will have to find some other way of supporting yourself. You will no longer be welcome here.' Assur's tone brooked no argument, and Freydis realised it was futile. She needed to speak to Joalf. There had to be something she could do to prevent this from happening.

'Ingolf will be coming for a visit in the next month or so, to finalise the arrangements,' Gyrid added. 'But we have plenty of time to make a few items for you to take with you. Linens and the like. And I will try to teach you more about household management. You must cease these silly bouts with Joalf. Now go, I will join you in a moment. We will begin with some cheese-making. That last batch you made was not as good as it should have been.'

Thus dismissed, Freydis turned to head outside. Too upset to be around other people, she pushed past Asmund, who threw her a sympathetic glance. It didn't help, because he wasn't in charge here. Not yet. And he'd never dare to oppose his father. He didn't have the guts. He was as much a pawn as she was.

Walking to the northern side of the sea stack, she stood close to the edge of the cliffs and stared out across the North Sea. It was incredibly beautiful, an endless expanse of blue and pewter that merged with the sky and clouds on the horizon. She'd often sat here and dreamed of the day she would return to her home, but apparently that had never been the plan. Her stepfather wanted her out of the way permanently, and no one cared what became of her. Except maybe Joalf, but he had no authority here.

It was hopeless.

Perhaps she ought to jump as well? No one seemed to want her anywhere. Not her mother. Not Assur and his family. Only Ingolf, a hateful man by all accounts. She lifted her chin. No, she would fight this somehow, but she had to make her plans in secret. Outwardly she would be the meek female they wanted, but they couldn't control her thoughts. And those were all of rebellion.

Dyflin
Gormánuðr (October) AD *875*

Storm had been told about the experience of time travel by both his sister, Linnea, and her friend Sara, but although he didn't doubt that they had done it, he was still filled with nervous tension as he prepared to attempt it himself. What if it didn't work? What if the axe he'd bought wasn't magical after all? Or perhaps only certain people were afforded the chance to travel through time, and he wasn't deemed worthy? By the time he actually tried it, he was jittery with nerves and had to take a moment to calm down using techniques he'd learned in the army, breathing deeply and clearing his mind. It almost felt like going into battle – or how he imagined that would feel, since he'd never actually taken part in a real one – and he needed to focus.

'Here goes,' he muttered, then cut the tip of his finger with the newly honed axe and recited the Norse words out loud. The effect was shockingly instantaneous – dizziness, morphing into a sensation of being cast into a whirling vortex, and extreme nausea. He had no idea how long this went on for, but eventually he blacked out.

He woke up fully expecting to be submerged in water, but

thankfully that wasn't the case. He had retraced his sister's last-known steps along the Liffey, and as it happened to be low tide, he'd decided to time-travel from its muddy shore. Naturally he didn't know whether the river followed the same course, or even where the tide would be when – or if – he arrived in the ninth century. He could have ended up right in the middle of it, but it was a risk he'd had to take. As he sat up and swallowed down the lingering nausea that always accompanied these magical journeys – or so he'd been told – he was grateful to find himself on dry land.

And it had worked! He had most definitely gone back in time.

He was sitting on the riverbank. The modern buildings and bridges were gone. Instead, along its edge, were a line of Viking ships and other assorted smaller vessels. There was no doubt about it – those distinctive sleek lines were unequalled anywhere else. He wanted to shout out with glee. *Actual Viking longships!* The re-enactor and history buff in him was jumping for joy and itching to go and check them out. As if that hadn't been enough to convince him, he saw men and women going about their business in the falling dusk, and they were dressed the same way he was. In Viking-age clothing. There wasn't a modern outfit to be seen anywhere. No cars, no high-rise blocks, no shops with large glass windows. There were only one-storey wooden buildings with smoke coming out of the gable ends, and a couple of fires further along the shore.

He had purposely chosen to time-travel at dusk. With a bit of luck, it would ensure that no one noticed his arrival, and he would also have time to familiarise himself with his surroundings without standing out too much. Brushing off the grass and mud from his trousers and tunic, he stood up and checked that he had all his gear. He'd come well prepared, with a sack of extra clothing, weapons hanging off his belt, and enough silver and gold to buy a small nation. He'd been buying plain, unmarked precious metal bangles and rings for months, amassing quite a collection, and he'd also found some authentic silver coins from the right period on the dark net, which he'd purchased as well. No need to advertise that fact, though, and he hoped he wouldn't have to defend himself against thieves.

As his eyes adjusted to the gloom of early evening, he wandered towards the nearest habitation. It appeared to be a large hut that sold ale. There were some raucous patrons sitting at tables inside, while others had spilled outside and were leaning against the walls. A game of dice was in progress at one table, and a fight broke out in another corner. Storm ignored both and walked up to a woman tapping ale into mugs from a large barrel.

'Pardon me, but is there somewhere around here I can find a bed for the night? I am newly arrived and do not know my way around.' He hoped his Old Norse was up to scratch – he and the rest of his family had been learning the language since Linnea married her Viking husband – but if not, they must get a lot of foreign visitors here, as the port was a hub for the slave trade.

The woman cast him a glance and began filling another mug before answering. 'Aye, if you carry on a bit further, there's Old Frida's. She lets people sleep in her hay barn for a bit of silver.' She looked him up and down, adding with a sly grin, 'Or you could always warm my bed for me.'

He suppressed the shudder that wanted to ripple through him. She wasn't old or ugly, but her clothing was filthy and worn, her hair unkempt, and she was missing a tooth. The word 'unsavoury' came to mind. There was nothing about her that would tempt him to touch her, but at the same time he didn't wish to offend her. He gave a non-committal smile and decided a white lie was in order.

'Thank you, but I doubt my wife would be best pleased if I did. My thanks for the directions.'

He didn't wait for her reply, but ducked out of the low doorway and strolled along the shore. A couple of times he stopped to admire the beautiful clinker-built ships, and to watch the comings and goings. He'd once helped to sail a reconstructed Viking ship, but seeing the real thing was still a thrill.

'I'm actually here!' he muttered, and couldn't help a grin from spreading across his face, despite the gravity of his mission.

He had been planning this for months now, and it was incredible that he'd actually managed it. The main obstacle had been finding a magical object to help him time-travel, but once he'd succeeded in locating that axe, everything else had fallen into place. The only problem had been to keep his plans a secret from Cian, but the guy was incredibly laid-back and didn't mind Storm staying with him until the axe arrived. As soon as it did, he'd told his friend he was heading back to Sweden. No one except for his parents would ever know differently. Once he'd changed into his Viking outfit, he'd stowed his bag in a locker at Heuston train station in Dublin. Hopefully, it would be safe there for the foreseeable future.

A group of urchins came running past him, and he recalled the real reason he was here. It wasn't to admire Viking ships, but to find his sister.

'*Hei!*' he shouted, and the boys stopped and waited for him to catch up. 'Can I ask you something? I'll give you a piece of silver to share if you answer truthfully.'

The children glanced at each other, then the tallest one nodded. 'We will. Ask away.'

'My sister came this way some months ago and I've lost touch with her. How would I go about finding someone who might have seen her?'

The boy shrugged. 'Lots of people come and go here. Wouldn't be easy.'

'She is very distinctive. Tall, with long curly hair of a vivid red colour. Definitely stands out in a crowd, so someone would have noticed her.'

'You should walk along the harbour here and ask the merchants. Some of them return regularly, so they might have been here and seen her.'

'Good point. And what about you lot? You're observant, are you not?' Storm knew that kids saw and heard much more than most adults gave them credit for. They were sharp-eyed and stored information like little sponges.

The boy conferred with his mates in hushed whispers, then turned back to Storm. 'None of us remember anything, but we could ask around for you. It'll cost you extra.' He held out his hand, and Storm fished a piece of silver out of his leather belt pouch. It was a quarter of a dirham – an Arabic coin: one of the ones he'd bought on the internet and which he'd cut into pieces.

'You can have more of that if you bring me useful information.'

The urchins' faces all lit up and they nodded as one. 'Where will we find you?'

'I'm told I can bed down at Old Frida's.'

'Yes, come with us and we'll show you the way.'

For their trouble, he gave them another quarter of the coin, and they promised to return as soon as they had any news for him. It was the best he could do for now.

Once he'd secured a place in Frida's hay barn with another piece of silver, he took a walk along the river. Whenever he came across a merchant ship or rowing boat, he stopped to speak to the owners. He asked the same question over and over again – had anyone seen a tall red-headed female six months ago. Unfortunately the answer was invariably no.

'If she was comely, she was probably sold as a thrall,' one man told him. 'Could have gone north, or more likely been taken to the south. The men around the Grikklandshaf are always on the lookout for women who don't have black hair. The fairer the better, and that goes for their skin as well. I've made huge profits there.'

His words made Storm shudder with revulsion. The trade in human beings was despicable in and of itself, but the fact that Maddie might have been one of the unfortunates sold that way was a chilling thought. The Grikklandshaf was what the Vikings called the Mediterranean. If she'd ended up there, he would have a hell of a job trying to find her.

'Damn!' he hissed to himself as he continued on.

In the end, he had to give up for the night as it was getting late. Since there were no street lights, the darkness was absolute, apart from the few fires that were still glowing. Before he lost his bearings completely, he returned to Frida's and bedded down for the night. He chose a spot against the wall and placed his possessions underneath the fragrant hay. He had no intention of being robbed on his first night.

The best thing about having been in the army was that he'd learned to sleep anywhere, and also that the slightest thing woke him instantly. When a hand was placed over his mouth and an arm wound round his neck from behind, he reacted instinctively. An elbow to the throat had his assailant gagging while trying to breathe past an Adam's apple that wasn't in the right place. A backwards kick also hit its target, and then a quick pull on the arm that was still around him had the man flipping into the nearest wall with a dull thud.

'*Stupid bastard*,' Storm swore in English, sitting up to make sure the would-be thief didn't have any accomplices. Fortunately he seemed to have acted alone.

Other people stirred around them, and there were some

mutterings, but no one came to his aid. The attacker was still trying to catch his breath. Having your Adam's apple bashed in was an unpleasant experience, but Storm had no sympathy.

'Get out!' he hissed. 'And don't come back. I'm a light sleeper, and next time I'll kill you.'

There was a little moonlight filtering into the barn through holes up near the eaves, and he saw the man's eyes widening in fright. Like a cockroach fleeing the beam of a torch, he crawled on all fours over the edge of the hay and then scarpered down a ladder. Storm swept the rest of the barn with a sharp gaze, but no one else was doing anything threatening. They were all there merely to sleep, same as him.

'Thank you for chasing him away,' someone said quietly. 'We would have been next.'

'You're welcome.'

With his fingers around the haft of the precious magical axe, he settled down to sleep again. It was fitful and light, however, as he was determined that no one was going to get the better of him. He wouldn't sleep properly until he'd found Maddie.

Chapter Three

Hrossey, Orkneyjar
Gormánuðr (October) AD *875*

'Do not even *think* about bringing that disgusting bird in here, girl! Leave it outside.'

Freydis reluctantly ducked back outside the weaving hut and held out her hand for her pet raven to step off. 'I'm sorry, Surtr,' she whispered. 'You'll have to sit out here while I try my best at weaving.'

'*Gwoark. Sorry. Sorry. Surtr is a good boy*,' the raven said.

'Yes, you are, but Gyrid doesn't appreciate you, I'm afraid.'

The large bird shook himself, as if disgusted at this turn of events, and hopped off her hand to perch on the roof. He made a noise deep in his throat that sounded more like a growl than cawing. It made her smile.

'I know, I know, but at least out here you'll have things to watch. And I'll bring you something to eat later. Now be good and don't attack anyone, please.'

She'd found him as a tiny chick near the cliffs two years previously. He'd been small, helpless and injured, and if she hadn't reached him first, he would have been devoured by a gull or some other large bird. He had been all alone, and she had assumed he'd fallen from his nest. There had been no way of resisting the little fluffy ball with a sharp, intelligent gaze. He had looked at her as if she was his saviour, and she'd accepted the job without hesitation, nursing him back to health. Assur and his wife had not been best pleased, but as always, Joalf had helped her. Together they had raised Surtr, and although his wing hadn't healed quite as it should, he was able to fly short distances. He still relied on them to feed him, though, and would never be able to fend for himself in the wild.

He usually came with her everywhere, but she could understand that Gyrid didn't want him near the looms, as he did have a tendency to defecate wherever he wanted.

She ducked inside, her eyes adjusting to the gloom. The only light came from the open door, and as it would soon be winter, it wasn't as bright as during the summer months. It was also cold, even though a small hearth piled high with smouldering peat gave out some heat.

'What are we making?' She tried her best to sound interested. Weaving was a tedious job, but it was better than sewing, which she was terrible at.

'A length of wool for a new *smokkr* for you. We need you to look your best for the wedding.' Gyrid pushed the shuttle through the warp and beat the threads into submission with her weaving sword, then moved the heddles – three horizontal bars at the front of the loom – with a swift efficiency Freydis had never quite mastered. 'Come, stand on the other side, then this will be much faster.'

They passed the shuttle between them and developed a steady rhythm. Freydis was grateful that at least she had been spared the process of creating the warp. The many threads that formed this were attached to the top of the upright loom and clay weights provided the necessary tension. Once it was set up, the weaving itself was fairly simple. You merely alternated the position of the heddles to produce the desired pattern. They were working on a herringbone twill, which was slightly more complicated than plain weave. This particular piece was two ells wide – approximately equal to twice the length between a man's elbow and the tip of his middle finger – and should be perfect for making a garment such as a *smokkr*.

After working in silence for a long while, Gyrid cleared her throat. 'I take it you were too young for your mother to have explained to you about the marriage bed and what your husband will expect of you? How to . . . er, make children, I mean.'

'She never spoke of it, no.' Freydis could feel her cheeks heating up.

'Well, you've seen the animals around here mating, have you not?' Gyrid wasn't looking at her, and Freydis realised the woman was as embarrassed as she herself was at having to discuss this. Presumably she felt it her duty to prepare her since Dagrun wasn't here.

'Yes. Are you saying it is the same for humans?'

'More or less. Except it is usually done from the front.' Gyrid's pale cheeks took on a red hue and she ducked her head, fiddling with the shuttle.

'Usually?' Freydis didn't understand, but perhaps that was just as well. However it was achieved, she didn't want to do it with Ingolf Gunnarsson.

'Yes, you'll see. It may be slightly . . . uncomfortable at first, but you will become used to it. As long as you don't try to fight him off. That would not be wise, as he'll have the right to do whatever he wishes. Try to be meek and obedient, that is my advice.'

Which merely proved that Gyrid didn't know her at all. *Meek and obedient? Hah!* Freydis had been a fighter all her life. It was a trait her father had encouraged and nurtured. How was she to submit to a husband she hadn't wanted in the first place?

No, there had to be another way. But what?

'What am I to do, Joalf? I can't possibly marry that man.'

Freydis was sparring with her mentor yet again, having successfully sneaked off to meet him on the mainland after finishing her chores for the day. Her focus wasn't really on the weapons training, however. It was firmly fixed on the unwanted betrothal, her mind going round in useless circles.

His mouth turned into a grim line, and he scowled. 'I don't know. You are certain you cannot go back to your mother and stepfather?'

'No, that is not possible. Assur said he had their blessing to choose a husband for me. They'll not go against his advice, else why would they have left it up to him?'

'True.' Joalf sighed. 'I could try to spirit you away from here, but it would be difficult at this time of year. The sea is treacherous from now until spring. It would be a huge risk to try and reach Skotland, especially as we'd have to attempt it in a small boat. I can't sail Assur's ship without the assistance of at least two men, even though it's not overlarge.'

Freydis's spirits sank, and she missed an easy opening, allowing Joalf to knock her sword out of her hand. 'Curse it!' she muttered, and flung herself down onto the grass, burying her face in her hands.

'Freydis . . .' Joalf's large palm settled on top of her head, as if he was trying to imbue her with his strength.

'It is so unfair!' she burst out. 'Why should I have to pay the price for Assur's debts? I know we're kin, but the relationship is not close. And he claims to have used up my entire dowry to pay for my keep. Surely that wasn't what it was for? I should have had my pick of suitors, had I wanted one. Now I'm supposed to settle for the most hateful man on the island.'

Joalf sank down next to her. 'I'll speak to him. Try to talk some sense into him. It might not do any good, mind, but I will do my best. If not, we'll think of something. Look at it this way – you're not a weak, helpless female, like Gunnarsson's previous wives. If the worst comes to the worst, you have strength and courage, and you can survive anything. Have I not trained you well?'

She leaned her head on his shoulder, affection for this gentle giant flooding her. 'You have, and I'm very grateful. Thank you. And you're right. Perhaps I will thrive as Ingolf's wife. If he hurts me, I'll hurt him back.'

'That's the spirit.' Joalf smiled. 'But I'll try to speak to Assur all the same.'

She could only hope he would be successful.

Dyflin
Gormánuðr (October) AD 875

Storm spent two days in fruitless searching. Asking endless questions and receiving negative answers in return. No one had seen hide nor hair of a woman of Maddie's description; it was as though she'd disappeared off the face of the earth.

Perhaps she had, and he was too late.

'No! I mustn't think like that,' he admonished himself. He couldn't give up so easily, but it was hard not to lose heart. She could be anywhere – a sultan's harem, a Viking jarl's estate, a Mediterranean vineyard, toiling in the hot sun . . . His imagination ran riot, but he reined it in. Speculating would only drive him mad. And he'd done enough of that during the months since she disappeared. Had imagined every possible scenario, then mentally flayed himself raw as he shouldered the burden of blame. He simply had to find her and make everything right again.

Dyflin was a bustling port, with a lot of comings and goings, so whoever had taken her could have merely been passing through. The static population didn't come into contact with everyone. Maddie was memorable, though, being so tall for a woman and with that untamed mane of long red curls. As he'd told his parents, Storm was sure she would have kicked up a huge fuss if anyone had tried to abduct her. He just couldn't imagine her submitting without a fight, and surely someone ought to remember that.

Returning to Old Frida's place at dusk on the second day, he was surprised to see the group of urchins he'd run into when he first arrived.

'Good evening. Come to try and earn some more silver?' he asked with a smile.

They were an appealing bunch, despite their worn clothing and grimy faces. He assumed they all had parents somewhere in the vicinity, otherwise they would have been sold as slaves by now. Their mothers probably despaired of them, as they should be out earning their keep rather than roaming the harbour. But perhaps they found odd jobs that way. Who knew?

'We've found someone who might help you,' the oldest said, acting as their spokesperson yet again. 'Come with us and we'll take you to her.'

'Her?' So far Storm had mostly questioned the menfolk. He hadn't wanted to be beaten up for treading on another man's toes if they thought he was propositioning their women. He was aware he had to be a lot more circumspect here, and not act according to his twenty-first-century upbringing in his interactions with the opposite sex.

'Yes, a wisewoman. Bothildr. Hurry!'

He was caught up in the boy's enthusiasm, and followed the urchins towards the other side of the port. It was like walking inside a swarm of buzzing bees. Now that they had something to show him, their excitement made them chatter and skip along, surrounding him completely. There was good-natured scuffling, giggling and teasing, and he smiled at their antics. It reminded him of his own childhood, and play-fighting with Maddie. She'd always been extremely fierce when sparring with him. At school, not so much, as she'd been bullied for her height and fiery hair. As they were so close in age, they had been evenly matched until he packed on more muscle in his late teens.

'We're here!' The oldest boy indicated a dilapidated hut with a flourish. 'Now will you pay us?'

Storm narrowed his eyes. 'Wait outside, please. If I learn anything useful, I'll reward you.'

He knocked on the door, which was standing open, and poked his head inside. 'Bothildr?'

'Yes, come in, come in. How can I help? Are you injured?'

An old crone sat on a stool next to a tiny hearth. It was smouldering fitfully and not giving out much heat, which might explain why she was wrapped in several blankets. A small and much-mended iron cauldron hung from a tripod over the meagre fire, and something bubbled in its depths, giving off steam. Bunches of herbs hung from the rafters, scenting the air with floral perfumes and some sharper smells he couldn't identify. It was like stepping into the lair of a witch from a fairy tale, and Storm was intrigued.

'No, but I seek information and I understand you might be able to help.' He stepped inside, ducking his head to avoid colliding with the lintel.

'Ah yes, the red-haired woman, was it? I remember her well. Head wound. But he looked after her. A good sort.'

'She was hurt? How? Why?' A fist of fear gripped his insides and twisted his gut. He'd hoped his sister – if it really was her they were talking about – had been able to defend herself. She was a martial arts specialist, after all, but this didn't sound good.

'Had been in a fight, or so he said. The injury was an accident. She was in the wrong place at the wrong time. Do not fret. She'll have recovered quickly.' Bothildr lifted a mug and took a sip of some beverage that steamed gently.

'And this woman, she was tall with long curly hair, the red of dark wine and copper mixed together?'

'Aye, that she was. Comely too, if you like them pale.'

'The man, who was he? And where was he taking her?' Storm didn't understand why, if Maddie had got herself mixed up in a fight, her opponent would then try to care for her when she was harmed. That made no sense.

Bothildr shrugged. 'No idea who he was. Never seen him before. He was just one of many who come here to buy thralls and provisions. He was going to Ísland, or so he said. Had a ship full of everything a settler would need. I'd bet anything he succeeded too. Determined sort.'

A settler bound for Iceland? This was curiouser and curiouser. A thought hit him. 'So he was taking her with him as a thrall? Had he bought her here?' If that was the case, at least he could buy her back. He could only hope she wasn't too traumatised by the experience.

The old woman pondered for a minute, then shook her head. 'I don't think so. He placed her in his own tent, you see. Was caring for her personally. A man wouldn't do that for a thrall, would he? He'd have left her in the care of others.'

'Hmm. Well, I thank you most sincerely. You have given me much food for thought and the only lead I have so far as to her whereabouts. Here, please accept this for your kindness.' He pulled a silver ring off his finger and gave it to her. It might be considered excessive payment for a few recollections, but to him, Bothildr's words were invaluable.

'Thank *you*, young man. May the gods go with you and assist you forthwith.'

As he emerged from the hut, optimism flooded him for the first time since he'd arrived here. As he recalled, Iceland wasn't massively settled at this time in history. It should be easy enough to find Maddie if she really was there. Now all he had to do was obtain passage on a ship heading in that direction.

He paid the urchins half a silver dirham each, then set off towards the nearest ships with a smile on his face. At last he was getting somewhere.

Chapter Four

Úthaf (North Atlantic)/Orkneyjar
Gormánuðr (late October) AD *875*

There were certain things you usually didn't consider when you lived in the twenty-first century. Such as the fact that travelling by sea in late autumn in an open boat was not the best idea. In fact, it was a downright crazy thing to do, even for an adrenaline junkie like Storm. He had always liked a challenge, and his parents said he'd been the type of fearless child who gave them nightmares. His motto was to try anything once, and if he didn't like it, move on. Anything from abseiling to skydiving and bungee-jumping, he'd done it, throwing himself into every activity heedless of the danger. But damned if this wasn't too much even for him. It wasn't a thrill in any way, but rather plain foolhardiness.

He sat huddled at the bottom of the ship, next to the railing, in order to escape the worst of the biting wind and sea spray, but it was a futile endeavour. There was no avoiding either of those things. He wished he'd had the forethought to just go back to his own time and travel to Iceland by plane.

Why on earth hadn't he?

Partly because he was here now, and a niggling voice inside his head had told him the time travel might not work a second time, something he couldn't risk. And also because he had wanted an authentic experience, and to follow in Maddie's footsteps properly. He hadn't thought it through, though. Impulsive and rash, that was what everyone had always called him. He was beginning to see why, even though he had tried to change his behaviour ever since his sister's disappearance. Losing her had matured him almost overnight, although sometimes, like now, he could still act recklessly.

He had managed to find passage on board a ship bound for Iceland, which was a miracle in itself. Most of the merchants in Dyflin had been on their way south, and not many of them had wanted to brave the North Atlantic – or Úthaf, as they called it – at this time of year. The owner of this vessel, Ófeigr, had already established a settlement in Iceland, and had come to buy more thralls and provisions to take back with him. His departure had been delayed by illness, which was the only reason he was so late in leaving. He still looked a bit pale and gaunt, but he was determined to go home before winter, come what may.

A blessing for Storm, although at the moment he was wondering if Ófeigr was quite sane attempting this journey now. If he hadn't been so desperate to reach Maddie, he would have waited until spring at the very least.

He huddled into the extra cloak he'd bought off one of his fellow travellers. The man had called it a *varafeldur.* It smelled like sheep, but it was keeping him relatively dry, so he wasn't going to complain about that. It was made of a type of material where the weaver had added little tufts of untreated wool to the plain weave at intervals. This created a sort of coarse rug effect, and because the tufts were unwashed, they retained the natural lanolin of the wool. That meant the cloak was water-resistant, just like a sheep. He was very grateful for that now, as without it, he would have been soaked to the skin.

'I can see land!' someone shouted, rousing Storm from his thoughts.

Ófeigr had brought a couple of men to help sail the ship and row if necessary, while he did most of the steering himself. They'd been heading in a northerly direction, passing the Isle of Man, Dumfries and Galloway, and sailing in between the Scottish islands and the Hebrides. Storm had to guess this, as the names in Old Norse were not familiar to him, but it made sense for them to go this way. Once past the top of Scotland, they were supposed to strike out across the Atlantic towards the Faroe Islands – Færeyjar sounded close enough that he was sure this was the place they were referring to – but they'd been blown off course. Right now, they weren't quite sure where they were, which didn't exactly instil confidence.

'Good!' Ófeigr called back. 'We had better look for a place to make landfall then. It is getting dark.' So far they had avoided being out at sea during the night, the men preferring to find a suitable beach somewhere to cook their supper and pitch their tents.

Several islands loomed out of the dusky autumn evening, some with soaring cliffs, others relatively flat. Storm didn't care where they were, as long as he could escape this ship for a while and get out of the biting wind. He was cold and miserable, and could barely feel his fingers and toes, despite wearing a hat, mittens and thick socks. He'd also put on two pairs of trousers – linen and wool – plus a shirt and two woollen tunics under a normal cloak and the *varafeldur*. It was still not enough.

They rounded a headland and saw a gap in between two large islands. Nestled in the middle was a smaller one, but it didn't look to have any suitable landing places, so they carried on northwards.

Without warning, another ship came hurtling out from behind the tiny island and gave chase. It took a moment for those on board to comprehend what was happening, but when they did, panic ensued.

'To the oars, everyone!' Ófeigr bellowed. 'Marauders! We cannot let them catch us.'

Storm was confused. Were they pirates, intent on stealing Ófeigr's cargo? He hadn't realised piracy was rife here, especially not at this time of year. From the conversations he'd overheard, he had gathered that hardly anyone went on long journeys in late autumn, so pickings for would-be marauders would be slim. However, that might make them more desperate, which was not a good thing. He jumped up and went to sit on a chest conveniently placed next to one of the oars. He fumbled with the leather binding that attached the oar to the ship, but managed to slot it into place at last. As soon as he had a steady grip on the handle, he put his back into it, like the others were doing. His heart rate sped up as they began to slice through the water faster. But would it be fast enough?

He didn't like the thought that they might be under attack at any moment. How did one fight off pirates on the open sea? It wouldn't be easy. There weren't that many of them to defend Ófeigr's possessions, and he doubted the thralls Ófeigr had bought would care which master they belonged to. They spent most of the time huddled listlessly at one end of the ship, their expressions blank or despairing. Why would they want to help?

'Faster! They're gaining on us!'

Storm increased his speed. It was understandable that someone would covet this cargo. Not just the thralls, but sacks of grain, bolts of cloth, and several caskets of more valuable items. A veritable treasure trove, in fact. They simply couldn't let it fall into the hands of men who had no right to any of it.

The ship was heavy, but somehow they managed to keep it going, and Ófeigr steered towards a rocky beach that appeared on their right. The other vessel was still gaining on them, but with luck it wouldn't reach them until they were on dry land, where it would be easier to fight. Storm checked to make sure his sword and axe were still hanging off his belt.

'Nearly there! Row harder! *Ein, tvei, ein, tvei.*'

Twenty yards from the beach, the ship hit something under the water and there was a horrible crunching sound as the planks ripped. Some were smashed to pieces, while others jerked up like a folding accordion. It didn't matter, though. Despite water rushing in, the hull held together long enough to propel them onto the shore. There it scraped over the stones and disintegrated even further. Everyone except the thralls scrambled out, vaulting over the railing. Storm turned just as the other ship drew up alongside them, and pulled his sword out of its scabbard. He was glad that he'd sharpened it the evening before.

He was vaguely aware of the sound of a cow horn hooting madly somewhere nearby, but there was no time to register anything more. The marauders were attacking, and he focused on the task in hand. In the army, he'd learned to switch off everything else and concentrate on the movements needed to defend himself. Although he had never been in a real life-or-death situation before, his body remembered the moves and executed them automatically. He slashed, parried, jumped out of the way of deadly blades coming his way, and generally did everything he could to stay alive.

There were too many of the attackers, though, and not enough of Ófeigr's men.

Anger fuelled Storm's movements. He'd come here to find his sister, and if he died on this godforsaken beach, it would all have been in vain. That thought made him redouble his efforts, but he wasn't sure it was sufficient. He killed or wounded several men – he didn't check whether they were alive or not, just moved on to the next one as soon as an opponent went down and stayed put. Still more kept coming at him. Just when he thought they were all doomed, he noticed a swarm of people come running across the beach, yelling at the top of their voices. The pirates paused, as if they hadn't counted on any further opposition, and Storm gathered the reinforcements had come to save Ófeigr's party.

Thank the gods!

As soon as the newcomers reached them, the odds turned in their favour. Someone ran up to Storm and began to fight alongside him. He faltered for an instant when he realised that it was a woman. There was no mistaking the long flaxen braids, or her delicate features. There was also no doubt that she was fierce, putting her whole heart into fighting the attackers. And she was doing a good job of it too.

'Die, *niðingr*!' she shouted, pushing back a youth with whom she was evenly matched. She obviously didn't expect him to fight dirty, however, as when the young man hooked his leg around the back of her knee, she fell onto her back, and he threw himself down on top of her, raising his sword.

Storm had just dispatched his current opponent, and now dived forward to grab the neck of the youth's tunic and pull him off. He smashed his fist into the guy's head and sent him stumbling backwards. 'Run!' he urged. 'You're losing, so escape with your life while you can.'

'Watch out!' The woman's widened eyes and her warning had Storm ducking out of the way instinctively. A sharp blade narrowly missed being buried in his back. Instead, it glanced off his forearm. He hissed with annoyance as a trail of fire blazed along his skin. It was only a surface wound, however, and nothing to worry about right now.

He grabbed the woman's hand and pulled her to her feet. Then he turned and booted his attacker in the face with a well-placed kick-boxing move. The man staggered and seemed to realise he was on the losing side. Without saying anything, he took off back towards the ship he'd arrived in. Soon it was pulling out of the bay and disappearing into the mist that was now rolling in across the sea.

'Good riddance,' Storm muttered, turning to see if the woman needed any more assistance. She was dusting herself off, but seemed O K apart from a shallow wound on her forehead that was dripping blood sluggishly down the side of her face. 'Are you well? Thank you for the warning. You saved my life.'

She blinked at him, as if she was surprised at his words. Why, he had no idea. Surely it was common courtesy to thank someone?

'Er, you are welcome. And thank you also for helping me.'

He smiled at her. 'I'm sure you would have managed on your own, but it seemed faster to pull him off you.'

'You . . . you believe I would have bested him?' Her blue eyes were huge in apparent astonishment. He noted in passing that they were beautiful, and surrounded by thick dark lashes. Surprising, considering how blonde her hair was.

'Of course. You have been well trained. You might struggle a bit against someone larger, but that boy was no bigger than you are. You were evenly matched.'

She seemed speechless, and a little frown appeared between her brows. It was adorable, and he had an urge to reach out and smooth it away. He restrained himself, as he didn't think she'd appreciate the gesture. Plus he couldn't go around touching random women here. That would definitely be frowned upon, he was sure.

He scanned the beach and saw that Ófeigr was being helped to his feet by some men nearby who were not part of his crew. There was blood all over his face and tunic, and he swayed and had to lean on someone. He must be in a bad way.

He turned back to the woman and asked, 'Where did you come from?' They were enclosed by soaring cliffs, but he couldn't see any buildings.

'We live up on the clifftop.' She waved a hand towards the top of a sea stack adjacent to the cove they were standing in. Now that he took in his surroundings more clearly, Storm could see a path snaking upwards. 'We've been attacked before,' she added, 'so there is always someone on lookout duty. When he saw what was happening, he blew the horn and we rushed down to help.'

'Well, I'm very glad you did. I need to fetch my things from the ship before it becomes completely inundated with water. We sprang a leak on the way in.'

'Oh no! That's not good.' She trailed after him as he walked to the shoreline and leaned over the gunwale to retrieve his sack of clothing. Everything else he owned was already somewhere on his person or hanging off his belt. 'Aren't you going to say anything about the fact that I'm a woman?'

'Eh?' Storm turned to stare at her. 'What do you mean?' He was puzzled by her words. She was very clearly a woman. Apart from the plaits and the delicate features, she was wearing typical female clothing, including a pair of tortoise brooches to hold her *smokkr* in place. While they'd been fighting, he had noticed she'd tucked her skirts into her belt, which made sense as they would have hampered her movements. She had been wearing trousers underneath, so it wasn't as if she'd been indecent in any way.

'Well, I . . . usually I'm told I should stay out of the way unless it's absolutely necessary for me to pitch in,' she said, kicking at a pebble near the edge of the water. It was a curiously bashful gesture, totally at odds with the fierce fighter he'd seen just a short while earlier.

He snorted. 'Why? In a fight such as that, it's good to have as many people on your side as possible. And you're clearly an asset, not a hindrance.' He shook his head. 'Forgive me, I don't understand.'

She gave him a strange look, then a small smile. 'No, I can see that. You are a most unusual man. I thank you for not thinking less of me for being a woman, and for your praise. Joalf will be pleased.'

'Who is Joalf?'

For some reason, he was suddenly jealous of the man. Was he her husband? Her master? Either would be disappointing. But now he caught on to what was happening here – sexism pure and simple. This was the Viking era, and presumably women were supposed to stay at home to cook and have children. She must be very strong-willed to go against the norm. As for himself, he had no problem fighting alongside females. It was an everyday occurrence in the army these days and he was used to it. They could be every bit as tough as the men. Just like his sister had always been.

'Joalf is my mentor. He's been training me since I was young.' She gestured towards a large middle-aged man with a bushy red beard who was part of the group helping Ófeigr.

'Oh, I see. He did it well.'

'Thank you. In fact, you can tell him that yourself. Come. We need to get your wound seen to. I'm assuming Assur will invite you all to bed down in his hall tonight.'

'Might be longer than that,' he muttered, glancing back at the massive hole in the ship's hull, but she didn't hear him.

Before they could climb the steep path, however, they were roped into helping to move the damaged ship. Someone took charge, and with muscle power from everyone present, they managed to pull it higher up onto the beach, out of reach of the tide.

'We'll come down and unload the cargo in a moment,' a man decreed. The woman whispered that his name was Assur and he was the owner of the settlement. 'It's not safe to leave it, in case those men return when it is full dark. For now, we need to see to the wounded. Follow me.'

Freydis scaled the path in front of the man who'd come to her rescue. She was still having trouble assimilating the fact that he had praised her fighting skills. No one other than her father and Joalf had ever done so. It was unsettling, and a little exhilarating.

'I'm Storm Haakonarson,' he said from behind her. 'What is your name?'

'Freydis Úlfsdóttir.' She saw no reason not to tell him. If these people were staying – and it didn't look as though they had a choice in the matter – he'd find out soon enough.

'Ah, so you are not Assur's daughter, then?'

'No. A distant relative. He is my mother's cousin.'

'I see.'

She glanced over her shoulder to find that he was following close on her heels. Her mind replayed the strange fighting technique he'd used on one of the marauders, and she couldn't help but wonder where he had learned to do that. She wanted to ask him about it, but now was not the time. He was bleeding and needed to have his wound seen to.

Once at the top of the cliff, she led him to the main hall. There was a small room at one end used for meal preparation and storage. She took him in there and told him to wait while she fetched water and a cloth. He did as he was told, gazing around the shelves as if he was curious about what they contained. The other wounded strangers were being tended to in the main area of the hall by Gyrid and some of the thralls. Freydis was happy to have Storm to herself, although she knew she probably shouldn't be alone with him. Hopefully no one would notice, as they were all busy with their own tasks.

'Let me see your arm, please. I'll need to wash it and bind it for you.' She dipped the cloth in the bowl of water she had brought back.

'It's nothing, but I suppose it wouldn't hurt to have it cleaned.'

He took off his shaggy outer cloak and shook the rainwater off before discarding it to one side. Another more conventional woollen cloak followed, then he undid his belt and dropped it, together with his weapons and whatever else was hanging off it, onto the floor with a clatter. He tugged two tunics and a shirt off with one quick move and stood before her bare-chested.

Freydis sucked in a sharp breath.

'What? Am I bleeding somewhere else?' He turned this way and that to scrutinise his torso and other arm, then frowned at her.

'N-no. It's fine. You were so quick, you surprised me, is all.'

Her voice was shaky, and her words were a lie. The sight of him in all his glory had almost rendered her speechless. She'd seen shirtless men before when they washed outside in the summer time, but this one was stunning, there was no other word for it. Muscular arms that flexed and bunched as he chucked his garments onto a nearby table. Wide shoulders and a broad chest tapering towards a stomach that was ridged with more muscle in an intriguing pattern. A smattering of chest hair in between his pectorals, and further down, a line of hair arrowing into his trousers. His skin was slightly bronzed, and there were strange swirling patterns all over one shoulder, down his upper arm and across half his chest. When she looked more closely, she could see that it was a drawing of a dragon. She'd heard of such things, images etched onto human skin, but had never seen it for herself.

He noticed where her gaze had gone, and his mouth quirked up in a half-smile. 'You've never seen *tattoos* before?'

'Tat . . . what?'

'These.' He pointed to the dragon. 'They are common where I'm from.'

She shook her head, trying to clear it. Her limbs were refusing to function normally, and she was acting like a ninny. 'No, I haven't seen their like.'

The pattern was intriguing. Dragons were symbols of many things – chaos and destruction, but also power, strength and courage, as well as protection. They were often carved onto the prows of ships to strike fear into enemies. She wondered why Storm would have such a thing etched onto his body. Did it have special meaning for him? She didn't dare ask. It was exquisitely rendered, and she would have loved to gaze at it some more, but that would not be seemly. Feeling her cheeks heat up, she took refuge in efficiency.

'Give me your arm, if you please,' she ordered.

By concentrating only on his wound, she managed to get her breathing under control. She'd had no idea that the mere sight of a man's chest could make her feel so unsteady. It was like receiving a kick in the gut. She washed his arm with lye soap, then dried it and applied a healing salve before winding a length of clean linen around it.

'There, that should do.' She was about to take the bowl and leave, but he put a hand on her wrist and stopped her.

'Wait. I have to return the favour. You're bleeding too.'

He wrung out the cloth and applied it gently to her forehead. Freydis had forgotten that she had blood trickling down her face. It occurred to her to wonder if she looked a fright, but then she kicked herself mentally. What did it matter? She had never cared before whether a man found her attractive or not. And Storm was a stranger.

'I apologise if I made you uncomfortable,' he murmured while he worked. 'I should have warned you that I was shedding my clothing.'

'It was nothing.' Or rather, it shouldn't have been a problem, but there was no point denying to herself that his nearness had affected her. He didn't need to know that, though.

His chest was right there in front of her eyes, close enough that she could feel the heat coming off his skin and smell his scent. Wind, brine, man and something vaguely spicy. She had the urge to lean forward and bury her nose at the base of his neck where it joined his powerful shoulders to take a deep sniff. Madness. She should move away, but her limbs refused to heed the frantic orders from her brain.

'Well, good. So you like my dragon?' His voice was as gentle as his movements, and yet Freydis's heart was still beating madly, as if it wanted her to flee. It was also an enticing sound, low and a little husky, and it sent a shiver shooting through her.

She glanced at his shoulder. 'It's . . . um, magnificent.'

When she dared to peek up at him, he was smiling properly. By Odin, the man was handsome. She'd never seen his like. Ingolf Gunnarsson was said to be good-looking, but Freydis would bet anything he couldn't compare to Storm. What made it better – or worse, if one didn't wish to be enthralled – was that he also appeared to be kind. He was a strange combination of ferocious and ruthless fighter with a soft touch.

She steeled herself and resisted the urge to stare at him some more. 'Thank you,' she said when he had finished his ministrations.

'No, thank *you*.' He bent to retrieve clean garments from his sack, and put them on.

Freydis watched the dragon disappear underneath his clothing and almost begged him not to cover it up. But that was foolish, and he wasn't hers to command.

'I'm going to get rid of this dirty water, then we had better go and find you something to eat. I assume you haven't had *nat-tverðr* yet?'

'No. We were looking for somewhere to make landfall, but then those men started chasing us.' He buckled on his belt and checked his weapons, then swung his two cloaks around his shoulders, fastening each with a brooch. 'I must go and help with unloading the ship first. I'll find you when we are done.'

'But your arm! Should you be lifting heavy objects?'

He stopped in the doorway and smiled even wider. 'I will be fine. It's just a scratch. May I leave my possessions here for now? They should be safe if I hide them behind this barrel.' When she nodded, he stuffed his bundle behind a large cask.

'I'll hang up your other garments to dry,' she offered.

'Thank you.'

When he disappeared into the night, Freydis stood for a moment trying to gather her wits. She had never found a man attractive before. Never understood what everyone was talking about when they whispered about desire. Now she knew.

Chapter Five

Hrossey, Orkneyjar
Gormánuðr (late October) AD *875*

Storm was surprised that the thralls were still huddled in a disconsolate group at one end of the damaged ship when he and the others returned to the beach. If it had been him, he would have taken the opportunity to disappear, but perhaps that hadn't occurred to them. Or maybe they were daunted by the fact that they were in a strange place and would have no idea how to escape and survive here. He asked someone if they could be cared for, and they were shepherded up to the top of the sea stack. Hopefully they'd be fed and given shelter. He decided to check and make sure later, even though they weren't technically his concern.

He worked tirelessly for what felt like hours, hefting cargo up the steep slope to the settlement. Assur found them an empty hut where the goods could be stored, and told them that the thralls were being temporarily assimilated with his own. Storm didn't mind the hard work. It felt good to use his muscles and get some exercise after days of inactivity on board the ship. The wound on his arm only pulled slightly and didn't bother him much.

'You'll be hard put to repair the damage before winter sets in properly.' Assur was standing next to one of Ófeigr's men, scratching his head as he surveyed the massive hole in the hull. Ófeigr himself was being cared for up at the hall. Being wounded on top of his recent illness had rendered him unfit to move for the moment.

'It'll take us a while, that is obvious,' the man replied.

'It's not just that,' Assur said. 'You simply won't find the materials needed here. There are precious few trees on these islands. All the timber we need is brought over from Hörðaland or Sogn, and this time of year no one is going to risk it.' He sighed. 'I think it likely you'll be stuck here till spring.'

Storm had paused to eavesdrop on their conversation, and his heart sank at hearing this. More delays? Just what he didn't need. What on earth were they going to do here for months on end?

An image of Freydis flashed through his mind, giving him a few ideas, but he shook them off almost immediately. He wasn't here to flirt with anyone. And he couldn't. This was the Viking era and no inappropriate behaviour would be tolerated. Besides, all he wanted was to find Maddie as soon as possible. Now another obstacle had been put in his path. It was as if the gods were conspiring against him. Were they making it deliberately difficult as a punishment for leaving her in the first place? He had to admit he deserved it if so, but it was still extremely aggravating.

He growled out loud with frustration as he strode up the path one last time and headed for the hall. There was nothing he could do about it if Assur was right. He'd have to accept a delay of a few months.

Once indoors, he was greeted with warmth and enticing cooking smells that made his mouth water. He hadn't eaten since daybreak and could kill for a decent meal. Spying Freydis over by the hearth, he went to join her and touched her arm lightly. She jumped, but he couldn't resist letting his fingers linger for longer than they should have. He removed them reluctantly. He should keep his distance.

'*Hei*,' he murmured. 'Did you mention *nattverðr* by any chance?' He gave her his best smile and saw her cheeks turn pink. For a woman who fought like a warrior, she was peculiarly shy around him.

'Oh, um, yes. Of course. Here, let me find you a bowl.'

She busied herself with filling a wooden bowl with some sort of stew, and broke off a piece of flatbread from a large roundel hanging off a hook nearby.

'I have a spoon,' he informed her, pleased that he'd had the forethought to pack one. It was made of horn and small enough to fit in one of his leather pouches.

'Good. Why don't you take a seat . . . er, somewhere.' Freydis looked around the crowded benches, frowning when she couldn't locate a free space.

'Don't worry. I'll find a place. Thank you.'

He took his food and his newly retrieved belongings and went to perch on the edge of a small dais at one end of the hall. He would have sat on the floor, he wasn't fussy, but this would do. While shovelling spoonfuls of stew into his mouth, he studied his surroundings. The building was run-down and patched in places, but for the most part it was clean. The flagstone floor was swept, and he didn't spy any cobwebs in the dark corners. There were people everywhere, talking, eating, waving their hands around as they made their points. The noise soared to the rafters, the cacophony of Norse words ringing in his ears. Thralls wove in and out of outstretched legs, serving ale. He accepted a cup when it was offered to him, and received a strange look in return when he said thank you with a polite smile.

It was slowly sinking in that he was in the ninth century. For real. He was sitting in an authentic Viking hall, surrounded by people dressed in the clothing of that era, all speaking Old Norse. Although he'd believed Linnea, his sister, when she'd told them she had travelled through time, a small part of him had still harboured doubts. Now he was here and could see for himself that the magic – if that was what it was – really worked. For someone who had grown up with parents who weren't just academics immersed in this time period, but enthusiastic re-enactors, it was a dream come true. He simply couldn't believe he'd been lucky enough to experience it. And instead of being cross that he was stranded here indefinitely, he ought to rejoice in his good fortune and immerse himself in Viking society while he had the chance. As long as he didn't stand out too much.

It was the opportunity of a lifetime and he determined to look on the bright side from now on.

Once his immediate hunger had been sated, his gaze returned to Freydis. She was still helping to serve food over by the hearth, together with an older woman who had to be Assur's spouse. The wife was richly dressed and had a haughty expression. There was a permanent scowl of dissatisfaction on her face, as if she disapproved of everyone and everything. He could see that Freydis was on the receiving end of several snarky comments, but the blonde warrior took it in her stride. Eventually the stream of people needing to be fed dried up, and she was able to grab a bowl of food for herself. She looked around for somewhere to sit, and Storm caught her eye, motioning her over by tipping his chin at her.

At first he didn't think she would come. She hesitated, but then straightened her spine and marched over, plonking herself down next to him.

'Don't think I've ever sat here before,' she said quietly, while moving a couple of inches away from him.

He regarded her with amusement. 'I don't bite, you know. Unless you ask me to, of course.'

'What? Why would I want you to do that?' Her expression was adorably flustered and confused, as if she had no idea what he was talking about.

He gathered she must be innocent and had never been with a man. He swore silently and told himself off for speaking without thinking. *Idiot!* Of course she wouldn't understand what he was referring to and he shouldn't have said it in the first place. That was a twenty-first-century reaction, one he had to learn to suppress. He simply couldn't go around saying things like that here.

'Ignore me, I was merely jesting.'

'Oh, I see.' She bent her head to concentrate on eating, but not before he'd seen her cheeks turn an even duskier pink.

He nudged her subtly with his elbow. 'You'll have to excuse me. I'm not used to the company of young unmarried women and I can be a bit of an oaf at times. I spend too much time with uncouth warriors.' That much was true anyway.

Her head came up and she sent him a sharp glance. 'What makes you think I'm not married?'

Storm stopped eating and considered how to put it so that he didn't offend her. In the end, he decided he couldn't say that it was the way she acted around him. That would merely make her even more self-conscious. 'Er, are you? If so, I apologise if I've overstepped somehow. Should I not be talking to you?' He scanned the room to see if any of the other men present were glaring at him, but couldn't spot anyone looking particularly belligerent.

She took another spoonful of stew and sighed. 'No, I'm not married, but I am betrothed, actually. At least I believe I am. It's . . . a strange situation.'

'How so?' He was intrigued now. 'Either you are or you aren't, surely?'

She took a bite of bread and chewed before answering. 'I shouldn't be discussing this with you, but I suppose if you're staying you'll hear the gossip anyway. As I said, Assur is my mother's cousin, and I was sent to live here when I'd seen ten winters. My father had died and my mother remarried a man called Bjarni. He was . . . apparently an impatient man, and didn't want me around. I believed this to be a temporary solution, but as you can see, I'm still here. I recently learned that I was never meant to return home. Although I would dearly like to, if only to make sure that my mother isn't being mistreated by that *aumingi*.'

'I see. That must have been disappointing,' he murmured, reaching out to squeeze her arm briefly. There was sadness in her eyes and her shoulders drooped as if in defeat. He didn't like to see her like that, although why it mattered to him, he didn't know.

'It was. Worse was to come, though. Assur informed me that the dowry my mother had sent with me had been used up to pay for my keep. He and his wife, Gyrid, have decided they no longer want me here. They have contracted a marriage for me with a man from a nearby island, Ingolf Gunnarsson. Assur is in his debt because of something that happened last year, and he seeks to repay the man with my hand in marriage.'

She had stopped eating and was staring into the distance, lost in thought.

Storm nudged her again. 'And how do you feel about that? Will he not make a good husband?'

To his surprise, she full-on shuddered, her whole body shivering. 'No, I don't believe he will.' She told him about the man's reputation and previous wives, ending with the one who had killed herself by jumping off a cliff.

Frowning, he stared at her. 'Can you not refuse? He sounds awful!'

She shrugged and put her stew down next to her, half eaten.

'How can I? I'm not wanted here and I have no way of earning my keep. Besides, it may all be rumours.'

'You could become a warrior.' Storm grinned at her. 'Go a-viking. You're fierce enough.'

That made a reluctant laugh huff out of her. 'Doubtful.'

'You can come with me. I'll protect you.' But they both knew he was joking. She couldn't do any such thing. 'What about that Joalf you were talking about earlier?'

'I have asked his advice. Not about going a-viking, but on how to escape this predicament. So far we've not come up with anything useful. He's promised to speak to Assur on my behalf, but it's probably pointless.'

'Well, let me know what he says. If I can help, I will. I owe you.'

'You do? No, I think we are even. You saved me from that youth.'

'And you warned me I was about to be skewered.'

'True. I still think I'm in your debt. And you've said nothing derogatory about me wanting to take part in the fighting. I'm grateful for that.'

He pointed at her bowl, which she seemed to have abandoned, as if speaking about her betrothal had made her lose her appetite. 'In that case, if you're not finishing that, can I have it, please?'

Freydis frowned at him. 'You want the rest of my stew?'

'Yes. No point wasting it, is there? I'm always hungry.' He held out his hand and she gave him the bowl with a perplexed smile.

'You are a very strange man.'

'You have no idea.'

But he wasn't going to tell her about himself. That was one secret he couldn't afford to reveal.

Freydis led the way to the weaving hut, with Storm right behind her. He and his companions had been allocated benches wherever one could be found, and she'd been told he was to sleep there. His nearness made her heart rate speed up, but then it had been erratic ever since he had first spoken to her. She was finding it difficult to absorb the fact that he had accepted her fighting skills without batting an eyelid. And the way he had talked about her options for escaping marriage with Ingolf was downright odd. Why was he on her side?

Most men would have taken Assur's part, believing that a woman should accept a marriage that was arranged for her. Within reason, of course. Unless Ingolf was proved to be an abuser of wives, he was ostensibly a good catch. Handsome, with a rich settlement and extensive trade connections, he ought to make someone the perfect husband. As his wife, she would rule over a large domain, with thralls and dependants to help with every chore. And yet that niggle about his supposed mistreatment of previous spouses would not go away.

It was too steep a price to pay for a life of luxury.

'Here we are.' She threw open the door to the hut and ducked inside, putting down the oil lamp she carried on a small shelf. There were two benches in here, and she placed a bundle of blankets and a fleece on one of them. 'You should be comfortable enough here.'

'Thank you.' Storm smiled at her, his eyes twinkling. She had noticed earlier that they were a very pale clear green, like water flowing over lichen. They were shadowed by long eyelashes and topped with slashing eyebrows, one of which had a scar running through it. His hair was shorn on the sides and back, but was long and curly on top of his head – a most unusual hairstyle. As she'd already noted earlier, he had broad shoulders and a muscular physique, and he was taller than most men. He was, quite simply, breathtaking, but that was neither here nor there.

'I will bid you goodnight then.' She backed towards the door, although she found it hard to tear her gaze away from him.

'Goodnight, Freydis. I hope to see you in the morning.' He picked up the fleece and spread it over the bench, while glancing at her over his shoulder. 'Perhaps you would allow me to train with you sometime? I feel the need to move after so many days on a ship.'

She stopped with her hand on the door. 'You wish to join me and Joalf?'

'Yes. If that's not too presumptuous? I wouldn't want to be in the way.'

'No, no, that would be . . . fine.' More than fine, but she refused to let on how her heart leapt at the thought. 'I'm not certain when our next session will be. Probably not for a few days, as there will be much to do with this influx of guests, but I can let you know.'

To be allowed to spar with someone other than Joalf would be amazing. He'd been wonderful, and she had learned a lot from him, but lately she'd begun to feel as if there was nothing further he could teach her. All they did was keep up the skills she had acquired already. Having seen Storm in action, she was sure he had a lot more to offer. The thought of that was exciting in the extreme.

'Good. I look forward to it.'

With a nod, she left him to bed down for the night, and returned to the hall and her own sleeping bench. As she snuggled under her blankets and closed her eyes, all she could see was Storm's face. The gods must have sent him here for a reason. She could barely wait for morning.

Chapter Six

Hrossey, Orkneyjar
Gormánuðr (late October) AD *875*

Storm woke early, feeling restless. After his time in the army, he wasn't used to inactivity, and apart from his brief stint rowing, and helping to unload the cargo last night, it had been days since he'd exercised properly. From Freydis's vague response regarding a training session, he had gathered that might not be happening any time soon, but he needed to move. Being in this strange time, it was imperative that he keep in shape so that he was ready for anything. He had already been in one skirmish; there was no saying when he would next need to fight. Time for a workout.

It was barely light outside, but he decided to go for a run first. Wearing two pairs of trousers – the linen ones that usually doubled as underwear, and thicker woollen ones on top – and a linen shirt, he left the weaving hut. Earlier, he had hidden his precious axe and his remaining silver on top of one of the roof beams, as he didn't want to take any chances of having them stolen. The door to the hut had no lock and he didn't trust the inhabitants of this settlement. The last thing he needed was to lose his time-travelling device or the riches necessary to search for Maddie.

He did a couple of stretching exercises, then set off. There were a few thralls awake and going about their duties as he jogged slowly towards the path down to the beach, but they took no notice of him. He picked up his pace and ascended the path on the other side in a burst of speed. Once at the top, he made his way along the edge of the cliffs at a steady clip, revelling in the sensation of being flooded with endorphins. He loved the rush of exercising, stretching his muscles and pushing his body to the limits. There was a chilly wind buffeting him, but he barely noticed as he eased into an even rhythm. Viking half-boots were not ideal running shoes, but the grass was soft and he had to make do. Eventually he turned back and made his way down to the beach, where the broken ship lay like a stark reminder of the difficulties he faced.

'Damn it all!' he muttered as he jogged back and forth across the sand, cooling down after his run. If those marauders hadn't chased them, he could have been on his way to Iceland by now. But the Norse gods had decided on a different path for him. He could only hope they would help him to reach Maddie eventually.

Merely running wasn't going to keep him in shape for fighting, so he started on a set of additional exercises. He practised martial arts moves and sword technique using a stick he found lying on the sand, then did some short sprints, digging deep to reach maximum speed, followed by press-ups and sit-ups in endless repetitions. By the time he was done, he was drenched in sweat and there was only one thing for it – a dip in the sea. He knew it would be freezing, but also incredibly invigorating. And it wouldn't be the first time he'd immersed himself in ice-cold water. During training manoeuvres with the army, he'd had to enter a lake in winter, and he'd survived. This wouldn't be any different.

Shucking off his shoes, socks, shirt and woollen trousers, he flung them onto the sand, and sprinted towards the water. Holding his breath, he threw himself under the waves and revelled in the shock of the glacial embrace.

It made him feel supremely alive.

'What in the name of all the gods is he doing?'

Freydis had slept badly, and eventually slipped out of the hall at dawn to go for a wander and clear her head before beginning her morning duties. Gyrid would have disapproved, but she'd been fast asleep on her bench. Freydis planned to be back before the woman awoke and noticed her gone. Instead of heading for her usual vantage point on the northern side of the sea stack, she had walked in the other direction, gazing at the mainland. While close to the edge, she'd happened to look down into the cove and spied a figure on the beach. She wondered why the guard on duty hadn't sounded the alarm. Either he was asleep, or the person below was not an intruder.

She stopped to peer down more intently. As she watched, the man came closer, and she recognised him. Storm. The man who had invaded her dreams all night and prevented her from sleeping properly. Now here he was in the flesh, running back and forth on the sand in bursts of speed. In between, he threw himself down either onto his back to crunch into a sitting position over and over again, or onto his front to push up and down on powerful arms. It was a mesmerising sight. Without thinking, she moved towards the path and headed in his direction.

Just as she reached the cove at the bottom, he pulled off his shoes and all his clothes except a pair of linen trousers and sprinted straight towards the water. Her breath became lodged in her throat as she watched the waves close over his head. Was he mad? He was going to freeze to death or drown.

She ran to the spot where he'd left his clothing and anxiously scanned the sea. To her immense relief, his head popped up and he began to clean himself with sand. His movements were rushed, yet she wanted to call out to him to hurry. He was facing away from her, though, and she doubted he would hear her even if she shouted her loudest. The longer he stayed in the water, the more dangerous it was. She had heard tell that a person's limbs could seize up in the freezing-cold sea, rendering them helpless and unable to move. They could then easily drown or be sucked out by the tide. She was just about to try screaming his name when he turned and waded towards the shore, stopping briefly when he caught sight of her. His mouth turned up into a smile and he lifted a hand in greeting, while carrying on with unhurried strides.

Freydis's mouth went dry and she felt her eyes widen as they glued themselves to his wet form. 'Sweet Freya,' she murmured, swallowing hard. He could have been the sea god Njord come to life, and for a moment she wondered if he was real or a figment of her imagination. Perhaps she was still in bed and dreaming? But no, her mind could never have conjured up this much detail.

His body glistened with water. It ran in little rivulets down from his powerful shoulders across his chest and into the defined ridges of his stomach. The linen trousers were more or less see-through, and Freydis tried not to stare at his nether regions. Skimming the most intimate parts of him, her gaze moved lower and she could see the material clinging to muscular thighs. He was sheer perfection. Although she was well aware that she ought to run away from the sight, her limbs refused to move. All she could do was stand there and blink at the vision in front of her.

'Good morning. Didn't expect to see you down here. Have you come for a swim as well?'

He'd stopped only a few feet in front of her, so close she could see the goosebumps erupting on his smooth skin. His nipples were puckered too, and the realisation that he must be freezing finally loosened her tongue.

'N-no! I was merely out for a walk,' she murmured, rushing over to where his clothes were lying in a heap on the sand. She picked them up and returned to his side to thrust them at him. 'Y-you should get dressed or you'll catch your death. Have you lost your mind? No one goes sea bathing this time of year.'

His smile turned to a teasing grin. 'They should. It's invigorating and a great way to wake up.' When she shuddered visibly at the thought, he chuckled. 'Oh well, I suppose I'll have to find another early-morning swimming partner then. A shame.'

'Put your clothes on,' she ordered between clenched teeth. The images conjured up by his words – of the two of them mostly naked and frolicking in the waves – were unsettling, to say the least. Another shiver rippled through her, but this time it was for a different reason. 'I'm serious! You need to get warm.'

His eyes twinkled with amusement. 'I will need to remove my wet trousers first. I cannot do that until you turn around.' He raised one eyebrow. 'Unless you want to watch?'

She hissed in an outraged breath but couldn't find the words to berate him. Turning, she faced the cliffs and ground her molars together. He was infuriating and fascinating in equal measure, and she shouldn't be here with him, alone on a beach before it was even properly light. And yet she couldn't bring herself to leave.

She heard a sigh. 'Forgive me. I should not have said that, even in jest. That was . . . badly done. As I said, I'm used to dealing with men. We tease each other mercilessly all the time.'

'Very well. You are forgiven.' But she wouldn't forget what he'd said. The idea of bathing with him was too intriguing.

There was rustling coming from behind her, and she folded her arms across her chest while she waited.

'There, all done. I'm decent. You can turn back now.'

When she merely threw him a glance over her shoulder, he moved to stand beside her, wringing out the wet linen trousers. 'Let's go. I'll race you to the top.'

'What?' She'd barely got the word out when he took off towards the path. '*Hei!* That's cheating,' she shouted, running after him.

He slowed down a tiny bit, but stayed a few steps ahead of her, his laughter floating on the breeze. A giggle bubbled up in her throat while she put her best efforts into catching up with him. He was teasing again, and she knew she would never reach him unless he let her, but it didn't matter. They were like children playing a game, something she only vaguely remembered from the time she'd lived with her parents. It was ridiculous for two adults to behave this way, but she couldn't deny that she was enjoying it immensely. For that moment in time, she felt carefree and happy.

When they were almost at the top, he came to an abrupt halt and she cannoned into the back of him. She was forced to grab his waist to steady herself, and he turned to catch hold of her wrists.

'Whoa, careful there,' he murmured. 'I'm sorry, I should have warned you, but I reckoned we had better behave in a more seemly manner up here in case anyone catches sight of us.'

'Definitely.' She was short of breath, but that could have been because of the way his hold on her made her skin tingle, rather than the race. Reluctantly she pulled her hands away. 'You should go and warm yourself.'

'I will, after I dunk my head in water that isn't briny. I don't like the feel of seawater in my hair.' He rubbed a hand through the longer tresses on top of his head, flicking droplets of water all around. Freydis's fingers twitched with the urge to do the same. She wondered what that would feel like, then buried the thought. She shouldn't be thinking of touching him in any way. 'Where are you going?' he asked.

'I have morning chores. In the hall.' She waved a hand in that direction.

'I'll see you in a while then.' He smiled at her and walked backwards for a few steps, watching her with those brilliant pale green eyes as if he didn't want to let her out of his sight quite yet.

'Yes, later.' She ducked her head and set off towards the hall without glancing at him again. It was an effort, but she had to break the hold his gaze seemed to have on her. He was a stranger. A man just passing through. She shouldn't be spending time with him at all.

But that was exactly what she wanted to do.

Storm went to dunk his head in a trough of rainwater, then returned to the weaving hut to get dressed properly. After folding his bedding neatly and hanging up his wet trousers, he walked over to the hall. Assur's wife, Gyrid, handed him a bowl of hot oatmeal with a dollop of butter, her expression no less sour this morning. He had some sympathy with her, given that she'd had all these guests foisted on her without notice, but he still felt she could have been more gracious about it. Not wanting to make matters worse, he thanked her politely, then sat down on the nearest bench to devour his breakfast.

Freydis was busy with chores, but she stopped briefly on her way past. 'Good morning. I hope you slept well. How is your wound?'

He gathered she was pretending they hadn't already seen each other earlier, and thought it best to play along. He didn't want to get her in trouble with old sourpuss, as he'd taken to calling Gyrid in his mind. 'Morning. It's fine, and I slept like a log, thank you.'

'A log?' She looked puzzled, and he gathered that simile wasn't used in Old Norse.

'Deeply,' he clarified. 'Although I had some rather vivid

dreams.' He winked, and watched as her cheeks turned pink once again. Jeez, did no one ever flirt with this girl? Then he reminded himself it wasn't the done thing here and he shouldn't either. *Damn it!* Why couldn't he remember that? She was just so adorable when she was ruffled.

Her reaction down on the beach had been interesting too. She'd been fascinated and delightfully flustered, yet totally unable to keep her eyes off him. And yesterday, when seeing to his wound, she'd stared at his naked torso as well. He wasn't shy, so he had allowed her to look her fill. Where was the harm in that? But he really must stop teasing her. It wasn't fair to toy with someone who didn't know the rules of the game. And he was following twenty-first-century rules, not those she lived by.

From now on, he'd behave himself.

'Um, so you don't need me to change your dressing?' she asked, glancing at his arm. He'd removed the wet bandage and noted that the wound was healing nicely. Seawater helped, as salt was good for speeding up the process.

'No, it's best to leave it alone, but thank you for offering.' Not that he didn't want her hands on him again, but it really wasn't necessary.

She glanced over at Gyrid, who was still scowling. 'I'd best get on. Perhaps I will see you later.'

'I look forward to that.'

He resisted the urge to wink at her again, but she was still watching him as she moved away and almost tripped over someone's feet as she bustled off, clearly rattled by his mere presence. It made warmth spread inside him to know that he wasn't the only one affected by the attraction between them. In different circumstances, he would have made a move on her immediately. She was gorgeous, with that long white-blonde hair he'd love to run his hands through, stunning blue eyes and an enticing figure. It was a potent combination, but he had to make do with admiring her from afar. She was taken.

Besides, he was hoping to leave this place as soon as possible. Finding Maddie was his priority, no matter how tempting it was to spend time getting to know Freydis. He couldn't allow himself to become diverted from his urgent quest. It was his sole reason for being in this century, and he mustn't forget that.

Once he'd eaten, he and Ófeigr's other men were called into a small room at one end of the hall. There they found the shipowner propped up in a bed, looking wan and exhausted.

'Ófeigr, are you well?' asked his right-hand man, Saemundr, frowning in concern.

'I will be.' The older man clenched his jaw and winced as he tried to move against the pillows. 'But I need to rest for a week or so. I received a wound to the leg and it has to heal.'

'We have worse problems than that,' Saemundr admitted, making a face. 'Assur tells me there are no planks available with which to repair our ship. And the damage is extensive – I've just been to have a closer look. There probably won't be any suitable wood until spring, when men from Hörðaland usually bring a few loads.'

Ófeigr cursed under his breath. 'You're saying we have to impose on Assur's hospitality until then?'

'I'm afraid so.'

He closed his eyes and sighed. 'Well, at least we have some provisions to contribute. Hopefully those at home in Ísland will cope without the goods we were bringing.'

Storm said nothing, but inside he was seething with impatience. *Damn it all!* He really didn't want to kick his heels here for that long. He had a sister to find, and he'd hoped to be back in the twenty-first century by the following summer at the latest. There were some posts coming up on the UN peacekeeping force that he wanted to apply for. What should he do now? Staying here would delay him for months, by the sound of it, and anything could be happening to Maddie in the meantime.

He could potentially use the magical axe to return to his own century, and then fly to Iceland, but again, the thought that the axe might not work a second time made him hesitate. He simply couldn't risk it being a one-time portal. As it was, he already felt the gods were toying with him. It wouldn't surprise him if they refused to make it work again. Not only that, but how was he going to bring such a dangerous weapon to another country? They'd never let him cross the border with an axe, a sword and a lethal knife.

Having considered the matter further, he decided there was nothing for it but to be patient. Hopefully Assur was wrong and they'd be able to get hold of the materials they needed. For now, though, he was stuck here. Perhaps there were other ships heading for Iceland from somewhere in the Orkney Islands. He'd have to try to find out. In the meantime, Ófeigr told them all to make themselves useful to their hosts, helping out wherever they were needed.

'We cannot expect to stay here for any length of time without doing our fair share of the work. No doubt there is hunting and fishing to be done, as well as slaughter and the like. I'll pitch in as soon as I'm able.'

They were dismissed, and glancing back at Ófeigr, Storm saw the man's hand shake as he tucked it under the blankets. Would he even survive the cold months?

It wasn't his problem. All he wanted was to reach his sister as quickly as possible.

He wandered outside, keen to escape the fug inside the hall. Too many people in too small a space. And interesting though it was, being in the ninth century felt very odd. He hadn't been here long enough to get used to it yet. His hands itched to reach for his mobile and check for messages and the latest news. He longed to grab a snack or a cup of coffee whenever he wanted to, without having to wait to be served, and with a choice of what to eat and drink. And although he'd often made do with primitive conditions when out on manoeuvres, he missed the creature comforts of his own time – warm, well-insulated houses, showers, proper toilets and a soft bed. He was a fish out of water here, and there was no one he could confide in. Not a single person who would understand or empathise.

That made him feel very alone.

For a while he walked around exploring the settlement, observing the various comings and goings. No one asked him to join in, and for now he held back from offering. The top of the sea stack was largely flat, and he headed for the northern edge of it. A cold wind buffeted his hair and clothing. It was exhilarating, making him feel truly alive. He made a mental note to wear his hat next time, though. For now, he couldn't be bothered to go back and fetch it.

Just as he passed the last of the buildings, a huge black bird came flying straight at him, making a strange croaking noise, like a creaky old door.

'Whoa!' He ducked instinctively, but to his surprise, the bird landed on his shoulder, gripping hard with large feet and flapping its wings until it gained balance. 'What the . . . ?' He froze, then turned to stare into the dark peppercorn eyes that were regarding him curiously, too close for comfort. 'Who on earth are you?'

To his absolute astonishment, the bird replied, '*Surtr. Surtr. Good boy!*' The words were perfectly recognisable as Old Norse, but Storm was having trouble believing they came out of that long curved beak.

'You can talk?' He gathered this must be someone's tame bird and not a wild predator as he'd first assumed. A huge smile spread over his features. 'That's amazing! Say something else. Surtr, was it? Speak to me.'

But the bird obviously wasn't in the mood. Instead it let out a *gwoark*, then made a series of clicking noises deep in its throat. Storm chuckled and tried to copy it, and the two of them ended up having a croaking and clicking competition, which was the most fun he'd had in ages, making him laugh out loud.

Carefully he reached out to stroke Surtr's blue-black feathers. The bird was some sort of crow. No, bigger than that. A raven, perhaps? It allowed him to touch it once, but grew impatient when he tried it a second time and shook him off. 'You are very beautiful,' Storm murmured. 'But I'm sure you are fully aware of that. Want to come for a walk with me?'

As he didn't expect a reply to that, he set off once again for the edge of the sea stack, the raven clinging to his shoulder. He stood there for a long time, watching the waves far below, the endless horizon, and the many seabirds swooping and diving through the air. Surtr sat still, clearly also observing everything. His gaze was intelligent, and Storm wondered what he was thinking.

'You want to join them, eh? Are you not able to?' He wondered if the bird was injured in some way. Was it his imagination, or was one wing slightly lopsided? 'I'll have to ask someone.'

When they'd both had enough of staring longingly out to sea, Storm slowly made his way back towards the buildings. As he rounded a corner, he almost walked into the solid figure of Joalf. He remembered him from the fight down on the beach, but they hadn't been formally introduced.

'Oh, I beg your pardon. Didn't see you there.'

Joalf grunted something, then did a double-take when he caught sight of Surtr. 'By Thor's hammer, what are you doing there, boy?' He glanced from Storm to the bird and back again.

Surtr made no move to leave, merely wriggled round to preen one of his wings. Joalf's mouth fell open. 'Well I never . . .'

'I hope I haven't done something wrong. He just came and perched on me. I didn't have the heart to tell him to go away.' Storm rubbed his chin, wondering if he should have tried to find the bird's owner to ask permission.

'No, no. He goes where he pleases.' Joalf was still staring at Surtr as if he couldn't believe his eyes. 'It's just that he's never taken to a stranger before. Not once. The only people he normally sits on are myself and his mistress, Freydis.'

'*Freydis. Treat. Treat. Gwoark.*' Surtr took this opportunity to join the conversation, and Storm raised his eyebrows at him.

'This is Freydis's bird?' It was his turn to be surprised. For some reason he'd thought taming a wild bird would be something a man might do, but that was sexist thinking. And he could definitely imagine Freydis having the kind of patience needed to train a raven.

'Aye,' Joalf confirmed. 'Found him when he was a chick, she did. Healed his broken wing as best she could. He's been with us going on four years now.'

'And she taught him to talk? That's marvellous! He's so clever, I can't believe it.' Storm grinned. He loved all animals, but had never met a tame raven before.

Joalf nodded. 'That he is. When he wants to be. Can be right ornery too.' He held out his hand. 'Here, Surtr, want to come and help me with my tasks?'

The bird put his head to one side, as if he was considering the offer, then deigned to hop down Storm's arm and onto the other man's hand. He made some more clicking noises as he climbed up to Joalf's shoulder.

The man shook his head. 'I still can't believe it. I wonder why he chose you?' He regarded Storm as if there was something strange about him.

There was, but Storm doubted the time-travelling magic had anything to do with this. He shrugged. 'No idea. Perhaps he was bored, like me.' He looked around at the hustle and bustle of the settlement. 'You wouldn't happen to know if there's anything I can help with? I gather we'll be staying for a while, and I'm happy to pitch in wherever I'm needed.'

Another considering look, then a nod. 'Come with me.'

Chapter Seven

Hrossey, Orkneyjar
Gormánuðr (late October) AD *875*

Freydis found herself occupied until late afternoon, when she was finally able to slip away from the hall. The extra thralls Ófeigr had brought had been put to work helping to cook supper, and all her other chores were done. Thankfully Gyrid was too busy directing everyone else to have time for another weaving session or lesson in household management. Freydis went in search of Joalf, and found him stacking peat inside a hut where it would be left to dry out before use. He wasn't alone.

'Storm? What are you—' She cut herself off. It was none of her business what he chose to do.

'Good afternoon! I'm helping Joalf while we waited for you to arrive. He tells me you were hoping to have a training session today.'

'Yes, but . . . you are a guest.' She frowned at him, but he didn't seem to notice and carried on with his task.

'Apparently we'll be staying for a lot longer than we thought. Our ship is severely damaged, and Assur tells us it will be difficult to find the right materials to repair it.' He sighed. 'We might have to remain here until timber loads arrive in the spring.'

'So I hear.' Earlier, she had vaguely registered the fact that Ófeigr and his men would be staying for several months. That meant they weren't just temporary guests, and they'd have to contribute to the running of the settlement any way they could. She hadn't thought they would start immediately, though, which was why she was surprised to find Storm hard at work.

'I offered Joalf my assistance,' he continued. 'Later I'll check if I'm needed elsewhere.'

'And right welcome it was too,' the older man said, his gaze approving. That in itself was cause for surprise. Joalf was a quiet man, not given to making friends or socialising overmuch. For him to take a liking to someone this quickly was very unusual. Clearly Storm's charming smile didn't just work on females. Not that she wanted to think about that . . .

'Hmm, well, that's kind,' she murmured.

At this point, Surtr, who had been perching on Joalf's shoulder, decided to transfer to his mistress instead. With a deep-throated cawing noise, he flapped over and landed on her, his feet gripping the material of her tunic. '*Surtr. Surtr. Good boy. Treat!*' he chanted.

Storm smiled at him, admiration in his gaze. 'He's such an amazing bird. You are very lucky to have him. I envy you.' He finished stacking the last of the peat and walked over to Freydis, hunkering down a bit so that he was eye to eye with the bird. '*Hei*, Surtr. Aren't you beautiful! Will you talk to me again? Or am I too much of a stranger?'

The bird peered at him, dark eyes glittering with intelligence. Then he tilted his head to one side and opened his huge, slightly curved beak. '*Good boy. Treat!*' he reiterated.

Storm spread his hands. 'Sorry, I don't have anything, but I'll be sure to save you something from my next meal.'

'Don't spoil him,' Freydis said, but at the same time she dug around in her pouch and produced a piece of meat she'd pilfered earlier while helping to cook tonight's stew. 'Here, this is all you get for now, you greedy bird.'

'Greedy bird! Greedy bird!'

The grin that spread over Storm's face was worth any number of stolen pieces of food. It made his ice-green eyes sparkle, and Freydis almost choked on her breath. She managed to turn it into a cough at the last moment.

'I hope we'll become friends, Surtr,' he told the bird.

'Looked to me as though you were well on your way already,' Joalf muttered.

Freydis turned to him. 'What do you mean?'

He nodded in Storm's direction. 'Ran into him wandering around the settlement with Surtr on his shoulder. They'd found each other.'

'What?' She stared at the newcomer and then frowned at the bird. 'But he's never . . .'

'Exactly.'

A look passed between them, acknowledging the significance of what had happened. She wasn't sure whether to be astonished or alarmed that her bird had decided to befriend a stranger. He'd always been shy with anyone other than herself and Joalf, but now he had voluntarily approached someone. It was uncanny. Almost like magic.

Storm, however, appeared oblivious to the fact that something unusual was going on, and reached out to stroke Surtr's soft head. 'Where exactly did you find him?'

Freydis took a deep breath and told the story of how she'd discovered the chick and rescued him, then hand-reared him. In the meantime, Joalf locked up the hut and went to retrieve their weapons. When he returned, the three of them headed for the mainland, still talking. Storm was full of questions, and she was happy to answer them. She gathered he was passionate about animals of any kind and abhorred their mistreatment. It was something she'd always been conscious of as well, although living on a farm she was pragmatic enough to know that most of them had to be killed in order for the humans to survive.

'Here we are,' Joalf announced as they reached the meadow where they usually trained. 'Shall we begin with our usual routines, and you can join in a bit later?'

Storm nodded. 'Yes, that would be good.'

As she hiked up her skirts and looped them through her belt, Freydis felt self-conscious for the first time in her life. It had never bothered her before, but having Storm watching her every move was disconcerting. She was aware that she ought not to show him her legs in this fashion, but he'd seen them the previous evening and hadn't batted an eyelid. Presumably it didn't bother him, so she wouldn't allow it to discomfort her either. To Storm's obvious delight, she transferred the bird to his shoulder, and tried to concentrate on sparring with Joalf. If she didn't look in Storm's direction, she could pretend he wasn't there. It wouldn't do to lose focus, or Joalf would take advantage.

As they went through their normal practice routines, Storm remained silent. He was leaning against a boulder, his arms crossed over his chest. It made his muscles strain against the material of his tunic, but Freydis refused to let this sight distract her. She'd seen brawny men before and he was nothing special. She ignored the little voice inside her head that said she was a liar, because he was like nothing she'd ever come across before.

'Good!' Joalf called out at last, before turning to Storm. 'What do you think?'

She felt her cheeks heat up as she waited for his verdict. It shouldn't matter to her, but it did, and she was afraid to hear what he had to say.

He pushed off the boulder and walked over to them, smiling. 'Yes, well done. You've got all those moves down pat. And I saw yesterday that you can use them in a proper battle situation, which is the real test. You kept your head under pressure. How are you at fighting without weapons?'

'Without?' She frowned at him. 'What do you mean?'

'There might be times when you'll need to defend yourself and you don't happen to have your sword to hand. Have you practised for such an occasion?'

'No. I assumed I'd only be fighting in smaller skirmishes like the one last night.' For the most part, she hadn't thought she'd be allowed to fight at all. She had tagged along with the men without being asked, and in the heat of the moment Assur hadn't thought to forbid it.

Storm shook his head and tutted. 'That won't do. Let me show you some weapon-free techniques. Joalf, can you take the bird, please?'

Surtr was made to hop onto Joalf's shoulder instead. The older man watched with interest as Storm gave Freydis instructions on how to handle herself if he charged her without any weapons, or came at her from behind.

'You are using their motion to your advantage,' he explained, and showed her what he meant. 'And you'll have the element of surprise on your side, as I'm fairly certain most of the men here won't believe you capable of hurting them.'

At first she was embarrassed to be grappling with him. Their bodies were in such close contact she could feel the heat of him through their combined clothing. But soon she forgot about that as she became fascinated by the moves he was teaching her – how a smaller person could unbalance someone bigger and heavier, how she could twist in certain ways to escape a tight hold, and which points on a man's body were the most vulnerable to attack.

'That's probably enough for today,' Storm declared finally.

Freydis bent over and placed her hands on her knees, breathing heavily. 'Where did you learn all this?' she huffed, looking up at him. He seemed not to have exerted himself unduly.

'You wouldn't believe me if I told you,' was his enigmatic reply.

Joalf came over and clapped him on the shoulder. 'Amazing!' he said. 'You'll have to show me as well.'

'I'd be happy to. Perhaps tomorrow? It's getting late and we'd best be heading back.' Storm looked at Freydis as she let down her skirts. 'Do most women here have trousers on underneath their tunics?' He sounded merely curious, and she gathered he didn't mean to be impertinent in any way. It was strange that he would ask – he ought to know the answer to that question already.

'In winter time, yes. It helps with keeping warm.' She didn't tell him she'd prefer to wear nothing *but* trousers, as she'd done when she was younger.

'When I first met Freydis, she was dressed like a little boy,' Joalf interjected with a teasing grin. 'Would have liked to throw her *smokkr* into the sea, so she would.'

'That was my father's fault,' she muttered. At Storm's raised eyebrow, she added, 'He raised me like a son, since I was his only child. My mother wasn't best pleased.'

'So you spent a lot of time with him?' Storm asked, picking up her sword and handing it to her.

'Yes, virtually all day, every day. We did everything together. Mother despaired of me ever learning any of the female tasks, as I was seldom indoors with her.'

She thought back to those happy, carefree times, when her father had taught her the skills she would need for survival, and for running their settlement. He'd instilled in her self-confidence and self-esteem, which might be why she was so reluctant to go along with Assur's marriage plans for her. She knew she was worth more than being used as payment in lieu of a debt. She was fully capable of making her own decisions, and she'd been raised to choose for herself. Her father would have consulted her wishes with regard to her future husband, and together they'd have chosen the best possible candidate. As it was, she hadn't even met Ingolf Gunnarsson, and what she'd heard didn't augur well. Her father would have wanted her to be a lot more cautious and not accept such an arrangement without due consideration.

Storm shrugged. 'It sounds wonderful, and where I come from, women wear men's clothing all the time, so it wouldn't bother me.' He chuckled. 'I doubt Gyrid would see it that way, though.'

'Definitely not. She's already cross about the fact that we train at all.' Joalf shook his head. 'Miserable woman. Let's go before she sends a search party to find us.'

The three of them scrambled down to the beach and then up again onto the sea stack. Freydis was tired, but in a good way. Her entire body was buzzing with excitement, and her brain went over everything she'd learned. Most of those moves would take a lot of practice, but she knew she could do it and was impatient to go through them again.

Storm was proving to be an absolute godsend. Thank goodness he was staying for the foreseeable future.

'Where have you been?' Gyrid's suspicious gaze darted from Freydis to Joalf and Storm, who had entered the hall behind her.

It was just her luck that the woman should happen to be near the door when they returned.

'I was outside with Joalf,' she prevaricated.

'And the other one?' Gyrid glared in Storm's direction. He was following Joalf over to a bench near the hearth. The two men were deep in discussion about something and thankfully didn't look her way.

Freydis shrugged. 'We met up with him outside.' It wasn't a lie, just not the whole truth.

'Well, I don't want you associating with any of the strangers. You are betrothed now. It is not proper for you to talk to other men.'

That was ridiculous. She spoke to the men in the settlement more or less every day, so why not the newcomers? But the others were nowhere near as handsome and charismatic as Storm. He drew everyone's gaze, something Gyrid must have noticed. She'd seen some of the married women eye him up too, as though he was a tasty morsel. It had made her insides clench, although it wasn't as if she had any rights over him.

'There can't be any harm in speaking to them in sight of a hall full of people,' she protested. 'What if they need my assistance with something – would you have me be rude and unhelpful?'

'That is not what I meant and you know it. Don't be insolent. Now come and help me with the *nattverðr* and stop gawking at him. He may be fine-looking on the outside, but you can never trust a man like that.'

Freydis decided not to argue. She would speak to whoever she wished, but from now on she'd have to be more discreet about it. While helping Gyrid with the last of the food preparations, she kept her eyes on the task at hand. Although supremely aware of Storm, who was now chatting with a few of the other men, she didn't look his way. In fact, she didn't intend to go near him for the rest of the evening.

But she would definitely find a way of continuing the training they'd begun. There was no way she'd miss out on an opportunity like that.

Storm had overheard Assur's wife when they'd come in, and had caught the woman's glare. He had no idea what he'd done to earn her enmity, but it was clear she didn't like him. Or perhaps she'd got wind of the fact that he'd been training with Freydis. If so, they would have to be more careful in future. The woman seemed to have it in for Freydis, which annoyed him. From what he'd seen so far, she worked extremely hard and never complained. What was Gyrid's problem?

He sat with Joalf and accepted a mug of ale from one of the thralls. It felt wrong to be served in this manner, but he couldn't kick up a fuss about it as that would make him stand out. Keeping a low profile and trying to blend in was the best strategy. He also refrained from staring at Freydis, even though his eyes wanted to return to her over and over again. She was beautiful, but completely unaware of it. It was the kind of natural beauty that came from within, not merely surface deep. He doubted there was a vain bone in her body, which only added to her allure.

He shouldn't notice her at all, but it was hard not to. Her blonde hair shone bright in the firelight, the thick plaits so long she could probably sit on them, and her graceful movements drew the eye. And he wasn't the only one aware of her appeal. Several of the other men cast longing glances her way, but she was oblivious. She'd said she was betrothed to someone already, against her will. That meant she was out of bounds in every way. And he was here to find his sister, nothing else. He needed to keep that in mind.

Some of Ófeigr's men joined them, looking downcast as they settled onto the benches either side of him and Joalf.

'It's going to be a long winter.' The corners of Saemundr's mouth were turned down and his shoulders hunched. 'Curse those marauders! Why can't they go and plunder further south?'

Storm was inclined to agree, although attacking anyone with a view to stealing their goods was despicable. It did seem disloyal to plunder their own people, but in the Viking age there were no

Scandinavian countries as such. Perhaps that meant no one felt any loyalty to those who spoke their own language and followed more or less the same social mores. The end result was the same – they were stuck here for the foreseeable future.

'Maybe we could go round all the nearby islands and beg or buy planks from every settlement?' he suggested. 'They might have one or two each, and then we'd have enough.'

'No point. I already asked Assur, and he says whatever planks they had would have been used by now to strengthen buildings for the coming winter. Besides, by the time we've done the rounds and carried out the repairs, it will be too late in the season to cross the Úthaf. We were already cutting it fine and taking a chance, leaving as late as we did.' Saemundr sighed. 'If only Ófeigr hadn't fallen ill at Dyflin. We weren't sure he would pull through, he was so sick.'

'Yes, a shame,' Storm agreed, although it had been to his advantage. Or so he'd thought. No one could have foreseen the predicament they now found themselves in. 'We will have to stay busy as best we can. There must be plenty of work in the settlement.' He for one would have to keep himself occupied, or he'd go mad thinking about the fact that he couldn't go after his sister any time soon. Feeling stuck and not being in control was something he absolutely hated. He was a man of action, not someone who sat around waiting for things to happen. It frustrated him no end that his hands were tied here.

'Yes, I'll do my fair share, but my joints always ache with the onset of the colder months, so I will stay indoors as much as I can. Maybe do some whittling and carving.' Saemundr held up a piece of wood he'd been working on with a sharp knife. 'Assur said there are always household items needed.'

'Hmm, I'm not very good at that and I prefer to be outdoors in any case. Can I help you again tomorrow, Joalf?' Storm turned to the older man, who had stayed silent during Saemundr's complaints.

'Aye. There are always tasks needing to be done. I'll look for you in the morning.'

Although Joalf was taciturn and not much of a talker, it felt as though they were becoming friends. Perhaps it was the surprise of Surtr seeking Storm out earlier, or his help in training Freydis, but he sensed that he had gained the man's trust. He hoped to keep it that way, or else the time spent here might become unbearable.

Chapter Eight

Hrossey, Orkneyjar
Gormánuðr (late October) AD *875*

Gyrid made sure to keep Freydis busy for the next few days. There were endless chores, as well as long sessions in the weaving hut. She claimed it was for Freydis's own benefit, as the cloth they were making would be hers, but Freydis wasn't convinced. It seemed a deliberate attempt to prevent her from seeing Storm, and even Joalf, whom she'd always spent time with each day.

On the afternoon of the third day, she finally had a few moments to herself when Gyrid was called away to deal with an emergency. One of the other women in the settlement had gone into premature labour, and anyone with experience of childbirth was needed. Freydis thanked the gods she wasn't one of them, and headed off in search of Joalf. Surtr, who had been waiting patiently for her outside the weaving hut, flew down to perch on her shoulder. He was making little noises to himself, and she gathered he was happy to see her at last.

'I'm sorry to have to ignore you all the time,' she murmured, and scratched the top of his handsome head. 'You should stay with Joalf, you know.' But Surtr seemed to prefer to keep watch over her, even if he wasn't allowed indoors.

'Freydis! We didn't expect to see you today.'

Joalf was the first to spot her as she came through the door of the building that doubled as smithy and carpenter's workshop. The settlement didn't have a resident smith at the moment, but Joalf was capable of making basic items. She'd thought to find him repairing cauldrons or other household objects, which was what he normally did for at least part of each day. Instead he was working the bellows while Storm banged away at something on the anvil.

Her eyebrows shot up. 'You're teaching Storm to work iron?'

Joalf chuckled. 'No, quite the opposite. He knows more about it than I do. Been trained by someone back where he comes from.'

Storm stopped what he was doing and nodded a greeting. 'So you finally deign to talk to us,' he said with a smile. It was clear he was teasing, and she didn't take offence.

'Why would I want to?' she countered, surprising herself with this comeback.

His smile widened. 'Good question.'

She threw a glance at the open door and grew serious. 'Actually, I'm not supposed to speak to you. Gyrid has been watching me like a hawk.'

'Just me, or both of us?' Storm asked, his eyebrows lowering into a V.

'Mostly you. She's never objected to me spending time with Joalf before.' Freydis sighed. 'It's on account of the fact that I'm betrothed. She says it wouldn't be proper for me to speak to unmarried men.' When he opened his mouth to protest, she held up a hand. 'I'm not to interact with any of the other newcomers either, so please don't feel singled out.' Although that was probably not true. None of the others made her heart beat faster, and somehow Gyrid must have sensed this.

'I see. That's a shame. I guess there won't be any more training sessions then.'

'Yes, about that . . .' She hesitated and looked to Joalf for support. 'Isn't there anywhere we could train in secret? I mean, not out in the open, but inside one of the buildings?'

Joalf stroked his bushy beard while he contemplated her request. 'Not sure. There's not much space anywhere except the hall, and you definitely can't do it in there.'

Storm stopped his hammering for a moment. 'Is there perchance a hayloft?'

'Yeees . . .' Joalf drew out the word and threw Storm a suspicious glance. He appeared not to notice.

'Well, that would make a great place to practise throwing someone down,' he explained.

'Ah, I see. Soft landing, eh?' Joalf's eyebrows lifted.

'Exactly.'

'Sounds perfect!' Freydis didn't care where they went as long as she got to practise those intriguing fighting techniques Storm had started showing her the other day. They could prove very useful if she came up with a plan for escaping the marriage to Ingolf. Leaving this place, whether alone or with Joalf, would be dangerous, so the more she learned, the better she'd be able to defend herself. 'How about now? Gyrid is otherwise occupied and hopefully won't come looking for me for a while.'

'Hold on. I'm nearly done.' Storm plunged the piece he'd been working on into a bucket of cold water, where it hissed and gave off a small cloud of steam. The noise made Surtr caw and shuffle on her shoulder, but he didn't fly away. 'How's this?'

He held up a beautifully crafted iron hook with the top curled into two ends that met in the middle. It was a lot more delicate than anything Joalf usually produced, and perfect for hanging cloaks and the like on the wall.

'How lovely! You are obviously quite skilled at this.' She took it from him and examined it more closely. 'Where did you learn? Were you a smith where you come from?'

He took the hook back and rubbed it dry with a piece of linen. 'No, I only did it for amusement. Someone taught me, but it is not my daily occupation.'

'Then what is?' Freydis was curious to learn all about him. How could anyone be this skilled and not do it every day?

'I'm a warrior. A fighter for hire.'

That made sense. He was good at that as well. Still . . .

'Well, I hope you make more pieces like this one while you are here. I'm sure Gyrid will like it.'

He made a face. 'I didn't exactly have her in mind, but if it makes her stop glaring at me, all the better.'

'Is that what she's been doing?' Freydis hadn't noticed, since she was normally the one on the receiving end of the woman's disapproval.

Joalf laughed. It wasn't something he did very often, but when it happened, it was a low rumbling sound that always made her want to join in. 'She's just jealous because she's no longer young enough to attract your attention.' He clapped Storm on the shoulder. 'Take Freydis to the barn and start the training. I'll be along once I've tidied up here and put everything away.'

'Very well, if you're sure.' Storm untied the leather apron he'd been wearing and pulled it over his head, hanging it on a nail on the wall. He gestured for Freydis to precede him. 'Show me the way.'

Freydis seemed a bit on edge as they set off. She kept scanning their surroundings as they walked between the buildings, as if she was afraid to be seen with him. He could understand it now that he knew Gyrid had told her not to spend time with him, or even talk to him. It was irritating, though. Where was the harm in just speaking to someone? Did the woman think he was going to seduce Freydis in a hall full of people? Ridiculous.

And yet he was still learning to navigate this new world he was in. There were probably nuances of behaviour he was unaware of, and he had to tread carefully. It wouldn't do to come across as disrespectful, and he didn't want to get Freydis in trouble. He'd follow her lead and be circumspect.

'Here we are.' She pulled open a heavy door and they entered some sort of barn or storage building. To their right was a ladder, and as soon as they'd closed the outer door, she began to climb it. She had to tuck her skirts into her belt first, and as he followed her up, he averted his gaze so as not to ogle her derrière. If she caught him doing that, she might be reluctant to train with him, and he really didn't want to make her feel uncomfortable in his presence.

They arrived on an upper platform that was chock-full of hay. It smelled amazing, like a hundred summer meadows all in one place. He drew in a deep breath, letting the scent envelop him. It was calming, and his whole body relaxed.

Freydis discarded the pouch that hung from her belt and re-tucked her skirts to keep them out of the way. Underneath, she wore trousers and a shorter long-sleeved tunic, exactly like his own, and not the usual long woollen dress. She should also have been wearing a long linen underdress – a *serk*. That was what Storm's mother and sisters had always worn during re-enactment get-togethers. Instead she had on what looked like a man's shirt, shorter than the tunic. There was nothing remotely sexy about either garment, but seeing her dressed like that made something zing through his veins. He ignored it and refrained from commenting on her attire this time.

'Let's spread out the hay a bit,' he suggested.

It was all piled up towards the back of the platform, leaving only a tiny part at the front bare. Storm pulled chunks of it out and scattered it to create a soft arena for them to work in. He made sure it was thick enough that if she fell, she wouldn't hurt herself. She quickly helped him and soon they were ready.

'Right. Now you're going to come at me as if you're attacking me, like last time. I'll show you again how I can use the momentum of your body to overthrow you. Ready?'

'Yes.'

At his signal, she rushed forward, pretending to brandish a weapon in attack. He grabbed her arm and flipped her easily, using a simple judo throw. She lay in the hay, blinking up at him. At their previous session, he had only showed her these moves in slow motion and never actually floored her. This time things would get real.

'What on earth . . . ?'

He smiled and reached down a hand to pull her up. 'Here, I'll show you slowly. It's very simple really.'

The lesson progressed, and he taught her various ways of unbalancing her opponent and using an attacker's own weight against them. She learned fast, and although her cheeks were pink with exertion, there was a sparkle in her eyes that made him grin. She was loving this and he enjoyed teaching her. A bit too much perhaps.

'One last throw. This one is a bit trickier,' he told her. 'Come at me from the side.'

She did as he'd asked, but as he went to flip her using his hip, she stumbled and the move went awry. He ended up tripping on her leg, and when she landed in the hay on her back, he fell on top of her.

'*Oof!*' She stared up at him, breathing heavily.

He became hyper-aware of the fact that their bodies were

touching virtually from neck to toe, and a shiver snaked through him. Her chest was rising and falling, her delicious curves plastered against him. He could feel them despite the layers of clothing in between them. It was somehow more sensual than being skin to skin, although why that should be, he didn't know. Yet he wouldn't have been human if he hadn't noticed, although he tried his best not to. Then he made the mistake of looking into her eyes. There wasn't much daylight in the hayloft, but he could still see the clear sky-blue of them. He'd heard the expression 'windows to the soul' but always dismissed it as nonsense. Now he wasn't so sure.

Without thinking, he reached out a hand to tuck a strand of hair behind her ear, while they continued to stare at each other. Everything around them faded into the background, and he could have stayed there for ever, content just to look at her.

'Storm?' Her tentative whisper pulled him out of his trance.

'Oh. Sorry. I . . .' His limbs felt languid, as if they were filled with treacle. He knew he ought to move, but he didn't want to. His gaze fell to her mouth. It was lush, pink and perfect. The urge to kiss her was so strong he almost flinched.

What the hell was happening?

The spell was broken by the sound of the barn door opening. 'Freydis? Storm? Are you there?' Joalf's voice echoed through the space.

They sprang apart as if electrocuted. Storm was on his feet in seconds, holding out his hand to pull her up as well. On autopilot he began to dust off the hay that stuck to the back of her clothing, and picked bits out of her hair.

'We're up here,' Freydis called. 'Wait there, we'll be down in a moment.'

Her cheeks were bright red and she wouldn't look him in the eye, but she didn't protest at his ministrations. Nor did she baulk when he picked up her pouch and held it out so she could slip it onto her belt quickly. While she busied herself with that, he put on his own belt, which he'd discarded earlier.

'So do you think you'll be able to use those moves now if anyone tries to attack you?' he asked, trying his best to sound casual. His voice was a bit gravelly, and he cleared his throat. He really hoped he wasn't blushing the way she was. Normally, nothing embarrassed him, but this was a situation he'd never found himself in before. The rules were different here, and he knew he'd crossed a line even if he hadn't acted on his thoughts.

'Yes. Thank you. That was extremely useful. I don't know where you learned, but I am grateful to you for teaching me.' She sounded calm and in control. He could see her hand shaking slightly, so it was probably an act, but he was glad Joalf couldn't hear that anything unusual had taken place.

'Any time. We'll practise some more another day. You go ahead. I'd better put all this hay back the way it was when we arrived.' He bent to do that, and heard rather than saw her climbing down the ladder.

Joalf's voice floated up to him as the two of them left the barn. 'I'm sorry it took me so long to get here. I was waylaid by Svein, and you know how once he starts talking he never stops . . . It's too late for me to join the lesson now and I heard Gyrid calling for you, so we'd better go and find her.'

Their voices faded and Storm sank down onto the hay, gripping his hair and tugging on it with his fists. 'That can*not* happen again,' he hissed at himself. Next time he'd make sure Joalf was with them.

He could not be trusted to be alone with Freydis.

'So did you learn anything useful?'

Joalf reached over and plucked a piece of hay out of her hair.

The gesture didn't give her goosebumps the way it had when Storm did it. With Joalf it was more of a paternal thing. He'd never been overly familiar or touched her much, but he showed her in other ways that he cared about her. Without him, her sojourn here at Assur's settlement would have been nigh on unbearable.

'Oh yes! It was unbelievable. He's a big man, is he not? And yet I was able to throw him to the ground with hardly any effort. I could probably even do it to you.'

She was still reeling from all she'd been taught. Bubbling with excitement. It was better to concentrate on that rather than the odd moment when he'd been stretched out on top of her. She tingled all over when she allowed herself to remember.

'That does sound good.' Joalf nodded. 'I want to learn too. Can't hurt.'

'You definitely should. I've never seen anything like it. I wouldn't have believed it possible if I hadn't tried it myself.'

'Hmm. Useful man. I can't quite fathom him out. He seems different somehow. And his speech is . . . well, sometimes he mutters in a tongue unlike any I've heard before.'

'Yes, I've noticed that too. Have you asked him where he's from?' Freydis hadn't had a chance to chat to Storm, and she had so many questions about him. She was hungry for every morsel of information, even though she was well aware she ought to stay away from him.

'He said Svíaríki, but I've known Svíar and had no trouble understanding them.'

Freydis shrugged. 'Perhaps he's spent time elsewhere.'

'Yes. He told me he's not one of Ófeigr's men. He'd merely bought passage on the man's ship.'

'To Ísland, was it?' She'd heard the other men talking about their homes across the sea.

'Aye. I haven't yet asked why he was heading there.'

'It is none of our concern.' Even so, she was curious and hoped Storm would tell them more eventually.

She was about to add something when the cow horn blared a noisy signal. They exchanged looks and started running towards the hall for their weapons. When they arrived, out of breath, they were met by Assur, who was exiting the main doors. He held up his hand.

'No need for alarm. Merely unexpected visitors.'

'Who?' Joalf grated out, huffing slightly from the exertion.

'Ingolf Gunnarsson. He must be here to finalise the betrothal and take a look at Freydis.' As if he'd only just noticed the state of her wrinkled garments, Assur frowned and looked her up and down. 'You'd best change into something finer, girl. He won't want a hoyden for a wife.'

She opened her mouth to tell him she didn't care, as she didn't want to marry the man in any case. But she knew she had to play along for now. She and Joalf hadn't yet come up with a workable plan, and it was best not to let on that they were plotting. The only way she'd ever escape was if she took everyone by surprise. By acting meek now, she could lull them into a false sense of security, and it would be prudent not to antagonise the man from the start.

'Very well.' She nodded curtly to both men and went in search of her best *smokkr* and some privacy in which to tame her hair. No doubt there was still hay in it. She'd need to comb and re-braid it to make herself presentable.

Once she was done, she returned to the main area of the hall and found Assur seated next to an imposing man with blond hair and a darker beard. Her kinsman beckoned her over, and she went, trying not to show her unwillingness.

'There you are! What took you so long?' He didn't wait for her reply, but turned to Ingolf and made the introductions. 'This is

Freydis, my cousin's daughter.' He didn't bother to tell her Ingolf's name. It was implied that she should be fully aware of who he was.

Ingolf rose to his feet and gave her a slight nod while his gaze roved from her head to her feet and back up again. The slow perusal made her grit her teeth, but she stayed outwardly calm. He was checking her over the way he would a brood mare, and she supposed to him that was all she would ever be. She stared back unflinchingly, although she wasn't as blatant about taking in his appearance. She had to admit, he was a handsome man, but she didn't feel even a tiny spark of attraction. Not the way she had with Storm earlier . . .

She buried that thought. It was something to ponder later. Now was not the time.

Ingolf smiled at Assur, then turned his charm on Freydis. 'I'm pleased to make your acquaintance. Come, won't you sit with us for a while?' He indicated a stool next to the two large chairs he and Assur were occupying. 'I was just saying I believe a wedding feast after Yule at the midwinter *blōt* would be best. Do you agree?'

'If that is your wish.' She bent her head, as if she acquiesced. In reality, she wasn't agreeing to anything, but he didn't need to know that yet. Yule was some way away, which could only be a good thing. There was still an outside chance that something might occur to stop the marriage from happening. Perhaps if she prayed to the gods and made a sacrifice, they would listen to her pleas. But deep inside she doubted it, and despair temporarily engulfed her, making her lungs constrict. She pushed the panic down. No, she had to take matters into her own hands and not rely on fate. And she would; she just hadn't figured out how yet. She forced herself to take calming breaths and not show any outward signs of distress. Ingolf, fortunately, appeared not to notice that anything was amiss.

'Excellent. That's settled then.'

After that, he and Assur lost themselves in a discussion about the political situation in Hörðaland and totally ignored her presence. She felt dismissed, but dared not move away in case that was seen as insulting. Taking more deep breaths, she stayed where she was and observed the comings and goings of the hall. She saw Storm enter after a while, casting a glance around, his eyes briefly resting on her before moving on. He was intelligent enough not to show any interest in her – if he had any, something she wasn't sure about – and went to sit with Joalf. They were soon laughing about something. She envied them. It must be so easy to be a man and never have to do something you had no wish to.

In fact, it was downright infuriating how Assur believed he had control over her life. If only she could teach him a lesson and find a way to disabuse him of that notion. Then smug Ingolf Gunnarsson could find himself another victim and Freydis could live her life in peace. Neither of them owned her, and in truth, she owed them nothing. No matter what Assur claimed, she had earned her place here with hard work, and she wasn't his to dispose of as he wished. Not without consulting her first.

What would her father have advised in a situation like this? 'Take charge of your own destiny' was one of his favourite sayings. Yes, that was what she had to do. She had to take back control from these men, and for all she cared, the pair of them could go and freeze for eternity in Niflheim, the cold and inhospitable world where evil men were sent after death. She had no doubt that was where they'd end up eventually, and if she had no other option, she'd hurry along their passage.

She would rather go down in a fight, taking them with her, than marry this conceited *argr*.

Chapter Nine

Hrossey, Orkneyjar
Gormánuðr/Frermánuðr (October/November) AD *875*

Storm studied Freydis's betrothed surreptitiously. The man looked like a grade A asshole. A bully of the highest order. He'd come across men like that before, both in the army and in civilian life. They thought themselves invincible and acted accordingly. This one was good-looking, in a smarmy sort of way. He sincerely hoped Freydis wouldn't fall for that, but so far it didn't seem that way. She was sitting still as a statue on that uncomfortable stool, her expression giving nothing away. At least she wasn't simpering at the man, thank the gods. Although it really shouldn't matter to him. He and Freydis were just friends.

'She doesn't want him, you know,' Joalf murmured. There was no one sitting close to them, but he clearly didn't want to be overheard.

'I know. She told me as much when I first arrived.' Storm was whispering, pretending to be sipping from his ale mug. 'What are you going to do about it?'

'Haven't decided yet. I hope he's not here to wed her on the spot, or we'll have to do something drastic.'

'We?' Storm raised his eyebrows at his companion.

Joalf's mouth tugged into a smirk. 'Aye. I've seen you looking at her. I reckon you'll help if I ask you to. I didn't like it at first, mind. I know nothing about you and I doubt you're looking to become a husband any time soon, but you care enough to assist us.'

'I do,' Storm admitted. He might not want to marry the girl, but he already liked her enough that he couldn't stand by and see her being forced to wed a man she didn't want. Especially not with all the rumours of violence circulating about Gunnarsson. It would be like sending a lamb to slaughter. No way.

'Well then, here's to success.' Joalf clinked his mug against Storm's and smiled.

Storm smiled back and echoed the toast. It might have been fate that had stranded him here, but perhaps the gods had had their reasons all along. He was still far from rescuing his sister, but here was another woman who also needed his help. Freydis was just as vulnerable, despite her fighting skills, and he was definitely beginning to care for her. How could he refuse to lend his assistance? That would have felt all kinds of wrong.

Freydis made sure she behaved impeccably during Ingolf's visit, and to her huge relief, he left the following day. He only spoke to her one more time, to say farewell.

'I will see you at the Yuletide celebrations. Assur tells me you will be going to Ranulf's hall, over on Mávey. I'll be there too.'

'Yes.' She nodded, even though this was the first she'd heard of it. Ranulf was a distant relation of Gyrid's, and they'd been to his settlement a couple of times over the years. She hadn't known they would be going this year, but it didn't matter. If Assur had decreed it, that was what would happen.

'Until then, farewell.' He gripped her face with both hands and placed a proprietorial kiss on her mouth, then turned to stride down the path towards the ship that was waiting in the cove.

She suppressed a shudder and made a beeline for the bathing hut. There was water and lye soap there, and she used it to scrub her mouth thoroughly. It was the only place she could do it in private, and she couldn't let Assur or anyone else see what she was doing. Ingolf's kiss hadn't been slobbery or unpleasant, merely impersonal and harsh, yet the imprint of it lingered. It was his way of branding her, she supposed. Her skin still crawled at the thought of it. Never again. She would not let him anywhere near her.

'So you really like him then.'

Freydis jumped, and almost dropped the linen sheet she was roughly drying her mouth with. Storm had stealthily entered the hut and pulled the door shut behind him. He was leaning against the door frame with his powerful arms crossed and his mouth quirked up on one side. Laughter danced in his eyes and she wanted to hit him.

'You find this amusing?' She threw the piece of linen onto the nearest bench, then stalked over to stand in front of him. Poking him in the chest, she added, '*You* don't have to marry someone against your will. Nor be kissed by them without any say in the matter.'

His teasing expression faded and he reached out to grip her upper arms. 'I'm sorry. That was insensitive of me. I have a habit of joking when I shouldn't. Forgive me? I meant only to lighten the mood.' His pale green eyes stared into hers and he did look very earnest.

She huffed. 'I suppose so. Now let me go.' Trying half-heartedly to tug herself loose, she stared at the floor.

'Are you sure you want me to? I taught you enough already that you could easily have made me.'

Her eyes shot back up to his. He was right. She was allowing him to manhandle her. Enjoying it, in some perverse manner. 'I . . .'

She couldn't deny that she ought to have stopped him. So why hadn't she?

He glanced at her mouth, as if he was contemplating kissing her himself. A thrill shot through her, all the air left her lungs and she blinked. What would that be like? Storm had a beautiful mouth, surrounded by a closely cropped beard that looked soft but would no doubt prickle if he touched his lips to hers. For some reason, she relished the thought of that. She wasn't at all repulsed by the notion of kissing him, the way she had been with Ingolf, but it wouldn't be right. She bent her head again, a deep sigh escaping her.

He let go of her arms and instead put both of his around her, pulling her close to his chest. 'You've had a horrible day and I reckon you need some comfort, am I right? Please allow me to hold you for a moment. Trust me, it will help.'

Her cheek had come to rest on his chest, close to his heart. She could hear its steady thumping and the sound was indeed soothing. Comforting. Calming. Almost of their own volition, her hands came up to rest on his shoulders. They were strong and unyielding under her palms, but reassuringly warm through the thick material of his tunic. She breathed deeply and inhaled the scent of wool, peat smoke and man. The unique blend that was Storm. It was perfect. Another sigh came from deep inside her, but this was one of relief, letting go of the tension that had been coiled inside her ever since she'd been told that Ingolf had arrived. Her entire body relaxed and melted into his. She felt his arms tighten around her, and he rested his cheek on top of her head. He didn't seem in any hurry to let go.

'How did you know it would make things better?' Her question came out as a hoarse whisper.

'My mother always says that this is the best way to recover from something awful. She's a very wise woman. You'd like her, I think.'

She could hear the affection in his voice when he talked about his mother. They clearly had a close and loving relationship, unlike hers with Dagrun. A woman she hadn't seen in eight years and who hadn't sent her more than a casual greeting. Even as a small child, she didn't remember ever being held like this, as Dagrun had never been particularly maternal. There were no memories of a warm embrace, only the occasional fierce hug from her father. But she didn't want to think about that now.

'Yes, I believe I would,' she murmured, slowly extricating herself from his hold. It went against her instincts. She would have liked to stay in his arms for a long, long time, but that wasn't prudent.

He smiled and brushed one of her plaits over her shoulder, bending to place a soft kiss on her cheek.

'I hope you feel better,' he said. 'I'll leave you for now, but you know where to find me if you need my assistance with anything.'

'Yes. Thank you.'

She watched as he let himself out of the hut, standing there staring into space for quite some time. If only she was marrying someone like Storm instead of Ingolf, life would be so much better.

Storm knew he probably shouldn't have hugged Freydis, but he didn't see the harm as long as no one found out. If ever a person had been in need of a bear hug, it was her. He had felt her relaxing against him and really hoped he had helped, if only in a small way. How could they do this to her? It was so unfair.

Before travelling back in time, he had never considered just how little autonomy women had in the past. Sure, he'd read about it, and heard feminists talking about how they'd had to fight for their rights, but here he was seeing it actually happening. And to someone he was starting to care about. That brought it home in a way no textbook ever could. Freydis, and the other females here, were expected to be guided by men, as if their intellect was somehow inferior. As a twenty-first-century man, he knew that was rubbish, but it was accepted here. No one questioned it, although from what he'd read, they trusted their women to look after their domains when they went trading or raiding. So why wouldn't they let them choose their own husbands?

Perhaps it was just Assur, and not everyone acted this way. The man was clearly in a fix, and had decided Freydis was his ticket out of trouble. Because she was stuck here, vulnerable and with no other relatives to speak up for her, he was taking advantage. Either way, she didn't deserve the horrible situation she'd been forced into, and he wished there was more he could do. If Joalf came up with a plan, he'd be all in, no doubt about it.

You just want her for yourself, a little voice inside his head needled him. He couldn't deny it. He wanted Freydis, no doubt about it, but he couldn't have her. She was nothing like the girls he normally picked up for a one-night stand in his century. Perhaps that was the draw. Wanting the forbidden. But he didn't think so. It was Freydis herself who attracted him. She was beautiful and fearless, but modest and unassuming at the same time. Both fierce and soft. Loyal, but with a stubborn and rebellious streak. All irresistible contradictions. Yet resist he must.

He'd lived life until now in a carefree manner, not taking his liaisons seriously, but he was in a different era. You didn't fool around without consequences, and Freydis being pure when she was married off would be a matter of utmost importance. Ingolf looked like the type of man who'd expect a chaste bride and know the difference if she wasn't. Or if not him, then whoever she married in the future. No matter how much Storm craved her, a quick tumble was never going to happen. Besides, his own reasons for being here should be uppermost in his mind, not getting involved romantically with a girl who was none of his business.

What was he doing getting sucked into this? It was madness. He should focus on surviving the winter. Go to Iceland. Find Maddie. Return to his time. Simple. Nowhere in that plan was there room for any complications, and Freydis was most certainly that.

Still, there was no way he could stand by and see her mistreated and coerced. As long as he was here, he'd do whatever it took to protect her.

'*Hei!* Where are you off to?'

Freydis jumped as Storm appeared unexpectedly from behind the corner of a building. Surtr, who was sitting on her shoulder as usual, cawed in welcome and flapped over to perch on him instead.

'Traitor,' she murmured, but couldn't help smiling at the way the bird leaned against Storm's fingers when he scratched the top of his feathery head.

'Going for a walk? May I join you? I need some fresh air. The hearth in the forge has been very smoky today and my lungs feel as though they are coated with sand on the inside.' He fell into step beside her.

'Yes, I feel the same. I've been helping with cooking all morning and I couldn't stand the fug in the hall another moment.' Freydis glanced behind her to make sure no one was watching them. 'Gyrid said I could go outside for a short while.'

'Good of her,' Storm retorted sarcastically. He sent a glare back in the direction of the hall. 'She treats you like a slave. If you ask me, she ought to be grateful to have your assistance.'

Freydis shrugged. 'It's just her way. She believes she is teaching me to be a good mistress of a household.'

'Hmph.' He changed the subject, clearly disagreeing. 'Where are we headed?'

'We? I don't recall saying you could come, but Surtr and I are going to the cliff edge.' She dared to tease him, and was rewarded with a big grin that made her insides flutter.

'Is that so?' He glanced at the bird, who was still on his shoulder. 'Well, I reckon I have his approval, so I'm tagging along whether you like it or not.'

'*Surtr, good boy*,' the bird muttered.

Storm laughed. 'That you are. Mostly.' He turned to Freydis. 'Did you know he stole a silver item I was mending yesterday? Joalf managed to get it back eventually, but he's a little thief.' He didn't seem angry about it, though, and Freydis smiled back.

'Yes, Joalf told me. Surtr likes shiny things, just like magpies.' They had reached the edge of the cliffs and she spread out a sheepskin she'd brought on the grass, being careful not to put it too close to the sheer drop. 'Will you sit with us?'

'I'd be honoured.' Storm sank down next to her, and they stared out to sea for a while in companionable silence. 'It's so beautiful here, isn't it. There is something very special about the light, and the air is so clear. I've never been to the Orkneyjar before.'

'No? I hadn't either until my mother sent me here eight years ago.' She couldn't help the tone of sadness that crept into her voice.

'That must have been so difficult.' He put his hand over hers where it was resting on the sheepskin. His palm was rough and slightly callused, but it felt warm and comforting, so she didn't pull away.

'Yes, it was. I had lost my beloved father six months previously, and then I was being taken away from the only home I'd ever known.' She fixed her gaze on the horizon, willing away the emotions rising inside her. 'I still don't quite understand it, because I tried not to be troublesome. Mother remarried quickly and my stepfather seemed not to mind me, but she claimed he wanted me out of the way. I mustn't complain. I've not been mistreated here. Well, until now . . .'

Storm's hand tightened on top of hers. 'They are still determined to make you wed Gunnarsson?'

'Yes. Perhaps I ought to try and make the best of it. As his wife, I'd be busy running a large household and perhaps having children. And as long as I didn't anger him, he would have no cause to abuse me. Assur might be right – his other wives must have been weak or incompetent. I'm neither.' If she really did have to marry him, there was no way she would let Ingolf browbeat her or destroy her spirit. He would soon learn that she was made of sterner stuff. But she was determined it wouldn't come to that. She'd find a way out.

'You're definitely not, but still . . . you shouldn't have to do something against your will.'

'No, but don't we all sometimes?' She turned to look at him. 'What about you? Joalf tells me you are searching for your sister. How did she come to be lost?' Joalf had asked Storm the previous day about his reasons for travelling to Ísland, and then reported back to Freydis. He hadn't shared any details, though.

He hung his head. 'It's a long story, and not one that paints me in a good light. Are you sure you wish to hear it?'

She turned her hand over under his so that they were palm to palm, then squeezed. 'Please, tell me.'

'Very well, but I'll give you a short version. We were visiting Dyflin with our parents, and I'd made some new friends. They wished to take me to a . . . gathering, where the ale flowed freely.

My parents were invited to take *nattverðr* with friends of their own, and I was left in charge of Maddie. I took her to the place we were staying, thinking she'd be safe there. I mean, she'd seen nineteen winters, so she wasn't a child, and she's as proficient at fighting as you are. I told her I was going out. She wanted to come with me, but . . . er, I didn't think it was the sort of place I should take a young unmarried woman. And I didn't want to spend the whole evening watching out for her. Selfish of me, I know. Maddie wasn't best pleased, but I never thought she would defy me. Apparently she did. Someone told us afterwards that they'd seen her leave, and then she disappeared. Vanished without a trace. It's taken me months to find even a hint of where she might have gone.'

'To Ísland?'

'Yes, I believe so, but I won't know for sure until I get there.' He shook his head. 'We would have been there already if it hadn't been for those marauders. Curse them!' When he glanced at her, the look in his eyes was so bleak she wanted to put her arms around him, the way he'd done for her the other day. 'I feel so guilty, Freydis. I should never have left her on her own,' he added in a hoarse whisper. 'She was my responsibility. I *have* to find her.'

She tightened her hand in his again. 'She was a woman grown, Storm. You couldn't have known she'd go wandering around at night. That was most unwise. And you *will* find her, I am sure of it. It might take a little longer than you'd envisaged, but if she is in Ísland, she's not going anywhere either right now.'

They both regarded the metallic grey water swirling far beneath them. The wind was fierce and the waves were high. It was an inhospitable expanse, and no one in their right mind would brave a week on the open sea this time of year.

Storm's expression brightened. 'You're right. I hadn't thought of it that way. Thank you!'

He brought her hand up to his mouth and kissed her knuckles, then let go. Despite missing his touch, Freydis felt content, because she had managed to comfort him. Now they were even.

For the next few weeks, Storm threw himself into work in the forge. He'd been attending Viking re-enactment camps with his parents since he was a baby, and although his first love had always been fighting, he had also learned blacksmithing. Weapons training and mock fights never took up the whole time during their stays at the various camps. He'd always been restless and not one for sitting still and doing nothing. When an older man had offered to take him on as his blacksmith's apprentice, he'd jumped at the chance. And over the years he had grown proficient enough to progress to doing it by himself. That came in very handy now.

'How long have you been putting off these tasks?' he teased Joalf. The man had a long line of items that needed either repair or remaking from scratch. Storm knew it was not Joalf's main occupation here in the settlement, and that it had been left to him when the previous smith had died of a sudden illness.

'*Þegi þú*, boy!' Joalf gave Storm's shoulder a playful shove. 'I do have other things to do, you know.'

Storm grinned. 'I suppose that is lucky for me. Now I can keep myself occupied too.'

It was fortunate in more ways than one. For one thing, it was a good excuse not to have to help with hunting, fishing or netting birds. These were necessary things if they were all to survive the winter months without starving, but Storm didn't like killing defenceless animals, even though he wasn't a vegetarian as such. For another, not only did it help him to stay out of Freydis's way, as she seldom came to the forge, but it was nice and warm in here. October had segued into November – or so he guessed, since he wasn't keeping tally of the days – and the weather was turning decidedly cold. Up here on the sea stack, the settlement was buffeted by icy winds and quite a lot of rain. On more than one occasion, Storm had taken his blanket and furs and spent the night in the forge rather than the draughty weaving hut. The walls in the hut had more than one hole, and although he spent some of his free time plugging them with moss, he hadn't yet located them all.

Another by-product of working in the smithy was that he was getting to know the inhabitants of Assur's settlement. Once they'd realised that there was someone who could do more than solder together a broken handle, they began to bring him other requests. Storm was happy to oblige. Working with iron was satisfying, and he'd always had an artistic bent rather than an academic one. With parents who were both archaeologists, it could have made him feel inferior, but they had never pushed him one way or the other. They were proud of his achievements, whatever they were, and he had grown up secure in his own worth. He realised now that was a gift he might not have appreciated enough. He'd tell them next time he saw them.

If he ever saw them again.

Not that they'd been proud of him lately. He cringed inwardly as he contemplated the many pointed silences and surreptitious glances he'd received since his sister's disappearance. He had let his parents down by not looking after her as he ought to have done, and the unspoken blame weighed heavily on his conscience. His foster-brother Ivar had told him not to take it to heart, and that they were just as much at fault, but Storm couldn't agree with that. They still loved him, and always would, but they were disappointed in him. How could they not be? He was twenty-one – almost twenty-two – and should have been more grown-up and responsible. Should have known better. Maddie going missing had acted as a cold shock to his system, making him mature almost overnight. There'd been no other option, and he had to make it right or he would never be able to look his parents in the eye again.

He and Freydis had had a few more training sessions in the hayloft, but Storm always made sure that Joalf was present. The older man wanted to learn as well, and although he didn't catch on as quickly, he did grasp some of the moves.

All in all, staying here over the winter was proving to not be as much of a hardship as he'd feared. Apart from wanting Freydis, he was enjoying it, and learning a lot about Viking society as well.

He'd be fine until spring. He had to be. As long as he could keep the dark thoughts and self-recriminations at bay.

Chapter Ten

Hrossey, Orkneyjar
Fremánuðr (November/December) AD *875*

'It's happened again! There's half a flock of sheep missing. And it's about to start snowing. I need everyone out looking for them! *Now!*'

Freydis was kneading dough in a shallow trough, up to her elbows in flour, when Gyrid came rushing over and shooed her out of the way. 'Go, girl. I'll take over here. I'm too old to go traipsing across the countryside in all weathers. Hurry! *Bóndi* can't afford to lose any more sheep.'

Dusting the flour off her hands, Freydis went to wash them quickly, then fetched her warmest cloak – one lined with fox fur – as well as a hat and mittens. She pinned the cloak shut, not wanting the cold air to be able to work its way inside. It was windy today, with flurries of snow already beginning to fall from the sky.

Why did the stupid sheep keep wandering off? Or was someone stealing them? When it had happened the previous year, they'd only recovered a handful. Hopefully this time the alarm had been raised more quickly and they would find them all.

She rushed out of the main doors of the hall and almost

collided with Storm, who came running from the direction of the forge. He was wearing the shaggy cloak he'd arrived in, and was pulling a hat over his unruly dark curls, then tugging on a pair of mittens.

'What is happening?' he asked, following her down the steep incline of the path. 'I was told to come quickly and dress warmly.'

'The sheep have wandered off. Someone went to collect them from the mainland to pen them in until the coming blizzard has passed, but most weren't where they were supposed to be. We have to find them.'

She was slipping and sliding in her haste to reach the bottom of the path, and Storm grabbed her arm when she nearly fell. As always, her skin tingled where he touched her, despite all the layers of clothing. She ignored the sensation, swallowing down the feeling of longing for more. He hadn't come near her since their chat on the cliffs, apart from their training sessions, and she understood why. The attraction between them was too dangerous. That didn't mean she had to like the fact that he kept his distance. She missed talking to him. She missed just being near him. *Skítr!*

'*Whoa*, take it easy. You breaking an ankle won't help,' he murmured, holding on to her until they reached the bottom of the slope.

He was right and she slowed down a little. It was harder going up the equally steep path on the mainland, and she didn't protest when Storm put a hand on her lower back and pushed to help her.

'Thank you,' she mumbled, ducking her head. The mere touch of his palm on her clothing had her feeling hot and bothered, and she was sure she was blushing. That wouldn't do.

'Any time. Can I go with you, please? I have no idea what I'm doing, and even if I did find a sheep, I'd probably get lost coming back.' He chuckled, but she could hear the truth in his words.

'Of course. Follow me.'

She noticed the direction other people were taking, and headed to the right along the coast as no one else had gone that way. She huddled into her cloak, trying to protect her face from the sting of the snow flurries, which were gradually increasing in quantity and ferocity. The wind was merciless, and she was very glad to be wearing a hat. She'd made it herself using the *nalbinding* technique, and it was nice and thick. Storm appeared to have a similar one, and she wondered who had made it for him. His mother? Sister? Beloved?

She knew he wasn't married, but did he have a special woman waiting for him at home? She hadn't thought to ask. What did she know about him really? Not all that much.

'Where did you get your hat?' she blurted, unable to keep her curiosity at bay.

'My hat?' He was keeping up with her, his long strides effortless. He threw her a confused glance. 'I bought it. Why?'

Freydis felt her cheeks heat up again. *Fool!* She shouldn't have asked. 'Oh, just wondered. I, er, made mine.'

He grinned at her. 'Trust me, if I'd made mine, it would have holes all over. I've tried my hand at *nalbinding*, and I'm useless.'

'*You* have tried that?' She was surprised. There were a few men who could do it, but mostly it was women's work.

'Yes, my mother made me and my siblings learn. They were all much better at it than me.'

'You have more than one sibling?'

'Mm-hmm. I have two sisters, although one is a half-sister. Linnea. And I have a foster-brother too, Ivar, but he's much older than I am. Fourteen winters my senior.'

It was nice to learn a few more facts about him, and the conversation no longer felt awkward.

'Where are they now?'

'Linnea is in Svíaríki with her husband, Hrafn, and their children. Ivar is, um, on a journey. As for Maddie, you know all about her.'

She had thought a lot about his tale of how his sister had gone missing. 'Do you think she's been taken captive?' she asked. It was something that could happen to anyone, she knew. The marauders who had chased Ófeigr's ship wouldn't have hesitated to grab as many people as they could to sell as thralls.

A frown marred Storm's brow. 'I don't know. An old crone I spoke to in Dyflin claimed she'd been in a fight – my sister, that is, not the crone – and a man had helped her and taken her on board his ship. She told me the man was heading for Ísland, but didn't believe my sister was his slave, as he was looking after her. It's the only lead I have to go on and I thought to follow them there. As I understand it, the island is not much settled yet. It shouldn't be too difficult to find one very red-haired female.'

'Oh, she doesn't look like you?' His hair had an auburn sheen in certain lights, but it wasn't red.

He smiled. 'We have similar colour eyes and are almost the same height. She is very tall for a woman. But otherwise, no, we're not much alike.'

'I have some half-brothers, apparently, but I've never met them,' Freydis blurted out. She hadn't meant to tell him, but since he was sharing, why shouldn't she?

He threw her a look full of compassion. 'Because you haven't been back to . . . where is it your mother lives again?'

'Sogn. And yes, that is the reason.' She clenched her fists inside her mittens as the old wound opened up again and flooded her with misery the way it always did. Why had her mother not sent for her? She could have done so at any time these past few years. Freydis wouldn't have been a burden – she'd gladly have helped out in any way she could – but it seemed her presence wasn't wanted. Well, so be it. There was nothing she could do but accept it. She locked the hurt away and attempted to sound cheerful. 'I hope to meet them one day. I'd like to get to know them.'

Storm murmured, 'I'm sure they would like you.' Then he added, 'What about Assur's son? I gather he is about your age, but I haven't seen you interact much. Are you close? You must have grown up like siblings.'

Freydis shrugged. 'Not really. He more or less ignored me when we were younger. I bested him in a fight once, and I think I dented his pride. Don't get me wrong, he's never been mean to me, and I believe he'd like to see me happy, but he has no say around here. I'm afraid he is rather weak and firmly under his father's thumb. And his mother's. Joalf was the one who looked after me right from the start. He's become like a father to me.'

'I'm glad. He's a good man.' Storm hesitated for a moment, then added, 'Do you think you might be able to go and visit your mother once you're married? Surely Gunnarsson would want to meet your kin.'

'I don't know. I can try to persuade him. I would dearly love to make sure my mother is well. Bjarni, her husband, has a temper on him, or so I've been told. Never saw any sign of it myself, the few months I knew him, but people change, I suppose. Mother said she was confident she could keep him sweet, but I'm not so sure.'

They plodded along in silence for a while, keeping their eyes peeled for any stray sheep, but the landscape around them remained empty.

'Are you really not going to try to escape the marriage to Gunnarsson?' Storm suddenly burst out.

'What?' Freydis stopped abruptly and turned to stare at him. She nearly shouted, 'Of course I am!' but hesitated before replying as she didn't want to give anything away at this stage. She didn't know if she could trust him. 'There is no escape. We both know that.' Turning away so that he wouldn't see she was prevaricating, she attempted to sound dismissive. In truth, she had been lying awake at night turning various plans over in her mind, but she hadn't discussed them with anyone other than Joalf. Had the man talked to Storm?

When she dared to look at him again, his mouth twitched, as if he was trying to suppress a smile. 'I'm not a fool and neither are you. There is no way you'll quietly accept your fate. You're too much of a fighter for that.'

'I . . .' She didn't know what to say.

He put a hand on her shoulder and gave it a squeeze. 'I won't tell anyone, you have my oath. And I'd be happy to help you. Just tell me what you need me to do.'

'Er, thank you.' She started walking again, scanning the clifftops, but there was nothing moving there. 'I don't have a plan as yet.'

'We'll have to put our heads together then. Now where are these blasted sheep? I'm freezing my . . . er, I'm cold.'

They passed the occasional hairy cow. They were a local sort with incredibly long coats that kept them protected through most types of weather. Ancestors of Highland cattle, Storm guessed, and presumably the snow wouldn't bother them. As they were black or brown, they were easier to spot than a sheep. How on earth were you supposed to find something white and fluffy in a blizzard?

He trudged after Freydis, letting her lead the way. As long as they stayed near the coast, he could still find his way home, but visibility was decreasing and he didn't want to chance getting stranded alone.

'There's one, look!' She pointed at something huddled next to a strange stone building.

'Are you sure?' He squinted through the rapidly falling snow but couldn't make it out.

'Yes, and there's another. Come!'

She began to run, and he increased his pace too. 'Wait, don't scare them off. I don't want to be roaming around for ever.'

Freydis didn't reply, but she did slow down, approaching the sheep with caution. 'Here, you try to grab one while I get the other.' She held out a length of rope to him and he took it. 'Bind this round its neck if you can.'

They reached the two sheep, which looked as miserable as Storm felt himself. Their eyes flickered with suspicion, but they didn't move.

'*Hei* there. Are you cold? We won't hurt you. Come now.' He tried to talk softly to the animal, and it appeared to work. The ewe – he assumed it was female, as it didn't have horns – allowed him to grab her around the neck, and he slipped the rope over her head and tied it in a secure knot.

'I've got this one,' Freydis announced. 'Can you see any more?'

He scanned the landscape, but the sky had darkened and the snow was coming down faster now. A strong wind whirled it into thick flurries. It was impossible to see anything. 'No. What is this place?' He looked up at the stone structure they were next to.

'Something built by the ancients, Joalf said.'

'Ah, a *broch*.' He'd heard about those. They were Neolithic buildings, and very ancient indeed. Even in this century, it was at least a thousand years old.

'A what?'

'Never mind. Why don't we take shelter inside until the wind subsides a little. We won't be able to see a thing, and I for one don't want to fall off the edge of the cliff.'

'Good idea. Er, you go first.'

'What, are you scared of spirits?' He chuckled, sending her a teasing glance.

'No, but if there are any, I'd rather you disturb them first.'

'Hah, you *are* scared.'

'*Fifl.*' She gave him a shove, and he laughed as he tried to tug the recalcitrant sheep in through an opening under a stone lintel.

The building appeared to be circular and fairly large. Perhaps as much as ten to fifteen metres in diameter. It was paved with stone slabs and divided into rooms by the same kind of material, interspersed with dry-stone walls. There was something that looked like a low, square trough in the centre of the largest room, and a half-broken staircase rising against the inner wall. Storm guessed the trough might have been a hearth, but it was empty now, apart from the snow gathering at the bottom. A smaller room off to one side was still intact, complete with ceiling, and he headed in there. He had to duck to avoid hitting his head on the lintel.

'This looks like the warmest place,' he called over his shoulder. 'At least the snow and wind won't get to us here.'

The ewe seemed to understand and followed him inside. Freydis and the other animal arrived a moment later. She looked around with wide eyes. 'Oh, it's beautifully made, is it not? How did they stack the stones so tightly?'

'They were master builders in *Neolithic* times.'

'Neo . . . what?' She frowned at him.

'The Stone Age. People who lived here at least a thousand years ago.' Or had it been Bronze Age? He wasn't sure, but it made no difference to Freydis. 'I can't explain. It is something I learned about a long time ago. Shall we sit down?'

Someone must have taken shelter here in the past, as there was a pile of old heather or grass in one corner. He handed her the rope holding his sheep for a moment while he took his *varafeldur* cloak off to shake it out the door. Melting snow flew everywhere, but the inside of the garment was mercifully dry and he knew the outside would soon be as well. After wrapping it securely around himself again, he grabbed a huge stone slab that had been leaning against the wall and manhandled it into place across the doorway. There was still a small gap at the top, but it helped to keep the worst of the weather out.

Without the wind whining around their ears, it was blessedly quiet. Storm sank down onto the pile of heather. Freydis followed suit, although he noticed that she made sure to leave some space between them. That wouldn't do, but he'd let her settle in before he did something about it. They would need to sit close together if they were to share bodily warmth, which was essential for survival in these sorts of conditions.

No need to spook her. She was probably nervous enough as it was, being stuck in this gloomy place with him. And who knew how long they'd have to remain here? He hoped it wouldn't be all night.

'Sit closer to me, please. We'll be warmer that way,' Storm said, beckoning her over.

They had both been quiet, lost in thought, and Freydis had no idea how much time had passed. Outside, the snow hadn't yet let up, and she could hear the wind keening around the stone structure. Thankfully, in here only the occasional draught penetrated, and her cloak had dried out.

She peered at Storm suspiciously, but saw no guile in his eyes. He was serious.

'I'm fine where I am,' she informed him, tugging closer the sheep she was holding on to. The ewe had been standing there as if unsure what to do, but now she seemed to accept her fate and lay down. Her woolly coat had glistened with melting snowflakes at first, but it was now dry. Freydis wondered if she could try to warm her feet underneath the animal, but decided against it now that the ewe had finally settled.

'I'm not dangerous, you know.' There was a teasing note in Storm's voice, and she glanced his way again. His eyes were dancing with amusement, and his mouth had that quirk that always made butterflies swarm in her belly. It was a welcome sight, even though it shouldn't be.

'I'm not afraid of you,' she retorted sharply. The asperity was more for herself, because she couldn't seem to resist the man's charm and she was fully aware she ought to.

'Ah, then perhaps you are worried I'll do something inappropriate. Is that it?' He was outright smiling now, and she smacked him on the arm. They both knew he could have done any number of things in the time they'd been sitting here, but he hadn't so much as nudged her with his elbow. She trusted him and was certain he'd never touch her without permission.

'What? No! Stop it, you provoking man. If I have to stay here with you for a while, you'd best behave.' Although a little voice inside her disagreed. She'd have loved him to misbehave, and she couldn't help but wonder yet again what kissing him would be like.

He chuckled. 'Very well, I'll try. But I'm serious about sharing warmth. It is necessary for our survival. Let me take this off and we can both huddle underneath.' He removed his shaggy outer cloak and turned it inside out so that the woolly tufts faced them. Then he draped it over their shoulders and pulled it snug, fastening it with a pin. 'There, how is that?'

His arm went around her waist and tugged her to his side. It felt only natural to lean her head against him. He was right – she was warmer already, although that might be because of how close he was. His unique scent enveloped her – clean clothing, a bit of peat smoke from the forge fire, and the man himself. It was enticing, alluring, and she wanted to bury her nose in his chest to breathe him in. She resisted.

'*Hei*, relax. I'm not going to molest you, I swear. I would never do anything you didn't want me to.'

That was the problem, though. She *did* want him to, and that was wrong.

She looked up and found him staring down at her. His eyes were a darker green in the dim light, but no less beautiful. His was a gaze a woman could drown in. And she would love to do just that.

He groaned and closed his eyelids. 'But don't look at me like that, please. You're making it very difficult for me to do the right thing.'

'What if I don't want you to?' she whispered, and his eyes flew open.

'Huh?'

Freydis was hot all over now with embarrassment, but she probably wouldn't have an opportunity like this again and she had to take it. 'What if I wanted you to kiss me? Just this once? And . . . um, nothing more.'

She was fully aware of where kissing could lead. After that cryptic talk with Gyrid, she'd asked some of the other married women in the settlement to explain better. They had obliged, with much laughter and some light-hearted teasing when her face had turned crimson at the mere thought of what they were describing. The fear of having to marry Ingolf and allow him to do those things to her had been uppermost in her mind for days. If she couldn't escape the marriage, he would have the right to kiss her and touch her whenever and however he pleased. Unless she took this chance, she would never know what it could feel like with someone she actually desired. She held Storm's gaze, trying to show him that she was in earnest.

He took a deep breath and regarded her for a long moment, then he nodded. 'I can do that. If you're sure?'

'Yes.' She made her voice sound decisive, even though butterflies were swarming in her belly.

He lifted her off the heather and sat her sideways on his lap. Then he put his arms around her waist and pulled her close, leaning forward to nuzzle her nose with his. It was a curiously intimate gesture that surprised her. Before she had time to comment on it, he smiled, then placed his hand on the back of her neck. Slowly, with his eyes open, he inched closer until his soft mouth met hers.

At first he kept still, the connection almost non-existent. Then he increased the pressure slightly and began to move his lips, brushing hers over and over again, as if tasting her. Little nibbles that sent tiny pulses of pleasure right down to her toes. All the while, he was gazing into her eyes as if gauging her reactions. When she didn't protest, his tongue darted out to lick the seam of her mouth, and she opened it for him. He delved inside, playfully licking against her own tongue, and a shiver raced through her.

It was delicious. It was wonderful. Sensuous and enthralling. For a while, she closed her eyes and lost herself in the sensations. She was drowning, but in the best possible way. She hadn't known it could feel like this. Hadn't known she wanted such closeness with a man. Any man. And yet this was perfect. She put her mittened hands on his chest and gave it her all.

After a while, he slowed things down, nipping playfully at her lower lip and dropping tiny kisses along her chin and behind her ear. Delicious warmth spread through her, and she couldn't stop a shiver from rushing through her.

'You like that?' he murmured, continuing his exploration down her neck. The edge of her cloak stopped him, forcing him to return to her mouth. He gave her one last toe-curling kiss before pulling back to look at her. 'Was that what you wanted?'

She could feel his heart beating madly through the layers of clothing and her mittens, although that might have been her own pulse thundering in her veins. 'Yes. Thank you.'

He laughed. 'Don't think I've ever been thanked for a kiss before, but it was my absolute pleasure.' As if what they'd done was perfectly normal, and nothing to remark upon, he simply held her and leaned his cheek against the side of her head. 'I'm warmer now, so I should be the one to thank *you*.'

Freydis didn't know how he could be so calm about this. She had never kissed anyone else, but he must have done so countless times. Perhaps it seemed like nothing to him. She'd do well to remember that and act as if it didn't matter to her either.

She allowed herself to revel in the comfort of being in his arms for a short while before moving off his lap and returning to sit next to him. He didn't let go of her entirely, and she was glad, as she wanted to prolong the contact for as long as possible. It was madness, but she doubted they'd ever be alone again in this way, and she wished to imprint the feel of him on her memory. If she ended up marrying Ingolf, at least she could close her eyes and picture a different man. It might help her to endure.

She glanced towards the door opening. 'It looks as though the snow has stopped. Should we try to head back?' It was the last thing she wanted, as it would break the spell of this magical moment in time, but it was becoming darker outside and they couldn't remain here all night. Gyrid would be incandescent with rage.

'Yes, let's. Will you be warm enough, or would you like to borrow my outer cloak?'

The kind gesture made her eyes smart with unshed tears. No one had ever been so considerate to her, except Joalf on occasion when she was younger. It made her emotional to think that Storm cared about her well-being. Still, she shook her head. 'I'll be fine. Mine has a fox-fur lining. But thank you for offering.'

He was such an enigma, this man. Tough warrior one instant, then solicitous and gentle the next. In between, he was mischievous and teasing. There were untold facets to him, all of which fascinated her. Under different circumstances, she would have liked to become much better acquainted with him, but first she had to find a way to extricate herself from her unwanted betrothal. And Storm might not want to know her in the same way in any case. He was going to Ísland as soon as he could. She had no place in his life, and never would.

They trekked back towards the settlement through a foot of snow, tugging the sheep with them. There was no one else about on the cliffs, and they didn't spot any other animals along the way. The walk seemed to take for ever, but at the same time they arrived back all too soon. Freydis was afraid this interlude would never be repeated, and something inside her protested vehemently.

Storm halted. 'You'd best go first. I'll wait a while so that no one knows we were together.'

'Very well. And . . . thank you.' She threw him a final glance, then pulled her sheep down the steep path from the mainland and up the other side onto the sea stack. They were both slipping and sliding in the snow, but somehow managed to stay upright.

She led the ewe over to a barn where Assur wanted them kept and was met by Gyrid. The woman scowled at her and looked her up and down.

'Where have you been all this time? I was beginning to think you'd run away.'

If only. But Freydis didn't say that out loud. 'Where would I run to in a blizzard?' she muttered angrily. 'I was searching for sheep along with everyone else. Here, this is the only one I found.'

'Take it inside.' Gyrid nodded behind her. 'I'm going back to the hall. Don't dawdle.'

The urge to do so anyway was strong, but there was no point. Riling Gyrid never served any purpose and only made matters more difficult. With a sigh of resignation, Freydis handed the sheep over to someone and made her way to the hall.

Storm waited for what he reckoned was a good ten minutes before making his way back to the settlement with the sheep in tow. It was a good idea to calm his mind and body before returning, in any case. That kissing session had stirred his blood, and although he was no longer as aroused, he was still restless and frustrated.

Damn it all, but I want her!

He'd meant to keep it light and teasing. Help her to create a memory of something that gave her pleasure, because he'd gathered that was what she was trying to do. But his good intentions had backfired and he had lost himself in her plush mouth. He definitely hadn't held back as much as he should have done, because she'd tasted and felt divine, and he couldn't remember ever enjoying a kiss that much. The way she had melted against him showed that they fitted together perfectly, their chemistry off the charts. Yet he was fairly sure she had no idea how rare that was or how much she was affecting him. She had likely never even been kissed properly before. In fact, he could tell she hadn't, although she'd caught on quickly.

She wasn't available, though, and he had to remember that. Not only was she spoken for – unless he and Joalf could help her escape Gunnarsson's clutches – she wasn't someone he could hook up with and discard the next morning. In twenty-first-century terms, she was serious girlfriend material, and he was surprised to find himself actually warming to that idea. Or he would have done, had he been in his own time.

He wasn't.

This was the ninth century, and there was no dating. If he

seriously wanted her, he'd have to woo her, ask her to marry him, and provide her with a home and a secure future, none of which were possible right now. Sure, he had plenty of gold and silver, and could probably establish a home for them somewhere. If nothing else, he could work as a smith, since he enjoyed that. The biggest factor, however, was that he would have to give up his life in the twenty-first century. That wasn't something he'd ever intended to do. Was he really going to lose sight of his objective in coming here in order to court a Viking woman?

He must be going crazy.

He shook his head. The question was academic, since there was no way Assur would want to break his arrangement with Gunnarsson. Judging by the latter's possessive handling of Freydis, he wouldn't let her go either, not for any reason. And despite their best intentions, Storm seriously doubted there was any way of extricating her from the marriage. It would go ahead and there wasn't a damned thing he or Joalf could do about it.

'Aargh!' he shouted out loud, startling the poor ewe, who jumped back. 'Sorry, sorry. It's fine. Come on.'

He descended onto the strip of beach between the mainland and the sea stack, taking care to keep his footing and making sure the sheep was OK following him. Then he slowly inched his way up the other side, his feet reluctantly carrying him back to a place where he wasn't allowed to touch Freydis. Nor so much as look at her, if that horrible woman Gyrid had any say in the matter. It was galling in the extreme.

'Focus!' he commanded himself. He was in the ninth century for a reason – to find and rescue his sister – and getting caught up with a beautiful girl was not his goal. He could not afford to be sidetracked.

Being with Freydis in any shape or form was a pipe dream. She wasn't for him and he'd better forget all about the sweet taste of her mouth, the soft feel of her curves against him, and the fresh, snowy scent of her hair . . .

'Get a grip, man!'

He stomped towards a barn whose door was partially open, releasing the sound of bleating. It would be best if he went to vent his feelings on a piece of iron. Sod the fact that it was already late.

Chapter Eleven

Hrossey/Mávey, Orkneyjar
Fermánuðr (November/December) AD *875*

A few more weeks went by, and Storm kept his distance from Freydis. He only saw her in passing, or across the room when eating in the hall. Ófeigr's men had settled into a routine, just like he had, taking on their share of the settlement's daily tasks. Ófeigr himself was still bedridden, although showing signs of improvement. At least he hadn't gone further downhill. Storm didn't see much of him or the others, as he spent most of his time in the forge.

'How have you survived this long without a smith?' he asked Joalf when the man brought him yet another household item to mend.

By now, he'd made his way through most of the backlog, and was happily creating new objects whenever he had a moment. He was even trying his hand at making jewellery, and had started by melting down an ugly gold ring he'd brought in order to fashion it into something more beautiful. He found goldsmithing a lot trickier than working with iron, so in the end he'd hammered it into a simple band and decided to just etch runes into the surface.

On impulse, he chose the words 'forever mine' in Old Norse. He figured he could sell it to someone who might want it for a woman they were courting. The fact that he'd actually had Freydis in mind was something he refused to acknowledge even to himself. He had no right to give her any such thing.

'We had one until recently,' Joalf replied, pulling him out of his reverie. 'A sudden illness carried him off, and Assur hasn't found a replacement yet. I don't suppose he'll look for anyone until you've gone now.'

The big man had taken to spending time in the smithy with Storm most days. As winter gripped the islands properly, there wasn't much he could do outdoors. He proved to be better at carpentry than smithing, and usually worked on something in the adjoining workshop.

'Lucky for you I'm not going anywhere for the foreseeable future then,' Storm smiled. He was teasing, but at the same time he was fairly content to stay here for now and work in the hot forge. It wasn't as satisfying as being in the army, protecting his country and the world from danger, but it was still enjoyable. In fact, it would have been perfect if he hadn't been plagued by thoughts of Maddie and his parents. The latter were no doubt wondering what had become of him, as he'd promised to return as quickly as possible. As for his sister, he'd tried asking Ófeigr's men if they recalled seeing a woman of her description. Since they came from Iceland, and it wasn't heavily settled as yet, he'd figured they might have come across her, but he had drawn a blank. He'd also questioned a few people from nearby islands who had visited the settlement, as they'd mentioned having been to Iceland during the summer. Again, no luck, although he continued to try and think of ways he could get news of Maddie.

Whenever he wasn't tormented by thoughts of his sister, he relived those magical moments in the broch with Freydis. He couldn't get their kisses out of his mind, no matter how hard he tried. It was fortunate that he had an anvil to pound. It was a good outlet for sexual frustration, which he was most definitely suffering from.

For the love of Odin, I have to stop thinking about her!

As if he'd heard Storm's thoughts, Joalf said, 'Freydis hasn't been herself lately. I worry about her.'

'Oh? How so?' Giving the piece of iron he was working on an extra hard wallop, Storm tried his best not to show how interested he was in news of her.

'That accursed marriage is coming closer. I know it's not to be until after Yule, but she'll be seeing Gunnarsson before then at the gathering on Mávey. She wants nothing to do with the man, but I can't see how she can get out of the betrothal.'

'The gathering?' Storm had vaguely heard talk about Yuletide festivities, but hadn't really paid much attention. Yule was Christmas, wasn't it? That word, which was the same as the one Swedes still used – *jul* – gave him a sharp pang of homesickness. He'd been sure he would be back in time to celebrate with his parents, but he couldn't see that happening now. How would they cope without any of their children at home for the holidays? They'd be miserable. Best not to think about that, as there was nothing he could do about it.

'Yes, the one we're all going to at Jarl Ranulf's settlement on Mávey in a few days' time,' Joalf clarified. 'Well, everyone except a handful of men who will be left behind to guard this place.'

'Oh, I hadn't realised that Ófeigr's men were invited too. I thought it was family members only.' He wasn't sure how he felt about having to be present when Freydis met up with Gunnarsson again. It would be sheer torture, and he'd want to throttle the man.

'No, no, you're all coming.' Joalf guffawed. 'Assur isn't going to pass up the opportunity of having someone else provide the victuals for the feast. He's too much of a skinflint for that.' He grew serious again. 'As for Freydis, I honestly don't know what to do. Time is running out, and so far we haven't been able to come up with any workable plans for putting a stop to the wedding.'

Storm knew all about that, as they'd tossed around a few ideas from time to time. The main problem was the fact that it was too dangerous to attempt a boat ride to mainland Skotland at this time of year. No matter where they hid her on these islands, Gunnarsson was bound to find her.

'Can you not try to speak up for her again?' he suggested, glancing at Joalf, who was frowning mightily. 'She told me she sees you in the light of a father. Tell Assur that is what you are, in effect, since she has no one else to support her.'

Joalf sighed. 'I have tried my best to fill that function, but I am not related to her by blood and have no actual say over her life. My connection to Assur – and thereby Freydis – is . . . complicated. Dagrun gave her into his care, to do with as he wished. I have seldom met such a callous woman, but from what little I saw, she was happy to be rid of her daughter.' He shook his head. 'Unbelievable.'

Storm's mouth tightened and he gave the piece of iron a vicious blow. 'That does sound awful. And yet from what she told me, Freydis is worried about her mother.'

A snort greeted his words. 'Yes, the gods only know why! Her new stepfather must be a piece of work, no doubt about it, although he hid it well the one and only time I met him. And he seemed pleased enough with his new wife. Dagrun is comely, I'll give her that. I doubt he'll mistreat her.' Joalf sighed again, even more deeply. 'I wish I could take Freydis away from here.' His fists clenched. 'And I would have done, had it been summer. I'd wager Assur suspects that, which is why he sprang it on us this time of year. He knows she's not a helpless female. There's fight in her, and she would have tried to escape. In this weather, though, it's nigh impossible to reach Skotland or the Suðureyjar, the group of islands west of there.'

There was a way, and Storm was seriously tempted to use his time-travel device, but it would have to be as a very last resort. Other people in his family came and went, and there was no reason why his axe shouldn't enable him to do the same. Although the magic might not work on Freydis, as she wasn't related to him in any way. From what he had observed, each time-travel mechanism could be used by one person and those who were linked to them – by blood or love. The way he felt about Freydis, she might qualify, but he wasn't convinced and really didn't want to risk it. They weren't in a relationship, and he had no idea how she felt about him, so there was a strong chance the magic would leave her behind and only transport him. That would only make matters worse. Besides, it didn't solve the problem in the long term. And anyway, where would he take her?

He shoved the glowing piece of iron into a bucket of water and watched the steam billow up with a drawn-out hiss as it cooled down.

'We will have to be vigilant at that gathering,' he said eventually. 'If you and I stay close to her, Gunnarsson won't get the chance to corner her alone anywhere. Then perhaps we can come up with some way of spiriting her away before the day of the nuptials. There must be *somewhere* she can hide until spring.'

'Hmm, maybe. I will certainly be sticking to her like a burr.'

'Then I'll do the same.' Storm smirked. 'If nothing else, it will irritate Gyrid no end, and it will be worth it to keep Freydis safe.'

The big man chuckled. 'Oh yes, that woman is not enamoured of you. The suspicious looks she sends your way! Honestly, you'd think it was a crime to be handsome.'

'You think I'm handsome? Aww, thank you. That is sweet of you.'

'*Fifl!*' Joalf smiled and gave him a small shove on his way past to fetch a piece of wood from the other half of the workshop. 'You know full well all the women ogle you whenever you enter the hall. If I ever see it going to your head, I'll be sure to knock you down.'

'You're too kind.' With a laugh, Storm danced out of the way of another shove.

Truth to tell, he hadn't noticed anyone else looking at him, because he'd been too busy trying not to stare openly at Freydis. She was the only woman in this settlement who had his attention, even though she was off limits. As far as he was concerned, the others didn't exist, and that wasn't like him. It was just as well, though, as he should be fully focused on finding Maddie, rather than flirting with anyone. His only goal was to survive the winter months and get himself to Iceland as quickly as possible. Still, since that was some way off, he might as well help Joalf protect Freydis in the meantime.

Where was the harm in that?'

'This is an impressive place!'

Freydis watched Storm take in the superior settlement on Mávey. It too was situated on top of a huge sea stack, but included much larger buildings than Assur's. She knew that the side facing the sea had spectacular cliffs populated by seabirds during the summer months. The ones with large strangely shaped orange beaks were particularly appealing, and she'd watched them last time they visited. She could have done with the distraction now. Her stomach swirled with apprehension, and she'd been unable to eat her morning meal. She simply wasn't hungry. Anxiety took up all the space inside her.

'It is,' she replied. 'The jarl, Ranulf, is a powerful man with allies back in Viken and Agder.' She knew this because Assur had impressed upon her the necessity of staying in Ranulf's good graces. It wouldn't do to anger someone that important, and they were honoured to have been invited to this gathering.

The journey along the coast had been unpleasant, in choppy seas, with an icy breeze and cold water spraying them from time to time. Freydis had barely noticed, however, her mind wholly on what lay ahead. She was dreading meeting Ingolf again, and wondered if he'd decide to claim her early, or if he'd adhere to the original agreement and wait until the midwinter *blōt*. She sincerely hoped it was the latter, as she needed more time to come to terms with her fate.

Or to find a way to escape it.

She had discussed the possibilities at length again with Joalf, but short of braving the sea between these islands and Skotland, they had been unable to come up with a single solution. Joalf was reluctant to risk their lives, but Freydis was growing increasingly desperate. She had decided that if there was no other way, she would try the sea route on her own. With the gods on her side, she might survive, and anything was better than meekly accepting the marriage. She knew Joalf had tried to intercede for her with Assur as well, but to no avail. There was simply no easy way out of the betrothal.

They were greeted by one of Ranulf's men on a small beach on the mainland coast. He indicated that they should make their way across a causeway, which was only accessible during low tide.

'It is safe right now,' he told them, 'but you'd best hurry before it turns.'

They picked up their belongings, with Joalf hefting a kist containing her clothing and other necessary items onto his broad shoulder. She fell into step behind him, and to her surprise Storm followed immediately after. She sent him a glance, wondering why he had suddenly chosen this moment to stay close to her. She'd barely spoken to him for weeks.

He checked to make sure no one was within earshot, then whispered, 'I'm going to help Joalf protect you while you're here. We'll make sure to keep you safe.'

'Oh.' She didn't know what to say to that. Protect her against what exactly? They couldn't deny her future husband access to her.

Another look back showed her that Gyrid was watching them with a frown, but she was too far away to say anything. Still, Freydis didn't want to annoy the woman unnecessarily.

'Try not to be too obvious, please,' she whispered. 'I don't trust Gyrid not to harm you in some way.'

Storm's eyebrows rose. 'You think I'm afraid of an old woman?'

'No, of course not, and I didn't mean her personally. She'd find some other way, or someone to do her bidding. Be on your guard, that is all.'

'Very well. You too.'

They didn't speak further, and once they arrived at Ranulf's hall, there were greetings, and the hustle and bustle of being assigned sleeping quarters. Freydis was put next to Gyrid in the main hall, while Joalf and Storm were shown to another building. She had expected as much, but it made her uneasy. Surely Ingolf wouldn't try anything with her guardian on the next bench? But she wouldn't put it past Gyrid to turn a blind eye. The woman was clearly dead set on marrying her off.

It was therefore a huge relief when she overheard someone saying that Ingolf wouldn't be arriving until two days hence, as he was busy with something in his own settlement. The reprieve gave her back her appetite, at least for that evening.

Ranulf's hall was enormous, as befitted a man of his apparent standing. A long rectangular raised hearth in the middle was flanked by two rows of paired posts that divided the building into three aisles lengthwise. The inside walls were covered with vertical planks, and the hall was open to the rafters, the cross-beams blackened by smoke. As usual, there were holes at either gable end to allow the smoke to escape, and the floor was covered in smooth flagstones. Shields and colourful hangings decorated the walls, and pillows and blankets provided even more splashes of gaudy colour. It was a warm and welcoming space, if a little too crowded for Storm's liking.

As he wasn't one of the important guests, he was seated down one end next to Joalf and two of Ófeigr's men, Saemundr and Olaf. Ranulf was sitting on a dais with his friends and allies. Assur was at that table, with Gyrid and Freydis not too far away. Gyrid, as usual, wore an expression of dissatisfaction, as if she felt it her right to be in a more exalted position. The sight made Storm smirk, but he hid it. As the two women were on the opposite side of the hall to himself and Joalf, at least they could see them. And that bastard Gunnarsson had yet to arrive, by all accounts. One less thing to worry about.

'She's receiving a fair few interested glances,' Joalf grumbled under his breath.

'Who, Freydis?' Storm wanted to say, *Duh, of course she is!* A beautiful girl like that – why wouldn't the men stare at her? Her pale blonde hair shone in the firelight, a beacon of loveliness that was difficult to ignore. And when she smiled, it hit you in the gut, even at a distance. He wanted to kick himself. He was no better than anyone else here, mooning over a woman who belonged to another man.

'Yes, I want to knock their teeth out,' Joalf snarled. 'I know what they're thinking.'

'I didn't take you for a violent man,' Storm teased. At Joalf's grumpy glare, he held up his hands in a peace gesture. '*Hei*, as long as they don't act on their thoughts, all is well, is it not?'

'I suppose. Watch her for a moment, will you? I'm going to the privy. Don't let her out of your sight.'

'Of course.'

Storm kept surreptitious watch over Freydis, noting the increasingly overt ogling she was receiving from a group of men halfway down the hall. It was late in the evening now, and they'd obviously imbibed copiously. The ale had been flowing rather freely all night, their host supplying an endless stream. And it was potent stuff. He himself had refrained from drinking more than one mug when he realised the strength of it. This was a new place and it behoved him to keep his wits about him. He only ever let loose when he was with friends he could trust.

The next time he glanced Freydis's way, she was on her feet, with her cloak around her shoulders, and heading towards the main doors. Without being too obvious about it, he rose to follow her, muttering something to Saemundr about having to take a piss. Joalf hadn't returned yet. Perhaps he'd been caught up in a conversation with someone. It was up to Storm to keep Freydis safe for now, but he hung back as she too visited the privy. Although he had told her he would be guarding her, it was better if no one else noticed him watching her every move.

She emerged alone and walked back towards the hall, her steps dragging as if she was reluctant to return. The privy was situated some way from the main residence, presumably to stop the stench from reaching those inside. He followed her at a leisurely pace, enjoying the fresh air after the musty atmosphere of the hall, but stopped and looked up when he heard her make a noise of surprise and dismay. His insides went cold at the sight of the group of men who'd been leering at her. They had come outside and now surrounded her on all sides. A planned ambush if ever he'd seen one.

Damnation!

'What have we here then? A pretty girl, all on her own. Just begging for company, I'd wager.'

'Yes, we've had our eye on you this evening. A rare beauty, aren't you, sweeting? And we're happy to share.'

Storm had gathered that they were merchants from Skotland, stranded in Orkney temporarily, like himself. They obviously weren't familiar with who was who on these islands, or they wouldn't be messing with a woman who was an honoured guest of their host. Or else they simply didn't care.

Freydis had frozen in the middle of the group, her head turning to take them all in. 'Let me pass,' she demanded. Her voice quivered slightly, but was loud enough to be heard. 'You surely don't want to molest a kinswoman of Assur and—'

'Who? Don't think we've had the pleasure of meeting him. No, we merely want to play a little. Where's the harm in that?'

'Leave me alone,' she hissed, sounding firmer.

'I don't think so.' One of the men guffawed. 'We've a notion to have some sport with you first. No one needs to know, eh?'

'Yes, we won't tell if you don't.' More drunken laughter.

Storm had had enough. He had to do something, and although he could probably have beaten them all up with help from Freydis, a fight would draw unwanted attention. Instead, he strode rapidly over to the men, barging two of them out of the way as he reached out to pull her back against his chest. He wrapped his arms around her waist and glowered at them.

'What do you think you're doing, bothering my wife? Leave her be this instant!' He kissed her cheek. 'Did they hurt you, my sweet?'

She shook her head, but frowned at him slightly. At least she was playing along, thank the gods.

'Your wife?' The men all peered at them, blinking like owls. The smiles slid off their faces and were replaced by varying expressions of confusion, outrage and surprise. A few of them were weaving, as if they couldn't stand up straight, and one knocked into his friend when he stumbled.

'Yes, Freydis Úlfsdóttir is my wife,' Storm stated through clenched teeth, waiting to see whether this information would have the desired effect, or if they were too far gone to care.

Another man leaned forward, narrowing his eyes at Freydis. He was having trouble focusing, and his head bobbed. 'You're married? Why were you sitting with that harridan, then?'

Storm felt Freydis take a deep breath, but she didn't move away from him or untangle his arms from her waist. She lifted her chin. 'Storm Haakonarson is indeed my husband. I was merely sitting with Gyrid because we had matters to discuss.'

There was angry muttering among the men, and one of them went to pull his sword from its scabbard, saying, 'I'll challenge you for her.' But he wasn't wearing a sword. None of them were, as everyone had been asked to either leave their weapons at home or in the safe-keeping of one of Ranulf's men. The jarl wasn't taking any chances, and didn't want any bloodshed during this gathering. Wise man. The drunkard frowned at his empty hand as if he couldn't understand where his weapon had gone.

'Go away, *aumingi*,' Storm snarled. 'And if you so much as look at my wife again, I'll gut you like a fish with my bare hands.'

More grumbling, but the men began to move back towards the hall, finally accepting that their planned sport wasn't happening. One of them caught hold of a passing thrall woman, who giggled at the attention, while another started singing a raucous ditty. Soon they'd seemingly forgotten why they had come outside in the first place.

'Are you well?' Storm whispered, keeping hold of Freydis in case her legs had gone weak from fright. She shivered against him, but he didn't know if that was because his lips brushed her ear as he spoke, or whether she was in shock. He was about to turn her around when another voice sounded from right behind him.

'Well, boy, now you've done it, and no mistake.'

He and Freydis both spun to face Joalf, who must have come up on silent feet. She disentangled herself, her face turning red in the light spilling out from the hall.

'What do you mean? I merely saved her from those louts, just as you asked,' Storm said.

'I could have handled them myself,' Freydis muttered. 'I was about to try one of those moves you taught me. I didn't need your interference.'

'Well, excuse me for offering my assistance to avoid the use of violence,' Storm huffed, crossing his arms over his chest, his mouth tightening. There was gratitude for you.

'That's not all you did.' Joalf regarded them both with a serious expression. 'You declared yourselves married to the other in front of witnesses. That means you are now wed. Man and wife.' He speared Freydis with a narrowed glare. 'You knew that, even if he didn't.'

'Eh?' Storm took a step back and looked from one to the other. Shock reverberated through him, and it took a while for the words to register. 'Married? Just like that?' No, impossible.

Not that he had any idea how marriages were performed in Viking times. He had attended a few during re-enactment weekends in the twenty-first century, but the people taking part had made up their own ceremony as no one knew what it entailed exactly. It had seemed like a fun alternative to an ordinary church wedding, whereas this was all too real.

Freydis's cheeks turned an even deeper colour, and she stared at the ground. 'You know there is a lot more to it than that, Joalf. Our families should have been involved in the decision, and a dowry and bride price agreed and so forth. Everything that's already been settled with Ingolf Gunnarsson. This was all pretend. Those men won't remember it in the morning. They were all in their cups.'

Ignoring his conflicting emotions, and concentrating on practicalities and possibilities, Storm mulled this over, coming to a quick decision. 'We can't be certain of that. Besides, Joalf witnessed it too, and any negotiations about dowries and things can be done later.'

She whipped around to face him, a V forming between her eyebrows. 'What do you mean? He would never hold us to it. I trust him with any secret. With my life even.'

'Yes, but don't you see? This might be the solution you've been waiting for. If we are now married, you can't wed Gunnarsson. Simple as that.'

'But—'

'Listen, I don't have a family here to speak for me, so I make my own decisions, and to all intents and purposes Joalf has been like a father to you. In my opinion he has as much right to agree to a marriage on your behalf as Assur does. You act for him sometimes, don't you, Joalf?' The older man nodded. 'Exactly. You told me you don't have a dowry, Freydis, and I'm happy to marry you without one. As for a bride price, I've no idea how much that is, but I'm certain I can provide it. Though come to think of it, Assur doesn't deserve to be given anything, since he's used up your dowry. That means we're even.'

Storm wasn't sure if he was doing the right thing by insisting, but now that he thought about it, it seemed so obvious. It might at least serve as a temporary solution, giving her a chance to escape Gunnarsson's clutches until she could leave these islands. There was no need for them to stay married for ever – in fact, given that he was supposed to be returning to his own century at some point, that might not be possible. And marrying her wouldn't be a hardship. Personally, he was all in. He'd been falling for her for weeks now, and strangely enough, the thought of being her husband didn't scare him. Not in the slightest. She might not feel the same, though, and it would be up to her to decide what happened in the future. For now, however, all they needed was to agree to be together. Thoughts of his quest to find Maddie, and his parents waiting anxiously at home for news, made guilt bubble to the surface of his mind, but he pushed them away. He hadn't given up on that. He *would* find her, but as he was stuck here anyway for a while, where was the harm in using this opportunity to protect Freydis?

She blinked at him, opened her mouth as if to say something, then shut it again.

'He's right,' Joalf acknowledged, rubbing his beard. 'But Assur and Gyrid aren't going to be best pleased. Not to mention Gunnarsson. He's going to be absolutely furious, and going back on their word to him is going to cause no end of complications. He'd have the right to demand compensation, something Assur can ill afford, but that's his problem. I'm with you – I think this is the best solution for now. You'd better make it real, and quickly.'

'Make it real? As in . . .? You think that's necessary?' The two men exchanged a loaded look.

'Yes.' Joalf's reply was emphatic.

'And you are in favour of this? Of me being her husband in . . . every way?' Storm couldn't believe it. Joalf was always so protective of his charge, he wouldn't hand her over to just anyone. He shook his head. This was too much. 'No, it must be Freydis's choice.'

'What are you talking about?' Freydis rounded on Joalf in exasperation. 'How can we make it any more real? If we're really going through with this, you said that declaring our intent in front of witnesses was enough.'

Storm coughed, while Joalf cleared his throat. 'He . . . um, ought to bed you too.'

She gasped, her eyes widening. '*What?* And you think this is a good idea? You, who've always protected me from everything, want Storm to . . . to . . . Now? Tonight?'

'Yes. I trust him.' Joalf looked at Storm, and he felt the older man's gaze probe right into his very soul. 'He'll look after you. Be a good husband.'

That trust was like a heavy weight settling across Storm's shoulders, but at the same time, he was honoured. He had no idea if he'd make a good husband, especially not in the Viking age. Marrying wasn't something he'd contemplated until now, but Joalf's faith in him made something warm stir inside him. Everyone had always seen him as a bit of a joker, someone who never took life seriously. Although he was well liked, he wouldn't have said that anyone believed him capable of shouldering great responsibility. Suddenly it was imperative that he prove them wrong and justify Joalf's belief in his integrity.

He reached out to take Freydis's hand. 'Seriously, we don't have to do anything tonight. We just need to make it look as though we did. And would it really be so bad, being my wife? I swear I'll not mistreat you, the way Gunnarsson is said to do with his women.'

He allowed his thumb to rub her palm, stroking it softly as if calming a skittish animal. They could work out the details between them later. Come to some agreement that suited them both. Right now, keeping her safe was more important than having everything figured out. To all intents and purposes they were married, and to hell with any consequences.

Her breathing was rapid, and he saw her swallow hard. 'I suppose not. Anything would be better.'

'It's so nice to be appreciated,' he joked, trying to keep the hurt out of his voice. Her words stung, but were no less than he'd expected. He was relieved to see a small smile curve her lips at least.

'I didn't mean . . .'

'I know.'

He returned her smile while trying to ignore the emotions churning inside him. The voice shouting, *What have you done? Put a stop to it right this minute!* The doubts beginning to rise up to half choke him. He pushed them down. This would work somehow. It had to. At the very least, they could stay married until such time as Gunnarsson lost interest. Vikings did have divorce, if a union proved to be a complete disaster.

'Where can we go to be private, Freydis?'

'I . . . I don't know. The bathhouse? I c-can't imagine anyone using it at night.'

'Excellent idea. We'll spend the night there with the door locked and everyone will assume we slept together.' He turned to Joalf. 'You'll have to be the one to accidentally find us tomorrow morning. Make it early, before most of the guests are up. That would be best, don't you think? And perhaps tell Gyrid that Freydis wasn't feeling well and has gone to bed down with some of the other women, otherwise she'll wonder where she is.'

'Yes, will do.' The older man came forward to give Freydis an awkward hug and Storm a slap on the back. 'Goodnight, and for what it's worth, I believe you'll suit very well. May the gods be with you.'

Storm kept hold of Freydis's hand and pulled her along towards the bathhouse. He plaited his fingers with hers, gripping tightly, and she squeezed back. It felt like a tacit agreement, as if she'd accepted this as inevitable. As for himself, he knew there was no turning back now. He'd wanted her ever since he'd arrived in the Orkney Islands, and although this was not how he had envisaged things working out, it was a good solution.

He'd do his best to be a great husband, then perhaps he could persuade her to make the marriage permanent. Deep inside, he was beginning to realise that that was what he wanted.

Chapter Twelve

Mávey, Orkneyjar
Frermánuðr (December) AD *875*

Freydis looked around the bathing hut, which had indeed been empty. There was faint moonlight coming in from an opening up by the roof, and some through the open door.

'We need more light,' Storm muttered. 'And it's freezing in here.'

'The hearth should be ready for use,' she said.

'Ah, yes.' He rummaged in his pouch and took out a fire iron and a piece of flint. He began to strike them together to create sparks, and soon he'd coaxed the kindling into flames that licked the dried peat someone had left ready to be lit. Presumably one of the thralls had laid the fire in preparation for the morning. 'That's better.'

The flames illuminated their faces, and for a moment neither of them spoke. Then Storm cleared his throat and moved towards the door. He closed and barred it before taking off his cloak, which he spread over one of the benches that lined the hut. He held out his hand. 'May I put yours on here too? It will make for a slightly more comfortable bed, although it's still going to be hard.'

Wordlessly she undid the pin holding her cloak in place and handed over the garment. He laid it on top of his own, fox-fur side up. Unbuckling his belt, he set that down on another bench. Without being asked, she did the same.

This situation was awkward in the extreme. She ought to be outraged at having been more or less tricked into marriage with Storm, but in truth, all she felt was excitement. He was her husband and she wanted to be his wife.

She wanted *him*.

'I'm sorry,' he said, a deep sigh escaping him. 'I had no idea my little ruse would land us in this predicament. Are you sure you want to go through with it? It's not too late to go back and hope those men don't remember a thing come morning. We can talk Joalf round. Or you can, at least. From what I've seen, he'd do anything for you. If you really hate the idea, we can—'

'No! It's fine.' She undid the tortoise brooches that held her *smokkr* in place. It would be too uncomfortable to sleep with them on. 'Like you said, it's one way of stopping Ingolf from getting his hands on me. Probably the only way, at this point.'

He came over to grasp her shoulders, gazing into her eyes. 'Don't worry. It doesn't mean you'll have to suffer mine on you instead. I'd never force you to do anything you're not comfortable with. We just need to appear convincingly in love tomorrow morning. And as if we've had a good night together. Can you manage that?'

She nodded. 'I . . . I think so. Can you?'

He gave her a look she couldn't quite interpret. 'That won't be a problem. So we are most definitely married? I've . . . er, never attended a marriage ceremony before, so I didn't think it would be that simple.'

'Well, like I said to Joalf, there's usually a lot more to it, but essentially if we're agreed on it, have declared ourselves husband and wife, and he bears witness to that fact, then yes, I suppose we are. We can try to sort out any other formalities tomorrow, preferably before Ingolf arrives. I don't think Assur will have a choice – he'll have to accept the marriage after we've spent a night together. I don't know what Ingolf promised him, but if you offer a bride price, that might help.'

Storm nodded. 'I can do that.'

Freydis bit her lip and noticed his attention drifting towards her mouth. His pale green eyes darkened as he stared at it. She hadn't been sure until that moment that *he* wanted to do this, but that was definitely yearning in his gaze. It would seem that he desired her, even though he was prepared to be considerate and not claim his marital rights until she was ready.

'I don't know what the future holds,' she added in a soft whisper, 'but I would much rather face it with you by my side. As my husband.'

'Very well.' He exhaled, as if he'd been holding his breath while waiting for her answer. 'Then let's try to get some sleep.'

Freydis hesitated. Would it really be enough to merely say that they had consummated the marriage? Ingolf was not a fool, and he might smell a rat. He could even go so far as to demand evidence. Some of the other women had told her there was a way of proving that you were a maiden. Presumably he could ask for her to be examined in such a manner. She shuddered at the thought and reached out to put a hand on Storm's arm, gripping the coarse fabric of his overtunic. 'Storm?'

'Yes?'

'I want you to claim me in every way. Now. Tonight.'

His eyes opened wide. 'What? Why?'

She clasped her hands together to stop them from shaking. 'I'm afraid that if you don't . . . if we don't . . . I mean, Ingolf could say our marriage isn't valid. Joalf was right about that. And I'm no good at lying. People can always tell when I'm prevaricating.'

Storm grabbed her upper arms and peered at her closely. '*Unnasta*, do you know what it would entail? For me to . . . er, claim you, I mean.'

She felt her cheeks turn crimson as she nodded. 'I do. Um, in principle.' Discussing this was embarrassing, but the fact that he was being kind to her and had even called her 'my dear' made her even more certain that it was the right thing to do.

He let go of her, closed his eyes and ran a hand through his unruly hair, turning to pace back and forth in front of her. 'I need you to be very sure, Freydis. This isn't something we can undo.'

Staring at the floor, she swallowed hard. 'I understand. Perhaps I'm asking too much. If you don't want me that way, that's fine. We can—'

'*Jesus*, woman! Of course I want to bed you. You're extremely desirable, and keeping my hands off you right now is testing my willpower to its very limits. It's you I'm worried about. I'm assuming it's your first time, and you cannot give that to me lightly. You . . . you might come to regret it.'

Freydis had no idea what the White Christ had to do with anything, but she could see that Storm was in earnest about the rest of what he'd said. That put her mind at ease.

'It is my choice and I want it to be you. No matter what happens in the future, or whether we stay married, I want this. Please,' she whispered.

He stilled and came to stand before her. 'Do you trust me?'

'Yes.'

'Good. Then if you're absolutely certain about this, I swear I will do my best not to hurt you, but there might be some discomfort. I'm . . . um, told it's inevitable, although only at first.'

'Don't worry about it. Just show me what to do.'

He swallowed hard, then cupped her face in his big hands and pulled her close for a kiss. His palms were warm against her cheeks, and his thumbs stroked her skin while his mouth slid against hers in a soft caress.

'We'll take it slowly. You like this part, right?' he murmured. 'What we did in the *broch*?'

'Mm-hmm.'

He took his time, kissing her over and over, raining light touches with his lips, as if she was fragile and precious. His rough stubble added a frisson of extra sensation, but she craved more. She became impatient and opened for him, inviting him in. She needed the kind of kisses they'd shared in the old stone building. With a groan, he obliged, tasting, teasing. He carried on kissing her until they were both shaking with need and quite out of breath.

'We're wearing too many clothes, *unnasta*,' he told her, his voice husky with desire. Suiting action to words, he kicked off his half-boots and tugged his tunic and shirt over his head. 'Sit, please.'

He gently pushed her down onto the bench and kneeled to remove first her shoes and socks, then the male trousers she was wearing under her tunic. She shivered, both from his touch and from the sight of his naked chest gilded by the light from the hearth fire. She hadn't seen him like this since the time he swam in the sea, but she had dreamed about it. The reality was so much better than dreams, though, and this time she could do more than look. *He's my husband.* The truth of that hadn't sunk in yet.

She reached out to run her fingers down his pectorals, swirling a tip round his nipples. Then she traced the intricate pattern he'd called a *tattoo*, her nails gliding along the painted dragon rampaging across his shoulder, arm and chest.

He drew in a sharp breath, but smiled up at her. 'Feel free to touch me anywhere you like. If you want, that is.'

Oh, she wanted to all right. He was so perfectly made, all hard planes and smooth skin, with that intriguing trail of hair leading down from his chest to the edge of his trousers. She would have liked to look at him and explore for ages, but for now she merely scraped her fingers down that trail to see if it was coarse to the touch. It was surprisingly soft, and she smiled when her questing fingers made him suck in his stomach. The sharply outlined abdominal muscles clenched, and she stroked her hand across them, marvelling at their firmness.

'Hmm, that might be enough for now,' he muttered, his voice like gravel.

He stood up and pulled her to her feet, then took hold of the hems of her tunic and *serk* in one go. They were whisked over her head in an instant, and she found herself standing before him wearing nothing at all. Her arms came up to cover her breasts instinctively, but he took her wrists in a soft grip and moved them away from her body.

'Don't. You're beautiful,' he breathed, almost reverently. 'Absolutely exquisite.' His eyes feasted on her, and although she ought to have been embarrassed, the heated gaze sweeping over her sent hot tingles shooting right down to her toes. It made her feel bold.

'Your turn?' She undid the drawstring of his trousers and hooked her fingers in the waistband. She couldn't help but notice that there was a bulge in the way that might prevent him from getting the garment off.

He smiled and grabbed her hand. 'Patience,' he huffed. 'Trust me when I tell you we want to take our time.'

'But I feel at a disadvantage,' she protested. She was bare and he wasn't. How was that fair?

'Fine, but please don't touch that yet . . .' he glanced downwards, 'or this will be over much too soon.'

She gasped as he removed his trousers, and couldn't help but stare at his manhood. She'd seen those of the animals on the farm, of course, but this was different. It was tempting to reach out and wrap her hand around it, but he'd said not to, so she refrained. 'Sweet Freya,' she managed. 'It's so . . .'

'Magnificent? Big? Impressive?' Storm was teasing in order to put her at ease, she could tell, but he spoke nothing but the truth. 'You can look your fill later.'

He gathered her close again, this time putting his arms around her waist and closing the distance between them. She found herself pressed against his hot skin. When he bent his head to kiss her again, she relished the feel of the hair on his body where it came into contact with her breasts and stomach. Her hands roamed over his chest again, then up to his muscular shoulders and arms and round to his back. The muscles there jumped as she ran her nails over him, and he groaned again. His hands cupped her backside and ground her centre against his hardness. The friction was delicious, and when he deepened the kiss, she became lost in a maelstrom of sensations.

At some point, he laid her down on the fox fur, covering her with his body. He didn't smother her, but made sure to rest most of his weight on his arms. Skilled fingers found their way to her most intimate places, and Freydis forgot both time and space. She moaned when he coaxed her to the brink of something wonderful, and hardly noticed when another part of his anatomy replaced the fingers. There was a slight sting as he sank into her, but he held still for a moment and allowed her to get used to the feel of him.

'Are you coping?' His question sounded strained, as if he was holding himself in check with a huge effort.

'Yes. I'm fine. Don't stop, please!'

A deep chuckle escaped him, but soon he was moving inside her, and she lost track of time. The wave that had been building swelled to a crescendo, and he used the pad of his thumb as well to help tip her over the brink. Stars exploded behind her eyelids and wave after wave of ecstasy coursed through her. She cried out, and soon he groaned his own release, although she vaguely noticed that he pulled out of her at the last moment, spilling his seed on her stomach.

Breathing hard, he moved to one side and gathered her close, holding her until they had both calmed down. Then he kissed her cheek and raised himself on one elbow to look down on her. 'Did I hurt you, my sweet?'

She smiled tremulously. 'No. You gave me great pleasure. I thank you.'

He huffed out a laugh and kissed her hard on the mouth. 'Believe me, the pleasure was all mine, but I am glad you enjoyed it.' Reaching up to push a strand of her hair away from her face, he added, 'Now you are truly my wife, and I will protect you with my life, you have my oath.'

Getting up, he found a length of linen someone had left in the hut and cleaned the mess off her stomach. His movements were gentle and caring, and she was grateful for his consideration. She didn't ask why he'd done what he did, although she understood it was so that she would not become with child. Their relationship was too new and she assumed he had his reasons. They lay snuggled together for a while, but despite the fire, the hut was cold, so eventually they got dressed before lying down again.

Storm felt dazed, and as if this entire evening was unreal. He couldn't get it through his head that he was married suddenly. Freydis's husband. And he'd made love to his wife. *Jeez, I'm even starting to think like a Viking.* Still, this was so much more than a hook-up or sleeping with a girlfriend. This was serious. It was going to take a while to sink in.

As he pulled on his tunic, he remembered something and dug around in one of the pouches attached to his belt. 'Ah yes, here.'

He pulled out the gold ring he'd made. The one with the runes hammered into its surface that spelled out the words 'forever mine'. He hadn't been able to make himself part with it, and instead had merely put it aside. Now it seemed fitting for the occasion. He held it out to Freydis.

'Please would you accept this as a wedding gift and wear it on the fourth finger of your left hand, if it fits? Where I come from, that signifies marriage.'

She blushed with pleasure and smiled at him, her gorgeous blue eyes shining in the firelight. 'Oh! Of course. Thank you. How . . . how thoughtful.'

He didn't tell her it was more of a claiming. Him showing the world that she belonged to him. It wasn't necessary, but it felt right.

'I'm glad you like it,' he said, lying down next to her and covering them both with one of the cloaks. 'Sleep now, my sweet. Tomorrow we have to face the consequences of what we've done, but we will weather that together.'

Storm had expected Assur and Gyrid to be angry, but he hadn't quite prepared himself for the almost incandescent rage the pair exhibited when informed of the unsanctioned marriage.

Joalf had come to knock on the bathhouse door just after dawn, and had led Storm and Freydis back to the hall. He'd been the one to inform his kinsman of Freydis's new status as Storm's wife, pretending he'd found them together quite by chance. Now he stood next to them in solidarity as Assur and Gyrid took turns to berate them.

'Of all the foolish things to do! You don't even know this man, Freydis. What kind of life can he give you? Does he even have any holdings of his own? A warrior for hire, isn't that what Ófeigr said he was?'

'He'll probably leave you behind in the spring, with a child in your belly and no way to support yourself. I know his type.' This was uttered by Gyrid with a particularly vicious sneer.

Storm was getting tired of being discussed as though he wasn't present, but he held his tongue. The man and his wife needed to vent their anger before they could calm down enough to see sense. Best to let them get it out of their system before he tried to reason with them.

'And you!' Assur turned on Joalf. 'What do you mean by encouraging this behaviour? I always thought you wanted the best for her.'

'I do,' the big man stated calmly. 'And marrying Gunnarsson isn't it. He would have destroyed her. I couldn't stand by and watch that happening. I told you not to pursue the match, but you wouldn't listen.'

'I don't believe this . . . My own kin, working against me! You knew how much was at stake here!' Assur was red in the face, and there was a very real possibility that he'd give himself an aneurysm or a heart attack.

Storm decided it was time to offer a sweetener. 'I am happy to pay you a bride price equal to whatever you had agreed with Gunnarsson. And I can assure you I'm not going anywhere without Freydis. She won't be left behind.' In fact, he was determined to remove her from here as soon as possible.

Assur scowled at him. 'That's not the point. How are we to explain matters to him?'

Ranulf, the owner of the settlement, had joined them and was listening with a scowl on his face. 'It seems to me that these young people have acted in haste. But it is Gunnarsson who should sort this out. His honour is at stake, and he'll be mightily offended. Lock them up until he arrives, then he can deal with the matter. Could be he'll take the girl despoiled or not.'

Assur grew pale at Ranulf's words. He was clearly terrified of

Gunnarsson, but that was his problem. Storm gave the jarl a death glare. 'He can't marry someone else's wife, and she's mine,' he snarled.

Ranulf regarded him coldly. 'I'm sure he could quickly make her a widow.'

'He can try.' Storm clenched his fists, but hid them in the folds of his tunic. He didn't want to show that the man's words were affecting him.

'What do you say, Assur? Shall we lock them up until tomorrow?' Ranulf smiled at his guest, clearly relishing the drama and the power he wielded here.

'Yes, let's,' Assur bit out. 'I've no doubt Gunnarsson will deal with them, although it's doubtful he will want Freydis now.' He glared at her. 'If nothing else, he can have you as a thrall, because you're not coming back to live under my roof again.'

Storm saw her flinch, but she didn't reply. He took her hand and twined his fingers with hers, giving them a squeeze. She sent him a grateful look.

'Joalf could do with cooling his heels as well,' Assur added. 'Take them away, all three.'

Ranulf called for some of his men and gave them orders. Storm and Joalf could have put up a fight, but by tacit agreement, they didn't. Together with Freydis, they were manhandled out to a storage hut of some sort, which was empty at present. With unnecessary force, the trio were shoved inside, and then the door was shut and barred from the outside.

Storm sighed and sat down on the nearest bench, pulling Freydis onto his lap. He wrapped his arms around her and held her close. 'That went well,' he said, his tone as sarcastic as he could make it.

Joalf chuckled. 'We knew how it would be. Assur is in Gunnarsson's debt, and he's a coward. Always has been. He knows the jarl won't be best pleased to be thwarted. That man is used to getting what he wants.'

'Not this time.' Storm was determined about that. 'I might surprise him if he tries to fight me for Freydis.'

'Don't.' Freydis's voice was hoarse, and she twisted to look at him. 'He won't fight fair, and no matter what you do, you'll never win. I've heard tell he isn't above having his men kill someone if he can't prevail himself.'

'I've heard that too,' Joalf chimed in. 'Best we find another solution.' He looked around. 'We need to escape. If we could get out of here, there's a chance you could row to Skotland. We were keeping that as a very last resort, but I don't see you have any other options now. The weather's not ideal, but hopefully it can be done.'

Storm had a better idea. He had no choice now but to use his time-travel device. First, though, they had to get back to Assur's settlement to retrieve it, along with the rest of his things and those of Freydis.

'What about you? Won't you come with us?' he asked the other man.

'No, I'm too old to go gallivanting about. Assur won't kick me out. Once he calms down, he'll realise I know all his secrets and he needs me to help run things. He's hoping Asmund will step up once he weds his betrothed, but the whelp isn't ready. He's never been allowed to decide anything and is too immature. It'll be a while before he learns how to take the reins. In the meantime, I do what is necessary, while giving Assur the credit.' With a small smile, he added, 'And I'll look after Surtr. You can return for him and me when you are settled somewhere.'

Storm didn't protest. He doubted the time-travel device would take three people – and a bird – and Joalf wasn't kin. He could only hope it would accept Freydis now that she was his wife.

He pushed her off his lap and stood up, taking in their

surroundings. The walls were made of stone and turf, and the door was fashioned from sturdy wood. Up at the top of either gable end, however, there was a large hole for smoke to escape when the hearth was lit. He eyed the holes, then estimated the distance from the front of the hut to the back wall.

'It could work,' he muttered.

'Hmm?' Joalf turned to see what he was looking at. 'What are you thinking?'

'That hole up there is big enough for me to crawl through. I'll need you to boost me up, then I can creep around to the front and let you both out. It will be faster than trying to break down the door, and quieter too. Gives us the element of surprise.' He reckoned the distance up to the smoke holes was approximately two and a half metres. He'd scaled much higher obstacles while training with the army. Their assault courses always included something like this.

'You think you can reach?' Joalf's expression was sceptical, but not disbelieving.

'I know I can. Here, stand with your back against the wall and put your hands out as if you're going to give me a boost up onto a horse,' Storm instructed. 'Let's hope there is no one outside. Freydis, please stand aside.'

He went to listen by the door for a moment, but all was quiet. This hut was over on one edge of the settlement, behind some larger barns. Hopefully most of the inhabitants were occupied elsewhere.

Starting from the door, he prepared himself for the jump. In a short burst of speed, he hurtled towards the other end of the building. Using Joalf's joined hands as a step, he propelled his body upwards and grabbed hold of the bottom ledge of the smoke hole. The wood surrounding it was rough, and he'd likely have some splinters, but he ignored the discomfort. He used the muscles in his arms to haul himself up until he was hanging with the upper half of his body outside. A quick look around showed that there was no one about, and he swung one leg over before gripping the eaves of the building to wriggle the rest of the way through. He pivoted outwards, then dropped to the ground, rolling as he landed in the yellowed grass.

Crouching down, he moved to the corner of the hut, peeking around it. Luck was on his side, and there was still no sign of anyone. He darted to the front corner and checked again – the coast was clear. Wasting no time, he ran over and lifted the heavy bar, then pushed the door open.

Joalf and Freydis must have been waiting immediately inside. He beckoned them forward with a finger on his lips to urge silence, then closed the door and put the bar back into place. The longer they could fool people into thinking they were still locked in, the better. Then he led them round to the back of the hut.

'Now where to?' he whispered as they huddled together close to the wall.

'Follow me,' Joalf answered. 'There's a secondary path down to the shore.' He scanned the sea and the beach over on the mainland, which was visible in the distance. 'Looks like we're in luck. The tide is out. We'll have to walk across boldly, and hope no one realises we shouldn't be there. As long as we don't meet Assur, Ranulf or any of the men who locked us in, we can pretend to be going about our business as normal.'

The others nodded, and they set off. Storm prayed to every god he could think of that they would come to their aid. He needed to get Freydis away from this place, and fast.

Chapter Thirteen

Mávey/Hrossey, Orkneyjar
Frermánuðr (December) AD *875*

It was broad daylight, and Freydis was convinced they would be caught and hauled back to captivity within moments. She cringed whenever she heard voices nearby, but the few people they met didn't give them a second glance. The meeting with Assur and Gyrid had been very early and most folk had been busy with their morning tasks, so perhaps they weren't aware that the trio were fugitives. The few thralls who had gone about their business inside the hall weren't likely to be around outside, and with any luck, Ranulf's men were eating *dagverðr*. Thank the gods Assur hadn't seen the need to post a guard outside the hut, as the door and bar were sturdy.

Joalf led them down a steep incline and along the bottom of the sea stack on the inland side. The causeway to the mainland came into view and they stopped to assess the situation.

'No one going back and forth at the moment,' he said, raising a hand to shield his eyes from the glare of the weak winter sun bouncing off the water.

'Let's take a chance and stroll across as if we have every right to.' Storm's mouth was set in a determined line. 'I'll go last, and if anyone comes after us, I'll try to fight them off. You run towards the boats. I'll catch up.'

Freydis didn't like that scenario, but kept quiet. They set off with Joalf in the lead, her in the middle and Storm bringing up the rear. She was slightly hunched over, as if expecting a blow, and realised it was because she was waiting for the metaphorical axe to fall. She made an effort to straighten up and walk with confident strides. If anyone in the settlement was looking, hopefully they wouldn't see anything amiss. After all, no one was forbidden from leaving unless they were thralls. People must go back and forth all the time on various errands.

Her heart was beating triple time and she almost lost her footing. Storm's hand came up to cup her elbow and guide her back onto the stones that made up the causeway. The water was lapping at the sides. It looked as though the tide had turned and was about to come in. They had been lucky with the timing. If fortune continued to be on their side, they would escape just as the waves came in and made passage impossible for anyone chasing them. No doubt Ranulf had boats on his side too, but most were moored by the mainland.

'Nearly there. Keep going,' Storm urged from behind, and she gritted her teeth and carried on. She was shaking now, but couldn't allow herself to slow down. Time was of the essence.

At last they reached the other side. A sliver of sandy beach with rock formations stretched to their right. The boats were moored where the sand met the water, and they hurried over to the smallest one. It didn't belong to them, but that was immaterial, since they were already in trouble. In silence, Joalf and Storm beckoned Freydis to jump in, then slid it into the water. Storm pushed off and vaulted on board after Joalf. The two men sat down side by side and took an oar each, rowing in tandem as if to an unheard beat.

'Can you huddle at the bottom, please, Freydis?' Storm said. 'Then if anyone is looking this way, it will appear as though there are only two of us. At a distance, that might fool them into thinking it's someone else.'

The bottom of the boat was mercifully dry, and she crouched down under the bench seat in the stern, covering her head with her cloak. She tried to make herself as small as possible, and prayed to the goddess Freya for luck, and to Ran not to drag them down to the bottom of the sea. The smell of brine was all around them, and the stench of fish wafted off the planks. Waves clucked against the hull, and seabirds screeched above them. But no one sounded an alarm, and she didn't hear any shouts calling them back.

After what felt like an eternity, Storm spoke. 'I think you can sit up now. We've rounded the cliffs and can't be seen from Mávey any longer.'

She unfolded herself, ignoring the strain in her muscles from sitting in such a cramped position, and took a seat on the bench at the back. 'Will they come after us, do you think?'

'Undoubtedly. But we'll be long gone by then,' Storm replied. He sounded confident, and she frowned at him.

'How can you be so sure? Crossing over to Skotland is difficult at the best of times, and it might not be possible today.'

He smiled. 'We probably won't be going there by boat. At least not this kind.'

Joalf turned to look at him at the same time as Freydis narrowed her eyes. What was he playing at?

He took a deep breath. 'It's time for the truth,' he stated, his expression serious now. 'There are some things I have to tell you both, and you will need to give me your oath that you'll never divulge what I say to a single person. Can you promise me that?'

'Aye.' Joalf's gaze was wary but intrigued.

'Yes, you have my oath as well.' Nervous tension gripped Freydis's insides, and she braced herself for whatever he had to say. Had he changed his mind about the whole marriage thing? Was she a fool for having given herself to him so easily? That thought sent a cold sliver of dread sliding down her back. But she couldn't regret it, no matter what happened. Last night had been so much better than she had imagined – wonderful, actually – and she wouldn't have wanted any other man for her first time. If that turned out to be her *only* time with Storm, so be it.

'Then I have to ask you this – do you believe in magic and the power of the gods?' Storm glanced between them, as if their answer was supremely important.

With raised eyebrows, Joalf nodded, while Freydis shrugged. 'Of course.'

'Good. Because I come from a time a thousand years into the future and I travelled to yours by way of a magical item. I believe it was forged by the gods, but I cannot say for certain. All I know is that it worked for me. Several other members of my extended family have done the same, with different magical objects, but I have never heard of anyone else managing it. Therefore, it feels as though we have been singled out for some reason as yet unknown, and this must be kept a secret.'

He stopped talking and looked from Freydis to Joalf and back again, waiting for their comments. They both merely blinked at him.

'The future?' she managed at last. That was the very last thing she would have guessed he would say. In fact, she could never even have dreamed of such a thing. 'Magic? You jest.'

He shook his head. 'No. I am serious. And because you are now my wife, I think the object will transport you to my time along with me if I ask it to. Hence we will disappear and no one here will be able to find us.' He turned to Joalf. 'I'm afraid I don't think it would work with you, as we are not kin or connected in any way, but you did say you were happy to stay behind, did you not?'

'Aye, but . . . you really mean it?' The big man had stopped rowing and was staring at Storm as if he'd grown three heads. There was an almighty scowl wrinkling his forehead, and his teeth were clenched. No one liked to be taken for a fool, and Joalf would never stand for that.

'I do. I know it is difficult to believe, and I don't blame you for being sceptical. No one in my family wanted to think it was real either. But we were proved wrong, and I will show you that I am telling the truth. If it doesn't work, you can laugh at me if you like, but I hope it will, as it's a much better option for escaping Gunnarsson's wrath.'

Freydis didn't know what to say. She wanted to believe him, but what if he wasn't right in the head? After all, what did she really know about him? He'd only been with them for a couple of months, barely that. He might be very good at hiding his real persona. And yet he seemed utterly sincere. Surely they ought to give him the benefit of the doubt. The gods were mysterious and mischievous, everyone knew that. Why should they not have created a device for travelling through time?

'I will wait to see if you can prove it,' she said at last.

'Fair enough. As I said, the object has a mind of its own and might not cooperate. In which case, we will be making that journey across the sea. Either way, we will return to the Orkneyjar when it is safe to do so, you have my word on that, Joalf.'

They rowed in silence after that. Storm figured the other two needed time to let his revelation sink in. If he'd been in their shoes, he wouldn't have believed it either. He'd laughed at the notion himself when Linnea had first time-travelled, but after meeting her Viking husband, and hearing other tales from her friend Sara, he'd come around. And now that he had experienced it himself, he knew it was real.

He could only hope the magical device would work for Freydis as well as himself. There was a lot more at stake now than when he'd first used it, and he couldn't help the anxiety that sent jitters through him. It had to work. If it didn't, he'd find another way, because he wasn't letting Freydis out of his sight until she was safe. Should the magic send him to the future on his own, he'd try to return immediately. Worst case scenario, if that didn't work either, he'd ask Joalf to stand by ready to take Freydis to Skotland.

Putting their backs into the rowing, they reached Assur's settlement an hour or so later. By that time, he was having trouble feeling the tips of his fingers, and his feet were numb too. Since they'd had to flee without collecting their belongings, none of them had their mittens or hats with them. It was pure luck that they'd been wearing their cloaks at least, but they were buffeted by an icy wind that froze them to the marrow. Though they'd done their best to cover their heads and wrap the ends of the material round their hands, it wasn't quite enough. A warming hearth was needed to thaw out their extremities, but there was no time for that.

Entering the bay, Storm had a flashback to the evening when he'd first arrived here. Yet again he was being pursued, straining to work his oar as fast as he could. Although no one was coming after them yet, as far as he could see, it was only a question of time. The two men dragged the little boat high up onto the beach, and he helped Freydis jump out. She was lithe and agile and could have managed on her own, but a possessive part of him he hadn't known existed wanted to put his hands around her waist to lift her over the side. *My woman. My wife.* The words echoed round his brain. Though he'd always shied away from commitment of any kind in the past, he found that he liked the thought of her being his. Relished it, in fact. He was definitely turning into a Viking, at least in his mindset.

Her cheeks were rosy. 'Thank you.' She made a show of brushing off her skirts, but it was clearly a ploy to avoid looking at him. He gathered she was remembering their night together and what they'd done, delayed embarrassment setting in. He wanted to put her at ease, but it would have to wait. They had more pressing matters to attend to.

'We had better hurry. They could arrive at any time. Freydis, I know you left some of your things behind at Mávey, but if there is anything here you want to bring with you, please go and collect it as quickly as you can. Your weapons and any valuables mainly. No need to worry about clothing. I can buy you new garments.'

The three of them hurtled up the path towards the settlement. A few people threw them startled looks, as they hadn't been expected back so soon, but thankfully no one stopped them. Surtr came flapping down off a rooftop and settled on Freydis's shoulder. He cawed at her and made clicking noises, bending his head to be petted, and she obliged.

'I missed you, beautiful boy,' she murmured. 'But I'm afraid I have to leave you again. Joalf will look after you, though. You be good for him, eh?'

The majestic bird said something Storm didn't catch, but he stayed on her shoulder while she rushed into the hall to grab whatever she wanted to bring on the journey. Storm himself hurried over to the forge, where he'd hidden his weapons and a pouch of silver. He hadn't wanted anyone to find them while he was gone, especially the magical axe. The extra clothing he'd brought to Mávey he would have to consider lost. No matter, it could be replaced in his own century.

'Thank the gods!' he whispered, as he retrieved his possessions from the top of the roof beam. The axe head glinted in the light streaming in from a vent high up in the wall, and the inscription seemed to wink at him. 'Yes, yes, I'll be using you in a moment. Please, please work for Freydis too, or I don't know what I'll do!'

He attached the axe to his belt with a leather loop, and threaded on the extra pouch of silver as well. His sword was slung across his chest in a baldric, and his long knife was suspended from the front of his belt in its sheath via another two pieces of leather. Quickly turning to the bench he'd been sleeping on, he retrieved the shaggy *varafeldur* cloak. He hadn't brought it to Mávey as it was a bit dirty, but he didn't want to leave it behind here. With a last look around, he sprinted over to the barn where he'd told Joalf and Freydis to meet him. As he ran, he heard angry shouting in the distance and gathered that Assur and Ranulf had almost caught up with them. It was time to test the magical axe.

'Don't fail me now, please!' he hissed at it. 'Odin Allfather, help me to bring my wife to safety, I beg you.'

He didn't know if the god was listening, but he sincerely hoped so.

Freydis raced towards the barn clutching a bundle that contained some spare clothing and her weapons. She didn't own any jewellery other than the ring Storm had given her, a small amulet in the shape of one of the goddess Freya's cats, and a silver bracelet, all of which she'd already been wearing. Surtr took flight and kept up with her in the air, and when she hustled in through the door, he dived inside after her. His feet clutched at the material of her cloak as he landed on her shoulder.

Joalf and Storm were already there, and the older man held out his hand to the bird. 'Come, boy. You need to stay with me for the time being. Your mistress will return for you, no doubt about it.'

Surtr tried to resist at first, pecking half-heartedly at Joalf's hand, but when the man pushed it closer, he grudgingly stepped off Freydis and inched up Joalf's arm.

Storm pulled his axe out of the loop on his belt, and the intricate silver pattern inlaid in the iron flashed in the light seeping through the doorway. He held out his hand, beckoning Freydis closer.

'Listen, *unnasta*,' he said. 'I'm going to use this to nick both our fingers, as the magic requires a blood sacrifice in order to work. When I do that, you will need to say a specific sentence out loud at the same time as me. Understand?'

'Yes. What do I say?'

His expression was dead serious, and she shivered as the enormity of what he was saying hit her. If he was telling the truth, they were going to travel through time. With magic. How was that possible? Dare she believe him?

'*Með blōð skaltu ferðast*,' he said.

She nodded and repeated the words quietly. 'Very well.' It still seemed far-fetched that this could possibly work, but she was determined to give him the benefit of the doubt until he was proved wrong.

Storm reached out to clasp Joalf's hand briefly. 'Thank you for everything. I swear I will look after Freydis to the best of my ability and be a good husband to her. We will return here when it is safe to do so, but if you need to escape yourself, head for her stepfather's place in Sogn, as we will likely go there first. Failing that, seek out my brother-in-law Hrafn's domains near Birka in Svíaríki. If you tell him I sent you, he and my sister will give you house room for as long as you need it. That is where I hope to end up as well eventually.'

'Will do. Go now. There is no time to lose.' Joalf went to close and bar the door, but they all knew that wouldn't hold for long if Assur was determined to enter.

The shouts outside were coming closer and rising in pitch. Freydis's stomach muscles cramped at the thought of her erstwhile betrothed's wrath at being denied her hand in marriage. She wasn't afraid for herself, but of what he would do to Storm if Assur caught them now. If nothing else, she hoped the magic worked for him at least.

'Are you ready?' Storm took her hand in his and plaited their fingers. 'Whatever you do, don't let go of me. On the count of three, say the words with me.'

He counted down, and on *þrír*, he used the lethally honed axe blade to make a small slash across the top of their fingers. She flinched, but he'd done it so quickly she barely had time to feel the sting of the cut. As drops of blood welled out, they recited the sentence together.

'*Með blōð skaltu ferðast.*'

Freydis heard banging on the door, and raised voices, but at the same time, a spinning sensation assailed her. She felt as if she'd entered a whirlpool as the world revolved around her at an ever-increasing rate. Nausea rose in her throat and she tried to swallow it down, whimpering in discomfort. She couldn't see anything because her surroundings were a blur. She closed her eyes. It didn't help, but through it all she clung to Storm's hand, her only anchor in this magical storm, concentrating on the feel of his callused fingers against hers. Finally the twirling became too much, and she sank into darkness and oblivion.

Chapter Fourteen

Mainland, Orkney Islands
December 2021

Storm groaned and sat up, gingerly moving his sword out of the way to stop it from poking into his hip bone. He wanted to throw up, but knew if he just waited a moment the nausea would pass. There was still a slight spinning sensation in his head, like the remnants of being on board a ship when you reached land. His brain was vibrating with the aftershocks of the time travel, and he raised his hands to hold on to his head.

A moan nearby had him opening his eyes, and his gaze collided with that of Freydis. Her pupils were dilated, almost obscuring the intense blue of her irises, and she blinked as if she couldn't focus properly. The mere sight of her had him grinning like a fool, and he let out a whoop of joy.

'It worked! You're with me!' He looked up towards the sky and shouted, '*Thank you, gods!* Thank you so much!'

'Shh, don't make such a racket,' Freydis complained, grabbing the top of her scalp with both hands. 'My head hurts and I think I'm going to be sick.'

She was kneeling in a huge expanse of grass. As he took in his surroundings, Storm realised they were still at Assur's settlement on top of the sea stack, only – hopefully – a thousand years into the future, because there were no buildings apart from the outline of one dwelling, the stone now covered in moss and grass.

'Stay still and it will pass,' he told her. 'The time travelling does that to your body, but you'll soon feel better, I promise.'

'Time travelling?' She looked up and glanced around. 'The barn is gone,' she whispered.

'That and everything else. Welcome to the twenty-first century. I think.'

She sank back into the grass, clearly stunned. 'I didn't think . . .'

'That it would actually work?' He chuckled. 'To tell you the truth, I wasn't sure myself. I mean, I'd done it once already, but I didn't know if it would happen again, or whether the gods would let me bring you. I guess they definitely consider us married.'

At the mention of the word 'married', she blushed. He found it adorable that this strong, courageous woman was embarrassed about their wedding night, but he didn't want her to feel awkward.

'*Hei*,' he said, reaching out his hand to take hers. 'It all happened so quickly. How about we take some time to just be friends before we rush into any more . . . er, marital activities. We don't know each other very well, and it would be good to grow comfortable in each other's company.'

It was the opposite of what he wanted really. Merely touching her hand had lust shooting through his veins, but he could wait. He would like her to desire him equally before he slept with her again. Then there was the added complication of his quest to find Maddie, and the fact that he hadn't intended to remain in the past indefinitely. Still, those were problems for another day.

Her gaze turned pensive and a small frown appeared between her brows. 'You don't want to bed me again?'

He almost choked. Trust Freydis to be direct about it. 'Quite the opposite, but I would prefer you to be a willing partner, not feel as though you had no other choice because of circumstances.' She opened her mouth as if to protest, but he held up a hand to stop her. 'We have plenty of time to become better acquainted. When you are ready to be my wife in every sense of the word, you can let me know. For now, we are essentially strangers bound together by a twist of fate. If we add, er, bedding, as you call it, to the mix, it complicates things. Let us take it slowly, agreed?'

'If that is your wish.' She hesitated, then added, 'I thank you for being so considerate.'

He shrugged and stood up, pulling her to her feet and steadying her when she wobbled slightly. 'Just pragmatic.'

'Where exactly are we? This looks like Assur's settlement – I recognise the views – but I can't see any habitation nearby.'

'No, me neither. I think it's still the same place, but in my century I don't suppose anyone lives here. We need to go over to the mainland and walk south to see what we come across. Once we reach the nearest settlement, I can find out more. I speak their language.'

'Oh. I hadn't thought about that. They won't understand me?'

He squeezed her hand, which was still in his as if she didn't want to let go. 'No, I'm afraid not. You might recognise a few of the words, but mostly it will sound strange to you. Don't worry, I will teach you.'

'Good.'

There was trust in her gaze as she smiled at him, and it almost floored him. He was responsible for her now – his *wife* – and she believed him capable of taking care of her. It was humbling and an honour. One he wasn't sure he deserved. But he'd sure as hell do everything he could to be worthy of her regard.

And perhaps he'd even win her love.

That thought brought him up short. Was that what he wanted? He honestly didn't know, but as with everything else, he put it to the back of his mind for now. There would be time enough to ponder such questions later.

They made their way down the path to the seashore. It was dangerous in places, as if it hadn't been in use much recently. Freydis couldn't help but compare it to the place she was used to. What had happened here? Why did Assur's descendants no longer live here? But a thousand years was a very long time, and there were likely none left. She wondered if Asmund had had any offspring. He was the couple's only surviving child, and although he had been Gyrid's pride and joy, he'd been a weak and ineffectual man. Freydis could have beaten him in a fair fight, although she hadn't tried it since that one time she'd bested him as a child. That would have been foolish in the extreme.

Once they had scrambled up onto the mainland, they walked along the cliffs in a southerly direction. It was still a wild and windswept place. The North Sea was a turbulent mass below them, pounding into the base of the cliffs with a muted rumble. The day was overcast, but thankfully it wasn't raining, and although the air was cold, there was no snow. There was a path through the grass and stones, as if people walked here a lot. She wondered why when there were no dwellings in sight. Was this place still used for grazing, perhaps?

Storm kept hold of her hand and she clung to him. He was still her only anchor in this new reality, and she wouldn't let go unless she had to. She wasn't sure if he'd been sincere when he gave that speech about not wanting to bed her until they were more comfortable in each other's company. It could be that he simply didn't desire her, now that he'd already had her once. Some men were like that, apparently, happy to move on when they'd sampled a woman. Or so she'd heard. Only time would tell, but she wouldn't be the one to instigate any further intimacy between them. That would be too embarrassing for words.

The light was fading by the time they came to a gate with a path on the other side. This led to what Storm called a *car park*, although she had no idea what that was or what the words meant. There was a track leading into it and a strange metallic object standing in a large square of flattened gravel. It had wheels of some sort and what looked like glass at the top, which meant you could see through it to the other side. Most peculiar. A man and a woman were putting something into the back of it. A sort of door was hinged open to show a storage space inside, like a metal kist. Storm walked up to them and spoke a greeting, then proceeded to talk to them, gesticulating with one hand.

At first they looked sceptical, but he soon had them laughing at something he said. Freydis, who'd kept her free hand on the hilt of her sword, relaxed. It didn't sound as though these people would be a threat to them.

Storm turned to her and smiled. 'These kind folk have offered us a ride to the nearest settlement. Will you trust me and not be afraid once we set off?'

'Why would I be afraid? And how are we to ride anywhere? They have no horses or oxen.'

He laughed. 'There's no need for either of those. You'll see. Come, climb inside.' He opened another door in the metal object. There was a leather-covered bench, smooth and shiny, and she slid onto it at his urging. He followed and shut the door behind him. Then he pulled out some kind of strap from behind her left shoulder and fastened it somehow, before doing the same to himself. 'That is to stop us from being thrown around too much,' he whispered. 'This, er, cart is going to move very fast, so brace yourself. I swear it is not dangerous.'

She said nothing, but couldn't help her eyes from going wide when the man and woman climbed into the similar benches in front of them and a strange noise started up. It was like the roar of a dragon that settled into grumbling underneath her. She wasn't scared, as Storm had told her there was nothing to be frightened of, but she was most definitely surprised and intrigued. Her astonishment increased when the cart began to move as if pushed by unseen hands. The man swivelled a round object, steering them onto the narrow track.

'You OK?' Storm murmured, taking her hand again to give it a reassuring squeeze. 'OK is a word from my time that means roughly "to be well".'

'I see. And yes, I'm . . . OK.'

She watched as the landscape began to pass by at dizzying speed, almost blurring her vision. The sensation of moving fast tickled her stomach, but it wasn't unpleasant. It made her want to laugh out loud, but she held it in, not wanting to draw attention to herself. There was nothing much to see outside, apart from a few dwellings that flashed by quickly. Dusk was falling and she didn't get a good look at them, but they were different to any buildings she'd ever seen before. It occurred to her to wonder what halls were like in Storm's time.

She assumed she would soon find out.

'You're doing well, *unnasta*,' he told her, giving her a smile and a kiss on the cheek.

His approval made warmth spread through her. Although she berated herself for being so silly, she couldn't suppress the emotion bubbling up inside. She wanted him to be proud of her, to like her. Maybe even to love her. Was that possible? Probably not. She had to be realistic. Most marriages were contracted for practical purposes, and he'd only wedded her to help her escape Ingolf's clutches. Although he did seem to care for her, as everything he'd done so far had been for her benefit.

Still, only a fool would hope for more.

The kind strangers let them off by the harbour in Kirkwall, the largest town in the Orkney Islands. That wasn't saying much, though, as it wasn't huge by any means. Storm had spun them a tale about how he and Freydis were re-enactors on their honeymoon after getting married in a Viking-type ceremony. He'd also told them they'd become lost while out walking along the cliffs and couldn't find their way back to the bus that would have transported them to the nearest town. He hoped there was such a bus – he was only guessing – but either way, the couple didn't question his story.

'Thank you so much, you're life-savers,' he told them as they hopped out of the car. 'Are you sure I can't pay you for petrol?' He'd offered, even though he didn't have any money with him. Luckily, they'd refused.

'No, no. Enjoy the rest of your stay here, and congratulations again on your marriage. Bye!'

They waved and sped off, and Storm turned to take Freydis's hand in his. Her fingers were still cold from their sea journey. He enclosed them with his, which had warmed up during their walk.

'Right, we'd better find a room for the night, then go and purchase a few things. No point going anywhere else today. I will need time to make arrangements for our onward journey.'

There were ferries from the island to Aberdeen or Scrabster on the Scottish mainland. His parents had made that journey a couple of years ago and had told him all about it. Storm wasn't sure that was the best route, though, and wanted to consider all options before making up his mind.

Freydis was absorbing her surroundings with wide eyes, no doubt wondering if she was dreaming. He knew it would take her a while to grasp the fact that they really had travelled through time. And there was a lot to take in here – his modern world must seem unreal to her.

Her gaze returned to his. 'Where will we go? Do you know anyone here who can offer us a bench for the night?'

He smiled. 'No, but I will pay someone. Come, let's see what we can find.'

The cathedral of St Magnus could be glimpsed in the distance, and he headed in that direction as it indicated the centre of town. They turned into a network of small alleyways and narrow streets. These were quaint and picturesque, and he could see why this place would attract lots of tourists during the summer season. Old-fashioned houses jostled for space along streets paved with large stone slabs. Now, in winter, it was fairly quiet, and only a few people were out and about. He and Freydis received some strange looks and a few smiles, but he walked with confidence and pretended he didn't notice. The islands were famous for their Viking heritage, so re-enactors couldn't be an uncommon sight.

Halfway up a small street, he spied a hotel sign on an old house made of local grey stone. 'This might be worth a try,' he said, stopping to look up at the facade and large sash windows. 'Come with me.'

He pushed the door open and tugged Freydis inside. There was a staircase straight in front of them, and the reception desk was tucked into an alcove to the right of it. There was no one manning it, but he tapped a bell and a woman came bustling out from a small office.

'Yes, can I help you?'

'We were wondering if you have a room for tonight, please.'

'I'm not sure . . .' Her expression was dubious as her gaze

flickered over their outlandish clothing. No doubt they were a little grubby, but hopefully that merely added to the authenticity of what she would perceive as a costume. When she spied Storm's sword and axe, her eyes grew wider, and fear flickered in their depths.

He rushed to reassure her. 'I hope you don't mind our little toys,' he joked, pointing to his weapons. 'We've been doing some re-enactment, but these are totally harmless, I can assure you. We're not allowed sharp edges. Don't want anyone getting hurt accidentally.' A complete and utter lie, as he could easily have sliced her through in seconds.

'Oh, well, that's good to know.' She relaxed fractionally.

'I'd be really grateful if you could check for any vacancies, please. We couldn't book ahead as I've lost my phone, but I'm happy to pay up front if there's anything available. One night is all we need.'

He rummaged in one of the leather pouches hanging off his belt. There was a false bottom inside, and underneath that he'd hidden a credit card for just this kind of emergency. He fished it out and was pleased to see it didn't look any the worse for having travelled all the way to the ninth century and back. Holding it up for the receptionist to look at, he gave her his most charming smile. It worked, and her demeanour thawed.

'Very well, hold on a moment.' She woke up a laptop with a mouse and clicked around on the screen while frowning at it. 'Hmm, yes. There is one room free on the top floor. Double with en suite. Would you like that?'

'Yes, please! Thank you so much. You're an absolute angel. Here, I don't care what it costs.' He handed over his credit card and hid another smile when the woman's cheeks turned pink at his effusive compliment. It didn't hurt to lay it on thick occasionally.

Freydis was standing silently by his side. He wondered what

she made of it all since she didn't understand a word of what he'd said.

'Here's your key. Your room is on the third floor. Breakfast is served from seven to nine. Have a nice stay.' The receptionist indicated the stairs, and Storm thanked her again before heading up. That was one hurdle they'd overcome, and he breathed a sigh of relief.

Despite the fact that the hotel was housed in an old building, their room was modern and functional, if a bit on the dreary side colour-wise. A lot of brown and beige, with a dull tartan carpet and matching curtains. A large double bed heaped with pillows dominated the space, and there were a couple of armchairs and a table tucked into a corner under the eaves. A nice, clean bathroom was visible through an open door, and Storm saw Freydis's eyes grow big again.

'What is that?' She pointed to the bathroom fittings – shower, toilet and sink – then blinked at the enormous mirror that reflected her face back at her as she peeked inside. She flinched. 'Sweet Freya! Is that . . . me?' She leaned forward again and studied herself. 'I've only ever seen my reflection in water. Never this clearly.'

Storm laughed. 'Yes, *unnasta*, that is most definitely you.' He came to stand behind her, winding his arms around her waist to pull her close. He couldn't resist resting his chin on her head and staring at the two of them. 'We look good together, don't you think? A handsome couple.' He smiled at her, a teasing glint in his eyes.

That made her smile and relax fractionally. '*Fifl!*' She smacked his arm but didn't wriggle out of his hold. Standing there with her back flush to his chest, everything suddenly felt right, and he squeezed her middle, then kissed her cheek before reluctantly disentangling himself.

'I'd better show you how all these things work.'

He proceeded to do so, and watched with amusement as she tried the taps, light switches and toilet flush. It was fun to see them from her perspective, not taking them for granted the way he always had in the past. He left her alone to make use of the facilities, then told her they were going shopping.

'*Shopping?*' She tried out the English word. 'What is that?'

'It is like going to a market to purchase various items, except the vendors' stalls are all indoors. Most of them, anyway.' He recalled a visit to York with his parents. 'Have you ever been to a large settlement with lots of dwellings? Like Jorvik or Skiringssal?'

'No, but I have heard of the latter.'

'Well, in those places craftsmen sell their wares directly from their workshops. That is similar to what we'll be seeing here, except the workshop itself will be hidden in a back room.' He couldn't explain a modern shop to her in any other way.

'Then lead the way. What are we purchasing?'

'Clothing and a few other items. And I need to make travel arrangements. What do you say we go and visit your mother and stepfather first? As it is the middle of winter, I doubt there will be anyone sailing to Ísland until spring. The search for my sister will have to wait, so we might as well go and see how your mother fares.'

There could have been some way of getting to Iceland while they were in the twenty-first century, then travelling back in time from there. However, that country would be knee-deep in snow, and it would be nigh on impossible to get around in order to find whatever settlement Maddie might have ended up in. Sailing round the coast was probably his best bet, at least as a starting point, and there was no point trying that until spring at the earliest. In the meantime, they could check on Freydis's mother and allay her fears on that account. If he'd understood correctly, the woman lived not far from present-day Bergen. He knew that Vikings had sailed from there to Iceland, so that would be ideal come spring.

'Thank you! I would like that above all things.' Her eyes shone with delighted surprise, which in turn pleased him. He loved to see her happy.

'Good, that's settled then.'

Something occurred to him that slightly dampened his spirits – no matter where they went, they didn't have passports. How would they get into another country without proper documents? He'd have to figure that out later.

Chapter Fifteen

Mainland, Orkney Islands
December 2021

Storm took her hand again as they exited the large dwelling house where he'd found them sleeping quarters for the night. Freydis was grateful for that, as she felt all at sea. Everything here was new and strange, and there was so much to learn and observe. The sheer size of the buildings was overwhelming, with several floors one on top of the other, as was the large number of them all crammed in together along these tracks. She was having trouble taking it in, and her mind was overflowing with new impressions and sights.

'You still OK?' Storm squeezed her fingers and dropped a quick kiss on the top of her head. His kind gesture made that silly warmth spread through her again, but she suppressed it. He was merely concerned about her, the way he would be with anyone else in her situation.

'Yes.' She recognised that word *OK* now, and resolved to absorb as much of his language as she could while she was here.

They emerged onto a wider thoroughfare lined with more buildings. Most had enormous sheets of glass at the front with displays of all manner of wares. As it was almost fully dark now, the merchants' booths were brightly lit from inside somehow. Freydis tried to remember to keep her mouth closed, as it had a tendency to drop open in awe. Storm had explained that glass was common in his era and no one thought it unusual to see such large expanses of it. She had only ever seen a small drinking vessel made out of that material, so to her it was incredible.

'Let's try in here.' He led her through doors that slid to the side of their own accord with a whooshing sound, startling Freydis. There didn't seem to be anyone there pulling them open, no matter where she looked. How very odd.

The inside of what he called a *shop* held racks filled with more garments than she'd ever seen in her life. 'Odin's ravens!' she whispered. 'Who has made all these? It must have taken years!'

Storm chuckled. 'No, the people here have tools that help make quick work of sewing. I'll show you sometime. Now, what is your favourite colour?'

'Blue.' Only truly rich people owned clothes that were a rich, deep blue rather than the pale colour produced by woad. She had always wanted cloth dyed with expensive imported indigo.

He picked something off a rack and held it up. 'Like this?' It was glorious, an almost blindingly azure colour.

'Oh yes! That is wonderful. But what is it?'

'A tunic of sorts. We call it a *hoodie*. And look, it has matching trousers with a drawstring. Here, I will show you how the fastening works on the tunic, then we can go and try things on.'

He picked out a pile of garments and headed for a series of little alcoves at the back of the room. Then he told her to go inside and strip naked before putting on some of the items he'd brought, and in which order they had to go.

'Shout if you need help,' he said. 'I'll be in the next one.'

Freydis reluctantly did as she was bid. The alcove didn't have a door, merely a flimsy hanging made of some sort of heavy material. She eyed it with misgiving and pulled it closed. She wasn't happy about being nude in a place where someone could enter at any time, but Storm appeared to think this was normal. It was also incredibly embarrassing to see her entire body in the large mirror that lined the inside of the space. She had never seen herself reflected in anything but small portions. Certainly not without clothes on. She hurried to divest herself of her normal garments, then slipped on the trousers and something he'd called a *T-shirt*. It was very flexible and moulded to her body like a second skin. She ran her hands over it, revelling in the softness of the material. She'd never touched anything so finely woven. It was almost a sensual experience, and she shivered.

'Are you dressed yet?' came Storm's voice from outside. 'Come out and show me, please.'

She pushed the hanging aside and saw his eyes open wide as he drew in a sharp breath. '*Whoa!*' He swallowed hard. 'I . . . er, should probably find a *T-shirt* in a different colour. That white is, um, a bit much.'

'How so?' She looked down, then realised what he meant. Her breasts and nipples were clearly visible through the thin material now that it was stretched tight across her body. 'Oh.'

'Yes, oh.' He closed his eyes for a moment as if praying for strength. 'Wait there, I'll find you another one.'

He disappeared and returned with a dark blue *T-shirt*, which he told her to change into. When she came back out of the booth, he said, 'Better. Now put on the tunic, please. Let's see if that fits.' He helped her thread her arms into the upper garment and did up the strange metal fastening for her. 'That's good.' He nodded approvingly and showed her that there was a hood that could be pulled over her head if necessary. 'Shall we purchase that?'

'Yes, please.'

'Try this as well, would you? It's instead of a cloak as it's so cold outside.' He held up an even longer tunic that looked to be made out of tiny down pillows all sewn together.

'What is that?'

'A *puffa coat*. It's very warm. You'll love it.'

She did. It was like sinking into a cloud, and here in the shop it was almost *too* warm. 'You're right. This is wonderful!'

He smiled. 'Good. You'll have to don your old garments while I pay for the new ones, then we can come back here and put them on again. Best if we don't walk around in the clothing from your time.'

They eventually walked out of the shop with several sacks each. These were made of an even stranger material and had little handles at the top. They contained both their old clothes and some more *T-shirts*, as well as something Storm had said were undergarments. 'I'll explain about those once we get back to our room.'

They strolled along the wide track. Freydis huddled into her *puffa coat*, her hands in the pockets she'd found on each side. She covertly studied the other people who were out and about. They were all dressed similarly to her, and no one gave them a second look any more. It was a relief not to be stared at, yet she still felt like a fish out of water.

Storm paused to look at a display of silver jewellery. 'Some of those are influenced by designs from your time. Do you see?' He pointed to a stunning brooch in the shape of a dragon twining around itself in sinuous curves.

'Yes, that is beautiful! I've never seen its like.'

He turned to her. 'Do you want it?'

'What? No! It must be worth a huge amount.' She could barely imagine owning something so valuable.

'Do not worry about that. If you like it, I'm buying it for you. I didn't give you a wedding gift, after all. Isn't that what I should have done?'

'Well, you gave me the ring.' She held out her hand and the gold band reflected the lights of a nearby shop.

'That was more a symbol of me claiming you. I've been told you should have had a proper gift when I asked for your hand in marriage.'

'I . . . well . . . that is to say, our marriage wasn't conventional,' she stammered. 'I didn't expect anything.' She couldn't resist adding with a smile, 'And you didn't actually ask.'

That made him laugh. 'True, but I should have done. You are worth a lot more than this paltry brooch, Freydis. Come, let's go inside.'

He put an arm around her waist and hugged her to his side briefly before ushering her in through the door. This one, thankfully, opened in the normal manner.

'You really don't have to,' she protested in a whisper, but he just smiled.

'I want to. Can't a man buy something for his lovely wife?'

'Now you're teasing,' she muttered. Her cheeks were becoming suffused with heat because his words affected her even though she knew he meant nothing by them.

He stopped and cupped her face in his hands, staring into her eyes. 'I'm really not,' he said, his voice a bit rougher than usual. Then he leaned in and placed a kiss on her lips, right in front of everyone. 'Now, no more protests, please, or I'll buy you a few other things besides.'

Freydis was so stunned by that unexpected kiss that she kept quiet while he haggled with the vendor. Instead of allowing the woman to wrap the brooch up, as she apparently wanted to do, he insisted on pinning it to Freydis's new tunic straight away. It glittered in the light as they exited the shop, and she swallowed down tears of joy. No one had ever given her such a fine gift, and she wasn't sure how to react.

She pulled him to a stop and made him turn towards her. 'Thank you, husband,' she said. 'You are most kind, and I shall treasure it always.' Then she stood on tiptoes and pressed a fierce kiss to his mouth, trying to show him how grateful she was.

The smile he gave her was almost blinding. 'You are very welcome, little wife. Now, how about we find something to eat?'

Down by the harbour, they found a cosy restaurant with a Viking theme, which amused Storm no end, especially when he spotted the sign featuring a helmet with horns. So clichéd and totally inaccurate historically. Still, if it drew in the tourists, who was he to complain? They settled at a table for two among shields, drinking horns, pretend weapons and other decorations that adorned the walls, and he ordered a selection of dishes for Freydis to try. The menu bore no resemblance to any Viking food he'd eaten, so presumably it was only the decor that was supposed to entice patrons. That was fine by him, as he craved some twenty-first-century cooking.

'We'll have chowder to start with, then a large portion of fries, a cheeseburger and some pan-fried sea bass. Oh, and the deep-fried halloumi, please,' he told the waiter.

'What would you like to drink?'

'Surprise us with a local ale of some sort.'

The waiter grinned. 'Two Red MacGregors coming up.'

'Thank you.'

When the drinks arrived, Freydis said, 'Wait a moment. Is that like the mead from my time?'

'No, more like ale. Why?'

Her cheeks turned pink. 'It's just that a newly married couple usually share a cup of mead to, um, signify their joining. It's part of the wedding rituals. I thought perhaps we could drink from the same mug in order to fulfil this tradition.' She ducked her head. 'But maybe that's silly.'

'No, not at all. I can buy some mead tomorrow if you like, but this will do for now. Here, you first.' He held out his glass to her and watched her take a sip, then took his turn. After he'd put the glass down, he took her hand across the table and gave it a squeeze. 'All good now?'

'Yes. Thank you for indulging my superstitions.'

'Not at all. I'm all for doing things right.'

The chowder was accompanied by chunky pieces of fresh white bread. He'd asked for two spoons, and they both dug in, occasionally dipping the bread in the creamy soup.

'Mm, this is so good!' Freydis closed her eyes and let out a sigh of contentment.

'It's only the beginning. Don't eat too much bread or you won't have room for the rest,' Storm warned.

'But I've never tasted bread like this. It's so light and soft.'

'I know. We are very lucky in my time, at least in this country and those nearby. There's never any shortage of food and the produce is of excellent quality.'

And had he ever been truly grateful for that? he wondered. Like everyone else, he'd always taken it for granted. He shouldn't have done.

They were soon sampling the other dishes he'd ordered, sharing the food as if they'd been a couple for years. It was strange, but at the same time very right. Storm decided not to overthink it. They had shared a lot more than food, after all. The ale was fruity and rich, and slid down their throats smoothly. When they couldn't manage a single mouthful more, they sat back and smiled at each other.

'That was the best meal I've ever had,' Freydis said. 'I don't know how you survived in my time if this is what you are used to.'

'It wasn't so bad. I've had worse.' And he had. Military rations while out on manoeuvre could be tasteless and boring, although nutritious. 'You and Gyrid are good at cooking,' he added. 'And some of the dishes we ate in Ranulf's hall were superb.'

'True. Well, I thank you for this. It is kind of you to provide for me.'

Storm chuckled. 'Isn't that what husbands do?'

'Yes, but . . .' She blushed and stared at the table, picking at some crumbs.

He reached across and put his hand over hers again. 'I'm teasing, but know this – I will always provide for you to the best of my ability. Here, it's easy, because I have wealth in this century. In your time, it might not be as straightforward, but I'll try.'

She nodded and gave him a small smile. 'Thank you. Again.'

'Don't mention it. Let's go back to the *hotel* and try to get some sleep. Tomorrow I have to find a way for us to journey to your mother's place.'

Sharing a double bed with Freydis was torture, but Storm was determined not to make love to her again until she was ready. She had felt that first time to be necessary, but there was no need for haste now. They really didn't know each other very well, and although he desired her something fierce, that was no reason to jump her the moment he had her alone in a bed. Although he'd had plenty of one-night stands and no-strings sex, that was different. Those encounters had been with girls who knew what they were getting themselves into, with no feelings attached. He was fairly certain Freydis would not see things that way.

That brought to mind another point – he would have to be faithful to her for as long as they stayed married. To his surprise, he didn't foresee any problem with that. He simply didn't want anyone else. The only woman he wished to sleep with was Freydis.

How this had happened, or why, he'd rather not examine in too much detail at present. Suffice it to say, he'd have no trouble being a good husband, a thought that made him want to laugh out loud.

Me, married at age twenty-one! Who would have thought it? If only my parents or siblings could hear that. They'd never believe it!

Perhaps he ought to tell them. He could easily contact his parents now that he was back in their century. But he wasn't planning on staying for long, so would it be cruel to give them false hope, in case he never made it back again? Besides, he had nothing much to report regarding Maddie, so was there any point? So far he'd failed in his quest, and they would be massively disappointed to hear how little he had accomplished. That he had, in fact, become totally sidetracked by his urge to protect Freydis. No doubt they would say he'd once again acted impulsively, not thinking things through. To a certain extent they would be right, but he couldn't see that he'd had any other choice. Would they agree, though? Probably not. No, he simply couldn't bear to talk to them right now. Much better to wait until he had at least made it to Iceland to see if Maddie was there.

After a restless night, he got up first and took a long, hot shower. Absolute bliss. Then he made himself and Freydis a cup of tea with the kettle provided by the hotel. He laced hers with plenty of sugar and UHT milk, and brought it to her as she sat up in bed looking delectably tousled.

'Here *unnasta*, I've brought you a hot drink. It is called *tea* and comes from a faraway land on the other side of Miðgarðr.' He set the cup down on the table beside the bed and brushed a tendril of hair away from her face, pushing it behind her ear. She had rebraided it before bedtime, but several strands had escaped during the night.

She blinked the sleep from her eyes and smiled. 'Thank you.'

Her smile hit him in the solar plexus, tugging at something

inside him. He ignored the strange sensation and went back to the armchair where he'd been sitting drinking his own tea.

'Would you mind staying here while I go out and try to find us passage to Sogn? It might be better if I'm alone.'

He'd been wrestling with the problem of how to get them to Norway. Without passports, there was no way they could fly or travel the normal routes. There would be border controls somewhere along the line. How on earth would he explain a woman who simply didn't exist in the twenty-first century? He couldn't. There was the possibility of hiring a private plane to fly them to Bergen, but again, someone was bound to want to check their passports when they arrived.

Briefly he considered doing that. They could sprint out of the plane after landing, then time-travel around a corner or in a nearby forest. But the chances of them being caught before they reached a private spot were too great. He couldn't risk it.

That left only one option – travelling by boat.

'Where are you going?' Freydis broke into his thoughts.

'To the harbour. I'll see if I can bribe someone to take us with them when they leave.'

She frowned. 'Why wouldn't they if you are paying for passage?'

'It's complicated, but in this century people cannot travel between places without something called a *passport*. It is an item that proves who you are, with your name and a few other details carved on it in our type of runes. Because you are not from here, I can't obtain one for you. And mine is in Dyflin so can't be used either.'

'How will you go about it then?' She sipped at her tea. 'Mm, this is delicious! So sweet.'

'As I said, I'm going to have to bribe someone. If that doesn't work, we may need to hire a boat.'

He could buy one, perhaps, but he wasn't sure he wanted to spend that much money. And taking a small boat across the North Sea in the middle of winter was probably not the smartest option either. Just as bad as rowing from Orkney to mainland Scotland in her time. He put down his cup and stood up.

'I'll try not to be too long. Promise me you'll stay here?'

'Of course. Go! I'll be fine.'

'OK. I'll be as quick as I can.' Before he could overthink it, he walked over to her and bent to give her a soft kiss. He saw her cheeks turn pink, but again ignored the sensation of warmth that spread through him.

He had more important things to do than moon about his wife.

Freydis stayed under the incredibly soft covers and sheets so white they were almost blinding. She finished the *tea*, a strange but not unpleasant beverage, and closed her eyes for a moment. A part of her would have liked to remain here in this room with Storm for ever. It was a safe haven, warm and comfortable, and when she lay down again and pulled his pillow into her arms, the scent of him was all over it. She breathed in deeply. It smelled clean, slightly flowery from the soap they'd been using, and of man. She loved it.

She loved *him*.

That was not something she'd ever expected to experience. She had heard about romantic love in the tales told by *skalds*, but most ordinary people married for convenience or status. Love or liking might or might not follow, and although most parents made sure both parties were happy with the spouse chosen for them, that wasn't always the case. As witness the callous behaviour of Assur and Gyrid towards her.

No one had selected Storm for her – unless the Norns had had a hand in it, weaving this into her fate – and their marriage had happened by chance. If she'd had a choice, though, she would probably have chosen him. There was no denying she'd been attracted to him from the start. Not only because he was handsome and charming, but because he had treated her as an equal. He had begun by praising her fighting skills, and at no time had he ever told her she couldn't do the same things as him. There was none of the condemnation or irritation she was used to, deriding the fact that she was less feminine than other women. On the contrary, Storm had seemed to revel in it and had taught her more, rather than telling her to stop.

It was incredibly refreshing and drew her to him even further.

Then there were those kisses they'd shared, not to mention the gentle way he'd dealt with their wedding night. She would always be grateful for that, and for him stepping in to save her from Ingolf, even if it was at great cost to himself. She'd stopped him from continuing on his quest to find his sister, but not once had he grumbled about it or blamed her.

'Aargh! Stop thinking about the man,' she muttered to herself, and flung back the covers. 'You're turning into a lovesick fool!'

He hadn't shown any signs that he was falling in love with her. In fact, he'd actually told her straight up that he wasn't going to bed her again unless she told him to. Therefore this attraction was one-sided, no matter if he showed small touches of care and affection. She would simply have to keep her own thoughts on the matter well hidden.

Chapter Sixteen

Mainland, Orkney Islands/Norway
December 2021

'You want me to take you to Norway and let you off somewhere along the coast? Why?'

The weather-beaten fisherman stared at Storm, scratching his head, his eyebrows lowered into a scowl.

'I know it sounds suspect, but there's someone after me at the moment. A guy with connections both here and in Scandinavia. Until I can prove myself innocent of what he's accusing me of, I need to lie low. If my wife and I enter Norway the normal way, he'll know immediately, and his henchmen will find us and hurt us. I'm pretty sure he has spies everywhere and he's probably hacked into the passport control database. The minute I show my passport to anyone, we're toast.' Storm was becoming an excellent liar, not something he was proud of. It was a necessity, pure and simple.

The man continued to stare at him, as if the words didn't quite compute. 'And who's to say this guy won't hurt *me* if I help you?'

'He'll never know. What possible reason would he have for looking at an ordinary fishing vessel? There's no connection between you and me.' Although there would be if Storm sent payment electronically, but he was hoping the man didn't think of that. And since his story was completely fabricated, there was no danger of the fisherman being harmed by the fictitious thug, though he might be caught by the Norwegian coastguard smuggling them in.

'He could be watching right now.'

'No, we've given him the slip, but it's only a matter of time before he catches up with us. It'll take at least a day or two, though. A friend of mine is leading him on a false trail.' Dear gods, but this story was getting convoluted. And why was he thinking in terms of gods, plural? He really was turning into a Viking.

'Hmph.' The fisherman still seemed unconvinced.

'Look,' Storm said, 'it's complicated and I'm really sorry to drag you into my mess, but I'll pay you well. And I swear, if you just drop us off somewhere, you'll never see or hear from us again. We don't even need to know each other's names. How much do you make from the catch you'll be bringing home? I'll give you double that amount. I can send half to your bank account as soon as I board your vessel, and the other half when we reach the coast of Norway.'

Thank goodness he had plenty of savings. Having always stayed with his parents whenever he was home on leave from the army, he'd been able to save most of his earnings for years. Some of it he'd brought to the ninth century in the form of silver and gold, but there was still quite a large chunk remaining. And before coming down to the harbour, he'd bought a cheap pay-as-you-go mobile. He'd be able to transfer money quickly using that and his banking app.

'Fine, I'll do it.' The fisherman stretched out his hand for Storm to shake and named his sum, his Norwegian accent strong even though his English was very good. Storm could have spoken to him in Swedish, but figured he didn't need to add that to the mix. It would only confuse matters. 'You'd better not come on board until after dark,' the man continued. 'I'll have a friend of mine pick you up in a rowing boat at the other end of the harbour.' He pointed southwards. 'His name is Alan and I'll make sure he's waiting for you at ten. Deal? You transfer half the money the moment you set foot on my deck, or you won't be going anywhere.'

'Deal.' They shook on it, and Storm breathed out a silent sigh of relief. This man had the only boat in the harbour with a Norwegian registration number. And thankfully, he was heading home this very evening. 'I'll see you tonight.'

He went back to the hotel with a spring in his step, and entered the room to find Freydis flicking through the information folder. Her eyes lit up at the sight of him, and he felt an answering smile spread across his face.

'*Hei*, you're up.' He went over to perch on the chair next to her. 'Did you manage to use the shower by yourself?'

'Yes, it was wonderful. I simply stood there for ages. And that soap – how do they get it to smell so strongly? The scent is still on my skin.'

He laughed and picked up her hand, giving it an exaggerated sniff while she tried to swat him away. 'Mm, yes, delicious! I'm glad you like it. And I have no idea how to make soap, so I couldn't tell you. One day we should learn. For now, we had better pack up our things and leave this room, or I'll have to pay for another night.' He nodded at the folder. 'Have you been reading about everything you can see around here?'

'Reading? No, these runes don't look like the ones I'm used to, although some appear to be similar. I was looking at the depictions.' She flipped the pages and pointed at a photo of the restaurant they'd been to the night before. 'How are they drawn? They are so lifelike. That looks exactly like the place we went.'

'They are not drawn. It is something called *photography.* I don't think I can explain it to you because it's not something I really understand myself. Anyway, let's get going.'

They packed everything they owned into the sacks they'd brought, including their weapons. It wouldn't do to walk around flashing sharp swords at people. Storm didn't think the Norwegian fisherman would appreciate them bringing such things on board either. After leaving the hotel, they spent the day wandering around Kirkwall. They had a leisurely brunch and later dinner, before hanging out in a pub until it was time to head over to the harbour. Before the shops closed for the day, they had purchased a large cool bag and filled it with food and drink for the journey, including a bottle of mead to share at some point. He guessed the fisherman wouldn't be feeding them, and although they might not be hungry because of the motion of the waves, it was good to be prepared.

Finally, ten o'clock rolled around and they waited at the southern end of the harbour. It was dark there, the glow of nearby street lights and the occasional building distant and faint. Closer to the main part of town, lights were reflected in the water, and the hulking shapes of boats lined the quayside. A quiet *slap-slap* of oars in water heralded the arrival of a small rowing boat. It drew up alongside them, and the man at the oars motioned for them to jump on board.

'Good evening,' Storm greeted him quietly. 'Are you Alan?' He received only a nod in return.

They settled in the stern, clutching their sacks, and Freydis scooted closer to him as if seeking protection. To reassure her, he found her hand and threaded his fingers with hers, holding on tight. He hoped the fisherman hadn't duped him and sent for the police or customs officers. They'd soon find out.

*

Freydis sat silent as the stranger rowed stealthily towards the mouth of the harbour. He'd not said a word since they climbed on board, and didn't appear to want to engage with them in any way. Storm had told her they would have to be alert to danger, but so far she didn't get the sense that the rower posed a threat. The crew of the fishing vessel might be another matter.

He had also warned her that what they were doing was outside the law of this land and the one they were heading to. It didn't faze her. There was apparently no other way because of those *passports* he'd mentioned. Freydis was pragmatic – she would do whatever needed doing. Worrying about whether it was legal or not was a waste of time.

Just outside the harbour, a large ship made of metal rode the waves, waiting for them. Freydis had seen others by the quayside earlier in the day, and Storm had explained that there were many shapes and sizes. Also that they were not propelled by oars or sail. How something so heavy could stay afloat was incomprehensible to her, but that didn't matter, only the end result. As the rowing boat pulled up alongside the bulky shape, a rope ladder was flung over the side. Storm guided her onto the first rungs and stayed close behind her as she ascended. She heard him thank the rower before following her up.

'*Evening*.' The man waiting at the top nodded to her as she swung first one leg, then the other over the railing.

Storm replied in her stead, as she wasn't sure what the word meant. She guessed it was a greeting, as he repeated it back. He'd taught her a few words of his language during the day, although he'd said it was one of two his family alternated between.

'My mother grew up in a part of this land and mostly spoke the Engilskr *tungu*, but then she met and married a man who lived in Svíaríki. That is where I and my siblings grew up, and the language there is different so we learned both. Strangely enough, they are both descended from yours.'

When the fisherman pointed towards the front of his ship and said, '*This way*,' she understood. Storm had taught her to say things like *this is a house*, *this is a table* and so on, and the word *way* sounded a lot like *vegr* in Norse. They followed him down a steep ladder into the bowels of the ship, where he nodded to a small room with benches either side. He indicated that they should make themselves at home.

'*Thank you*.' She and Storm said the words at the same time, as she'd learned them earlier, and he sent her a small smile in acknowledgement.

Storm added something in his language, and fiddled with a small device that lit up in the semi-darkness. He'd told her it had to do with payment, so she didn't question him. Once he was done, the fisherman seemed satisfied and they entered the cabin. The door to the space slammed shut, but she didn't hear a lock or bar and breathed out a sigh of relief. She placed her sack on the floor under one of the benches and sat down. Storm did the same.

'Well, we made it this far.' He slung an arm around her shoulders and pulled her into his side. 'Are you OK?'

'Yes. On edge, as I'm not sure whether we can trust him, but we are here now.' She wanted to add that as long as he was with her, she would be fine, but thought it best to keep that sentiment to herself.

'Indeed. He said we have to stay below deck, which is fair enough, as we don't want to be seen. We might as well lie down and rest. Shall we take turns to stay awake so that we cannot be taken unawares?' He retrieved his knife from his sack before replacing it under the bench. 'Best to have a weapon of some sort to hand.'

She nodded. 'Good idea.'

'You sleep first then. I'll keep watch.'

As she lay down, she heard the noise of what Storm had called an *engine* – the mysterious force that would propel them across the sea. The entire hull of the vessel reverberated with it, clunking loudly, and she became aware of the motion of the ship as it began to move. She clutched her stomach, queasiness assailing her, but as long as she was lying down, it might be bearable. As if he felt the same, Storm went through a tiny door she hadn't noticed before and emerged with a bucket.

He gestured to the door. 'There's a privy in there if you need it, but this might be faster in case you feel sick suddenly. I'm going to put it between us. I have a feeling the sea might be rather rough this time of year.'

'Thank you.'

'Come here.' He squeezed in next to her on the sleeping bench and put his arms around her. 'I'm sorry we have to travel like this, but it was the only way I could think of. Your time is so much easier when it comes to borders between territories.'

'It's fine.' She scooted closer to him and tentatively leaned her head on his shoulder. The muscles of it were solid and unyielding underneath her, but he held her gently. She loved how protected and safe it made her feel.

She closed her eyes and prayed to Njord, the god of sea and winds, for a bearable journey.

'I never want to set foot on a ship again, for as long as I live.' Storm groaned and sank to the ground, his stomach still roiling while everything underneath him appeared to undulate. 'I am so grateful to be on land. Thank you, Odin!' He wasn't normally religious, but it felt right to thank a Viking god, since he assumed they were behind the magic of time travel and had been helping them so far.

'And thank Njord for getting us here safely,' Freydis added, kneeling beside him. Her face was as pale as he assumed his was – more a sickly shade of grey than anything else – and her eyes were bloodshot. There were dark circles under them too, and he had no doubt his looked the same. It had been a very long journey.

Another friend of the fisherman's, this time a Norwegian, had come out to meet the ship in a small boat with an outboard motor, somewhere along the coast in the archipelago just north of Bergen. After Storm had sent the second payment to the fisherman's account via his mobile, he and Freydis had been ferried to dry land and left near the edge of the shore in an uninhabited area. The owner of the smaller vessel had taken off with a curt goodbye, and now they were alone.

According to his phone, it had taken them about sixteen hours to get here. Sixteen incredibly long, tortuous hours. No more than half an hour had passed before extreme seasickness had set in for both of them. Storm didn't normally suffer from motion sickness, and would probably have been fine if they'd been out on deck. However, they couldn't risk being seen and had to stay out of sight while the fishing vessel got under way, pitching and dipping in the rough seas. Being cooped up below deck without access to fresh air or sight of the horizon, all they could do was feel the motion. The constant shuddering of the hull and the stench of fish and diesel that permeated the ship didn't help in the slightest. They'd ended up taking turns to use the bucket and the toilet until they were both too empty and exhausted to do anything other than dry-heave. Even water didn't remain in their stomachs for more than a few minutes at a time, but they'd tried to stay hydrated nonetheless.

'Thank all the gods that is over with!' Freydis drew in a deep breath. 'What do we do now?'

Storm got to his feet, as sitting on snow was not the smartest idea. There wasn't a great deal of it, but it was enough to cover the ground, and the cold penetrated his clothing. 'I assume you would recognise the landmarks around the settlement where your mother lives, yes?'

'I would. My father used to take me with him when he went to market. He taught me how to find my way home from the coast.'

'Good. Then if, as you say, it is in Sogn, it's north of here. We will walk in that direction until you see something familiar.' It might not be the best plan, but it was the only one he could come up with. 'We'd better have something to drink first to settle our stomachs.' He opened the cool bag and extracted a soft drink, pulling the tab. 'Here, have some of this. It has lots of sweetness in it, which will give us strength.'

She took a large sip, then hiccoughed as the fizzy bubbles hit her throat. Storm chuckled. 'Sorry, I forgot to tell you to take it slowly.'

'What *is* that?' She peered at the can as if it was magical.

'I honestly can't explain it to you, but it helps you recover from stomach upsets.' He hadn't the faintest clue how sparkling soft drinks were made, other than the fact that you added carbon dioxide somehow. They finished off the drink between them, then he picked up the cool bag and his sack, which he hefted over his shoulder. 'Let's go.'

It was around two o'clock in the afternoon, and he reckoned they had at least a couple of hours of daylight left. He had no idea how far they'd get, but he hoped to find a town or village along the way with accommodation for the night. There was no point renting a car – and he couldn't anyway, since he didn't have his driving licence with him – or taking a bus. If they did, Freydis might miss the landmarks she was looking for. Also, they had entered the country illegally, to all intents and purposes, and it would be prudent to stay away from the main roads for a while in case anyone had spotted them. It was best they continue on foot. It didn't bother him. He'd been on many a hike when training with the army. He could only hope Freydis would be able to manage, but she was strong and fit and never complained.

She stood up and grabbed her own sack. 'Lead on.'

The way she trusted him to do the right thing was unnerving, but at the same time it gave him confidence. Unlike his parents, she believed in him. Was willing to follow him wherever he told her to go. That was a precious gift, one he hoped he was worthy of.

It was fully dark by the time they entered the outskirts of a small town. They'd crossed a long bridge – the Nordhordland Bridge – onto a large island, then a smaller bridge back to the mainland and a little place called Knarvik. It had been too early to stop there, so they'd carried on northwards and ended up here in Alversund. They found a hotel, and to Storm's relief there was a room available. Because he spoke to the receptionist in Swedish, which the Norwegian woman understood perfectly, she didn't ask for ID of any kind, another thing to be thankful for. Scandinavians generally trusted each other, and they didn't need visas between their countries. He supposed not many tourists came in the depth of winter, so perhaps she was glad to have some guests.

'What is that?' Freydis whispered, while the receptionist typed something into her computer. 'Why is that tree covered in lights?'

Storm glanced at the Christmas tree she was staring at. It occupied a corner of the reception area and was covered in twinkling lights and shiny baubles. He had completely forgotten that they were approaching that time of year. Now he registered the slightly over-the-top decorations all around them. It was strange to think that he wouldn't be spending the festive season with his family, but he didn't really mind. He had more important matters to see to.

'It's our way of celebrating Yule,' he told Freydis in a low voice. 'Putting up little lights and shiny decorations is part of it. I'll tell you more about it later.'

There was a restaurant in the hotel, and they ate a quick meal. By this time, they were both starving, and wolfed down plates of steak and chips.

'I'm going to sleep well tonight,' Freydis said with a yawn, when they'd retired to their room. 'Don't think I did more than doze off a couple of times on board the ship.' She threw herself down onto the bed and spread her arms and legs like a starfish. The sight made Storm smile, but also stirred his baser instincts, so he quickly looked away. Freydis and a bed were a dangerous combination.

'Me neither. But first I'm having a long shower and brushing my teeth.' He'd shown her how to do the latter in Kirkwall, and she'd seemed intrigued and eager to learn.

'Good idea. You first.'

'We could do it together.' The words slipped out before he had time to think about it, and he swore under his breath. He must be more tired than he'd thought.

Freydis shot up into a sitting position, staring at him with big eyes. 'What?'

'Nothing. Forget it. I shouldn't have said anything.' He busied himself pulling clean underwear and a T-shirt out of his sack, but stilled when her arms came around his waist from behind.

'Is that something you want to do? Be naked with me under the rainfall?' Her voice sounded hesitant, unsure, and quivered slightly as if she wasn't certain she wanted to hear his answer.

Storm sighed and pushed his fingers through his hair before facing her. She kept her arms around him and they were chest to chest as he gazed down on her. 'Yes, Freydis. It's something I would like very much. But I said I wouldn't pressure you. Our marriage is new and we can go slowly. You didn't choose me to be your husband. I was more or less foisted on you.'

He allowed his hands to rest lightly on her hips, but didn't pull her any closer. If he did, she would know exactly how much he wanted her to take a shower with him. And more. Much more. Odin's ravens, but she was so beautiful. He could drown in those sky-blue eyes of hers, and as for that lush, kissable mouth . . . No, he wouldn't go there.

She tilted her head to one side and regarded him with a solemn expression. 'You didn't choose me either, Storm. I don't know if you resent having a wife suddenly, when you had no intention of marrying anyone. At least, not at that precise moment in time.' She blushed and lowered her gaze. 'I enjoyed what you did to me during our wedding night, though, and I wouldn't mind doing it again. You can see to it that I don't become with child, if you don't want me to, like you did then. I would understand.'

Something in her tone rang alarm bells in his mind. She sounded sad. Resigned. Frowning, he lifted her face up by putting his fingers under her chin. 'You think I don't want children with you?'

'I . . . I assumed not, since you . . . well, I noticed you didn't spill your seed inside me. That . . . that was intentional, was it not? Maybe so you can divorce me when Ingolf is no longer a threat.' Her face was flaming now, and she tried to turn away from him. He didn't let her.

'*Unnasta*, that was only because we were in a precarious situation. Getting you with child would have complicated everything. I thought it best to wait until our future was more settled. In truth, I would love for you to bear my children.' He was astonished at how true those words were, even though he hadn't contemplated having a family for many years to come. With Freydis, the thought didn't scare him at all. Weird. 'Now is not a good time, though, wouldn't you agree? I have no fixed abode to offer you, and I'm still intending to search for my sister. That could take months, years. I want you to come with me, and all this travelling would be onerous for a pregnant woman. Not to mention that I would worry about you, as it could be dangerous.'

She nodded. 'Oh. I see. You're right. Waiting makes sense when you put it like that. I'm a little past the usual marriageable age, but I'm not too old yet. A few more years shouldn't make a difference.'

That made him laugh. 'Freydis, you are very far from old! Here, in this time, you wouldn't usually marry for several years yet. So no need to worry on that score. But you believe me, don't you? I was only looking out for you, not trying to slight you in any way.'

'I believe you.' Her words were a mere whisper, but he could see that he'd allayed her fears, and that pleased him. She hesitated, then blurted out, 'Does that mean no washing together?'

He grinned. 'Far from it, if that's really what you want. In fact, give me a few minutes and I can make sure we'll be able to do whatever we want without worrying about children.'

Most public restrooms had condom machines, didn't they? He hurried downstairs to see if this proved to be true of the ones near the hotel foyer. He sincerely hoped so. People accused him of being impulsive and reckless, but if Freydis truly wanted him, where was the harm in them sleeping with each other?

They were man and wife, after all.

Chapter Seventeen

Norway/Sogn/Langnes
December 2021/Hrútmánuðr (late December) AD *875*

Freydis didn't know where her courage had come from. She'd never in her life solicited a man's attention, and to ask to be naked with one – well, she was astonished at herself. The impulse had been so strong, though, she couldn't stop herself. And she'd wanted to know where they stood, as Storm had acted mostly like a concerned brother throughout their journey.

Now she knew – he wanted her.

'I mustn't read too much into it,' she admonished herself. He'd not refuted the suggestion that he aimed to divorce her once the threat from Ingolf was gone. Yet he hadn't said he would either.

She took a deep breath. *Stop!* The Norns had already woven her fate, and speculating about it would not do any good. *Accept whatever happens.* That was what her father had taught her. You fought as best you could for what you wanted, but in the end, the outcome was up to the gods.

When Storm returned, he held up a row of little shiny packages. 'We're covered,' he said, grinning, and she nodded even though she didn't really understand. Then he seemed to notice that she was standing in the same place where he'd left her. His smile dimmed. 'Have you changed your mind? You're allowed to, you know. As I said, there is no rush.'

She shook her head and walked over to him, putting her hands on his chest as she looked up at him. She smiled. 'No, I haven't. Shall we bathe?'

He threw the packages onto the bed and wrapped his arms around her before bending to take her mouth in a fierce kiss. 'We shall indeed.'

He tugged down the fastening of her tunic – the thing he called a *zipper*, which fascinated her – and shucked it off her shoulders. He became distracted by the sight of her chest encased in the figure-hugging *T-shirt*, and reached up to touch her breasts, palming them and rubbing her nipples through the thin material, which made the sensations all that more intense. Freydis let out a little moan.

'Take it all off,' he whispered hoarsely, and gripped the hem of the garment. She helped him pull it over her head, then set to work on the drawstring of her trousers.

'You too,' she urged, when he merely stood there watching her.

'What? Oh. Yes.'

His clothing disappeared in record time, and then she was the one staring at him. It was much lighter in this room than the bathing hut where they'd spent their wedding night. She could see every inch of him now, and he was beautiful yet masculine and exuding latent power. Those wide, muscular shoulders and broad chest, strong arms, and a stomach that appeared to be carved out of rock made excitement fizz in her veins. And the soft trail of hair leading down to his manly parts, as if pointing the way to pleasure, urged her gaze to settle there. She swallowed hard and reached out a hand to touch. His abdominal muscles twitched, as did his manhood, making her smile.

'You are sensitive,' she commented.

'To your touch – always.'

He let her explore for a while, and her fingertips drifted up across his pectorals, running along the dragon pattern etched into his skin. 'I like this,' she murmured. 'I want one too.'

'You do?' She thought there was amusement in his voice, but then he grasped her hand and stopped its movement. 'Enough. Time to bathe, and then we can enjoy ourselves all night.'

Freydis wasn't sure what he meant. Surely the act of love couldn't be drawn out for that long? But she trusted him, and there was no time to think about it anyway, as she was being urged into the bathing room. As the hot water cascaded down on them and he locked his lips with hers, she forgot everything else and just gave in to pure sensation. It was utter bliss.

'I don't understand. Gyrid said usually only animals do that from behind, and yet . . .'

Storm was spooning a very sated Freydis and chuckled at the confusion in her voice. 'You can do it in any position you want, *baby*. Front, back, sideways, against a wall – the possibilities are endless.' He hugged her close and breathed in her unique scent, his arm wrapped around her middle. 'Poor Gyrid has probably never had a man wanting to do any of it with her. Her loss. The main question is, did you enjoy it?'

She glanced at him over her shoulder, cheeks flaming. 'You must know I did.' Seeing his no doubt smug expression, she elbowed him lightly. 'Infuriating man!' she huffed.

He laughed, earning himself another glare. 'I'm sorry. I wasn't trying to annoy you. It was a serious question. If you hadn't liked it, I wouldn't do it again. I'd try something else. Just give me a few moments to recover.'

'What? You want to . . . ? But we just finished!'

'Trust me, we are nowhere near finished, *unnasta*.' He nuzzled her neck and kissed his way down her shoulder and back up again. 'We have to make up for lost time. It's been days since we were married, and I've wanted you ever since.'

'I see.'

She didn't sound reluctant, so he continued kissing and stroking her until he was ready to show her another way of making love. She seemed to enjoy that one as well, especially since he encouraged her to be on top. Afterwards, she flopped down onto his chest, breathing hard. Her glorious hair was spread around them like a curtain, as he'd insisted on unbraiding it before washing it in the shower. He stroked his hand down the long, silky tresses, which were now dry, and relished the sensation. It was gorgeous. *She* was gorgeous. And all his.

'That was . . . beyond anything. I had no idea.' She looked up and rested her chin on his chest. 'Thank you for letting me . . . um, be in charge.'

He leaned up to kiss her. 'It was entirely my pleasure, *baby*.'

She tilted her head. 'What does that word mean? You said it earlier too.'

'It's an endearment, like *unnasta*. Literally, it means an infant, but it is used by people in my time for those they love of any age.'

He saw the startled question in her eyes – did he mean that he was in love with her? Since he didn't yet have an answer to that, he chose to pull her down for another scorching kiss instead. Wisely, she didn't pursue the matter, and he was grateful.

Was he in love? He wasn't sure, but it certainly felt as though he was well on his way towards that state. He hadn't had a steady girlfriend since high school, and had been content with brief liaisons, but this felt different. Quite apart from the fact that they were technically married, which ought to have scared the hell out of him yet didn't, this was a real relationship. They were forming a bond, mental and physical, and growing closer each day. Friends as well as lovers. But it was too soon to talk about a forever. He preferred to carry on living in the moment, leaving the future to take care of itself.

To distract her further from such a dangerous subject, he made love to her again – slowly and gently this time – and then they both fell into exhausted slumber.

A week later, Freydis finally spotted a landmark she recognised. 'Storm! I know where we are. This is close to Langnes.'

They were standing at the mouth of a wide fjord, and she knew that if they continued along the southern side, they would eventually arrive at a smaller offshoot that led to her childhood home. The settlement was situated on a long spur of land sticking out into the water, hence the name, which meant 'long peninsula'.

'You are sure?' Storm's eyes lit up, the weariness of travelling on foot for so long disappearing from their depths.

'Yes, definitely.' She pointed to the other side, which from here could only be reached by boat. 'See that tiny island there? It was one of the sights my father told me to look for.'

'Thank the gods for that! I thought we'd be walking for another week at least.' He set the sack he called a *cool bag* down and opened it to pull out one of those bubbling drinks he liked so much. Freydis still wasn't convinced, and preferred her beverages to slide smoothly down her throat without attempting to go up her nose along the way. 'This calls for a celebration.' With his usual consideration, he handed her the drinking vessel first.

'Thank you.' She had learned to take small sips, and relished the sweetness that lingered on her tongue. Storm had told her it wasn't good for her teeth, but that as long as she made sure to brush them each morning and night, it wouldn't do her any harm.

'So which way now?' He took his turn drinking, while glancing around the area.

'Inland. If we carry on along this side of the fjord, we will reach Langnes before nightfall.'

'Good. We had better make haste then. It is probably best not to arrive unannounced after dark.' He finished the drink and packed away the empty container. Before he closed the *cool bag*, he extracted a piece of *chocolate*. That was one type of food she had come to appreciate very much. 'This is the last of our food, so we might as well finish it. I'm going to leave the *bag* here, although it goes against everything I've been taught.'

'What do you mean?' Freydis frowned at him, puzzled, as she accepted her share of the sweet treat.

'In my century, far too many people throw rubbish everywhere instead of only on the designated midden. And as I've told you, we have materials like *plastic* that do not become one with the earth again. Not ever. So by leaving this *cool bag* here, I am adding to the destruction of nature. Unfortunately, it cannot be helped. And who knows? Perhaps we will come this way again some other time and I can retrieve it. In fact, I'll make a point of it.'

Freydis nodded. It all sounded strange to her, but she understood the gist of it. She swallowed the last of her *chocolate*. 'What about our clothing?'

'We'll have to leave that here too and change back into the garments of your era. I'll stuff them into the *bag*.'

There was still snow on the ground, and an icy wind whipped the coastline, so stripping down to nothing was not an appealing prospect. It had to be done, though, and Freydis didn't complain. She donned her old clothes, which felt strangely abrasive after the feather-light touch of the *T-shirts* she'd been wearing for the last two weeks. Her cloak, when she had fastened it, also seemed rather inadequate compared to the *puffa coat* with its feather lining. And she disliked the feel of the skirts restricting the movement of her legs, but she gritted her teeth and told herself she'd soon become used to it again. She had grown soft in Storm's time. That would never do.

'Are you ready to travel back in time?'

Storm had changed into his outfit too, complete with belt and weapons. The sight of them, as well as the feel of her own sword and knife, sent a wave of familiarity through her. She'd missed being armed and ready to defend herself, even if she could have used Storm's defensive techniques at a pinch. They had found time to practise them a few times along the way.

'I'm ready.' Although she was not looking forward to the extreme dizziness and nausea, the end result was all that mattered.

She was going home.

Hours later, they rounded a bend in the shoreline and Langnes came into view. Freydis stopped, her throat suddenly tight, and gulped for breath. 'There it is,' she croaked. 'My home.'

As if he understood that her emotions were unsettled upon seeing the place after so long, Storm took her mittened hand in his and gave it a squeeze. 'Let us hope they have enough *nattverðr* to share with us. I could eat an entire horse right now. Time travelling certainly makes you hungry, eh, *baby*?'

The endearment, and the support that emanated from him, was enough to steady her, and she managed a small smile at his attempt at humour. 'It does indeed. Come, husband *mín*.'

He grinned at that and followed her towards the settlement. It was dusk, and only a few people were out and about. There was smoke coming from the gable ends of the main hall, and light spilling through the half-open door. Voices could be heard inside, while from other buildings came the sounds of cattle and sheep.

A couple of dogs barked as they caught sight of the newcomers, and came rushing towards them.

'*Hei, hei*, we are friends, not foe,' Storm told them calmly, while taking off his mitten so he could stretch out a hand for them to sniff. Freydis followed suit, and the canines settled down, although they continued to bark intermittently.

The noise brought a man running. 'Good evening,' he said, peering at them. 'Where have you come from?' Then he did a double-take and looked closer. 'Young Freydis? Is it yourself? By all the gods!'

She smiled. 'It is. I'm happy to see you looking so well, Trond.'

In truth, the man had aged a lot in the eight years she'd been gone, but at least he was alive and he'd recognised her. That had to be a good sign.

'And right pleased I am to see you too.' He beamed at her. 'I thought you'd settled elsewhere.'

'Yes, well, I did. This is my husband, Storm Haakonarson. We have come for a visit. Is . . . is Mother here? And *bóndi*?'

'Of course, of course.' He nodded at Storm. 'Pleased to meet you. Let me take you both inside. You must be frozen to the marrow.'

He led the way into the hall, and the chatter stopped abruptly as he made his way towards the dais at the other end and everyone noticed the newcomers. Freydis held her head high, preparing herself mentally for this meeting with Bjarni and her mother. She had no idea what kind of welcome she would receive, and clenched her fists in the folds of her cloak to keep her expression calm. She wasn't a vulnerable ten-year-old any longer, nor was she alone.

'*Bóndi*! Mistress Dagrun! Look who I found outside! And all grown up too.'

She saw the moment her mother caught sight of her, and her heart sank when Dagrun's eyes narrowed. There was no welcoming smile on her face, no cry of joy, just a stillness as if she was weighing what to say. Disappointment flooded her. Assur had been right. Her mother didn't want her back and had never intended to send for her. Those had merely been empty words. She took a deep breath and smiled as if nothing was amiss and she didn't care, but inside she was screaming.

'Mother. Bjarni.' She gave them each a deferential bow, and was pleased to find that at least her stepfather looked happy to see her.

He stood up, nearly overturning his chair in the process, and smiled at her. 'Freydis! This is an unexpected pleasure. What brings you here? I was sure your mother said you'd married and were settled in a new home.'

'I did, yes. May I introduce my husband, Storm Haakonarson?' She indicated the man who was standing close behind her, his chest touching her shoulder in solidarity and his hand resting lightly on her lower back as if to ground her. 'We are on a journey and had hoped to travel to Ísland, but the weather has been against us so we thought to visit you for a while until sailing conditions improve. I hope you don't mind.'

'Of course not.' To her surprise, Bjarni appeared sincere, and gestured for someone to make room at the table. 'Come, sit. We were about to start the evening meal. You are most welcome to share it with us, and to stay for as long as you need to. Is that not so, *víf*?'

He looked at Dagrun, who hadn't said a word so far. At this direct appeal, she managed a tight smile, although it didn't reach her eyes. 'Of course. Do join us, Freydis, and . . . Storm, was it?'

She frowned at his name, as if it was wrong. To her it probably was. Freydis guessed Assur must have informed her of the impending nuptials to Ingolf. Her bringing Storm instead was confusing, but she had no intention of explaining right now. That could wait.

'Thank you.' She gave Bjarni a genuine smile, grateful for the warm welcome. The hall was, after all, his and not her mother's. She had to remember that. 'We would be delighted.'

Handing her cloak and sack of possessions to Trond, who promised to put them somewhere safe, she took Storm's hand and went to sit down at the table.

This stay should prove very interesting indeed.

Chapter Eighteen

Langnes, Sogn
Hrútmánuðr (late December) AD *875*

Wow, what a bitch! That was the only thought running through Storm's mind, as he concentrated on his food while Freydis made small talk with her stepfather. Her mother hadn't been the slightest bit pleased to see her. Rather, she'd been downright rude. What was up with that?

He listened in on the conversations around him and learned that Bjarni and Dagrun had two little boys – Birkir and Baldr, aged around six and eight respectively. They were sitting nearby with a nursemaid of some sort, and every time he caught them staring at him, they giggled. He winked back, making them smile. Bjarni appeared to treat his wife kindly, deferring to her opinion from time to time, and she looked well fed and sumptuously clothed. The hall they were in wasn't huge, but it couldn't be described as small either. It was decorated with carvings and tasteful wall hangings, and was comfortable and warm. Food appeared to be plentiful, if a bit boring, and the ale was flowing.

In short, Dagrun had everything she could possibly wish for, so why the animosity towards her own daughter? He couldn't figure it out.

'Where do you hail from, Storm?' She had suddenly leaned forward and was talking to him along the table, in front of her husband and Freydis, whose conversation stopped abruptly. Her gaze was speculative, as if she was gauging his worth.

'Svíaríki,' he replied calmly. He wasn't going to let her faze him. 'My kin own a prosperous settlement not far from the trading place called Birka. We will most likely settle there with them once we've completed our travels.'

He had made that up on the spur of the moment, as he hadn't given much thought to what would happen when – if – he found Maddie. Originally he'd intended to go back to the twenty-first century, of course, but now he wasn't so sure. There was no rush to decide, though.

'I see.' Dagrun continued to spear him with her intense gaze. 'So you will rely on your kin to provide for the two of you?'

'Not at all.' He clenched his jaw to stop himself from snapping at her. She was deliberately baiting him. Judging by the small gasp from Freydis's direction, she'd come to the same conclusion. 'I am well able to provide for my wife and any children we may have. I have enough riches for us to set up our own home, should we so wish. I've been a mercenary, but I am also a blacksmith. I'm assuming Freydis would prefer me to stick to the latter profession, at least until she tires of me.' He smiled teasingly at her and leaned over to kiss her cheek, which made her blush.

'*Fífl*.' She swatted his arm playfully. 'Of course I won't tire of you.'

He knew they were only putting on a show, but the words warmed him. Dagrun, however, did not seem impressed.

'A blacksmith? I see. A . . . worthy occupation.' It was clear she didn't think so, not by a long shot.

Storm ignored her barb and turned his attention to his food, as if he'd grown weary of her questions. Thankfully, Bjarni must have caught on to the underlying tension. He defused it by asking Freydis about Assur and her time in the Orkney Islands. Dagrun didn't say another word for the rest of the meal, and when they were done, she retired to a private chamber at one end of the hall. Bjarni frowned at her departing form, but said nothing. Instead, he called another woman over.

'Bodil, can you please find my daughter and her husband a suitable bench for the night? I'm sure they'd like to retire after their long journey.'

Storm saw the gratitude in Freydis's expression at the fact that the man had called her 'daughter'. It would seem her stepfather had more affection for her than her own mother did, which was very sad. There was nothing they could do about it, however, until or unless they found out what had caused such animosity. Perhaps the woman was just a cold fish, in which case it was a lost cause. It made him angry on Freydis's behalf, and a wave of protectiveness washed over him. He wanted to shield her from hurt, and he would, to the best of his ability. She was his woman, no matter how caveman that sounded.

They followed Bodil along the row of benches, and soon gathered she was one of Dagrun's cronies, since she didn't seem pleased to have to accommodate them. With a few curt words, she forced some other people to move their belongings, then nodded at the single free bench space.

'There's not much room here, as you can see. You'll have to share,' she informed them tersely. The challenging look she shot their way indicated that she thought this some sort of punishment.

Storm gave her a wide smile and a wink. 'Thank you. I like nothing better than sharing a bench with my lovely wife. That's definitely not a hardship.' His meaning was clear, and made

Freydis turn bright red. It also had the effect of wiping the smugness off Bodil's face, which pleased him no end.

'I bid you good night.' The woman stomped off, and Storm chuckled.

'Sour old biddy,' he muttered, putting his arms around Freydis to hug her close. 'Are you OK, *víf mín*? That was a very trying meal, but I think we survived.'

She nodded against his chest and hugged him back while letting out a long sigh. 'It was indeed. I knew coming back here might be difficult, but I had hoped for a little more . . . warmth. I'll admit to being surprised it came from my stepfather. I have no idea why he's been painted in such a bad light by Assur and my mother. Still, at least now I know where I stand. There is nothing here for me long-term, but we will have to remain for a while. Do you mind? I'd like to at least spend some time getting to know my little brothers.'

He kissed the top of her head and rubbed soothing circles on her back. 'I don't mind at all. Whatever you need. There is nowhere we need to be until spring. There won't be any ships to Ísland until then, so we'll have to stay here at least a couple of months.' He indicated the pile of sheepskin pelts and blankets a thrall had just brought. 'Shall we bed down for the night?' he whispered. 'I want to hold you.'

'Yes. You have no idea how good that sounds right now.'

They divested themselves of their weapons and outer tunics, hanging them on hooks on the wall above the bench before crawling under the blankets. Storm made sure he was on the outside and curled around Freydis, holding her close. All he wanted was to make her feel cherished and safe. There were tender emotions rising inside him, and he let her feel them in the way he held her. He sensed she needed someone on her side right now, and he would be that person for her.

He moved her plait out of the way and kissed her cheek. 'Sleep well, *baby*.'

The following morning, Freydis decided to take a quick walk around outside before *dagverðr*. Storm insisted on accompanying her, and she had no objection to that whatsoever.

'Does it look the same?' he asked, taking in their surroundings.

'Yes, more or less.'

She couldn't fault the way Bjarni ran things. Nothing was in disrepair, the animals and people seemed content and well fed, and everything had an air of prosperity. She was pleased that her father's legacy had not fallen into the hands of someone who'd run it into the ground. Bjarni was a staid and serious man, not the opportunist she had thought when he'd married her mother mere months after her father's death. She had done him an injustice, as had Assur and Dagrun, it would seem.

What she had viewed as harshness as a child appeared to be nothing more than a firm hand and a wish to have things done properly. Thinking back, she had probably tried her stepfather's patience with her hoydenish ways. And as a newly married man, he might also have been trying to stay on his wife's good side. Freydis suspected now that any punishments she'd been given had been at her mother's instigation, not his. She saw no sign of him being unduly severe with his own children. They were little mischief-makers, but seemed happy and carefree.

Storm interrupted her introspection. 'It's a beautiful place,' he commented, taking a deep breath as if appreciating the sharp, fresh air that seared their lungs. It came back out in a cloud, reminding her that they shouldn't be standing around. It was too cold for that, but she wasn't quite ready to head indoors yet.

Steep mountains cradled the still waters of the fjord, with trees and bushes clinging to the sides. At the moment, everything was covered in snow, and the waterfalls that normally cascaded down the sides had frozen into shiny sculptures. The tranquil scene was reflected in the mirror-like surface of the fjord, which was only icy around the edges. Looking at it was soothing and refreshing.

'It is. I always loved it here.' She swallowed down the lump of nostalgia lodged in her throat, but he noticed it anyway.

'And it all belongs to Bjarni, through his marriage with your mother?'

'Yes.' She shrugged. 'At least that's how I believe it works. Father always said his domains would be mine one day, but Mother told me that the dowry she sent with me was my share of this place.'

'Hmm.' Storm appeared deep in thought for a moment, then, pulling her in for a sideways hug, he smiled. 'Well, no matter where we end up, Langnes will always be here and we can visit any time. I'm sure Bjarni wouldn't mind.' He wisely didn't mention her mother.

'You're right.' And the fact that he'd said 'we' when referring to their future gave her hope. They might find a place that was equally as stunning in which to make a home. Langnes belonged to her past. Now it was time to look forward.

Freydis was grudgingly invited to join her mother and the other women as they settled down to their tasks inside the hall. It was too cold to be outdoors unless you were doing manual labour of some sort, and they were all busy with various stages of cloth production. Every household needed its own material in order to make clothes, bedlinen and sometimes sails. The women were currently working with wool, but at other times it could be flax instead. For the first couple of days, no one spoke to her, other than to give brief instructions on which wool to use, or what other task needed doing. It was as if they were all waiting for Dagrun's permission to be friendly. Freydis decided her best course of action was to ignore the tense atmosphere and wait it out. If it was some sort of game her mother was playing to test her fortitude, she refused to show that she cared.

Finally, after two days of pointed silence, Dagrun addressed her. Freydis had just taken the spindle offered to her by a scowling Bodil and settled down to spinning woollen yarn without complaint. It wasn't her favourite thing to do – none of the female tasks were – but at least she was competent at it these days. Gyrid, for all her faults, had been a patient teacher, and had refused to give up until Freydis became proficient enough. Her mother's voice rang out, making her look up.

'I see you have finally learned *some* womanly pursuits, *dóttir*.' The comment was made in an acid tone. 'Assur's wife must have managed to instil a few things, proving that going away was good for you, just as I thought.'

She spoke as if Freydis had merely been sent away to learn about household management. Yet she'd had no intention of bringing her daughter back. It rankled, but Freydis decided not to rise to the bait.

'It has been eight years, and I am a little more mature these days,' she said lightly. 'You'll no doubt be surprised to learn that I can manage most female tasks.'

'That does indeed astonish me. I despaired of you ever learning anything worthwhile.' The implication being that fighting, hunting, fishing and husbandry, the things her father had taught her, were not.

Freydis gritted her teeth and carried on spinning. She was aware of Storm sitting nearby, helping someone to whittle new spokes for a rake. No doubt he was listening, and she wondered what he made of the conversation. He had deflected her mother's barbs nicely the night they'd arrived, but it was embarrassing to have him witness more of the humiliating comments. What if he started to resent having a wife who wasn't perfect at running a household? He'd seemed fine with it before, and he had admired her fighting skills, but perhaps he hadn't considered the matter properly.

'What I don't understand,' her mother carried on, 'is how you came to marry a mere blacksmith, rather than the prosperous jarl my cousin selected for you. It makes no sense. You could have been the mistress of a huge estate. Several, even. But perhaps your skills weren't quite up to par.'

'That was not the reason. Quite simply, I refused Ingolf Gunnarsson. The man may be a jarl, but he is despicable. Besides, Storm and I had a . . . um, prior arrangement. I had already given him my word.' That was a lie, but no one here would ever know, and hopefully her husband wouldn't enlighten them.

Dagrun tutted. 'I am disappointed in you. A girl in your position should have been eager to make the best possible match. You ought to have been grateful to Assur.'

'Really? And what position would that be?' Freydis gripped the spindle so tightly her knuckles were white. 'The one where my entire dowry had disappeared because your cousin used it to pay for my keep? I owed him nothing, and I worked hard for as long as I stayed with him and his wife. The fact that he put himself in debt to Ingolf was not my problem. I was not a chattel for him to use as payment.'

Her mother threw her an incredulous glance. 'Such disrespect to a man who took you in without complaint!'

'He was obviously well paid for his hospitality,' Freydis muttered. 'I'm lucky Storm did not mind taking a wife who was entirely without dowry. The gods only know why Ingolf wanted to do so.'

At this point, Storm surged to his feet and came to stand behind the stool she was sitting on. 'I'd thank you to stop insulting my wife, Mistress Dagrun,' he growled. 'As I believe I informed you, I am not a *mere* blacksmith, and she has not in any way married below her status. Unlike Gunnarsson, I will cherish her and treat her well. But I gather it might have suited your purposes better for him to have killed her, the way he did his other wives. Seeing as how she, rather than you, probably should have inherited this property from her father. Isn't that how it is?'

Dagrun's mouth had fallen open, and her eyes were shooting daggers at him. 'How dare you!'

'How dare I speak the truth?' He shrugged. 'I'm always in favour of honesty. I simply want to make it clear that Freydis will not be challenging you or your husband for ownership of Langnes. She doesn't need it, so you can stop with the vitriol. She is not a threat to you. She has me and my family now, and we will provide well for her. I can see that Bjarni is a good man, who probably believed whatever tale you spun him about the inheritance. He is taking excellent care of this place and he is welcome to it. But one more word out of you, disparaging Freydis, and we might reconsider. Have I made myself clear?'

Freydis was staring at him in astonishment as well. It hadn't occurred to her that Langnes should have been hers, even though her father had told her so. She had assumed he was mistaken, and had understood from her mother that they shared ownership after her father's death. Her portion was the dowry that was sent with her to Assur. But she had never actually seen the amount and had no way of knowing what a settlement like this was worth, nor what a widow was entitled to.

Dagrun stood up abruptly and threw down the spindle she had been wielding. 'All I see is that Freydis has married an insufferably conceited man. I shall speak to my husband and ask him to send you on your way.'

'You do that. I'm sure he'll reconsider when I ask him for the full amount of Freydis's dowry, rather than the pitiful pile of silver you no doubt gave Joalf. And make no mistake, I can check with the man myself to verify it. He is a friend of ours.'

With a shriek of annoyance, Dagrun stomped off towards her sleeping chamber, Bodil hot on her heels.

Freydis looked up at Storm. He placed his hands on her shoulders, leaning down so they could speak without anyone else hearing their conversation. 'Did you make all that up on the spur of the moment?' she whispered.

'No. It's been gnawing at me since we arrived here, and listening to your mother only made my suspicions solidify. There had to be a reason she wanted you out of the way, and that seemed the most likely one. Her reaction confirms that I was right.' He sighed. 'Do you want to challenge her legally? I assume there is a *þing* around here to decide such matters.'

'I don't think so. If Bjarni had been an evil man, I might have considered it, but I have no wish to live here. Especially not if I have to share the running of the place with my mother.'

'Good. Then we will leave as planned and I'll make sure you never want for anything.' He fixed her with a stern gaze. 'But if she *ever* speaks to you like that again, please fetch me, because I won't stand for it. You've done nothing to deserve such treatment.'

She smiled at him, her heart overflowing with gratitude and love for this man. 'Thank you. Thank you for being on my side.'

'Always.' He captured her mouth with his, uncaring that they had an audience, and didn't stop kissing her until she felt it all the way down to her toes. Then he went back to his whittling, while Freydis carried on with her spinning, heart beating furiously.

No one said a word, but a couple of the other women smiled at her, and eventually began to talk amongst themselves again. Freydis took this as tacit approval, and relaxed for the first time since she'd arrived here.

Chapter Nineteen

Langnes, Sogn
Hrútmánuðr (late December) AD *875*

'Storm, might I have a moment of your time, please?'

Bjarni had approached him as he stood down by the edge of the fjord, contemplating the stunning scenery. He'd needed some fresh air after being cooped up in the hall for days. Sitting still wasn't his thing. Never had been.

'Of course.'

The man sighed and stared out across the water. 'It has come to my attention that you had words with my wife yesterday. And also the gist of the argument. I confronted her about it, but she's refusing to speak to me.' He rubbed his beard. 'She's . . . a difficult woman, in many ways. Proud to a fault, as her father was a powerful jarl of illustrious lineage. Quiet and taciturn too, but she has been a good wife to me and has given me two fine sons. She runs my household with efficiency and doesn't question my judgement. I've never had cause to doubt her integrity before now, and it didn't occur to me that what she told me about her daughter was untrue.'

Storm shrugged. 'Why would it? Freydis wasn't your child, and no doubt you felt it was up to Dagrun to decide her future.'

'That is so. She was a most unusual little girl, having been more or less raised as a boy by her father. I have no idea what he was thinking, but I didn't know how to deal with her. She was continually challenging our authority, insisting on doing things the way she'd been taught. When Dagrun suggested she might benefit from being away for a while in order to learn how to behave properly, I thought it reasonable. With the example of others before her, I believed Freydis would come to realise that her upbringing was not normal. Then she would understand that she needed to conform.'

'I see.' Storm understood the man's point of view, but he hadn't been in full possession of the facts. 'The only problem was that Dagrun had no intention of ever bringing Freydis back here. She spent years waiting to be summoned, but no word came. To say she was disappointed would be an understatement.'

Bjarni nodded. 'I've gathered that now. However, her mother told me she'd had word that the girl was extremely happy where she was and wanted to remain there. Then we had a message to say that a brilliant match had been arranged for her with a very important man with vast estates. I was pleased for Freydis and assumed she was happy with the arrangement. Dagrun implied as much, and I didn't enquire further. I should have done. I'm sorry. It was my responsibility.'

'No, I understand why you didn't. You trusted your wife, and why wouldn't you?'

They stood in silence for a moment, then Bjarni turned to him. 'Do you wish to take the matter to the *þing*? We would need to bring the man who fetched Freydis back here so he could testify as to the amount he was given for her dowry. Or Assur himself, although I'm not sure I would trust him since he is obviously in cahoots with Dagrun. I am a fair and honest man. I have no wish to swindle my stepdaughter out of any part of her inheritance.'

Bjarni rose in Storm's estimation, although he already liked him. 'You should really speak to Freydis herself about this matter. As her husband, what is hers is now mine, but I wish her to have the final say.' Although in this era a woman's property became her husband's upon marriage, Storm had no intention of making this decision unilaterally. 'I don't think you need to worry. As I told Dagrun, we didn't come here to challenge you or make demands. Freydis merely wanted to visit her mother and spend some time in her childhood home. Also to meet her half-brothers. I and my family have enough wealth to provide for her. We don't need any part of Langnes.' He gesticulated to the prosperous settlement. 'If you had mismanaged it or treated the people here badly, it might have been a different matter. As you clearly haven't, I think she'll be happy to leave it all in your hands. Come spring, we'll be on our way. But do please talk it over with her to make sure. I don't want to influence her either way.'

The older man let out what sounded like a heartfelt sigh of relief. 'Thank you, that is most generous of you. I am very grateful to you both for being so reasonable, and I shall definitely have a word with Freydis to confirm her wishes. If matters stand as you say, I will express my gratitude to her personally as well. I'll make sure Dagrun behaves better towards her from now on, and you are welcome to stay for as long as you wish.'

'Excellent. I'm glad the matter has been cleared up. Now all we have to do is survive the boredom of the next few months.' Storm stomped his feet to try and bring some warmth to his frozen toes. He hated having to wait around, but there really wasn't anything he could do until they could find passage on a ship headed for Iceland. That would be in two months' time at the earliest, or so he'd been told. No point enquiring about Maddie here either, as he doubted she'd have journeyed via Norway. That would have been an unnecessary detour. 'I don't suppose you have need of my help with anything other than whittling? I'm a man of action, and sitting indoors all day is going to be the death of me. Although I have to warn you, I am not over-fond of hunting.'

Bjarni smiled. 'I know what you mean. I cannot abide inactivity either. Did you not say you were a blacksmith? Perhaps you could help old Orm in the smithy? He does well enough with most things, but he's getting on a bit and could probably do with assistance when it comes to heavier items. Shall we go and ask?'

'Yes, please! That would be perfect.'

A winter spent in a smithy sounded much more appealing and would make the time go faster. Despite the new accord with Bjarni, he couldn't wait to leave this place. The gnawing worry of what was happening to his sister ate away at him and gave him no peace. The next few months were going to feel like years, but there was nothing for it but to endure.

Langnes, Sogn
Einmánuðr (March) AD *876*

The weeks passed slowly, time dragging its heels, at least for Freydis. She didn't see much of Storm during the day as he was busy helping out in the forge, but he made a point of sitting with her in the evenings. He always included her in discussions and board games, and she was content, but she would have preferred to spend all her time with him rather than with the other women as was expected. Dagrun wasn't outright antagonistic any longer, but then again, she wasn't friendly either. It was as if she resented having had her plans disrupted and being found out in a lie, instead of being grateful that she hadn't been punished for her misdeeds.

Freydis alternated between being angry about it and feeling apathetic. The damage had clearly been done when she'd spent most of her time with her father as a child. Dagrun must have felt left out, and now it was too late to repair their relationship. If she hadn't had Storm, she might have been more upset, but as it was, she didn't need her mother. Besides, Bjarni and her two little half-brothers more than made up for Dagrun's coldness. Whenever she could escape for a while, Freydis spent time with Birkir and Baldr, teaching them sword techniques and archery. Bjarni didn't mind, and in fact he often came to join in. The four of them were forming strong bonds, which pleased her greatly.

She knew her sojourn here was finally coming to an end when it was time for the *Dísablót*, which was celebrated at the end of the winter, just before the summer half of the year began. Festivities were held to honour the female deities and spirits, the *dísir*, and it was hoped that the sacrifices made would help the coming year's harvest. A number of animals were slaughtered, and there would be feasting in the hall for everyone.

'I'm so pleased I get to experience a proper *Viking* celebration,' Storm commented as they took their places at the table on the dais alongside Bjarni, Dagrun and others.

'*Viking?*' Freydis raised her eyebrows at him. 'What do you mean? We're not going a-viking now.'

He bent to whisper so that only she could hear his words. 'It's what the people of my time call you and yours. You know, instead of for example Engilskr, to us you are Víkingar.'

'How very odd. And what have you been told about our feasts?' She took a sip of mead, which had been served for this special occasion. It was sweet but potent, and slid smoothly down her throat.

He grinned. 'That they can become rather raucous. A lot of ale or mead is consumed and there is singing, dancing and *skalds* reciting epic tales. Perhaps other things happen afterwards as everyone gets a little carried away . . . You did say this *blót* was about fertility, did you not?'

'No! I said harvest.'

She knew her face was becoming flushed at his teasing, but he was conjuring up images in her mind that she'd been trying to suppress for weeks. The look in his eyes told her that he too was thinking about bedding, and a shiver of delight ran through her. There was desire in his gaze, and she didn't mind in the slightest. She wanted him, all of him, every time he was near, but she wasn't sure if he felt the same. They had never discussed it, and she didn't dare bring the matter up.

Since they'd returned to her time, he had only made love to her a few times, and always carefully withdrawn so as not to get her with child. Being surrounded by others every night made it awkward, and she'd missed the wild abandon of the encounters they had had in his century. Trying to do it quietly in a hall full of people wasn't very satisfying.

'Perhaps they *will* get carried away later,' she murmured. 'We could try to find somewhere a little more private.' She smiled back and dared to lean over and kiss him on the cheek. She didn't often initiate physical contact between them, but sometimes she couldn't resist. He was simply so overwhelmingly gorgeous, and for now at least, he was hers.

'Oh? That sounds like an excellent idea.' He nuzzled her neck and kissed her below the ear, a sensitive spot as he well knew. Excitement shot through her. She had wondered if his ardour had cooled now that they'd been married for a few months, but evidently that wasn't the case. 'I look forward to it.'

He drank some of his mead and made a satisfied noise. 'Mm, this isn't bad.' He helped himself to the dishes being brought round by the thralls, and offered her a piece of roasted meat that he'd cut off with his eating knife. 'Here, you must try this. It's delicious!'

She opened her mouth and took it with a laugh. 'There's no need to feed me like an infant. I have my own portion.'

He deliberately licked the fingers that her lips had touched and sent her a smouldering glance. 'Maybe I want to,' he said. 'I like looking at your mouth.' He leaned forward and kissed her. 'And touching it,' he added in a husky whisper.

Freydis shook her head at him. 'Later,' she promised. She hoped he would kiss her a lot more thoroughly, and if not, maybe it was time she asked for what she wanted.

The combination of mead and ale was quite potent. By the time the evening was drawing to a close, Storm was pleasantly buzzed. He felt at peace with the world, and even managed to smile at Dagrun, who was her usual surly self. Her husband was a saint to put up with her, but perhaps she showed him a different side when they were alone. He hoped so for Bjarni's sake.

He turned to look at his own wife, and a bolt of lust shot through him. Here was a woman who was never sour, and always happy to see him. They had fun together and hadn't argued a single time so far. The way people lived here, though, did not give anyone the privacy needed for a proper relationship. Not to mention the fact that he'd had to leave any remaining condoms behind in his own century. He'd tried to keep himself in check since they'd arrived, and had only succumbed a few times. His arguments against having children at this stage still remained, but damn it all, keeping his hands off her was proving painfully difficult. Literally.

Tonight he was determined to get her alone and have some fun. To that end, he took her hand in his and whispered, 'Time to go.'

Her startled gaze flew to his, but then she caught his meaning. 'Oh. Yes, of course.' She scrambled off the bench and followed him as he made his way outside. No one paid them any attention, as the noise levels were still high and everyone was either drunk or asleep at this point.

'Where are we going?' He felt her shiver at the sudden blast of cold air that hit them when they stepped outside the main door.

'The forge. It will be empty at this time of night, and I want you to myself. You'll be making a lot of noise.' He knew he sounded smug, but he had no doubt he could make her feel good enough to be loud about it. It wouldn't be the first time, after all.

'Th-there's n-no sleeping b-bench in there.' Her teeth were chattering, and he slung an arm around her shoulders while hustling her towards the forge building.

'We don't need one. You'll see.'

Their progress was somewhat erratic. There was still a little bit of snow on the ground, and some icy puddles, and they both slipped a couple of times and had to lean on each other. Freydis giggled, and he felt like laughing himself as the world tilted slightly.

'Whoa! Careful there.' Perhaps he was more drunk than he'd realised. Mead and strong ale were not the best combination, but he felt good and mostly in control of his limbs.

They stumbled into the dark forge and he slammed the door shut and barred it. He doubted anyone else would come here tonight, but he didn't want to take any chances. There was moonlight shining in through the air vents in the gable ends of the building. Although it wasn't much, it was enough for them to see what they were doing. He wrapped his arms around Freydis and their mouths collided as if they were starved of each other.

Storm's head was spinning, but he didn't know if it was from the alcohol or the desire rushing through his veins. He ignored it and concentrated on the beautiful, vibrant woman in his arms. *My wife. Mine, all mine.* There was immense satisfaction in hearing those words running through his mind. He'd never wanted anyone as much as he wanted her right then. She seemed just as eager, tangling her fingers in his hair to inch him closer.

'Mm, you taste of mead,' he murmured, stroking her tongue with his and biting gently on her lower lip. It was plump and luscious – her whole mouth was – and he couldn't get enough of it.

She giggled again. 'You too. It's even better this way.'

'Hold on.' He let go of her for a moment and fetched one of the leather aprons that were hanging on hooks on the wall. He spread it over an empty workbench, then pulled Freydis over to stand before it. 'There, wouldn't want you to get splinters. Now take off your *smokkr*, please, *unnasta*.'

Shucking off his own belt and overtunic, he dropped them on the floor and helped her pull the dress over her head. It too was discarded unceremoniously. Walking her backwards into the bench, he rained kisses on her mouth, neck and shoulders, as far as her *serk* gave him access. At the same time, his hands roamed underneath it, lifting the hem until he could reach the drawstring of the trousers she wore. He pulled at the fastening and they dropped down.

'Storm?' He heard the question in her voice and smiled against her silky skin.

'I need those off as well, *baby*. Step out of them, please.' He bent to help her, and had to tug off her ankle boots too in order to get the trouser legs past her feet.

Once her lower half was bare, he lifted her onto the workbench and stepped in between her legs, stroking his way up the inside of her smooth thighs. 'Now I'll show you we don't need a bed. Are you ready, sweet wife?'

He felt her tremble in anticipation. 'Yes! Yes, I am.'

The slamming of a door and loud voices shouting outside woke Storm. He winced and raised his hands to cradle his head. It ached like the very devil, and the slightest sound reverberated around the inside of his skull like a symphony orchestra in full flow, complete with cymbals.

'*Jesus!* What happened?' he muttered, but he was well aware of the cause of this pain. Mead and ale in copious quantities. It had seemed like a good idea at the time. Now he was not so sure.

He became aware of the armful of warm woman snuggled up to his chest, and images from the night before assailed him. Stumbling through the cold night, the dark forge, making her moan his name in ecstasy as he . . .

'*Shit!*' he breathed. In his inebriated state, had he given any thought to birth control?

The answer was a resounding no.

Swallowing a groan, he closed his eyes and berated himself. He vaguely remembered thinking that it didn't matter any longer, because Freydis was his wife. Since when did he start reasoning like a Viking male? He must have been here too long. However, he liked kids, and the few times he'd given any thought to the matter in the past, he'd decided he wanted a family. He just hadn't thought it would be quite so soon. He was only twenty-two, having recently had a birthday – although he'd missed the actual day, since he wasn't keeping track exactly – and not really father material.

Then again, he hadn't believed he was husband material either, and he wasn't doing too badly at that.

Maybe he was panicking for nothing. She might not be pregnant. It wasn't always a foregone conclusion. Some couples took ages. Besides, he'd been playing Russian roulette the few times they'd made love before, as the withdrawal method wasn't foolproof. Still, it was better than nothing, which was what he'd practised last night. Several times, if he recalled correctly.

This time he did groan out loud.

'What ails you, husband?' Freydis turned in his arms and peered at him through half-open eyelids. 'Do you need anything?'

'No. Thank you. I'm merely a little . . . tired.'

She smiled. 'Is that what you call it? I'd say your head is pounding mightily. I should perhaps fetch you a bucket. You are rather pale.'

She reached up to stroke his cheek, and he caught her hand and kissed the palm. 'Why are you not suffering?' he grumbled. 'You shouldn't be this cheerful. I swear you had your fair share of mead.'

Her smile widened. 'I did, but I drank it more slowly. I've had it before and know its possible effects.'

'Well, good for you,' he snarked, then instantly regretted his surliness. 'Sorry. Ignore me. I am not at my best this morning.' He didn't add that he was lamenting his actions after the drinking more than the alcohol itself. She didn't need to know that.

'I'm going to leave you to rest.' Freydis sat up and swung her legs over the side of the bench they'd slept on. There had been one in the forge after all, right at the back. 'Call me if you want anything. I'll be nearby.' She leaned over and kissed his cheek, whispering, 'And thank you for last night. It was . . . enlightening. I'll never be able to enter the forge again without remembering what you did to me on that workbench.'

'Me neither,' he mumbled.

Damnation. What if she was with child? He sighed. No point fretting about it until she confirmed it. That could potentially slow down his quest to find Maddie, as he'd have to take into account the needs of a pregnant woman and travel more slowly. Yet Freydis was strong and healthy, and might be fine. Either way, he wasn't leaving her behind, no matter what. Hopefully the gods would be on his side in this as well.

Chapter Twenty

Langnes, Sogn
Gaukmánuðr (April) AD *876*

Four weeks after the *Dísablót*, Storm set off for the coast to try to find them passage to Iceland. Bjarni was going to visit one of his brothers, who lived further north, and had offered to take Storm with him as far as the mouth of the fjord.

'From there you can make your own way to the nearest coastal settlement. From what I hear, there are several ships a year that leave for Ísland. It has become a desirable destination, what with land being scarce around here.'

'Thank you. I'll see what I can find.'

Storm said farewell to Freydis in private, pulling her into an empty storeroom to kiss her goodbye. 'I'll try not to be too long, *unnasta*,' he promised. 'I would take you with me, but I think it will be faster if I go on my own. If I can't find passage immediately, we wouldn't have anywhere to stay while we wait. As a man, I can bed down anywhere – someone's barn perhaps – but if you come along, we'd have to pay for proper accommodation. I'm not sure that *hotels* even exist in your time, do they?'

'You're right,' she reluctantly admitted. 'But hurry, please.

Being here alone with my mother, and with no Bjarni to act as a buffer, is going to be painful.'

'I'm sorry. Not long now until you can say farewell to her for good. Take care of yourself while I'm gone. I'll miss you.' He gave her another fierce kiss, then forced himself to walk away.

It felt wrong to leave her. They'd been more or less joined at the hip since their hasty marriage, and he was used to it now. He didn't worry about her being harmed physically, as she was more than capable of defending herself against Dagrun. Mentally was a different matter.

'She'll be fine,' he muttered to himself. She was a strong woman and wouldn't be cowed.

And it was only for a few days.

'Mistress Dagrun, you have visitors.'

A thrall walked up to the group of women working on the various stages of cloth production. Freydis didn't always join them, but she had done so today. She needed something to occupy her to stop her fretting about Storm. He'd been gone three days now, and she was beginning to worry that something bad had befallen him. Surely it wasn't that far to the nearest coastal settlement

Stop it. He was fully capable of taking care of himself. She was acting like a fool.

She looked up to see who might be passing by Langnes. Visitors were few and far between, and usually consisted of relatives, or pedlars hoping to sell some of their wares. Today's guests were neither.

At the sight of the two men walking towards her, she froze, the spindle almost falling from her suddenly numb fingers. Assur and Ingolf Gunnarsson were sauntering through the hall as if they were very sure of their welcome. Judging by the smile that lit up Dagrun's face, they hadn't miscalculated. Them being here was definitely not a coincidence. In fact, it would seem they had been expected and eagerly awaited.

Freydis sucked in a sharp breath as her mother threw her a triumphant glance before standing up to greet the two men.

'Cousin, how lovely to see you after so long. You have timed your arrival perfectly.' Dagrun turned to Ingolf. 'And you must be Jarl Ingolf. Welcome to our hall. I'm sorry my husband isn't here at the moment. He is visiting kin up the coast. Can I offer you some refreshment?'

'No, thank you, cousin. We won't be staying long. We have merely come to fetch the jarl's recalcitrant wife-to-be.' Assur fixed Freydis with a savage glare. 'She's caused us no end of trouble. Now she's coming back with us.'

Freydis didn't reply. Her gaze was darting around, trying to find a way to escape, but they were blocking the route to the only exit. She was trapped. Plus, she didn't have her weapons on her. She hadn't seen the need for them here in her childhood home. Bile rose in her throat, but she pushed it down, clenching her hands around the spindle. Perhaps she could poke their eyes out with it? But she'd only manage one before the other grabbed her. It was no use. And Ingolf was astute; he would have brought backup.

Trying to steady her breathing, she sent Dagrun a murderous look. 'I suppose I have you to thank for this, Mother. Trust me when I say you will rue this day. I curse you and hope the gods are listening.'

Dagrun flinched and went pale, but she drew herself up to her full height. 'I have only your best interests at heart. You will want for nothing. Besides, it doesn't merely benefit you, you know. Do stop being so selfish and think of your family for once! Having such an illustrious connection . . .' she paused to smile obsequiously at Ingolf, 'will be an advantage for us all. Perhaps aid your little brothers in future. I really don't understand why you would throw away such a wonderful opportunity. Now go! You will soon be wed to the jarl and he'll keep you in check. You'll have no opportunity for mischief.'

'No, but my husband will know something has happened to me and he'll take revenge in my stead. I hope he strangles you with his bare hands,' Freydis snarled. 'It is no less than you deserve.'

Through her haze of anger, she was beginning to understand her mother's motivation. During her stay at Langnes, she had overheard Dagrun lamenting the fact that she had married beneath herself when she was wedded to Freydis's father. She came from a powerful family herself, and had no doubt assumed she would have an equally prominent husband. Unfortunately for her, she had several older sisters, and she'd ended up with Úlfr. He hadn't been a bad match, but he was completely uninterested in currying favour with anyone or socialising much. Dagrun must have been sorely disappointed.

And now she seemed determined that her daughter should make up for it. *Unbearable!*

'Where is the man?' Assur surveyed the hall, as if he expected Storm to be sitting somewhere calmly while all this was happening.

'Unfortunately he's gone off to the coast for a few days, but you'll no doubt meet him on your way back and can dispatch him then.' Dagrun made it sound as if it would be an easy feat.

Dispatch him! They were planning to kill Storm? Freydis's entire body turned cold, and she shuddered as chills raced down her spine. She would have to warn him somehow. Not that he'd go down without an almighty fight, but knowing Assur and Ingolf, they hadn't come alone.

'Pack your things, daughter,' Dagrun ordered. 'My cousin is clearly in a hurry.'

'Don't *ever* call me daughter again! You are nothing to me but a *niðingr* from now on. No mother would act the way you have. I hope never to set eyes on you again.'

Freydis headed for her sleeping bench. She briefly considered trying to make a run for it, but decided it would probably be better to bide her time and go with them without putting up any resistance. If she bolted now, she doubted she'd get far, whereas there might be an opportunity for escape later. Swallowing down a curse, she pulled out her sack of belongings. It wasn't large, as she didn't own much. She picked up her cloak and fastened it with a pin. Even though the weather had warmed up considerably, it would still be cold at sea.

Before she could react, Ingolf had grabbed the sack and turned it upside down, making everything tumble out.

'You can't bring these,' he said, and put her knife and sword aside. 'Assur tells me you have skill with weapons, and I'm not foolish enough to trust you with any.'

It was a wrench to leave behind the sword her father had given her, but there was no point arguing. The only thing she could do right now was suffer in silent dignity. She wouldn't give her mother the satisfaction of seeing her crumble, so she merely sent her a death glare before heading for the door.

But inside, she was crying.

'Bjarni! If I'd known you were rowing up the fjord today, I'd have hailed you.'

After securing passage on a ship bound for Iceland, Storm had walked back through the forest without bothering to check. He had thought Bjarni was planning on staying away longer, and it had seemed faster to go back to Langnes on foot to bring Freydis the good news as quickly as possible. As it happened, the two men arrived almost simultaneously, and ended up walking into the hall together.

It was ominously silent. Storm halted just inside the main doors, which had been standing open. A sixth sense made him cautious. He glanced over to the corner where the women sat, working industriously at their spinning and weaving. They weren't gossiping as normal, and the only one who looked vaguely pleased was Dagrun. His insides clenched. Something wasn't right.

She caught sight of them and stood up. '*Bóndi*, you are back.' Putting down her work, she moved towards them, but she kept her gaze on Bjarni. 'I thought you would be gone for longer. I trust all is well with your brother?'

'Yes, thank you, he and his family prosper.' Bjarni too must have picked up on the strange vibe in the hall, as he looked around with a frown. 'Where are the boys? Are they outside training with Freydis?'

'No, Trond has taken them fishing.'

Storm couldn't stay quiet any longer. 'And where is my wife?'

Dagrun finally deigned to look his way, and there was a gleam in her eyes that gave him the creeps. 'She's gone back to her rightful husband. They left yesterday. I thought you would have encountered them along the way.'

'*What?*' He was aware that he was bellowing, but the rage that rose inside him was immediate and red hot, and could not be contained. It had to be unleashed. 'What do you mean? *I* am her husband, no one else.' But he was very much afraid he understood exactly what she was saying.

'Dagrun? What have you done?' Bjarni gripped her upper arms and gave her a little shake. 'Storm is Freydis's husband. They've been together for months, you know that.'

Laughter bubbled out of her, and Storm wondered if she was slightly unhinged. How could she laugh about this matter? *The complete and utter bitch!*

'Don't be a fool, husband. My cousin promised Freydis to Ingolf Gunnarsson, a rich and formidable man, long before she ran off with this . . . this blacksmith. The jarl will be powerful kin for us, and the connection could be extremely useful in future. Think of the boys. Why, he might have them to stay with him when they're older, and introduce them to influential people. Or even help us make great matches for them when it comes time for them to be married.' Her disdainful gaze swept over Storm as if he was something foul she'd stepped in. 'They merely came to take her back to her rightful place. She's lucky he is still willing to have her.'

'Have you run mad, woman?' It was Bjarni's turn to yell, and his face turned dark red. 'You had no right to meddle in this matter. How did they even know she was here?' He was still gripping her arms tightly, but she seemed not to notice or care.

'I sent Assur a message, of course. Remember that pedlar who came a while back? He said he was heading to the Orkneyjar, and I paid him to call in on my cousin with a greeting from me.' At last she appeared to notice that her husband was not happy, and frowned at him. 'What does it matter? You have always said Freydis is my concern, and I had only her best interests in mind. She will thank me one day.'

'Odin's ravens! I've had quite enough of this. For months I've turned a blind eye to the way you've been treating her, hoping you would see sense, but no more.' Bjarni started to walk towards their bedchamber, dragging his wife along with him. 'You can stay in here until I decide what to do with you, but rest assured, I no longer wish to be wedded to you.'

Storm wanted to shout *Hooray!* and *Take that, you evil witch,* but kept his mouth shut. Bjarni was acting exactly the way he ought to, and it was immensely satisfying to finally see him put his foot down. The man had been way too lenient with his wife up until now. He was clearly someone who disliked conflict, so it had taken a lot for him to get this riled up. Dagrun had definitely gone too far this time.

She turned pale, stumbling as his strides were longer than hers. 'What? You cannot mean that! I merely wish my daughter to have the best possible life. As the wife of a rich jarl, she'll have everything she could ever need. Luxurious garments, people at her beck and call, jewels and—'

'Yes, she'll have everything except the husband she's already chosen! Everything except happiness. And she'll be wedded to a man who's already killed several wives, by all accounts. Or at the very least driven them to take their own lives. *That*'s what you want for your daughter? You are not in your right mind. Well, let me tell you, you're not staying here.' He shoved her inside their chamber and slammed the door shut, securing it with a bar.

She started banging on it, shouting, 'You can't divorce me! If you do, you lose Langnes. And what of the boys? They'll need their mother.'

'Langnes is mine whatever happens,' Bjarni retorted, 'because it mostly belonged to Freydis and she has said she's happy for me to keep it. You can go back to your high-and-mighty kin, if they'll have you. As for the boys, I'd rather they grew up without a mother than have you as an example of how to behave. *Skítr!* I cannot believe this!'

He slammed his hand onto the nearest table, then paced up and down for a moment, trying to calm down. Storm took no notice. He was more concerned with his own wife. While watching Dagrun receive her just deserts, he had momentarily forgotten the main problem here – how to retrieve Freydis. Now the enormity of what had happened slammed into him once more, almost knocking the air out of his lungs. She was gone. Taken by those ruthless pigs. And they had a whole day's lead on him. *Damnation!*

Bjarni stopped before him. 'I take it you're going after her?'

'Of course. I'll need to go back to the coast to find passage. There is no time to lose. The sooner I can reach her, the better. There's no saying what that *niðingr* Gunnarsson will do to her.' He was so furious he was shaking, and worry for Freydis had him in knots.

'I will come with you to the Orkneyjar. We can take my ship.' Bjarni's mouth was a grim line of determination.

'Are you sure?' Storm hadn't expected this. He was grateful enough that Bjarni had taken his side and finally seen fit to punish his wife. He deserved better than someone like Dagrun. He was a good man.

'Yes. You'll need assistance. I'm not as young as I was, but I can still fight. We can bring a few of my men as well.'

'Probably better to attempt to rescue Freydis by stealth, just the two of us. The jarl will be expecting us to pursue them, but he has countless men at his disposal. I doubt he's worried. Any force we can muster will be puny in comparison. We could never hope to win that way, and he knows it.'

'Very well. That makes sense, if he's as powerful as you say.'

Bjarni shouted for one of his men. 'Sigfast! I'll be going away again and I don't know how long for. I want my wife to be kept locked in our chamber. You may give her food and drink as normal, but she's not to set foot outside that room, understand? When I return, I will divorce her and personally escort her back to her father's hall. Until then, she can stew. Oh, and she's not to see or talk to my sons.'

Storm went to collect the belongings he'd left behind when he went to the coast. He hadn't wanted to carry everything. On the sleeping bench he had shared with Freydis, he noticed her weapons lying discarded, and he added them to his sack. She would need them as and when he caught up with the bastards who'd taken her away.

He hoped she would use them to kill at least one of them while he dealt with the other.

Úthaf (North Atlantic)/Orkneyjar

Freydis sat at the front of Ingolf's ship and stared resolutely forward. She hadn't so much as looked at either of the two men who had come to fetch her since they set off. She'd refused to speak to them as well, not making a single sound even when Ingolf backhanded her across the face. She had contented herself with sending him another fierce glare, hoping he could see the extent of her hatred for him. She wasn't afraid of him. The only thing that scared her was the fact that they were planning to kill Storm.

She heard them discussing it now, and their words sent icy shivers of dread shooting through her.

'He's bound to come after her. He'll know where she's been taken,' Ingolf stated. 'But we will be waiting for him. Unless he turns up with an entire shipload of mercenaries, he won't stand a chance.'

'Aye. Then once you've made the girl a widow, you can wed her.' The smug satisfaction, as well as the ingratiating way Assur spoke to Ingolf, grated on Freydis no end.

'Not immediately. I'll have to wait and see if she's with child first. I refuse to acknowledge another man's offspring. If she is, I'll get rid of it at birth. Easy enough to leave it on the cliffs for the ravens and gulls to take care of.'

Freydis choked on a gasp at his chilling words. She had heard of the practice of *bera út* – when an infant was left somewhere to die of exposure or be eaten by wild animals or birds – but she'd never known anyone who'd actually done it. It was despicable. The thought of anything like that happening to a child of hers made her want to kill Ingolf with her bare hands.

He went on as if he hadn't just uttered such vile words. 'I'll keep her somewhere safe until we can be certain. That gives us time to deal with her man as well. He'll never find her, even if he escapes us.' He chuckled, as if he was relishing the coming confrontation.

And he probably was. He seemed the type of man to thrive on a challenge. His goal was to be in control of everything and everyone.

Someone needed to stop him.

Once they arrived in the Orkneyjar, after a long, cold and tedious journey across the sea, it became clear that the person who'd be thwarting him would not be Freydis. At least not immediately. She was taken to a remote island and locked in a small hut that was part of an isolated farmstead. No matter how she tried, there was no way out, and she was powerless against the guards who oversaw her incarceration. There were always two of them, and it was evident that Ingolf wasn't taking any chances.

How was she to escape from here? She had to find a way, because the thought of Storm walking into a trap turned her stomach. She couldn't bear it if he died because of her.

Chapter Twenty-One

Langnes, Sogn, Norway
Gaukmánuðr (April/May), AD *876*

Storm and Bjarni were heading for the Langnes jetty when a small ship hove to and a man jumped out. Shielding his eyes with one hand, Storm stared as a familiar figure came striding up the hill.

'Joalf! By all the gods! What are you doing here?'

He ran to meet the older man halfway and gave him a bear hug without considering whether that was the done thing in Viking times. Joalf's expression registered surprise, but he allowed it and hugged Storm back briefly.

'Good to see you as well. I'm glad you're still here. That means I'm not too late.'

The joy of reunion melted away as Storm remembered where he'd been going. 'Too late to warn us of Assur's imminent arrival, you mean?'

'Aye.' Joalf looked from one man to the other, as Bjarni had now reached them. 'I take it I'm wrong. *Skítr!* I overheard the messenger saying that you were visiting Dagrun, and Assur left soon afterwards to see Gunnarsson. I came to tell you and Freydis to leave, in case they were coming to look for you. I'm guessing my ship wasn't as fast as theirs.'

Bjarni shook his head. 'I'm afraid not. They came yesterday. I'm Bjarni, Freydis's stepfather. And you are?'

Storm remembered his manners. 'Oh, sorry, this is Joalf, the man who looked after Freydis during the time she was away. He's been her mentor and like a father to her. Without him, she'd have been miserable.'

The older man's cheeks turned ruddy. 'Storm exaggerates, but yes, I've kept an eye on her since she arrived at Assur's settlement. In fact I was the one who fetched her from here.'

'Thank you,' Bjarni said. 'I'm glad someone had her well-being in mind.' He sent a quick glare in the direction of the hall.

A flapping sound and a hoarse cawing noise interrupted the conversation. Bjarni jumped back as a large black shape landed on Storm's shoulder.

'What in the name of all the . . . ?'

'Surtr!' Storm was overjoyed to see the bird again, and smiled as he stroked its soft head feathers. 'How have you been, boy? You got to travel all this way, eh? Lucky you.' He turned so that the raven was facing Bjarni. 'This is Freydis's pet. We had to leave him behind when we came here, and we've missed him.'

'*Surtr. Good boy. Surtr. Treat! Hei, hei.*'

Bjarni looked, if possible, even more startled, but also intrigued. 'How marvellous! He talks? I've never seen a pet raven before. And it is a lucky omen too.'

'How so?'

'Having a raven accompany you into battle is auspicious. A sign that victory will be yours. You may not be heading for a battle as such, but it will still be a fight.'

'Really? I've never heard that.' Storm was even happier to see Surtr if that was true.

'I have,' Joalf said. 'But tell me more about what has been happening here. There's no time to lose.'

Storm quickly explained what had occurred, and Dagrun's part in it all.

'Unbelievable!' Joalf was appalled. 'So they are only a day ahead of us? We might be able to catch up.'

'No. They'll be expecting us to come after them,' Storm said. 'We have to be cleverer than that. What we need is a plan.' He mulled over their options, then turned to his host. 'Bjarni, while I appreciate you wanting to come with us, I think it might be best if you stay here. I'll have Joalf now, so I'm not alone. Two can be stealthier than three, and he can always return here if anything should happen to me. I believe we must sneak in somehow, so the fewer of us the better. What say you?'

'That sounds reasonable, although I am loath to let you face danger without more assistance. But very well, I'll stay behind. I can make sure no one comes sniffing around here to see if you've returned. They may send men to kill you if they think you are likely to come back.' Bjarni looked at Joalf. 'Do you wish to have a meal and rest before you set off again?'

'Thank you, but no. Time is of the essence. Are you ready to go?' Joalf asked Storm. 'I have all the victuals we'll need for the journey.' He gestured towards the small ship, where two men from Assur's settlement waited. Storm assumed they were loyal to Joalf and had agreed to come with him. He couldn't have sailed the vessel on his own; it was too big for that.

'I'm ready.' He turned to Bjarni. 'I thank you most sincerely for everything. You've been nothing but kind since we arrived here. I am glad Freydis was able to spend time getting to know you and her brothers. If I manage to free her, we will return to visit when we are able. In the meantime, I'll send word if I can.'

'Please do. I'll not rest easy until I know you are both safe. May the gods be with you, and be careful!'

To Storm's surprise, Bjarni gave him a hug and slapped his back. It made him smile, despite the gravity of the situation, and he followed Joalf down to his ship with determination. He was going to save Freydis one way or another, and prove her horrid mother wrong. *He* was the best husband for Freydis, and he wasn't about to let her go. Not ever.

Orkneyjar
Gaukmánuðr (April/May) AD *876*

The journey across the sea took longer than expected because of contrary winds, and it was several days before Storm and Joalf arrived in the Orkney Islands. They began their search for Freydis by stopping at a few of the settlements along the coast near Ingolf's domains. They had decided that there was no point going there directly, as they'd both no doubt be killed on sight. They were now at the third such homestead without being any the wiser, and impatience was making Storm's stomach churn.

'A new bride, you say?' The wife of the homestead's owner frowned at them. 'I've not heard anything about that. I know the jarl was rumoured to be betrothed to someone back during the Yuletide festivities, but nothing came of it and he celebrated with us alone.'

'So you've not heard tell of him bringing a woman to his hall recently?' Joalf asked.

'No. Why do you wish to know?' The husband was regarding them with suspicion.

Storm shrugged. 'It is merely that a woman has gone missing from one of the northern islands. Someone said they'd seen the jarl's ship near there around the same time, and we thought we'd try to find out more.' He spread his hands and adopted an innocent expression. 'It's not that we're accusing him of anything, but I've been told he is a tad . . . er, prickly, and we'd rather not ask him directly.' He smiled. 'We'd like to keep our heads attached to our bodies, if you know what I mean.'

That made the husband and wife relax. They exchanged glances. 'That's true. He can be quick to ire, that's for certain. But no, we've not heard of any newcomers at all. As far as we know, the jarl's been busy overseeing his estates.'

It was disappointing, and when Storm and Joalf left the settlement, they were both grim.

Storm helped to row the ship far enough out to sea that they could hoist the sail. Then he went to sit with Joalf, who was steering. The other two men stayed at the front, talking to each other. Storm knew they couldn't overhear, as the noise of the wind and waves was strong today. And even if they could, they'd keep it to themselves. Joalf had explained that they were his friends, and not particularly happy with Assur.

'This isn't working,' Storm said. 'We have to try something else.'

'What, though?' Joalf sighed and adjusted the steering oar.

'Let us head back to Assur's place. He should be home by now, and he won't expect us to go there. If we arrive at night, we can take him by surprise and try to force him to reveal her whereabouts.'

'Ingolf could have men lying in wait there.'

'Only one way to find out. I would bet the majority of his men are guarding him and Freydis, wherever she is.' Storm raked a hand through his hair, which had grown considerably since arriving in the ninth century. He'd had to start tying it back, but the breeze from the sea wasn't helping.

'Very well.'

It was full dark when the ship's hull scraped onto the sandy bay below Assur's settlement. As Storm, Joalf and his two friends jumped out, swords and battleaxes at the ready, a couple of shadows detached themselves from the edge of the cliffs and came hurtling towards them.

'There he is!' one of them shouted, pulling out a sword that glittered in a sliver of moonlight. 'Get him!'

More dark-clad men came running, but Storm didn't count more than six in total. Rather than ponder the odds of the four of them besting the larger group, he went on the attack. It had been months since the previous fight on this beach, but he had spent part of each day at Langnes doing weapons training with Bjarni and his men. His body remembered all the moves, and he executed them perfectly. There was no thought to danger, only a strong urge to vanquish these men who threatened his way forward.

Who dared to stop him from finding his wife.

Joalf and the others were not as young as he was, but they held their own, and in the end, the skirmish was over surprisingly quickly. Four of Ingolf's men lay dead or dying on the sand, while the other two were badly wounded. Storm held his sword to the throat of one of them. 'Do you yield?' he snarled.

'Yes, yes. I'm tired of hanging around this cold, damp beach anyway,' the man muttered, his expression surly but resigned.

'Now tell me where Ingolf has taken my wife,' Storm ordered. He lowered the sword and gripped the man's throat with his hand instead.

'I've no . . . idea. Can't . . . breathe.'

'*Tell me!*' Storm let go and instead put both hands on the man's shoulders to shake him roughly.

Gulping down air, the man shook his head. 'I can't. We were dropped off here first. Thought he was taking her home.'

Storm could see that this was the truth. He growled with frustration.

Joalf came up behind him. 'Leave him. Let's try our luck with Assur, assuming there are no more welcoming parties waiting for us.'

'Fine.'

The path up to the top of the sea stack was clear, and no one lay in wait for them when they got there. All was quiet, and the only sounds came from the hall. The evening meal was in full swing. When they threw open the doors and stepped inside, a hush fell on the room. Storm and Joalf strode down the middle towards Assur and Gyrid, while their two companions stayed by the doors. They'd agreed to take care of anyone who tried to sneak up on them from behind.

'Let me handle this, please,' Joalf hissed.

'That's probably best, or I'll kill him before he so much as utters one word,' Storm agreed, his blood already at boiling point out of sheer frustration.

'Joalf!' Assur blanched and stood up, trying to gather his composure. He began to bristle. 'So you have deigned to return my ship, I take it? How dare you use it without my permission?'

Storm and Joalf stopped in front of the table, and the older man crossed his arms over his chest. 'That's what you wish to discuss? The whereabouts of your ship? I dared because you went too far, *brother*.'

'Brother?' Storm blinked at his companion.

'Half-brother really, but yes, unfortunately we shared the same father,' Joalf muttered. 'It's not something I'm proud of, so I rarely mention it.' He glared at Assur. 'I told you not to betroth Freydis to that *aumingi*, but you wouldn't listen. Then you have the audacity to abduct her from her rightful husband, this man.' He pointed at Storm. 'I should drag you before the *þing*! Or would you prefer to meet me in *einvigi*? I'd happily fight you one on one.'

Assur held his hands up, looking like he was trying to pacify a roaring lion. 'Now calm down. There is no need for this. You know Ingolf was within his rights to take her back. She ran away from a formal betrothal. She was already his.'

'No. She never agreed to it. Never said the words. It was all your doing.' Joalf reached across the table and grabbed the front of Assur's tunic, leaning close to his face. 'Tell me where he's hidden her, and I'll let you live.'

'I . . . I don't know.' Assur gulped, his face ashen.

It was the wrong answer. Joalf's meaty fist connected with Assur's cheekbone with a resounding crack, and the man shrieked.

Gyrid jumped to her feet and started to wring her hands. 'Joalf, please, stop this! I'm sure we can come to some arrangement—'

'*Þegi þú*, woman!' Joalf snarled. 'Just shut up, for once in your life! You're afraid I'll take the settlement away from your coward of a husband and you'll be out of a home. Believe me, it is very tempting right now, and it would give me great pleasure to see the back of you!'

'You . . . you can't. It would go to Asmund in the first instance.' Gyrid drew herself up to her full height, which wasn't much. Clearly she was willing to fight for her cub.

'Asmund isn't ready to run this place. We all know he's never been allowed to think for himself. It's always you or his father telling him what to do,' Joalf sneered. 'If I was in charge, I'd teach him properly.' He turned back to his half-brother. 'Now tell me where she is!'

'I'm serious! I have no idea.' Another punch, this time breaking Assur's nose. 'Stop! Stop! He . . . he said something about hiding her at a remote farm. Really, I don't know which one.'

Joalf stared into his half-brother's eyes as if to make sure this was the truth. Then he punched him again for good measure, a forceful blow under the chin that had Assur's eyes rolling up into his head. Joalf turned to stare down the rest of the assembled company.

'If anyone here knows Freydis's whereabouts, tell me now, because if I find out later that you knew, I will kill you. You have my oath on that.' He swept his gaze around the hall, but no one said a word. 'Very well. Asmund, lock your parents in their chamber. You're in charge here until I return. And I *will* return to run this place, as well as teach you how to take over one day. My mother may not have been married to mine and Assur's father, but I'm the eldest son and have as much right to this place as he does. He's been mismanaging it for years. Does anyone wish to protest against this? I'll take on any challengers.'

Again, silence reigned. Asmund stood up and came to stand next to Joalf. 'You heard the man. Help me put my parents in their chamber.' There seemed to be a new purpose in the young man's gaze, as well as determination. Storm could see that he would do his best to run the settlement until Joalf returned.

Hopefully, that would be soon.

Freydis was going out of her mind. She tried to keep herself occupied with weapons training – using an old stick she found on the floor in lieu of a sword – and strengthening exercises, but the days were still interminable. And the hut was too small for her to move around much, making her feel as though she'd soon start climbing the walls. It was unbearable.

The elderly couple who lived on the remote farmstead brought her two meals a day and a flagon of spring water, always accompanied by the two guards Ingolf had left behind. At first Freydis had tried to talk to them, thanking them for the food, but they didn't respond. With scared glances at the guards, they kept their expressions carefully neutral. It made her want to scream.

'You could at least let me out each day for a walk,' she

grumbled to one of the guards when a week had passed. She knew exactly how many days she'd been here, as she had scratched a line into the wooden wall each evening. 'Your master wouldn't want me to waste away in here, now would he? There's no point in that if he aims to marry me. You need to keep me healthy.'

The guard frowned, but didn't reply, merely shut the door. She guessed they had their orders and were determined to follow them come what may.

'There must be a way out,' she muttered, searching the interior yet again for clues as to how she could break free.

When she and Storm had been locked in with Joalf, he'd scaled the wall and wriggled out of the smoke hole. Unfortunately, that was not an option here. For one, the hut wasn't big enough for her to be able to sprint and take a running jump, and for another, the hole itself was too small. Not even she would fit through it. The *jötnar* take it!

Where was Storm? Had they captured and killed him yet? It was driving her demented not knowing. The only thing keeping her spirits up was the thought that if he *was* dead, there'd be no point in keeping her hidden away. Ingolf could bring her back to his hall and keep an eye on her there if she was a widow. Therefore her husband must still be out there somewhere, looking for her.

But what if he wasn't? What if he'd decided being married to her was too much? He hadn't planned on it in the first place, and now that spring was here, he could simply carry on with his quest to find his sister. If he then disappeared back to his own century, she was as good as widowed in any case. Free to marry Ingolf.

The mere thought of it made bile rise in her throat. 'Never!' she vowed.

Although she wouldn't jump off any cliffs to escape the jarl, she would fight him to the death. If she was the one who perished, that would be preferable to a life as his wife. And hopefully she could at least wound or maim him.

The door opened unexpectedly, and the old woman came in. She hesitated just inside the threshold, then came forward. 'Lift your skirts,' she demanded.

'What?' Freydis blinked at her in confusion. What was she talking about?

'I have to check whether you are having your monthly courses.'

Of course. How could she have forgotten that conversation on the ship? A shudder went through her. Another reason why she'd rather fight him to the bitter end. 'Why should I?' she responded, lifting her chin.

The old woman sighed. 'If you don't, those two out there,' she jerked a thumb over her shoulder in the direction of the guards, 'will come in and do it for you. Wouldn't you rather show me yourself?' Something in Freydis's gaze made her take a step backwards. 'And if you think threatening to harm me will help you escape from here, you are mistaken. They don't care about my life any more than yours, so killing me would accomplish nothing.'

Unfortunately, Freydis believed her.

'Very well.' She lifted her *smokkr* and *serk*, then tugged on the drawstring of the trousers she was wearing underneath. Shoving them down part way so she could see that there'd been no bleeding, Freydis glared at her.

'Satisfied?'

'Aye. I hope for your sake you're not with child, though.' The woman shook her head. 'That infant will have a very short life.'

Freydis ignored the words, even though they made her gut clench. She pulled her trousers up and retied them at her waist before dropping her skirts. As the old woman left, she frowned after her and began to count in her head. It *had* been a while since she'd last had her courses. And more than four weeks since the *Dísablót* and that magical night in the forge. Was it possible . . . ?

'Sweet Freya!'

She put a hand on her flat abdomen and cradled it gently. Yes. Yes, it was, but only time would tell. It could simply be that all this upheaval had wrought havoc with her body. Either way, she wasn't about to tell anyone here her suspicions. She didn't put it past those men to kick her in the stomach and be done with it. In fact, she was surprised Ingolf hadn't done so already.

She had to be grateful for small mercies.

Chapter Twenty-Two

Orkneyjar
Gaukmánuðr (May) AD *876*

'Do you think this will work?'

Storm was crouching in the dark with Joalf behind a barn not far from Ingolf's hall, peeking out from time to time at people coming and going to visit the privy. It had been two weeks and they'd drawn a blank in their search of all the small islands they could find around here. His patience was at an end. He had to find Freydis *now*, before it was too late. The gods only knew what was being done to her.

'If we can grab the right man, then yes,' Joalf whispered back. 'I'll recognise one of his most trusted men when I see them.'

'Well, I wish they'd hurry and come out.'

It felt like there were ants crawling up his spine. This long wait was unbearable, and they could be discovered at any time. The two of them were taking a huge risk coming here. They were lucky they'd been able to slip past the guards on the landward side. Ingolf must have assumed they would come by boat, as most of his men were on the shore side of his settlement. Instead, they had left their little ship half an hour's walk away and circled round to the back.

At least another interminable hour crawled by, and it was getting late. Or early, rather, as it had to be well past midnight. But just as Storm was about to give up, Joalf grabbed his sleeve. 'There. That one,' he hissed. 'That's Svein.'

A man in a russet-coloured tunic with fancy braided trim glittering with silver thread was headed for the privy. He was alone, and his gait was unsteady. *Excellent!* Storm and Joalf followed him to the foul-smelling latrines, situated as far from the hall as possible. They checked that no one else was around, then waited for the man to come out after doing his business. As soon as the door opened, Storm rushed up behind him and put one hand over his mouth, while grabbing him in a headlock with his other arm.

'Come with us or you're dead.'

The man tried to struggle at first, but Storm tightened his grip on his windpipe and he soon stopped. He dragged him into a nearby field and luck was with them. There were no guards posted here. Not a soul to hear any noise they might make.

'Keep walking, Svein,' Joalf said, pointing the sharp end of his long knife into the man's side. 'And not a word if you wish to live.'

Storm let the man go, but kept an eye on him. He didn't doubt he could catch him if he decided to run, especially since Svein was inebriated, but it would seem he wasn't dumb enough to try that. They marched him in a circuitous route back towards their ship, stopping about halfway there. Storm turned to grab the front of his tunic.

'Where is Ingolf keeping Freydis?' he snarled.

'I've no idea. *Oof!*'

'Try again. We know you were with him and that he's left her at a remote farmstead. Which island?'

'Don't know the name of—*Aargh!*'

Storm had punched him in the face, and at the same time Joalf's knife sank into the man's side. 'Start talking,' Joalf advised.

'I'm happy to gut you, piece by piece, but I won't make your death quick.'

When Svein hesitated yet again, Storm lost it and started raining blows everywhere he could. Stomach, ribs, face, and even a kick to his private parts that had the man howling and doubling over. Eventually he reined himself in and stopped.

'Well? I can go on all night if that is your wish. Joalf hasn't even started with the knife yet. Is it really worth it? There are hundreds of women on these islands. Ingolf doesn't need mine. I understand his pride has been hurt, but he'll get over it. Do you want to die for the sake of a woman who means nothing to you?'

Svein wiped away the blood dripping from his nose with the sleeve of his tunic, then his gaze swept between the two of them. 'Fine,' he muttered. 'She's way up north, on a tiny islet off the east coast of Westrey. I don't think it even has a name.' He scowled and raised his chin. 'Kill me now and be done with it. You know I cannot return looking like this, or he'll know you've been here. Or at least he will once he returns.'

'True, which is why you're coming with us. Walk.' Joalf pointed the knife at Svein's ribs yet again. 'We'll drop you off somewhere along the way.'

'He's away, you say?' Something about that made Storm anxious.

'Not yet. He's abed for now, but he's leaving at dawn. I'm to stay behind. Said he'd be back in a day or so.' Svein shrugged. 'And no, he didn't say where he was going.'

'He'd better not be going to see Freydis, or he's a dead man.'

But Storm had a horrible feeling that was exactly where Ingolf was heading.

Two weeks. Two incredibly long weeks, and Freydis was no closer to finding a way out. The old woman had come to check on her twice more, but there was no sign of any bleeding. There was a distinct possibility she was with child, but she couldn't be sure. She hadn't had any of the usual symptoms the women back at Assur's settlement always talked about. No nausea or vomiting, and she was eating as normal. All she could do was wait and see.

She was lying on the rustling straw mattress, willing herself to sleep for a while in order to pass the time, when the door opened. Lifting her head, she expected to see the old woman again, although it wasn't long since she'd had her morning meal. Instead, the sunlight was blocked by a large figure silhouetted in the doorway, one she recognised all too well. She shot to her feet and backed up, watching warily as Ingolf pushed the door shut and turned to face her.

'Good morning.' The predatory smile he gave her had her nerve endings on full alert. 'I thought I would come and see how you fare.' He didn't come any closer, but Freydis could see in his eyes that this was deliberate. They both knew he could advance at any time. He was toying with her.

She stared at him, but didn't reply.

'Cat got your tongue? Or did I wake you from a sweet dream about your dead husband?' He chuckled, the sound sending frissons of fear and revulsion down her spine.

She wanted to shout and scream, but he was baiting her on purpose, so she refused to give him the satisfaction. Whether Storm was dead or not, she wouldn't react, since that was what he wanted.

He scowled. 'I see you're still not reconciled to your fate. I thought as much, so perhaps you need a lesson to remind you who is your master now. I won't lie with you yet, not until we know for certain that it's safe, but there are other things I can do to you.' He smiled again and flexed his fingers. 'Undress.'

She shook her head and lifted her chin in defiance. If he wanted her clothes off, he'd have to remove them himself.

His mouth tightened in annoyance, and he clenched his fists. 'I see. Well, I shall enjoy it all the more if you resist.'

He moved swiftly towards her, and she knew it was now or never. Gathering her strength and concentrating hard, she rushed forward to meet him halfway. Using the momentum of both their bodies, she performed one of the manoeuvres Storm had taught her, flipping Ingolf onto his back on the floor. She stomped hard on his manly parts, and as he bent over to grab them with an unearthly shriek, she kicked him in the face. There was a satisfying crunch as she broke his nose, or at least rearranged it for him. While he was still processing that latest blow, she ducked down to pull his sword from its scabbard and ran for the door.

'Eirik! Gorm!' he bellowed. '*Stop her!*'

Before he had a chance to even get to his feet, she had the door shut and barred from the outside. One of the guards – she thought this one was Eirik – came running, but thankfully the other must have been occupied elsewhere. He stopped at the sight of her brandishing a sword, his eyebrows rising to his hairline.

'What in the name of . . . ? Where is Jarl Ingolf?'

She lunged at him without a word, nicking his hand as he fumbled to pull out his own sword. He yelped, but managed to extract his weapon. They fought in silence, his expression becoming more and more grim as it dawned on him that she wasn't the easy opponent he'd thought her.

'Why, you little *bikkja*,' he panted. 'We should have beaten you daily to sap your strength.'

'*Argr*,' she shot back. 'You're definitely cowardly enough to hit a defenceless woman. But now you're going to pay for it.'

He was tiring, she could tell, and his concentration was slipping, but she was having some trouble herself. Ingolf's sword was a lot heavier than her own, and it was taking all her strength to wield it. This would need to be quick, or her muscles would give up. A feint to the left, then a vicious downward slash, and she opened up a huge gash in his left thigh. His leg crumpled and he fell to the ground, cursing loudly.

As Freydis looked around, searching for some way off the island, the other guard came charging towards her from the main dwelling. He was bigger and stronger than his companion, and she wasn't as confident she could best him, especially as she was already panting from the effort of using the hefty sword. She had no choice, though. It was either that or be captured again.

To her dismay, a further two men came running from the direction of the small beach she remembered from when she'd arrived. They must have come with Ingolf and had heard the commotion.

'*Skítr!*' She couldn't overpower three warriors single-handedly. That simply wasn't possible. All might be lost, but she was determined to make a stand and fight to the end. She'd see her loved ones in the afterlife, and if Storm was already dead, as Ingolf had said, they would be reunited soon.

Gorm advanced on her, but ducked with a grimace when there was a sudden flapping of wings just above his head, followed by a harsh cawing noise. A pair of sharply taloned feet grabbed at his hair, making him cry out in pain.

'*Ow!* What in the name of Thor . . . ? Get off me! Off, I say!'

'Surtr!' Freydis had never been so happy to see anyone in her life. If he was here, it meant help had arrived. 'Good boy! Get him,' she encouraged the bird, who was doing his best to peck out Gorm's eyes while hovering in front of the man's face. Somehow the raven managed to stay out of reach of the lethal sword being brandished at him. Freydis helped by slashing at the guard's hand with her own weapon.

Shouts came from the beach. Two more men appeared, and Freydis's heart leapt with joy. 'Storm! Joalf! Over here!' she yelled.

Storm, being much younger than his companion, reached Ingolf's men first. He didn't hesitate, but started fighting them both until Joalf joined him. Freydis needed to concentrate on her own foe. Gorm had an even more determined expression on his face now, and was flailing his arms to chase Surtr away. He likely knew that if he could capture her, Storm and Joalf would give up.

Well, she wasn't going to let him. And Surtr was nothing if not tenacious. She trusted him to help her win this fight.

Storm fought like a madman, aware that time was of the essence. He had to defeat these two goons before the third man got his hands on Freydis. She could hold her own, he knew that, but she'd never fought anyone as big as her current opponent. She probably wouldn't be able to carry on for much longer, even with Surtr providing a distraction. He needed to hurry. And no doubt Ingolf was around here somewhere as well. It was merely a question of time before he joined the fray.

'Hold on, *unnasta*!' he shouted, hoping that a bit of encouragement would spur her on. 'I'm coming!'

Thankfully his opponent had been caught off guard, and Storm was able to sink his blade into his shoulder. That made the man drop his weapon, and Storm used his fists and the hilt of his own sword to render him unconscious. A quick glance to the side reassured him that Joalf had the other man under control, then he was sprinting towards Freydis. She was breathing heavily, and red in the face from exertion, but he couldn't see any blood on her. *Thank the gods!*

'*Hei, hei! Treat!*' Surtr evidently thought he had earned a reward, but the fight wasn't over yet.

'Enough, boy,' Storm told the bird. He didn't want him hurt accidentally. 'Go to Joalf, please.'

By some miracle, the raven listened and flew off to harass

Joalf's opponent. Freydis's adversary must have heard Storm coming, because he backed off and tried to face them both. Storm and Freydis advanced on him together, forcing the man to choose who to fight first. It was impossible for him to engage with two people at once, and it wasn't long before he too was down, bleeding profusely from a wound to the stomach. He sat on the ground cradling his abdomen while Storm gathered Freydis to his side with one arm around her waist and gave her a fierce kiss. As he breathed in her unique scent, the knot inside him loosened, and he heaved a sigh of relief. She was safe.

'Are you well, *baby*? Have they hurt you?'

'No, I'm unscathed.' Her voice was a little shaky, but that was understandable. 'I locked Ingolf in there.' She nodded towards a nearby hut. 'He's alive, though.'

'A shame.'

'I broke his nose.'

'Did you now? Good.' Storm grinned at her and felt pride coursing through him. That was his wife: strong, resourceful and a fierce fighter. He should have known she'd be OK. But oh, the relief of finally having her in his arms again.

The man on the ground cursed. 'You'll not get away with this.'

'Would you rather we killed you?' Storm snarled. 'Because that can be arranged.' He lifted his sword as if contemplating a *coup de grâce*.

The man flinched. 'No, no,' he muttered.

Storm crouched in front of him and looked him in the eyes. 'Listen to me. You tell your master that he is lucky to be alive. I should kill him for what he's done to my wife, but I am a magnanimous man and I will let the matter drop as long as he leaves us alone henceforth. But make no mistake, if he comes after us again, I will gather a mercenary force and attack him. I have the necessary silver and I will not hesitate to take away all he holds dear. It will happen when he least expects it, and I'll not be merciful again. Do I make myself clear?'

'Yes.'

'Good. All I want is my wife, nothing else. I really don't think that is too much to ask.' He could have gone into the hut and killed Gunnarsson, but the man was presently unarmed and, by the sound of it, injured. That would have made Storm no better than that coward. Hopefully the jarl had learned his lesson.

He took Freydis's hand and twined their fingers together. 'Come, *unnasta*, let us leave this place. Joalf is waiting.'

The older man had finished off his opponent and was standing guard over the unconscious men. An old man and woman peered out of the doorway of a larger house, their gazes flickering across the scene. They must be the owners of this remote farmstead, and by the looks of things, they weren't doing too well. Perhaps Ingolf had paid them for taking care of Freydis. It wasn't Storm's problem. He felt very little concern for them, given that they'd been part of the scheme to hold his wife captive.

He watched as Freydis greeted Joalf with a fierce hug, but they didn't linger. The sooner they left this place, the better.

'Are you sure we are safe here?'

Freydis was lying in Storm's arms on his bench in the weaving hut at Assur's settlement. She'd been surprised to be taken there, and even more astonished to find Asmund in charge, with a surly Assur lurking in the background. Gyrid too had seemed unusually subdued, and barely greeted her. Storm had explained about Joalf challenging his half-brother, but she'd been too exhausted to take it all in. Now it was the morning after their arrival, and Storm had just made love to her, gently and with reverence, as if she was precious. And he hadn't held back.

'Yes, it should be fine. Joalf has posted guards. If anyone

arrives, they'll blow that horn. Everyone here has been told to be wary of strangers, and never to venture onto the mainland alone. If Ingolf is stupid enough to try to attack, he will be met with fierce resistance.' Storm chuckled. 'I should think being bested by a woman in a fight is something he'd rather not have anyone find out about, though. You did well. I'm proud of you, *baby*.' He pulled her close for another kiss, which led to other things. It was a while before they could talk again.

'What happens now?' Freydis asked. She had made herself comfortable with her cheek against his warm chest. His heartbeat thumped steadily, a reassuring sound, and yet she still wasn't quite sure where they stood. He was holding her now as if he'd never let go, but was that merely a reaction to the fright of her abduction? She didn't dare ask. Her fingers idly traced the pattern of his *tattoo*, while she wondered whether to say anything about the possible pregnancy. She still hadn't had her monthly courses, yet she didn't feel any different from normal. It was too soon to say, and there seemed no point in mentioning it until she was sure.

Storm sighed. 'I still want to go to Ísland. We could get there faster if we found passage to Sogn from here, but Joalf tells me that Ófeigr's ship is being repaired. He is feeling better at last and is planning to sail home as soon as he can. I already paid him to take me with him, and he can easily fit you on board as well. It would make sense to wait until he is ready to leave.' He stroked her hair, tangling his fingers in the long tresses. 'There is also the fact that Joalf needs us here for the next few weeks. I know he would say he'd cope very well without us, but Assur and Gyrid are going to be difficult until they learn to accept that they are no longer in charge.'

'That's true. I've known for a while that Joalf is Assur's half-brother, but he never appeared to want any part in running this place. He was always content to stay in the background.' She had thought it was because he had no rights to ownership, but Joalf had told her on the way back here that this was not so.

'Our father decreed on his deathbed that we should have equal shares, but I told Assur I was happy for him to manage it on his own, as long as I could stay here and live my life the way I wanted. But I can't stand by and watch him destroy our father's legacy. It is time to take a stand.'

And that, apparently, was what he had done.

'He still doesn't really want to be in charge,' Storm said, 'but he's determined to teach Asmund how to do it properly. Then he'll fade into the background again. The man likes peace and quiet, and to be left alone.'

'Yes. That's why he never married, or so he told me once. He wanted to be free to do whatever he wanted. You're right, though, we should stay and help him until everything has settled down. How long will it be before Ófeigr is ready to sail, do you think?'

'He said four or five weeks, depending on how the repairs go. He's still trying to source more planks, and he is waiting for a man to come over from Westrey. They need an expert shipbuilder or the hull won't withstand the Úthaf.'

'Very well. I'm happy to wait, as long as you are. I know you're anxious to reach your sister.'

He flipped her onto her back and leaned over her to kiss his way down her neck. 'I don't mind staying for a while, if you promise to sleep here in the weaving hut with me. I'm not letting you out of my sight for a single moment.'

She was more than happy with that. And she noticed he hadn't said anything about divorcing her now that the threat from Ingolf appeared to be gone. She would never beg him to stay, but there was no way she'd be bringing it up. As long as he wanted her to be his wife, she would be. She only hoped it was for ever.

Chapter Twenty-Three

Hrossey, Orkneyjar
Sólmánuðr (June/July) AD *876*

Four weeks turned into five, then six, and still Ófeigr's ship wasn't ready. The damage to the hull had been extensive, and it was difficult to repair without taking the entire ship to pieces and starting from scratch. The master shipbuilder had finally arrived and was hard at work directing the others, but it would take time.

Storm didn't mind. Apart from the guilt for not rushing to find Maddie by any means, he was happier than he'd ever been. He was busy in the forge most days, making iron nails for the ship repairs. When he wasn't doing that, he was helping Joalf with other tasks. The two of them, together with Freydis, were also training Asmund in fighting techniques. The young man had been taught by Assur and his men for most of his life, but they weren't as good and he still had a lot to learn.

And his nights were spent with Freydis, alone in the weaving hut. They made the most of the privacy, and he had stopped worrying about getting her pregnant. It no longer mattered. Almost losing her to that swine Ingolf had made him realise he was head over heels in love with her. One way or another, he wanted them to stay together – whether it was here in her century or in his was unimportant. They could work that out at some point. For now, he was content to be her husband in the Viking age. He hadn't told her he loved her. It was too soon, and seemed like a step too far as yet, but he would when the time was right. And she hadn't mentioned being with child, so he assumed it hadn't happened. As and when it did, he'd be pleased. Somewhere along this roller-coaster journey back in time, he'd matured enough to feel ready to be a father.

The thought made him smile as he wondered if anyone in his family would believe that. He'd simply have to prove to them that he had finally grown up.

Towards the end of what Storm believed must be June – here called *Sólmánuðr* – they had other things to consider. Visitors arrived with news from what he thought of as Norway, although here they called it Hörðaland, since the unified country of Norway did not exist at this time. A loud discussion erupted in the hall that night over mugs of ale.

'That upstart King Haraldr Hálfdanarsson wants to rule over everyone, including you here in the Orkneyjar,' declared the new-comers. 'There are rumours that he and his allies are preparing to take on the rulers of Vestfold and Denmark in a sea battle. Both sides are actively recruiting men to fight for them. If he wins, he'd be your overlord. It is time to take action. You must help us stand against him.'

Storm gathered that Vestfold was somewhere in the region of modern-day Oslo, and that another king by the name of Hjorr was leading that faction.

'Who is this Haraldr?' he asked Joalf. He'd never paid as much attention to history lessons as his siblings, but he'd heard of Harald Fairhair and Harald Hardraada. Could this be one of them?

'He is the son of Hálfdan Svarti – the Black – of Hringaríki,'

Joalf told him. 'At present, he rules most of the western and central parts – Rogaland, Hörðaland and Sogn among them. And he has other powerful men on his side, like the jarls of Trøndelag and Møre. He's been a king since he was a mere ten winters, and has a reputation for being ruthless and violent. Now he wants more. Everything, in fact.'

'I see. And that affects these islands?'

'Yes, we are part of the trading routes that are necessary for that part of the country. The Orkneyjar would become one of his domains.'

'How likely is he to win?' Storm had studied battle tactics from history, and knew that large naval clashes were unusual in this era. He'd heard of sizeable armies fighting on land, but not at sea.

Joalf shrugged. 'Who knows? It is said that Haraldr has a large naval base at Hafrsfjordr, but King Hjorr will have Danish ships and warriors on his side.'

Assur was mostly quiet these days, sulking in the background, but he became fairly vocal in support of joining the fight. 'The last thing we need is a new overlord,' he argued. 'That could be costly, and things are good the way they are at present. Change always brings chaos.'

Joalf reluctantly agreed, and Asmund seemed eager to fight. Perhaps he wanted to show everyone that he had the necessary courage to be a good chieftain. Personally, Storm thought the young man was too inexperienced and lacking in combat technique. It wasn't up to him to dissuade him, though.

When Ófeigr weighed in as well, swearing that King Haraldr was out to rule Ísland too, something that couldn't be tolerated, the matter appeared to have been decided. They were all going to take a stand with the Vestfold chieftains.

'Will you help us, Storm?' Joalf asked. 'I know this isn't your fight, but we could do with someone with your skills.'

He didn't see that he had much choice. If he refused, he'd be considered a coward. Joalf was his friend and his wife's de facto father. He owed him big-time for helping to rescue her. The only possible downside that he could see was that Bjarni might be on the opposing side, since he lived in Sogn. Hopefully he'd consider himself too old to fight and would send others in his stead. Storm didn't want to meet Freydis's stepfather in battle when he'd been so kind to them. He kept this thought to himself, or else the others here might think him untrustworthy. And if Freydis hadn't thought of it herself, it was better not to point it out.

'Very well,' he agreed.

'If he's going, I'm coming too,' Freydis declared. A mutinous glint in her eyes warned Storm not to outright forbid it.

He wanted to, but he kept his mouth shut. The thought of her going into battle made him ice cold with fear, but at the same time he knew she'd be safer with them than left at home. At least then he could keep an eye on her and shield her from harm as much as possible. And having spent her whole life trying to prove she was as capable as the men around her, how could he deny her the chance to convince them? It had never occurred to him to tell his female colleagues in the Swedish army that they shouldn't be there. They were every bit as determined as he was, and although physically weaker, they could hold their own.

But they weren't his wife. The woman he loved.

He managed to keep his thoughts to himself, but he would be watching her like a hawk.

Hafrsfjord
Heyannir (July) AD *876*

'How the hell did I get here?' Storm muttered to himself as he sat in Assur's ship getting ready to row towards the nearest enemy.

He'd only been supposed to go back in time to find his sister, not get married and end up taking part in a naval battle.

It was mind-boggling, but unfortunately all too real.

They were in a large bay apparently called Hafrsfjordr, which they'd entered through a narrow passage that he had mistrusted on sight. Only one ship at a time could get through, and it took for ever. If King Haraldr had chosen this place for the battle, he had done well. His opponents could easily become trapped if they all tried to retreat at once. From a tactical point of view, it was brilliant. Not so much for the side Storm was on, though. He had a bad feeling about this. It didn't help that their ship had been one of the first to enter, which meant they were now far away from the possible escape route.

The bay was surrounded by hills, and he glimpsed large groups of people on their tops and sides. He assumed they must be backup, in case the fighting ended up on land. King Haraldr wasn't taking any chances. If he was beaten back that far, he'd have reinforcements coming to his rescue.

The side Storm was on did not. 'I don't like this,' Storm whispered to Freydis, who was seated next to him on the *kist* they were using as a bench. 'That Haraldr is a canny one. I think we've walked – or sailed, rather – into a trap.'

She had Surtr on one shoulder and was absently stroking the bird's shiny chest. The raven didn't appear to be fazed by anything going on around him, but Storm hoped he would have the sense to keep out of the way once the fighting started. He hadn't wanted to bring the bird in the first place, but Joalf had reminded him that it was said to be good luck for a warrior to have a raven when going into battle. For Freydis's sake, he'd bring anything that would push the odds in their favour. And to be fair, the bird had been helpful when they'd rescued her from Ingolf.

He frowned now and turned to gaze at the hundreds of ships

that were lined up to face their contingent. Their distinctive prows and shapes marked them out as typically Viking in style, and some had beautifully carved sterns. No doubt they were designed to intimidate, but it was the massed ranks of men that sent a chill racing through Storm. There had to be literally thousands of them. A formidable sight. The sun's rays were bouncing off a terrifying array of lethal weapons – swords, axes, spears and knives – and their owners meant business. They were here to annihilate their opponents. No quarter would be given.

'We're evenly matched, as far as I can see. He doesn't have more men than our side,' Freydis commented.

'No, but if things go badly for us, we won't be able to escape.' He sighed. 'Never mind. We are in the thick of it now. There's no going back. But please, stay by my side. Promise?'

She nodded, and he gave her a swift, hard kiss.

'Hold on tight to your shield.'

They each had a sturdy wooden shield that had been painted white for the occasion. It was to show their allegiance to the Vestfold men, who all had the same.

The sound of horns rang out, then a rhythmic banging on the shields started up. Surtr squawked and flew up to perch on the rigging of the ship's sail. With thousands of men joining in, the din was deafening, but Storm didn't mind. He recognised it for what it was – a tactic to psych everyone up and whip them into a frenzy, ready to fight. Adrenaline surged through him. He'd felt this way during mock battles and manoeuvres when he was training with the Swedish army, but the feeling had never been this strong. This was not a game or practice round. It was cold, hard reality. He heard howling too, and gazed in surprise at groups of half-naked men with animal pelts across their shoulders. They must be the berserkers he'd read about. Hopefully he wouldn't come across any of them. They looked half crazed with bloodlust.

A swishing noise took them by surprise, and a shower of arrows came winging their way towards them as if conjured out of nowhere. Storm raised his shield instinctively, pulling Freydis to his side to protect her. Assur's ship was to one side, which meant they escaped the worst of it, and only one man was hit. He toppled overboard, joining hundreds of others from their line-up. A battle cry rose, and everyone set to and rowed full tilt towards an opposing ship.

'Watch out – *incoming*!' Joalf yelled, as their hull scraped against that of another vessel.

In the next instant, hooks were thrown across to keep them from drifting apart. Men swarmed over the railing, and Storm jumped to his feet, pulling out his sword. Freydis did the same, and they were soon engaged in hand-to-hand combat with a whole host of fierce-looking Norsemen. He tried to concentrate on his own battle, while still keeping an eye on his wife. So far, she was holding her own, but there was no denying the fact that she was smaller than most of their opponents. Fortunately she was soon duelling with a youth who couldn't be more than sixteen. Storm relaxed – she could easily best him. He closed his mind to anything other than survival, and practising everything he'd ever learned. Utilising every technique, modern or Viking, he managed to stay relatively unscathed. His body was operating on autopilot, doing what was necessary without pondering the reality of blood, gore and death.

After what seemed like an eternity of fighting, he had a moment in which to take in the scene.

It was a disaster, as far as their side was concerned.

'*Shit!*' he muttered in English, as his gaze swept across the bay. King Haraldr was clearly winning. Huge swathes of the Vestfold contingent were being routed left, right and centre. When he glanced to his right, he thought he caught sight of a familiar face. *Ivar?*

He blinked. No, it couldn't be. What would his foster-brother be doing here? But unless the light was playing tricks on him, it was definitely him. And he was on the opposing side, which could only mean one thing – Storm, Freydis and their allies were about to be vanquished. Ivar was a historian. He'd know full well who was going to win this battle, as he'd no doubt read about it. There was no way he'd fight for the losing side.

He wanted to shout out his brother's name, but knew that he was too far away to hear, especially with all the noise going on around them. It was impossible to catch his eye either, and Ivar disappeared from sight, engaged in his own battles.

'*Fuck!*' Storm ground his teeth in frustration. He had to get Freydis out of here. *Now.*

At that moment, a larger ship rammed into them, and he stumbled. There was an ominous groan from the hull, then shouting from Assur and Joalf. 'To the oars! Row towards land!'

He grabbed the back of Freydis's tunic and pulled her down to sit beside him as he quickly fitted their oar into place. They both took hold of it and began to row without a word, putting their backs into it, even though they were still breathing heavily from all the fighting they'd done. Surtr swept down on silent wings and landed on Storm's shoulder. The raven's hefty body felt reassuring, and calmed Storm's tumultuous thoughts. It was like a sign from the gods. They would be OK if they could just escape from here.

'Are you hurt, *unnasta*?' he whispered, checking Freydis from top to toe for injuries. She had some minor scrapes, but he didn't see any large bloodstains.

'No. Bruised and a bit battered, but I'll live. You? That's quite the black eye you'll be sporting soon.'

Someone's elbow had rammed him in the face at one point, and he knew he would have a shiner. 'Eh, it's nothing. I'm fine. But we need to get out of here. Our side is losing badly.'

'You're right. We should stay and fight to the end, but . . .'

'No. This is not a cause worth dying for. We're leaving.'

The ship's hull scraped against sand, and everyone got up and jumped over the side onto an island on the outer side of Hafrsfjordr. It wasn't a moment too soon, as the bottom of the vessel was rapidly filling with water. Storm vaulted the gunwale and turned to help Freydis. She could have managed by herself, but it grounded him to have his hands around her waist momentarily. He needed the contact.

Their respite was short-lived. Some of Haraldr's men were swarming the island in pursuit, intent on wiping out all trace of their enemies. It wasn't long before they were fighting for their lives yet again. Somehow Surtr hung on to his shoulder, pecking angrily at their opponents if they came too close. It made them hesitate and gave Storm an advantage.

'Good boy, Surtr,' he murmured. He was tiring of this, and he could see that Freydis was exhausted. He needed to get her away from here.

'Joalf, I'm going to try and take Freydis to the other side of the island and hope someone can pick us up. She's flagging fast and that won't end well. Come with us? This is pointless.'

The older man shook his head. 'No, I'll stay a while longer. I cannot abandon Asmund, but I'll try to make him leave soon too. If we make it out alive, I'll see you back in the Orkneyjar, agreed? Take care of my girl.'

'Will do.' They only had time for a quick hug, then Storm was herding Freydis away. Before they'd gone very far, however, a familiar voice rang out.

'Where do you think you're going? Only cowards escape from a battlefield.'

They turned to see Ingolf Gunnarsson with a smirk on his face, and it was the last straw. Storm literally saw red. This man had threatened and kidnapped his wife, and kept her prisoner for weeks. Now he was impugning their honour and standing in their way. Enough was enough. This had to end now. He strode forward and knocked Ingolf's white shield out of his hand with a lightning-fast roundhouse kick.

'Oh, a man without a white shield. Must be an enemy. That means I can kill you, *niðingr.* And it will be my absolute pleasure.'

'Why, you—'

Ingolf didn't have time to say anything else as Storm attacked. Surtr flew up into the air and flapped over to Freydis, leaving him to move freely. Renewed energy flowed through him, giving him the strength to rain down blows on the hateful man. They slashed and parried with their swords, but Storm was impatient and flung his own shield away, drawing out his axe instead. He'd trained to fight with both weapons, one in each hand, and that was what he did now. Since Ingolf no longer had his shield, and only seemed able to use one weapon at a time, he didn't have any defence against the two-pronged assault. Storm didn't hesitate to use kick-boxing and martial arts moves as well, not giving Ingolf even a second to regroup. Moments later, the man was sinking to the ground, his eyes glazing over. It was done.

'Good riddance,' Storm snarled. He'd done so much killing by now, he was becoming numb to it. He reflected briefly on the fact that he had turned into a fully fledged Viking, with their mindset and ruthlessness. Although the twenty-first-century part of his brain rebelled against this, he knew it was necessary in this age and there was no point dwelling on it. Here, you did what you had to, and that included ridding the earth of scum like Ingolf.

Freydis had hung back, and didn't say anything. He saw the relief in her eyes, though, and knew she wouldn't mourn Ingolf or blame Storm for killing him. Taking her hand, he guided her across the rocky surface of the island. Once on the other side, they saw a few ships heading off into the distance. Not many had escaped, but some must have made it out of the narrow fjord opening.

They began to wave at the fleeing vessels, shouting for someone to come and pick them up, but most ignored them. Storm had just about given up hope when another ship came into view. One that was clearly on its way towards the battle rather than sailing away from it. And miracle of miracles, he recognised the sail.

'Ófeigr! Over here! Stop!'

Would they hear him? He began to pray to every god he'd ever heard of.

Chapter Twenty-Four

Úthaf (North Atlantic)/Ísland
Heyannir (July/August) AD *876*

Freydis was so tired she thought she'd never again be able to move. She couldn't believe how lucky they'd been. Ófeigr's ship hadn't been ready until the very last moment, and unexpected winds had blown him slightly off course so that he and his crew had arrived late, not realising the battle was more or less finished. Fortunately, they'd seen her and Storm waving at them and pulled in to take them on board. And now they were all on their way to Ísland. As they'd intended to continue on their homeward journey after the battle – having thought they would be on the winning side – the ship was already loaded with provisions and all their belongings.

'No point dying for a lost cause,' Ófeigr had said pragmatically when informed how matters stood. 'I might as well go home and make sure my domains are safe. You are welcome to stay with us as long as you need.'

It was six days before they sighted land, and soon afterwards they were pulling into a little bay covered in black sand. Freydis leaned against Storm as they made their way up a slight incline to a strange building made out of turf. It was the largest one of many, and people came swarming out to greet them. She watched in silence as Ófeigr's family welcomed him home, and then she and Storm were introduced to his wife, Catla.

'Welcome, welcome. Come inside, do. You must be sorely in need of some victuals and a long sleep. I know I was when I first made that crossing. This way, please.' The woman eyed Surtr with some misgiving and added, 'Er, will the bird be coming inside?'

'No, he'll wait out here.' Freydis motioned for Surtr to hop onto the low-hanging turf roof. 'Won't you, boy? Be good now and I'll bring you a treat soon.'

'*Treat! Treat! Caaaww!*' The raven seemed to understand and went to perch near the doorway.

They were soon fed and slightly re-energised, and then Catla urged them to come and take a bath in the settlement's hot spring. 'It feels wonderful, and so refreshing. You'll love it!'

'You go first, *unnasta*.' Storm pushed Freydis gently towards the woman. 'I'll go in with Ófeigr and the others when you're done.' Freydis wished she could have bathed with him and him alone, but that would have been impolite, so she nodded her acquiescence.

Catla had been right, and sinking into the hot, vaguely smelly water was an incredible experience. Exactly what her sore muscles needed. The older woman didn't join her, but waited on a bench that had presumably been put there for people to leave their clean clothes and drying sheets on. Freydis was too tired to worry about being seen naked by a stranger, and hadn't hesitated to pull off every last garment. They all needed to be washed too. Thankfully, she and Storm had stowed their belongings on Ófeigr's ship before heading for the battle, as they'd planned on leaving with him afterwards in any case. She was grateful for that, as it meant she had a change of clothes to put on once she was done here.

She scrubbed herself with soft sand from the bottom of the hot spring, and also used the lye soap Catla had provided. When she was done, and couldn't justify lingering in the blissful heat any longer, she dragged herself out and reached for the length of linen to dry her body.

Catla tilted her head and studied her with a small frown. 'You didn't mention that you're expecting. How far gone are you?'

'What?' Freydis's head came up and she stared at the woman. 'I . . . I'm not sure.' She swallowed hard and looked down at her abdomen. There was a small but distinct bump now, hard to the touch. She could no longer fool herself that it was mere anxiety that had kept her courses away. 'About fifteen or sixteen weeks, maybe more,' she whispered, admitting it out loud for the first time.

'That's what I thought. Your first?'

She nodded, and sank down onto the bench, wrapping the linen sheet tightly around herself. 'I honestly didn't know for a while. I went through a . . . harrowing experience, you see. I thought perhaps the fright had jolted my body out of rhythm. Also, I've not been sick or felt different in any way. Perhaps just a little more tired than usual.' In a whisper, she added, 'No one else knows.'

'You haven't told your husband?' Catla sounded both kind and concerned. 'Perhaps you'd better do so, and soon. I'm surprised he hasn't noticed for himself.'

Freydis was too, but then again, the bump still wasn't particularly noticeable, unless you looked closely. Or, as in Catla's case, had seen something similar many times before. 'Yes, I'll tell him tomorrow. For now, I just want to sleep.'

'Very well. Let's go and find you a bench.'

*

Storm woke the next day feeling a hundred per cent better. He was still sore and bruised, and there was a possibility he had a couple of cracked ribs, but he was alive. And what was more, so was Freydis. He swore he'd never again let her take part in anything so dangerous. It was going to give him grey hairs. If he told her how much he loved her, perhaps he could persuade her to stay at home in future. Provided there were any more battles to fight, although he sincerely hoped there weren't.

Another positive was that they were finally in Iceland. He'd been trying to get here for the best part of a year. If his sister really had come here, he could only hope her trail hadn't gone cold, and that she was still alive and well. He was eager to set off and ask at every settlement along the coast, but he was aware that both he and Freydis needed to rest and recuperate first. Another couple of days wouldn't make any difference after so long.

They ate a hearty breakfast of barley porridge with butter, and Storm released a sigh of contentment as he handed back his empty bowl. 'Thank you, Mistress Catla. That was exactly what I needed.' He turned to his wife, who'd been uncharacteristically quiet. 'Want to come for a stroll along the coast with me? We can have a look around.'

She nodded and followed him outside.

They walked side by side, and he took her hand, revelling in the way her smaller one fitted his so perfectly. 'Did you sleep well, *baby*? I guess it will take a while for us to recover from that battle. And for my face to go back to being handsome,' he joked. He pointed to the black eye, which was fading but still a very pretty purple colour, or so he'd been told. There were no mirrors here, which meant he couldn't check for himself. Smiling at Freydis, he kissed her cheek, but she didn't smile back. Instead, she seemed nervous about something.

Once they were out of earshot of the settlement, he pulled

her to a halt. 'What's the matter? Do you have an injury you haven't told me about?' Worry flooded him, but he tried not to leap to conclusions. Surely she would have told him if she was hurt? It had been over a week since the battle, after all, and she'd seemed fine.

'No, it's not that. I . . . have something I need to tell you.' She cleared her throat and stared out across the sea. 'Storm, I'm with child.'

'Huh?'

The words didn't register at first, but when they did, he felt as though someone had punched him in the gut. 'You're pregnant?' His mouth had fallen open and he had to make a concerted effort to close it. 'With my child?'

She frowned at him. 'Of course with your child. Who else's would it be?'

'No, yes, sure, I . . . Good. That's good! I'm glad. I mean . . . a child. *A child!*'

A baby. They were having a *baby*. Holy shit! This was huge.

He was momentarily lost for words, and her gaze became uncertain as she studied him with those cerulean-blue eyes. 'I know this wasn't what you wanted, but lately it seemed as though perhaps you'd changed your mind. You . . . we weren't as careful.'

He *had* changed his mind, and he was filled with joy at the thought that he was going to be a father. It had always been a possibility, and he shouldn't be surprised, but he was. Pleasantly so. A grin tugged at the corners of his mouth, but then another thought intruded on his happiness and his smile faded.

'Wait a moment. You knew you were with child and you still went into battle with me? *Freydis!* The child could have been hurt! What in the name of all the gods were you thinking?'

The enormity of this slammed into him, making him almost

breathless as his protective instincts rose to the fore. If he'd known, he wouldn't have let her put herself and the baby at risk. No way. The mere thought of what could have happened had cold chills racing down his back. He could have lost everything in one fell swoop.

She took a step back, as if his question was a physical entity pushing her away. 'I . . . I wasn't sure. I've not had any of the usual symptoms. I only had a slight suspicion. And—'

He interrupted her. 'A suspicion you should have shared with *me*! Do you think for one moment I would have let you join us if I'd had even an inkling that you might be with child? I would have stowed you somewhere safe for the duration!'

He saw her flinch, and realised that had come out a bit more forcefully than he'd intended. Still, he couldn't stop the words from tumbling out. His emotions were all over the place, and he was unable to control them. It wasn't anger, because she must have had her reasons, but disbelief that she could have been so reckless. And fear. Complete and utter raw terror at what could have happened.

Jesus! She could have killed their baby. Might already have damaged it. No, that didn't bear thinking about. She was safe now, and seemed healthy. He had to hope all was well with them both. That was the only thing that mattered, and from now on he'd make absolutely sure she didn't exert herself in the slightest. He'd take care of her. Treat her as if she was made of porcelain.

'*Unnasta* . . .' He reached out for her, but she held up her hands to stop him.

'Don't!' Her eyes filled with tears, and remorse flooded him. Had he been too harsh? But he couldn't have stopped his reaction if he'd tried. It was pure caveman instinct to want her and his offspring to be safe. She'd taken an unnecessary risk, but the main thing was that she was OK.

'I didn't mean . . .'

Freydis took a deep breath, although it didn't stem the tears that were now spilling down her cheeks. 'I know I should have stayed behind, but I couldn't bear to let you go and fight on your own. I wanted to be by your side. I'm so sorry . . .' Without waiting for his reply, she swivelled round and ran back towards the settlement.

Storm cursed in every language he could think of, while kicking at a clump of grass. '*Damn it!*' he muttered. This should have been one of the happiest days of his life, and now he'd spoiled it. He'd have to go after her and make things right. Show her that he wasn't angry or blaming her, just concerned. But it might be a good idea to let her calm down a little first. It was probably better for the baby if she wasn't agitated.

He would follow her in a while and tell her how pleased he was that they were to become parents. It was the single most incredible thing that had ever happened to him.

Freydis was shaking all over and sobbing uncontrollably when she made it back to the hall, but she didn't want to go in there. Everyone would know she was upset, and she couldn't deal with anyone right now. She hadn't cried in years, but these tears were impossible to stem and she needed to let them out. Her emotions were all over the place, and it felt as though she had no say over them.

Turning right, she headed off towards the cliffs on the opposite side of the settlement. She had to be alone. Wanted to wallow in solitude. *How could she have been so stupid?*

Storm was right, and she couldn't blame him for being incredulous and questioning her actions. She should have told him, and first and foremost she should have shielded their child. He was a grown man. It wasn't her place to protect him in battle. To think her presence could have influenced the outcome in any way was simply ludicrous. She should have trusted him to look after himself and return to her. But she'd been unable to watch him leave without her.

She sank down onto a tuft of grass, pulling her knees up and burying her face in her hands. 'I just wanted to be near him,' she whispered as the tears continued to flow. If he was going to die in battle, she'd wanted to die with him.

Admit it, a little voice in her head prodded. *That's not the whole truth. You wanted to prove to everyone that you were every bit as good as Assur and his men.* For years they'd derided her for wanting to learn to fight. Taunted her. Said it wasn't her place and that a woman had no business learning weapon skills. The battle had been her chance to show them how wrong they'd been. To be of help, and stand shoulder to shoulder with the other warriors. And Storm had seemed to understand, because he hadn't told her no. He'd been on her side.

Not any longer. She doubted he would trust her in future. She had ruined everything, and all because of reckless pride in her fighting skills.

'I'm such a fool!' she berated herself.

Sweet Freya, but she loved him so much. Thinking back, it had probably been love at first sight, because Storm was the only man to ever treat her as a true equal. Once she'd begun to get to know him, that first infatuation had turned into so much more. She'd seen the man he was – strong, kind, determined and capable – and fallen for him more each day. Now he was lodged deep within her heart, and no other man would ever compare.

But the expression on his face when he realised what she'd done had almost slayed her. Disappointment and shock – she'd seen those emotions flashing in his eyes. There was no way he would ever love her now. He would definitely divorce her. And he'd probably disappear back to his own time as soon as he had found his sister, if indeed she was here on this island.

Would he take their child with him? She didn't think he'd be that cruel. As far as she had heard, nursing mothers had the right to keep a child until it was at least a year or two. And she wouldn't let him. She'd fight tooth and nail to keep her baby. Joalf would help her if she appealed to him for assistance, she was certain. He'd always been on her side. Hopefully she and Storm could come to some sort of agreement, though. She swallowed hard. No, she couldn't lose their child as well – it would be the only thing she'd have left to remind her of him.

By the time he returned to the settlement, Storm had calmed down. Freydis was nowhere in sight, but eventually she appeared, her eyes red and her cheeks blotchy. It was clear that she'd been crying, and he couldn't bear it. He wanted to take her in his arms and comfort her, but when he held out a hand to her, she didn't walk into his embrace the way she normally would.

'Freydis,' he murmured. 'I'm sorry. I overreacted. You surprised me, is all. I am very pleased about the child. It's excellent news. Can you forgive me?'

She turned a sad gaze on him, and he could see that she didn't believe him.

'Of course. I . . . I understand. And it won't happen again. I'll be very careful from now on.'

Without looking at him again, she entered the hall. He followed, not sure what to say or do. They had never argued about anything before, and he could tell he had hurt her. But other than apologise, which he'd done, what more could he do? Perhaps the pregnancy hormones were making her extra sensitive. He would leave her alone for now, but soon he would try to talk to her again to make things right.

They both tried to act normal, but everyone must have noticed that they were subdued. Thankfully, no one commented on this fact, and people left them alone. When it came time to go to bed, Storm lay down behind her and took her in his arms as usual. Although she was stiff at first, she relaxed into his hold as sleep claimed her. He pulled her close and prayed to all the gods that he could keep her and the baby safe from now on.

He tried to talk to her again the following day, but it was as if she wasn't really listening. She registered his words and nodded, but some part of her had retreated inside her mind and he couldn't reach her. Storm didn't know what to do, but after another day of her avoiding him, he decided they might as well start searching for Maddie. They would be alone for a while on the journey, and he might have more of an opportunity to make her listen.

'Please may I borrow a rowing boat?' he asked Ófeigr. 'It will be slow going, but at least I won't miss any settlements along the way. And I'll bring it back to you as soon as I can.'

'Of course. I'll have Catla pack you up some food for the journey. You should be able to purchase whatever you need along the way too, as long as you have some silver. And people here are hospitable. They'll find you a place to sleep at night.'

'I do have silver, thank you.' He had plenty, as he hadn't had to use much as yet.

He informed Freydis that they would be leaving the next morning. She looked startled at first, as if she'd been sure he was going to leave her behind. Then she nodded and went to pack her meagre belongings. That expression on her face made him frown. How could she think he was going to abandon her when she was carrying his child? What did she take him for? He'd provide for them both, no matter what. He had to make her understand that, but how? There had to be a way to get through to her.

They set out just after dawn, with him rowing and Freydis

sitting in the stern. Surtr clung to her shoulder, unusually quiet and subdued, as if he too could sense his mistress's misery. For some reason that made Storm feel even worse, but he wasn't sure how to break the ice. Instead he resorted to practicalities.

'Tell me whenever you spot a settlement, please,' he said. 'We'll stop at each and every one.'

'Very well.'

She wasn't crying any longer, but he'd noticed she was very pale. He wanted to ask if she was feeling OK, if being pregnant was giving her any problems, but he couldn't get the words out. She'd said she was fine and hadn't had any of the usual symptoms. He had to believe her. He didn't even know how far along in the pregnancy she was, but he couldn't bear to ask. It might upset her again, and that was the last thing he wanted to do.

They made landfall several times during the course of the day, but no one had seen or heard of a tall, red-headed woman. By nightfall, his arms and shoulders ached from rowing, and he just wanted some food and a bed. They rounded a headland and saw lights in the centre of a large bay.

'We'll stop here for the night,' he said. 'Hopefully they'll at least have a barn we can sleep in.'

It turned out to be a large settlement, with plenty of space and a sleeping bench to spare. A richly dressed man welcomed them and offered hospitality. 'I'm Ingolfur Arnarson of Vik. Come in and meet my wife, Hallveig Frodadóttir. She'll have some stew for you in a trice.'

Another Ingolf, but at least this one was friendly. Storm thanked him, and settled near the hearth with Freydis by his side. After a day at sea, they were both windblown and ready for a hot meal, and he saw her sway with exhaustion. He berated himself for not noticing earlier. He should have been more considerate. Having accused her of not thinking of their child's welfare, he was guilty of the same thing by not looking after her properly. He determined to speak to her tomorrow, come what may. It was clear they couldn't go on like this.

The stew, served with pieces of flatbread, was delicious and exactly what they needed. 'Thank you so much. We are most grateful.' Storm handed his bowl to a thrall who'd been waiting nearby.

'You're very welcome,' Arnarson replied. 'What brings you here? Are you from one of the settlements out east? I'm assuming you didn't come all the way across the sea in a rowing boat.' He smiled.

'No, we've been staying with Ófeigr Guðfreðarson and he lent us the boat. I'm searching for my sister, who went missing last year. I don't suppose you've seen a tall woman with long, curly red hair?' He was tired of asking the question, and was beginning to think he was on a wild goose chase.

'Hmm, that sounds a lot like Geir Eskilsson's wife.'

'Eskilsson?' Storm recognised that name. Linnea was married to a Hrafn Eskilsson, and he had brothers. He couldn't remember if she'd mentioned a Geir, but surely it couldn't be a coincidence?

'Yes. They live north of here, at Stormavík. You should be able to reach there tomorrow, then you can see for yourself.'

'Stormavík?' So like his own name. How peculiar. But it was a lead at last and he beamed at the man. 'Wonderful! Thank you, we will definitely go there and ask.'

He couldn't quite allow himself to hope that it really was Maddie, but a little bit of optimism ran through him anyway.

May the gods be on his side.

Chapter Twenty-Five

Stormavík, Ísland
Heyannir (August) AD *876*

'We need to talk. Can you come and sit at the back of the boat, please?'

Freydis's head swivelled. She'd been waiting for Storm to speak to her the whole of the previous day, but he hadn't. Now he'd taken her by surprise. He had stopped rowing for the moment and was looking at her. Without replying, she forced herself to half stand up and move past him, climbing over the bench he sat on. She tried not to touch him, but it was impossible to get by without gripping his shoulder briefly. The feel of his solid body under her fingertips made her long to hold on tightly, but she knew she didn't have the right. Taking a deep breath to ready herself for confrontation, she sank down on the bench at the back and faced him.

This was it. He was going to tell her he wanted that divorce. She clenched her fists, hiding them in the folds of her skirts, and braced herself for the blow she knew his words would deliver. Having had a few days to think about it, however, she was determined to fight back. She acknowledged that she'd been at fault in not telling him about the pregnancy, but was it really such a crime? Besides, she had been careful to protect her stomach during the battle, and nothing had happened to her. As far as she could tell, the baby was still there, and she herself was hale and hearty.

'I'm sorry about the way I reacted when you told me the news,' he said quietly, starting to row again but staring at the bottom of the boat rather than at her. 'Your announcement came as a shock, and I just couldn't believe you would jeopardise our child's life like that.'

She could only nod. Since he didn't see that, as he still wasn't looking at her, she forced out a few words, her voice hoarse. 'I know, but—'

He continued without letting her finish, raising his eyes at last. 'Are you well? Did you take any blows to that part of your body?'

She blinked at him. He sounded genuinely concerned, and she wasn't sure what to make of that. All the arguments she had prepared in her mind disappeared, to be replaced by confusion. 'Um, I'm fine. And no, I kept the shield in front of me the whole time. I only had bruises and cuts on my arms and legs.'

'Good. That's good.'

How was she supposed to reply? Was he still angry or not? She couldn't tell. He was silent for so long, she couldn't stand the tension. 'Are you divorcing me?' she blurted out.

'What? No.' He frowned. 'I would never abandon a woman carrying my child.'

The relief was palpable. She gulped in air, the constriction around her lungs easing up. *Thank the gods!* He wasn't leaving her. Yet. But she needed more clarification.

'Wh-what about when the child is born? Will you leave then?' She shouldn't push him, but she needed to know. Had to prepare herself so that she could try to change his mind, somehow. It was better to have time to come up with valid arguments than to have it sprung on her at a future date. She couldn't live with the uncertainty a moment longer.

His expression turned darker. 'Freydis, I'm not going anywhere. Not without you and the child. You're my wife and we'll be a family in . . . how long exactly? When is it due?'

A family. He wanted them to be a family. But only for the sake of the child. She pushed down the irrational disappointment. This was more than she'd expected. More than she deserved. She should be grateful, but instead his words made anger burn inside her. Why would she want him to stay out of obligation? That was almost worse than him abandoning her.

'Around Yule, I reckon,' she told him curtly. 'Perhaps a week or so beforehand.'

'OK.' He nodded. 'OK, that gives us time to get used to . . . to everything.' His gaze became stern. 'But from now on, you will take the utmost care of yourself, do you hear me? No heavy work, no rowing, no fighting. Pretend you are carrying a fragile glass vessel inside you, and act accordingly.'

'Of course I'll be careful, but for the love of Freya, I'm as strong as an ox! Women have been bearing children since the beginning of time. We are able to go about our work as usual until the birth. There's no need to fret.'

He opened his mouth as if he was going to argue about it, then thought better of it and stayed silent.

Good. She was pleased that he was so concerned about his offspring, but she wouldn't let him dictate her every move from now until Yule. That would be unbearable, and she wasn't stupid. If she felt tired, she'd rest. If not, she would carry on as normal.

At least their child would not be unwelcome, and he wasn't leaving. She would have to be content with that for now.

*

Storm wasn't sure their little talk had cleared the air as much as he'd hoped. Freydis remained silent for the rest of their journey north, and he had no idea what else to say. Baby steps, he told himself, then almost chuckled at the unintended pun. They had some work to do to repair their relationship, but there was plenty of time. He decided to raise the subject again another day. For now, he had other things to think about.

As they entered the mouth of the fjord Arnarson had described as the place where they'd find Stormavík, butterflies danced in his stomach. He really didn't want to get his hopes up, but it was difficult not to. The name Eskilsson echoed inside his skull, as if the gods were teasing him. Would it prove to be a red herring? Surely Hrafn's younger brother had been called Geir, or was that merely wishful thinking? The only other Eskilsson sibling he'd met was Rurik, but he was almost sure a Geir had been mentioned.

'Do you see a settlement?' he asked Freydis. She was still facing him, which meant she was the one who could see the way forward while he had his back to their direction of travel.

'Yes, over there.' She pointed to the left.

He glanced over his shoulder. There was a smaller offshoot of the fjord, dotted with tiny islands and with a little peninsula jutting out into the water. A group of turf buildings could be seen on the other side. As they rounded the tip of it, they found a secluded bay with a strip of sand suitable for landing their boat. A large ship was already there, dragged high up so as not to be sucked out to sea by the tide.

He adjusted their course and made landfall. There was a moment of déjà vu. Someone blew a cow horn, just like they'd done when he'd first arrived at Assur's settlement, but this one wasn't quite as loud. He jumped out of the boat and pulled it up onto the sand before helping Freydis out. By the time they were both standing on the sliver of beach, people were walking towards them. They seemed in no rush, presumably because two people arriving in a small vessel didn't present much of a threat, but their expressions were wary.

First to reach them was a man with sun-streaked dark blond hair tied back in a ponytail. He was as tall as Storm, with broad shoulders, and looked to be strong and fit. There was a definite resemblance to Hrafn, Linnea's husband, whom he'd met on several occasions. Also to Rurik, who was married to Linnea's friend Sara. He was about to greet the man when his eyes were drawn to a red-headed whirlwind sprinting down the slope from the main building. He blinked, making sure he wasn't seeing things, then felt a huge grin spread across his features.

'Storm! *Storm!* I can't believe it!' Maddie threw herself into his arms and nearly knocked him over. He stumbled back a step, then gripped her tightly round the middle and swung her around.

'Maddie, at *last*! Where the *hell* have you been, brat?' he said in English. 'We've been so worried.' He put her down and hugged her close, rocking her in his arms and soaking in the peace that settled over him. He'd found her, and she was alive and well. *Thank the gods!*

'Here.' She leaned back and grinned at him. 'I've been here the whole time. Didn't Ivar tell you?'

'Ivar? No, I haven't seen him.' Except perhaps he had. Not long enough to speak to, though.

'Ahem.' The blond man had come to stand beside them, frowning and with a frosty glare. 'Would you care to explain why you're manhandling my wife?'

Storm had been concentrating on Maddie and had forgotten everyone around them. Now he became aware of the fact that they had an audience. Not just this man, but a group of other people who had approached silently behind him. And then there was Freydis, who was waiting quietly on his other side.

'My apologies. I'm Storm Haakonarson, Maddie's brother. You must be Geir? Hrafn's brother, right? I've met him a few times.' He let go of Maddie and gave her husband a slight bow. 'Forgive my manners. I've been searching for this troublesome little thing for nearly a year and had given up hope of ever finding her again. You can imagine my relief at this moment. I've been going out of my mind with worry, and feeling so guilty for losing her in the first place.' He turned to his sister. 'I'm so sorry, sis. I should never have left you behind. You have no idea how much I've regretted my actions that night.'

'Don't be sorry. If you hadn't, I would never have met Geir. We can talk about that later, but seriously, you did me a favour.' She grinned at him, and he felt the weight lift from his shoulders.

Geir's expression had thawed. 'Another brother?' He raised an eyebrow at Maddie, who laughed. 'And "little"?'

That made Storm smile, as his sister wasn't exactly tiny.

'Yes, but there won't be any more,' Maddie said. 'I only have two, and now you've met them both.' Cryptically, she added, 'And I won't be leaving with this one, I promise.' She turned to Storm to explain further. 'Ivar was here not long ago. He came with Hrafn on a trading journey.' Throwing Geir a teasing look, she added, 'My dear husband thought he was an old suitor of mine at first.'

'Well, how was I supposed to know?' Geir grumbled. 'You have a habit of throwing yourself at strange men.'

'*Fifl*.' She went over to put her arms around his waist, then rose on tiptoes to give him a quick kiss. 'Only when I'm related to them.'

'Hmph.' Geir pretended grumpiness, but Storm could see the love in his eyes as he looked at Maddie. It warmed him that she'd found such happiness. Which reminded him . . .

He turned to put a hand on Freydis's arm and drew her forward. 'This is *my* wife, Freydis Úlfsdóttir. Freydis, meet my sister Maddie and, apparently, my brother-in-law Geir Eskilsson.'

Maddie's eyes lit up. 'Oh, how wonderful! Another sister. Welcome to the family, Freydis. I hope you've both come to stay for a while. But where are my manners – please come up to the house and have some refreshment.'

She led a bemused-looking Freydis up the slope, and Storm fell into step with Geir behind them, followed by everyone else. He was introduced to some of them but didn't register their names. That would no doubt come later.

'So you've not seen Ivar?' Geir enquired. 'And you've been looking for Maddie for a year?'

'Nearly, yes. I started in Dyflin, which is where she went missing. I'm assuming you were the man who rescued her there when she was hurt. I spoke to an old crone who told me she'd patched her up after a fight.'

'Indeed. She wasn't fighting with me,' Geir explained. 'I tried to help her when she was being assaulted by four men. She was holding her own, but it looked like she could do with some assistance. Unfortunately, one of them managed to hit her over the head by mistake. He was actually aiming for me. As she was injured, I couldn't leave her behind, so I took her with me to Ísland. We . . . er, reached an understanding eventually, and were married at the end of last summer.'

'I'm glad. She looks very happy. Was Ivar well when you saw him?'

'Yes, but heading back to Hörðaland.' Geir smirked. 'I believe there was someone he was anxious to return to.'

'Ah, I see.' Storm decided now was not the time to mention the battle they'd both taken part in. He wasn't sure whether Ivar had survived, and he didn't want to put a damper on things now that he'd finally found his sister. Today, celebrations were in order.

*

Freydis had never had a sister, and it was strange to be addressed as such. Maddie was friendly and chatty, and not at all how she had imagined her. Although she had the same wild curls as her brother, hers were an extremely vivid red, and very long. And they both had green eyes, of slightly different hues. There was a sibling resemblance, but not so much that you'd notice it if you didn't already know they were related.

'Come in, come in. You must be tired from your journey. How far have you come today? And why were you in such a tiny boat? What was Storm thinking? Surely you didn't row all the way here from the mainland?'

Maddie lobbed a steady stream of questions at her, and Freydis answered as best she could. It was all a bit overwhelming, and she also felt as if she was here under false pretences. Storm might have said that he wouldn't abandon her and their child, but they were far from a normal married couple and their relationship was strained. It was very different from the easy camaraderie and love Maddie and her husband so clearly had for each other.

A stab of jealousy shot through her, but she pushed it down. Most people did not have marriages like that, and she shouldn't expect it either. Although she'd thought for a while that was where she and Storm had been headed, it wasn't the case now. Perhaps there was a chance they could go back to their earlier friendship, at least, but it might take a while. Time would tell, and it was something she could mull over later. For now, she had to concentrate on what Maddie was saying.

One of the other women of the settlement produced mugs of ale and little oatcakes. Freydis nibbled hers, while continuing to answer Maddie's endless stream of questions. Storm took a seat beside her and held up a hand at his sister.

'Enough, *sis*! Let poor Freydis breathe for a moment, will you?

There's plenty of time for talking. And she needs to rest. She's in a . . . um, delicate condition.'

Freydis's cheeks heated up. She hadn't expected him to announce that so publicly or so soon, and with what almost sounded like a proud note in his voice. Was he actually truly happy about her pregnancy? He'd said so repeatedly during the last few days, but she still wasn't sure if she dared believe him. It had to be wishful thinking on her part, although he *had* seemed pleased when she'd first mentioned it. Before he realised what she had done.

Maddie, seated on her other side, completely missed any dark undercurrents. She squealed and gave her a fierce hug. 'How wonderful! Congratulations! I can't believe I'm going to be an aunt again.' She leaned forward and punched Storm on the arm. 'You dog! You didn't waste much time.'

'*Þegi þú!* Just shut up,' he muttered, chuckling. 'Says the woman who got married before me.' He glanced around, as if to make sure no one could overhear them. 'And what on earth were you doing travelling back in time by yourself anyway? You couldn't have waited for me? I left you alone for one night. *One!*'

Maddie squirmed a little. 'I was only going to go for a walk and have a quick look around in the ninth century, then come back, but it didn't work out that way. I swear I didn't do it on purpose. And then . . . I wanted to stay.' She sent her husband a heated glance, making it clear what her reason had been. 'Anyway, I've been back to tell Mother and Father. If you'd stayed put, you would have known I was safe.'

He hung his head. 'I've been feeling so bad, and they blamed me even if they didn't say so outright. It *was* my fault you left, because I abandoned you for the evening. I had to try to find you or I couldn't have lived with myself.'

Freydis remembered him telling her that he'd gone to drink ale with his friends, and that was when Maddie had disappeared.

She knew he felt responsible, but Maddie shook her head, obviously disagreeing.

'They shouldn't have blamed you,' she said. 'Sure, I was a little miffed at being left behind when you went out with your friends, and it might have contributed towards me wanting an adventure, but it wasn't your fault. Not at all. Geir and I believe it was fate. Or the gods meddling, perhaps.'

Storm's expression showed that Maddie's words had lifted a load from his shoulders, and he blew out a breath of relief. His sister obviously didn't blame him, and here they were together again, and all was well. Freydis was glad for his sake. The siblings were close. Not merely in age, but in every way. She could tell. And being the elder by a year, Storm must always have felt responsible for his sister. No wonder he'd been devastated to lose her.

'Now, no more talk of guilt. Tonight we are celebrating,' Maddie declared. 'Freydis, why don't you lie down for a rest while we prepare some extra-special dishes for *nattverðr.* Come, Liv has cleared a space for you and Storm.'

She stood up and pulled Freydis to her feet, leading her to a comfortable sleeping bench in a corner of the hall and gently pushing her down onto a soft sheepskin.

'Sleep.' She smiled and bent to give Freydis a hug. 'You have to take good care of my niece or nephew. I'll wake you when it is time to eat. I'm so pleased you're here.'

Freydis did as she was told. She really was very tired, and her sister-in-law's affection warmed her heart. She couldn't wait to get to know her better.

As they settled into life at Stormavík, it amused Storm no end that his sister had named the place after him.

'No, I didn't,' she protested when he teased her about it, her cheeks flushing pink. 'It's very windy around here, that's all.'

'Sure it is.' He chuckled, and ducked the punch she aimed his way.

'OK, fine. I missed you, all right? It was a weird time for me. At the start, I wasn't sure I wanted to stay and I was homesick. No need to look so smug about it.'

That made him laugh outright, but to placate her he said, 'I would have named a place after you too, Mads, you know that. I missed you terribly, and I was so afraid for you. Anything could have happened.' He still shuddered to think of the possibilities, but mostly he forced himself not to imagine it.

'Yes, well, everything is fine now. It's in the past. Let's talk about the future instead. What are you going to do next? Are you staying in this century?'

They were sitting on a bench outside the main door of the hall, and Geir had wandered over to join them. 'Yes, what are your plans, brother?'

The two men had quickly bonded, and Storm liked Geir immensely. He was quiet and capable, and besotted with Maddie. All good qualities. He went about everything he did with confidence, without bragging about his skills. And he balanced Maddie out perfectly, while allowing her to be herself. It was clear that she had blossomed and come out of her shell. Her geeky teenage years were over, and in their stead there was a self-assured young woman. It was lovely to see.

'Well, I was wondering if you'd mind us staying here for the winter? Freydis is due to give birth around Yule, and I don't want to risk taking her on any more long journeys right now. If you don't have enough food for us, I could go down the coast and try to buy more provisions. I brought silver aplenty and would be happy to contribute. We wouldn't want to be a burden, or deprive you and your people in any way.'

'You're very welcome to stay for as long as you wish,' Geir said.

'We've done well this year and the harvest will be good. There's always hunting and fishing too. You could help with that. We'll be fine. What say you, *ást mín*?'

'Yes, of course you must stay.' Maddie smiled and leaned her head on Storm's shoulder. 'It's so wonderful to have you here, and I'm enjoying getting to know Freydis.' Her smile dimmed. 'She does seem a little . . . quiet, though. Is everything all right between you?'

'Maddie,' Geir muttered in warning, and sighed.

'I know, I know, it's none of my business, but I hate seeing her so down.' Maddie frowned. 'And it's not good for the child. She should be blossoming right now.'

A pang of guilt shot through Storm. They'd been here a few days now. Although he'd slept next to Freydis every night, they were still not back to how they had been before. He'd tried to be solicitous and not make any physical demands of her, but something was still bothering her. He needed to find out what it was.

'No, you're right. We had a . . . disagreement, but it's time to set things right. I'll talk to her, I promise.'

'You want to chat about it?'

'Maddie, cease your meddling!' Geir stood up and pulled his wife to her feet. 'Sorry, brother. I'm going to take her away now.'

Storm laughed. 'Please do. I know you mean well, Mads, but I can handle this on my own.'

At least he hoped he could.

Chapter Twenty-Six

Stormavík, Ísland
Heyannir (August) AD *876*

'Freydis, would you like to go for a walk? I'm told there is a spectacular view from the cliffs over the sea.'

'What?'

She'd been sitting on the bench outside the hall, sewing a tiny tunic. She hadn't yet felt her child fluttering inside her, but her little bump was growing and her breasts were sore and sensitive. There was no denying the fact that she had to prepare herself for becoming a mother. That included making garments and whatever else the child would need. Normally she disliked sewing of any kind, but when it was for her baby, it was completely different. Maddie had kindly given her a length of linen and one of wool for this purpose.

Storm was standing before her, impossibly handsome as usual. She had to look away before he saw the love shining out of her eyes. He'd never be hers properly, but she couldn't help wanting him. She longed for his touch, but he'd merely held her carefully each night, without doing anything else. Apparently he hadn't believed her when she'd told him she was strong and healthy and wanted to carry on as normal. That included lovemaking, which he hadn't seemed averse to before. Perhaps it was time to clarify a few things.

'You've been sitting here working for hours.' He held out his hand. 'Come for a walk. A little exercise will do you good, and you can rest your eyes.'

She stood up and put away her sewing, determination flowing through her. A walk on the cliffs was the perfect time to find out if he was merely being careful for the sake of the baby, or if he'd lost interest in her now that she was with child. If it was the former, he was going to get an earful. She grabbed his hand, and to her surprise he didn't let go. Instead, he twined his fingers with hers the way he used to.

He led her along a path that snaked from the back of the settlement up a hill towards the coast. They walked in silence, and she revelled in the feel of his callused hand gripping hers. What did it mean? What was he doing?

When they were far from the dwellings, up on top of the cliffs, he stopped and turned towards her, studying her expression. There was a strong breeze, and the smell of the sea hung in the air. Seabirds squabbled and swooped nearby, and down below the waves were capped with white foam. She was only vaguely aware of their surroundings, because her heart was pounding and her mind whirled. Why was he looking at her like that?

Little tendrils had worked themselves loose from her plaits. In vain she pushed them behind her ears, but they didn't stay put. Storm reached out to help, his fingers caressing her cheek as he smoothed her hair back.

'Freydis,' he said, his voice husky. 'Tell me what you're thinking, please. Have you not forgiven me yet? I didn't mean to be harsh, I swear.'

'I . . . What?' She wobbled slightly, and his hands moved to her waist to hold her steady. 'Shouldn't it be the other way around? I thought you were the one who hadn't forgiven me for putting our child at risk, although I swear I didn't do it intentionally. I was as careful as I could be.'

He lifted her chin with his fingers. 'I know you didn't do it on purpose, *unnasta*. You just weren't thinking clearly. It happens. Sometimes we act recklessly without considering the consequences. Believe me, I'm the last person to blame anyone else for that. All my life I've been told I'm impulsive. I jump into things feet first without reflecting on the possible outcome. I really can't fault you for doing the same. It was just that I couldn't handle the thought of you or the child being hurt. It scared me stupid and I reacted without thinking, turning into some sort of overprotective beast. I'm so sorry, *baby*.'

'So what are you saying?' She couldn't take her eyes off his. They were a mesmerising clear green in the bright sunlight, and they were boring into hers as if he was searching her soul.

He cupped her cheeks with his warm palms. 'I'm saying that I want us to go back to how we were before that stupid argument. No! Actually I want to go even further.' He took a deep breath. 'Freydis, I love you. If we weren't married already, I'd want to marry you now. I can't wait for us to be a family, and if you'll have me, I will try to be the best husband, and the best father I can to our child.'

Her heart stopped for a moment, then started up again, beating so fast she thought it would explode. 'You . . . you love me?' She couldn't take it in.

She'd expected a serious discussion on how they would manage once the child arrived. How they could learn to co-exist amicably, at best. And she'd come prepared with counter-arguments, hoping to persuade him to want her again, at least at night. Instead, he'd made her speechless.

He nodded. 'I do. Could you ever learn to love me back, do you think? I know you were more or less coerced into marrying me. I don't suppose I'm the sort of husband you had envisaged.'

Her mouth stretched into a huge smile. 'Oh, but you are! And I already love you. Have done from the very first time we met, I believe. I . . . Are you serious?'

He was grinning now, and instead of answering, he took her mouth with his in a fierce, possessive kiss that sent shock waves all the way down to her toes. His tongue demanded entry, and the kiss became passionate and all-consuming. Lightning bolts of desire arrowed through her, and she clung to him, fisting her hands in his tunic to pull him even closer. The taste of him, the feel of him – she'd missed it so much. Being in his arms made everything right in her world. There was nowhere else she'd rather be.

His hands soon moved further down, roaming her body, until the only thing they could do was give in to the explosive attraction between them. It was summer – even though that wasn't saying much here in Ísland – and there was soft grass beneath them. No one was nearby or likely to see them. It wasn't long before they were both mostly undressed and on top of a pile of clothing, enjoying each other beneath the sun. Storm worshipped her with his fingers, mouth and tongue, and Freydis wondered if she'd died and gone to Valhalla. He coaxed her towards dizzying heights, and as her body shattered into a million fragments of exquisite pleasure, she was sure she had never been so happy in her entire life.

Storm was hers, and he loved her. Nothing was more important than that.

'Are you alive, *ást mín*?' Storm dropped a kiss on her cheek and hugged her close, shivering a little. The air was decidedly fresh.

Summer here was more like early spring back home, although the sun did provide some warmth.

'Mm-hmm.' He'd never called her 'my love' before, and she closed her eyes to savour the moment.

'I hope we didn't hurt the little one,' he murmured. 'I didn't mean to get so carried away.'

She turned her face to smile at him. 'It's fine. The other women have been telling me I shouldn't be afraid to carry on as normal in every way. I told you, we are not as delicate as we might look. In fact, it is good to stay active in every way.'

'Glad to hear it.' He reached out and placed his large hand on her abdomen. 'It's becoming noticeable now. How does it feel?' His voice was low and filled with reverence, and it made her heart beat faster again.

'I've not felt the child move yet, but I'm told there will be a fluttering sensation soon. But my . . . er, these are sore.' She gestured to her bosom and saw his eyes light up with appreciation.

'And getting bigger, if I'm not mistaken.' He bent to trail his lips across them, making desire stir inside her again as his rough stubble grazed her skin, leaving a delicious tingle in its wake.

'That pleases you?' She'd been afraid he would find her body repulsive once it began to change.

'Oh yes.' He glanced up at her with a mischievous grin. 'You have no idea. I'm going to have a very hard time keeping my hands off you.'

She decided to throw caution to the wind and twined her arms around his neck. 'Then don't, husband *mín*,' she whispered. 'Perhaps I don't want you to.'

With a growl he pounced on her again, and it was some time before they were dressed and sitting next to each other on the grass. Neither of them was ready to leave yet and return to the others.

Storm dug around in his leather pouch and held something

out to her – a gold ring that winked in the sun's rays. 'Here, this is for you. My mother told me that when she was expecting me, my father gave her a ring as a thank-you gift. I want to do the same. You don't know how grateful I am that I found you, and that you're carrying my child. You have changed my life. My entire world, in fact.'

Emotion rose in her throat, and she had to swallow down the lump. 'You've already given me a ring, and a brooch, and you don't have to give me anything else, but thank you. It's beautiful.' It was a simple shape, but inlaid with a swirling pattern of snakes or beasts wriggling in and out of each other.

'I know I don't have to. I *want* to.' He leaned over to kiss her. 'And I'll give you one for each child we have in the future. I want at least four, maybe more.'

'Storm!' She laughed. 'Let's get this one birthed before we start talking about any more.'

'Very well, but I'm looking forward to having a family with you.'

'Me too.'

She couldn't wait to be the mother of his child.

Stormavík, Ísland
Hrútmánuðr (late December) AD *876*

Freydis's contractions began the evening after the Yuletide festivities. Storm had discussed the matter with her beforehand, and she didn't protest when he stayed by her side, keeping an eye on proceedings. Giving birth was a risky business. There was no way he'd let anyone touch her without being clean and sterilised. He only hoped nothing went wrong, but he had stashed his magical axe nearby just in case so that he could transport her to a twenty-first-century hospital if need be.

'Push now. You're doing well.' Lif, the wife of Stormavík's blacksmith, was in charge, having had several children herself. She seemed to know what she was doing, which was good. Storm had been trained to assist at childbirth during his time in the army, but he'd rather not have to put his skills to the test.

Maddie was also present. She was pregnant herself, almost five months along and positively radiant with happiness. Storm had gathered that she and Geir had had trouble conceiving, and he was pleased that his sister was getting her wish to become a mother. For now, however, he was concentrating on his wife.

'You're so courageous, my love,' he whispered, wiping her sweating brow with a damp cloth and giving her a quick kiss. 'It will soon be over. Here, squeeze my hand when the next wave hits you.'

She *was* brave, gritting her teeth against the pain and pushing as hard as she could. Her grip on him was so fierce, his fingers were going numb, but he didn't mind. She was the one suffering right now; it was the least he could do. Maddie had taught her to breathe through the contractions, and that seemed to help a little. Cursing under her breath also let off steam.

'If you think I'm doing this thrice more, you're mistaken,' she hissed.

Storm hid a smile. He knew she'd change her mind once the baby was in her arms and the ordeal had faded from her mind. If not, he'd take her to the future, where they could drug her to the eyeballs next time. For her first time, she'd insisted on staying in her own era, giving birth the traditional way, surrounded by family. And she and Maddie had really bonded, becoming sisters in every way that mattered. Storm didn't protest, as it was up to her. As long as she was willing to have his babies, he didn't care where it happened. He wanted a big family, and so did she. They'd agreed on that.

This baby would have to be an only child for a while, though, as they had decided to make their home in the future. In order to travel there, the child had to be old enough to say the magic words. That meant they'd have to wait at least two years to put their plans into action. He hoped he could keep her from getting pregnant again that long.

Much as he liked it here, Storm didn't want a permanent life in the ninth century. Farming wasn't for him, and although he enjoyed working as a blacksmith, it was more of a hobby and not what he wanted to do every day. When he'd broached the subject with Freydis, she had astonished him with her enthusiasm for living in his century. She'd been seriously impressed with all she had seen on her brief visit, and wanted to experience more. He had various ideas for what they could do once they were back in the twenty-first century, but there was no rush to decide.

'*Aarrgghh!*' With a final push and a hoarse yell, Freydis finally managed to propel the baby out of her womb and into Lif's waiting arms. She wrapped the child in a linen towel, and it let out a strong cry.

'You have a healthy son. Congratulations!'

'Oh, wonderful!' Maddie bent to hug Storm, then grasped Freydis's hand. 'I'm so happy for you both.'

'A little boy!' Storm helped Lif place the bundle in Freydis's arms. He watched her hold their son with tears pricking his eyelids. 'Thank you, my beautiful wife.' He kissed her tenderly, then the downy head of his small child.

'What will you call him?' Maddie asked, watching as Lif expertly cut and tied the umbilical cord, then took the baby away for a moment to clean him up.

'That's for you to find out at the naming ceremony.' Storm winked at her. 'It's a secret until then.'

Freydis looked up at him. 'You've decided then?'

To his surprise, she had told him he could choose their baby's name. It was apparently the custom. They'd announce it formally once she'd had a short rest.

'Yes, but if you don't like it, you must promise to tell me.'

'I will like it, I'm sure.'

When both mother and baby had been cleaned up, and it was just the three of them in Maddie and Geir's bedchamber, which they'd borrowed for the occasion, Storm lay down beside his wife and son.

'Gods, but I love you! Both of you,' he whispered as they snuggled together. 'You have no idea how much. Thank you so much again for this gift.'

'My pleasure. He's absolutely perfect, isn't he?'

'Yes, just like you.'

Storm put his arms around both of them and watched over them as they slept. They were a family now, and he'd keep them safe no matter what.

Later that day, everyone gathered in the hall to watch the naming ceremony. Storm had been told that this involved Freydis feeding their son for the first time while everyone watched. He wasn't best pleased about that, but to his relief, she hid her breasts under a shawl so that no one else could see much. It was probably silly to be so alpha possessive, but he couldn't help it. She was his, and he didn't want the other men here to get even a glimpse of her.

The little one was more than ready for a feed, judging by the angry noises he'd been making. Thankfully, he settled down as soon as he started suckling, and for a while, blessed silence reigned. It was an emotional moment. Storm thought his heart might burst with pride and joy.

When the baby had had enough at last, Freydis handed him over to Storm. He cradled the tiny head carefully, reverently.

Smiling at everyone, he raised his voice. 'I'd like to present to you mine and Freydis's son, Wolf Stormsson. May he thrive and grow as big and strong as his father and uncles!'

A loud cheer from the assembled company startled the baby and made him cry again, but Storm shushed him and rocked him against his shoulder. Rubbing his son's tiny back, he succeeded in burping him, and he didn't care one bit that a little of the milk ended up on his tunic.

He smiled at Freydis. 'Will it do, my love?' He saw that she was looking slightly puzzled, so he explained, 'Wolf is the same as Úlfr in my language. I thought to honour your father. Did I do the right thing?'

'Oh!' A blush of pleasure spread across her cheeks and her eyes glowed. 'Thank you! Thank you so much. Yes, that's absolutely perfect. I love it.'

'Good.' He sat down next to her and gave her a long, deep kiss. 'And I love you.'

Wolf began to grizzle, and Storm could feel something damp through the blanket. 'Ah, time to change your clout, methinks.' He looked over at Lif. 'Can you show me how to do it, please?' He would have been perfectly able to change a modern nappy, but the Viking version was something he had yet to learn.

Everyone in the room except for Maddie went quiet and stared at him with wide eyes and open mouths.

'You . . . you're going to change him yourself?' Lif blinked, as if she wasn't sure she was hearing right.

'Of course. I mean to help out in every way with my son. He has two parents. No point in only one of them doing all the hard work.'

Out of the corner of his eye, he saw a few of the men squirming, but Geir was giving him a wide grin. 'By all the gods, I'll come and learn too. You're right. I want to be involved in every way.'

Lif shook her head and muttered, 'The whole world's gone mad.'

Storm ignored her, and followed her to the nearest bench, where she proceeded to show him how to change a nappy ninth-century style. He had a go himself, and although he could probably do better, he considered it a reasonable effort for a first time. He'd get better with practice.

Geir was watching his every move. 'He's so unbelievably tiny! Not sure our big hands are made for this task.'

'He'll soon grow. And I want to bond with my son whenever possible.'

'You're right. I'll be doing the same. And if anyone tells me it's women's work, they can go jump in a bog.'

Storm laughed. 'Exactly.'

Dry clothes and clout in place, he lifted Wolf and cradled him to his chest. He couldn't care less what anyone here thought – he was going to be a hands-on dad. He and Freydis were a team, and equals in every way, just as she'd always tried to prove.

She was definitely right about that.

Epilogue

Eskilsnes, Svíaríki
Midsummer AD 887

'Did you ever, even in your wildest dreams, imagine we'd end up here?'

Haakon Berger was standing with his wife, Mia, and their friend and colleague Lars Mattsson, looking out over the grassy area in front of Eskilsnes, the home of their daughter Linnea and her husband, Hrafn. They were in the ninth century, at a feast in honour of their other daughter, Maddie, and her husband, Geir. The couple had recently made the move back to Sweden after selling their Icelandic settlement to a friend. From now on, they'd be living at the farm Geir had inherited from his aunt, not far from here.

With their son Storm and foster-son Ivar both living mostly in the twenty-first century, a stone's throw from Haakon and Mia's summer cottage by Lake Mälaren, they finally had their whole family within reach. At least, as long as they were prepared to do some time-travelling, which was not a problem since Haakon had found them their own magical device a few years ago. Storm, Ivar and their families were here today, and so were

Lars's granddaughter Sara and her husband, Rurik, with their children. Since Rurik was Hrafn's brother, it felt like they were all kin, as the Vikings would say.

Also present was Ivar's ancestor – now blood brother – Thorald, with his family, and Hrafn's best friend, Haukr, and his wife, Ceri, as well as a huge warrior by the name of Holger, with wife and kids. He was a friend of Rurik's from his days fighting with the Great Heathen Army over in Britain. Some of Hrafn's trading partners had come too, including his now grown-up foster-son, Kadir. That young man had originally come back from Byzantium – or Miklagarðr, as the Vikings called it – with Linnea and Hrafn. Once he was old enough, he'd moved to the trading town of Aldeigjuborg in Garðaríki – present-day Russia. There, he didn't stick out as much, since other traders often came up from the south. He still saw his Swedish family as often as he could, so that he had the best of both worlds.

In short, it was a huge gathering of absolutely everyone connected in any way with Haakon and Mia and their family. They couldn't believe their eyes. It was almost too much to take in. Lars appeared equally stunned, although he grinned widely when he caught sight of his namesake, Sara's oldest son, who was chasing after his youngest brother, a four-year-old tearaway.

'I'm so happy, I feel like I should go and make a sacrifice to the gods,' Mia whispered. 'Look at all those children! Our grandchildren and their friends. Having been an only child myself, I never thought I'd have a family as big as this. It's quite simply breathtaking.'

Apart from Kadir, Hrafn and Linnea had four children. Ivar and his wife, Ellisif, had two, while Storm and Freydis were the happy parents of five, as were Sara and Rurik. Geir and Maddie had their hands full with two sets of twins. That made sixteen grandkids in all (including Kadir), and since Sara was like an honorary daughter, it felt as though her five little ones were partly theirs as well and added to the tally. Watching them all running around having fun was wonderful. It was complete and utter chaos, in the best possible way.

Haakon put his arm around Mia's shoulders and drew her close. 'Yes, who would have thought this was how our life was going to turn out? It all started with your ring.' He glanced at the golden serpent wrapped around her finger, glinting in the sunlight. He had a replica on his own finger, and could have sworn it tightened momentarily.

'Mm, it's magical for sure.' Mia lifted her hand and kissed the snake's tiny head. 'Thank you,' she murmured. 'We really can't thank you enough.'

'I second that,' Haakon agreed, and bent to kiss his wife, the love of his life. As always, she melted into his embrace, and they forgot the rest of the world for a moment.

They counted themselves the most fortunate people ever. The Norns had outdone themselves when deciding the destiny of Mia, Haakon and their descendants, who were all extremely grateful for the incredible gift of their large time-travelling family. Later, when the festivities had died down a little, the entire group would go to the sacred grove and give thanks to the Norse gods and the three weavers of Fate.

As for Haakon and Mia, they quietly thanked the gods every day.

Acknowledgements

This is the final book in the Viking Runes series, and it's going to feel very strange to leave this fictional world and the characters I've lived with for so long, but I think I'm leaving them in a good place. And who knows, perhaps I'll return to them in the future? Time will tell. I want to say a big thank you to my lovely editors Nicola Caws and Kate Byrne, who have both worked with me on this story, together with their team at Headline. As always, many thanks to the cover designers Caroline Young, Sarah Whittaker and Emily Courdelle for the gorgeous covers – I love the way they all match so well – and to the wonderful narrator of all my audiobooks, Eilidh Beaton, whose Old Norse is now near perfect! Huge thanks also to Lina Langlee, my fabulous agent, for encouraging me to write about our heritage. I love working with you all!

As with the other books in the series, I tried to find a unique location/setting for this one and ended up choosing the Orkney Islands for the most part. I knew that the Vikings had been connected with those islands for a long time, and they were a very important part of their trade network. The only problem was that I'd never been there, and as you've probably gathered by now, I like to visit the locations of my books if at all possible. Thankfully, my husband was easily persuaded to take a trip up to Orkney, as he'd never been there either. We went on an epic road trip all the way to the north of Scotland, before taking the ferry from Scrabster, and we thoroughly enjoyed every moment. So a massive thank you to Richard for indulging my travel whims, and I'm glad you liked it too!

As ever, thank you to my lovely friends – Gill Stewart, Sue Moorcroft, Myra Kersner, Henriette Gyland, Tina Brown and Carol Dahlén, plus the Word Wenches mentioned in the dedication. I am so grateful to have you all in my life – you're the best!

A special thank you to Natalie Normann for help with all things Norwegian. And thank you to Dr Joanne Shortt-Butler for helping me with Old Norse words, phrases and pronunciation, as well as special research into Viking marriage customs – you really helped to put my mind at ease regarding this plot line.

To Josceline and Jessamy – love you!

And last, but not least, a massive thank you to all the readers, reviewers and book bloggers – I'm so grateful for your support and really hope you enjoy the conclusion to this series!

Christina x

P. S. If you want to keep up with news, behind-the-scenes information and special deals, please sign up for my newsletter – you'll find the details here: https://tinyurl.com/mr3fu9ch

Bonus Material
Courting Estrid

Birkiþorp
Late June AD *896*

'I'll only stay for a couple of weeks, Mother, I promise. I . . . need to get away.' Estrid clutched her father's big silver cloak pin in one hand and a bundle in the other. It was dusk and she was standing at the edge of the forest next to their neighbour Haukr's property. Thankfully, no one was about other than herself and her mother, Linnea.

'All right, Estrid, but be careful, please.' Linnea gave her a hug. 'You know I worry whenever you go to the future.'

'No need. I'll be fine, and Grandma and Grandpa are there. They'll look after me.' Although she was really hoping they had work to do so they'd leave her alone for a while. She needed to lick her wounds.

She had just watched her little sister Hrefna marry Cadoc Hauksson, and her cousin Gytha wed his brother Bryn, in a joint ceremony. Both girls were younger than herself by almost five winters. It should have been her in that hall, celebrating with all their relatives around them, having a wonderful time and looking forward to a bright future with an adoring husband by her side. Only, she'd never found any man who fit that description.

It wasn't that she was unattractive – quite the opposite, judging by all the attention she received wherever she went. But her father was a wealthy and influential man, and Estrid's dowry large. That meant she had never quite been able to bring herself to trust that anyone wanted her for herself and not merely the riches or connections she could bring. It was frustrating.

And she'd never been in love.

With a mother who had travelled through time to find her soulmate, Estrid could at least escape for a while and spend some time in the twenty-first century with her grandparents. They would spoil her and look after her, without sending her searching or pitying looks, or expecting anything else from her. It would be peaceful. Fortunately, her parents understood and let her go.

The magical brooch performed its function, and soon she found herself stumbling up the slight incline towards her grandparents' summer house by Lake Mälaren. Luck was with her, and the lights were on inside. When she knocked on the back door, she was greeted with open arms.

'Estrid, sweetheart! To what do we owe this pleasure? Is everything all right?' Her grandfather Haakon hugged her tight.

He and her grandmother, Mia, both spoke passable Old Norse, but during her many visits Estrid had learned Swedish so that they could be more comfortable. She replied in their language. 'All is well. I just needed to escape for a while. I'll fill you in if you make me some of that lovely hot chocolate, please.'

'Of course.' Mia beamed at her, and she was ushered inside for a long catching-up session.

Mia and Haakon worked in the city but spent weekends and holidays at the cottage. They were due to leave for work the following day, but were happy for Estrid to stay on. They knew she could look after herself and could obviously see that she needed to be alone.

'If you need anything or want us to come and pick you up, you know how to reach us.' Mia gave her one last hug before they left. They'd taught Estrid to use the ancient telephone at the cottage, but she usually avoided it. There were only so many strange objects she could handle at any one time, and the twenty-first century was full of oddities.

She spent the next day just lazing in the sun and swimming in the lake, trying not to think too much or do anything other than exist. By evening, hunger drove her inside to put on the strange clothing that was always kept here for visitors from the past. Blue trousers that hugged her backside, with even smaller ones underneath, and a soft shirt that clung to her curves a little too much. Once dressed, she wheeled out an old bicycle from a shed. She'd learned to ride it many summers ago and preferred it to learning how to drive a car. It wasn't that she was afraid, it just seemed too strange.

Mia and Haakon had left her a small square card made of plastic to use when shopping, so no one took much notice of her in the food market and she set off for home with two bags full of produce. Everything she'd need for a few days, including chocolate, which she could never resist. It was getting late as she pedalled along the tiny country road towards the cottage, and she enjoyed the peace and quiet as there was no one else about. Or so she'd thought. As she passed a house set back from the road, a huge motorcycle suddenly came hurtling out of the driveway, taking the corner at a precarious angle. The rider obviously hadn't seen Estrid in the half-light of the summer evening, and had to swerve to avoid hitting her.

'*Aaaah!*' She was so startled, her bicycle wobbled and she lost control of it, ending up in the ditch. Her shopping bags miraculously stayed intact, but the same couldn't be said for her dignity or one scraped knee. Untangling herself from the bike, she jumped to her feet and shouted, '*Aumingi!*' at the motorcycle rider, who had skidded to a stop some fifty yards down the road.

He turned around and drove back towards her, slowly this time, and came to a halt nearby. After kicking down the stand, he pulled his helmet off and dismounted, jogging over to where Estrid was now busy righting the bicycle and picking up her grocery bags.

'Are you OK? I'm *so* sorry! Here, let me help you with that.' The man tried to grab the handlebars of her bike, but she pushed him away with a hard shove to the chest.

'No! I'll do it myself. Go away, *fifl*. You've done enough.'

He blinked, startled by her vehemence. 'Really, I'm very sorry. I should have looked properly before driving out of the gate like that, but I was so pissed off with someone, I wasn't thinking straight. I know, I know, it's not an excuse, and you have every right to be angry. I gave you a fright. Hell, I scared myself too! Please, let me give you a hand to try and make up for it.'

A quick glance showed her that the man was wearing an expression of contrition that looked sincere, but Estrid's limbs were still a bit unsteady and she didn't like it. Normally, she wasn't afraid of anything and stayed calm in a crisis, but he had definitely scared her. If they had collided, things could have been serious. Also, she disliked being seen as incompetent at anything or vulnerable in any way. It rankled that she'd let herself be so startled, she had lost control of the bike. She ought to be tougher than that. It was embarrassing in the extreme.

'Thank you, but I can manage.' She hauled the bicycle up onto the road and hung the two bags off the handlebars. 'You can go now.' She vaguely noted that he was very tall and rather good-looking, in a scruffy sort of way, but she didn't want to stare at him. The sooner he left, the better.

'You're not hurt?'

'A few scrapes and bruises, that's all. Nothing I can't handle. It's fine.' She refused to mention that her pride had taken the largest hit. 'Just be more careful in future.'

'Oh, I will, but . . .' He hesitated, clearly reluctant to go, but Estrid turned her back on him and hopped onto the bike. She started pedalling away before he could say anything else. When she glanced back after a while, he was still standing by the side of the road staring after her with a frown marring his features. Hopefully, he'd leave soon and she could forget about the embarrassing encounter.

And so would he.

Estrid made her way back to the cottage. She hadn't reckoned on having such an eventful evening and looked forward to finally eating her supper. She'd only just started preparing it, however, when there was a knock on the door. Since she was alone in the house, she called out, 'Who is it?' without unlocking the door.

'The guy from the property down the road. We, um . . . met earlier.'

She opened the door and the man who had almost run her over stood outside, bathed in the light that spilled out from the cottage. This time Estrid allowed herself to study him properly. She took in how big he was – both tall and wide across the shoulders. He was also remarkably attractive, with beautiful greenish eyes, a slightly turned-up nose that gave him an impish look, full lips, long golden-brown hair pulled into some sort of knot on his head, and matching stubble. Estrid reckoned he topped her own father by at least a handspan, which was impressive.

'Hey,' he said, looking a little wary as if he wasn't sure how he'd be received. 'I just wanted to come and check on you. Make sure you're all right. I know you said to leave you alone, but I feel so guilty. I'm not normally that reckless, I swear.'

By this time, Estrid had calmed down and acknowledged to herself that she'd overreacted during their previous encounter. Anyone would have ended up in the ditch when faced with a motorcycle coming out of nowhere at full speed. It didn't signify incompetence on her part. 'I'm fine. No harm done.'

He breathed out, his relief palpable. 'Good. I'm glad. And I'll make sure we put up a sign to tell our members to be careful when exiting that gate.'

'We?' Estrid wondered if he was the ruler of some tiny kingdom. It sounded like it, but as far as she knew, they didn't have those in this era.

'Oh, the motorcycle club. I'm the leader and that's the gate to our club house.' He stuck out his hand. 'I'm Henrik Törn, by the way. As in the sharp parts of a bramble,' he added with a smile. 'Strange, I know.'

'Ah, *Thorn*,' she muttered, translating it into her own language without thinking.

'If you want to say it in English, sure. I don't mind. And you?'

She wasn't speaking English, but decided not to tell him she'd said his name in Old Norse. 'I'm Estrid.'

'With an E? Not Astrid? Hmm, unusual, but I like it.' He was staring at her with an appreciative glint in his eyes, but for once, she didn't mind. Instead of feeling like a brood mare under inspection, his perusal made her heart beat faster. She stared right back.

'How did you find me?' She was sure she hadn't told him where she lived.

'Oh, there are only two houses down this lane, and since the lights were on in this one, I took a chance. You live here? I don't think I've ever seen you before.'

'No, this cottage belongs to my grandparents. I'm just visiting. Oh, and my uncle owns the other house you mentioned.'

'Ah, I see.'

They studied each other for a moment longer and Estrid wasn't sure what she was expected to do now. He'd checked on her and she had reassured him she was unharmed. Was there more? Social interaction in this century wasn't something she knew much about. In the end, she did what anyone in her time would do – extend hospitality.

'Would you like to come in? I was just about to have some hot chocolate and cheese sandwiches. You're welcome to join me.'

Törn looked startled, then his smile widened. 'Sure, thanks. That would be great. If you're certain you don't mind? I didn't have dinner yet so I'm starving.'

'No, please, come in.'

Perhaps she ought not invite a strange man into the house, but she didn't feel threatened and she knew how to handle herself if he should suddenly decide to attack her. He didn't seem the type, though, and she reckoned she was safe with him. Soon, they were seated in the glass room at the back of the house, which her grandmother called a 'veranda'. Estrid loved it as it was warm and cosy, yet you could see all around you. Törn seemed to agree.

'This is a wonderful place, isn't it? Fantastic views over the lake.'

'Yes, it's my favourite room in the house,' Estrid agreed.

'And man, this is delicious! I haven't had hot chocolate since I was a kid when my gran used to make it for me.'

'Really? I have it whenever I can.' Estrid couldn't imagine living in the twenty-first century and not having this beverage on a regular basis.

He grinned at her, his eyes twinkling. 'Have a sweet tooth, do you?'

Thankfully he didn't appear to require a reply to that as she wasn't quite sure what he meant. How could your teeth be sweet? Although her Swedish was good, some of the phrases people used went over her head.

'Tell me more about this club of yours,' she suggested. She wasn't sure what a club was but gathered it was something like a *hirð*, a band of men bound together, in this case presumably by their love of motorcyles.

Törn made a face. 'Not much to tell. It was started years ago and my dad used to run it. I sort of inherited the leadership from him when he passed away. To tell you the truth, I'm sick and tired of it, and I'm not sure it's what I want to do any longer.' He shook his head. 'Actually, it's becoming more and more difficult to keep control of the members. Don't know if I can be bothered, you know? But on the other hand, they'll never let me go. I know too much.'

'How do you mean?'

He hesitated. 'I shouldn't really tell you, but the club is involved in some shady stuff. Nothing terrible, but not within the law. I want nothing to do with it, but I've no idea how to escape. They'd always find me if I tried to leave.'

Estrid didn't ask what sort of 'shady stuff' he was talking about. Probably better not to know. She could think of one place he could go where his friends would never find him, but doubted he'd believe her if she mentioned it. Most people had trouble grasping the concept of time travel.

'Well, I hope you find a solution,' was all she said.

'Yeah, me too. Listen, I'd better go back to make sure there's nothing bad happening. Can't trust any of them, especially if they've been drinking.' He stood up and carried his plate and mug into the kitchen. 'Thanks very much for feeding me, and apologies once again for earlier.'

'You're welcome.'

Estrid walked him to the door. When she'd opened it, he turned to look down on her. 'It was lovely meeting you.' Before she had a chance to protest, he bent to give her a soft kiss, then he melted into the night. She stood still, putting her fingers to her lips where she could still feel the imprint of his mouth on hers. He'd barely touched her, but a tingling sensation spread right down to her toes. She'd been kissed before, but never had it affected her like that.

She must be tired, she decided. It had been a long day.

Estrid was lying on a towel on the jetty the following day, basking in the warm rays of the summer sun. She knew she ought not to, as usually only thralls had tanned skin and she was turning a deep shade of gold, but it was so nice she couldn't resist. And it didn't really matter anyway as she wasn't hoping to attract anyone at home. She almost laughed out loud at the thought of them seeing her in the tiny bathing garments Mia had bought for her. They were barely more than a few triangles of cloth tied on with string. Anyone in her time would be scandalised.

She sat up in an instant when the planks shook beneath her, and grabbed the knife which she had placed under the towel in case it was needed. Squinting into the sun, at first, she only saw the outline of a huge man, but when she heard his rumbling voice saying 'Hey', she relaxed and allowed the knife to stay hidden.

'Törn! What are you doing here?' She hadn't expected to see him again, although a part of her had hoped he might stop by. Especially after that brief kiss. The incident with the motorcycle was more or less forgotten.

He put his hands in the pockets of his trousers and looked slightly sheepish. 'I, um, wanted to check on you again, to make sure there were no ill effects. You know, after yesterday. But if you'd rather I didn't bother you, just say, and I'll leave you to your sunbathing.'

'No, it's fine. Come and sit down if you want.' She spread out the second towel she'd been using as a pillow. The jetty could give you splinters if you didn't have a barrier against it.

'OK, I'd love to.'

To her astonishment, he shucked off his shirt in one swift motion, flinging it over his head and onto the grass nearby. His shoes and socks followed, then he unbuttoned his trousers and pushed them down his legs, leaving only a pair of very small black ones that moulded to his shape. Estrid just blinked and couldn't take her eyes off him. He was magnificently made and his many muscles rippled in the sunlight under smooth, tanned skin.

He caught her staring and grinned. 'What? You've never seen a nearly naked man before?'

'Er, no.'

'Huh?' He stopped what he was doing and his smile faded. 'Are you serious?'

'Yes.'

'Oh, shit, I'm sorry. I didn't mean to embarrass you. Should I get dressed again?' He held his trousers in front of him as if unsure what to do.

Estrid shook her head. 'No, it's fine. Leave it.' She swallowed hard. If only she could stop staring perhaps this wouldn't be so awkward.

'O-kaaay.' He put the trousers on the ground and walked over to sit on the towel next to her. 'So are you part of some sort of cult or something?'

'No.' Not that she knew what that was. 'It's just that my parents are a bit strict about my interactions with men.'

'Interactions, eh? I see. Well, please tell me if I make you feel uncomfortable. I really wouldn't want to do that.'

'Don't worry about it.' Estrid lay down and closed her eyes and she heard Törn do the same. A few moments later, she felt his fingers reaching for hers and twining with them.

'I really wanted to see you again,' he said, his voice low and mesmerising. 'You were so fierce last night, when we first met. You really took me by surprise, in the best way possible. I'd half expected tears when I scared you like that, to be honest, yet you told me off. Quite rightly, too. I'm a big guy, and most people don't stand up to me. It was refreshing.'

She scoffed. 'I'm not that delicate. In fact, I'm usually tough and fear nothing. I was surprised, is all. I can look after myself. My uncles trained me in self-defence and my father taught me how to wield a knife properly.' Not all girls were brought up that way, but in her family they believed it was necessary.

'Oh yeah?' His fingers squeezed hers and didn't let go. 'Well, I was impressed.'

They swam in the lake and lazed about in the sun for the rest of the afternoon, and Estrid liked the way Törn treated her as a friend. There was none of the usual reserve she always felt from the men who courted her. Instead, he started a water fight, then challenged her to a swimming race. When she protested that he'd let her beat him on purpose, he just laughed.

'I'm trying to be a gentleman,' he told her. Although she didn't know what that was, she gathered he meant he was being noble because she was a woman.

'You don't need to be,' she retorted, but didn't understand the heated look in his eyes when he replied.

'Oh yes, I do.'

Törn ended up staying for supper again, although this time he offered to cook. He made them something he said were 'omelettes', light and fluffy eggs with added ingredients and cheese. A mixture of raw vegetables called a salad was added, and some bread warmed in the oven. Estrid enjoyed the meal very much and said so.

'I'm glad.' He grinned. 'I'm doing my best to impress you.'

'Are you? Why?'

'I would have thought that was obvious. I like you. Really like you. And I want to get to know you better in every way.'

His words made her shiver, whether with anticipation or excitement, she wasn't sure. 'What if you find out things you don't like about me?'

He shrugged. 'Doubtful. From where I'm sitting, you're pretty much perfect.'

She rolled her eyes. 'I didn't mean the way I look. Men are always commenting about that.'

'I bet.' He frowned. 'You don't have a boyfriend already, do you? Or a husband? I mean, you would have said, right?'

'No, I don't. I've never had one.' She knew about boyfriends, as Mia had told her how these matters were conducted in this century. It seemed strange to her that you would try out several men – or a whole lot of them in some cases – in order to find one that suited you. Although it sort of made sense if it helped you to end up with one you were truly compatible with.

Törn stared at her as if she'd sprouted wings. 'What? How is that possible? Is this to do with your parents again?'

'In a way. I . . . come from a place where it is frowned upon. You marry one person and that is it, mostly, unless you later find you have a very good reason for divorce.'

He shook his head as if he couldn't quite take this in. 'But you're gorgeous! How is it that you're not married already then? You're not too young, are you?'

'No, I've seen . . . I mean, I am twenty-four.' She remembered at the last moment that people here didn't count age in winters but in years. 'As for why I'm not married, I haven't found a man I trust yet.'

'Trust? What about attraction? Like, I'm insanely attracted to you right now. I'm sure I can't be the only one.'

'There have been a few I could possibly have imagined myself marrying, but as I said, I didn't trust their motives. They might genuinely desire me, but I have other . . . advantages they could be coveting more.' She decided to come clean since he didn't look as though he understood what she was talking about. 'Look, my father is very powerful and rich, and anyone who marries me will benefit from that. How can I be sure that's not their primary motive for wanting to wed me?'

'Ah, I see.' Törn smiled. 'Well, believe me, that is the last thing on my mind when I look at you.' He sent her a glance that was so heated she felt it burn all the way down to her toes.

'Er . . .'

'Sorry, I'm making you uncomfortable again. If you've really never done this before, I can't imagine how you feel about me hitting on you.'

It was Estrid's turn to frown. 'You're not hitting me. I wouldn't let you. Like I said, I can defend myself.'

He tilted his head to one side. 'I know. That's not what I meant. Am I right in thinking Swedish is not your first language?'

'Yes. I mean, it isn't.'

'Then what is? You only have a very soft accent.'

'Um, Icelandic.' Mia and Haakon had told her this was the closest living language to hers in this era.

'That makes sense. So when you say my name, is that in your language? And by the way, I like how it sounds. Thorn.' He put a hand over one of hers on the table and without thinking she turned hers over so their palms fitted together. Heat flared between them again.

'Yes, *Thorn*. So if you're not about to hit me, what did that mean?' She gazed into his eyes, which were fixated on hers.

'That I was flirting with you. Trying to get you to reciprocate my attraction so that I can touch you a little. Like this.' He nodded at their joined hands. 'And perhaps more?'

'Oh. Good.'

He huffed out a surprised laugh. 'Good? You don't mind?'

'No.' A part of her was appalled at her forwardness. She would never have behaved this way in her own century. Perhaps the freedom here was going to her head, but she wanted this man to touch her. More than she'd ever wanted anything.

'Well, then . . .' He stood up and came round to her side of the table, taking her hands to pull her onto her feet. 'Can I kiss you?'

She nodded, and his arms came round her waist, drawing her close. This time when his mouth came down on hers, it lingered. He dropped tiny kisses all along her lips, then licked the seam. When she gasped and opened up, his tongue met hers, tentatively at first, then moving more confidently. He must have realised she had no idea what to do, because he murmured, 'Play along with me, baby. Just do the same as me.'

She didn't know why he was calling her a baby, but it sounded like an endearment so she took it as such. She learned quickly that kissing with tongues was a game she enjoyed. Very much so. Their kisses became deeper, more demanding, and she twined her arms round his neck. Instinctively, she stood on tiptoes and tried to get even closer to him, rubbing against him in the process. He groaned.

'Baby, if you do that, I won't be able to be a gentleman for much longer.'

'Um, what?'

He bent his head and whispered in her ear, 'I'll want to take you to bed and I don't think you're ready for that yet. Not if you've never been kissed before.'

'Oh, right. I'm sorry.' Embarrassingly, she was sure that physically she *was* ready for him to bed her, but she barely knew this man and appreciated his restraint. She tried to pull away, but he held her tight and stroked her cheek with his thumb, while gazing into her eyes.

'No, it's fine. I want to teach you things, and that means I have to tell you how you're affecting me as well. I loved it when you rubbed up against me, but it has consequences.' He pushed her gently against his lower half, where she could feel exactly what he meant. 'I don't want to scare you so we'll take it slow, OK?'

'Thank you.'

Törn came over every day for the rest of that week, sometimes in the afternoon, sometimes later. He told her he wasn't working at the moment as it was the summer holidays, which seemed fortuitous as normally he wouldn't have been able to spend so much time with her.

Estrid looked forward to his visits with anticipation fizzing through her veins. She knew it was probably wrong, but she couldn't help herself. Each time he came, his lessons in touching progressed a little further, but he kept his word and continued to act as a gentleman. A part of her was beginning to wish he wouldn't, but the more sensible part was appalled at herself.

'My grandparents will be coming tomorrow for a few days, so I won't be able to see you then,' she told him on the Thursday. Ordinarily, the days of the week meant nothing to her, but she knew this because her grandmother had telephoned to remind her.

'Damn, that's a shame.' Törn looked chagrined, then frowned. 'You don't want them to know about me visiting you? Is it because I'm a biker? Not everyone likes us and I guess your grandparents might not think me good enough for you.'

Estrid felt her cheeks heat up. 'No, that's not it. I'm just not sure what I'd tell them. I mean . . . what are we doing? Are you . . . er, courting me?'

He chuckled. 'I suppose you could say that. I'm serious about wanting to be with you, as a couple I mean. My friends would call it "dating exclusively".'

'What does that entail?' She wished she had paid more attention to the relationship customs of this era, but it had never affected her before.

He pulled her into his arms and gave her a soft kiss. 'It means I want you to promise to be mine and not so much as look at any other man. And I'll be yours, never noticing any other women. It usually also means we'd sleep together, when you're ready for that.'

'For ever?'

He shrugged. 'Most people don't make that sort of commitment until they've been together for a while.' He leaned back and his gaze searched hers intently. 'But I get the feeling that's not good enough for you, am I right? You need more from me.'

She bit her lip. She was aware that in this time there were ways of preventing pregnancy, which meant couples could sleep together without any consequences. It was like being married, but many times over. She wasn't sure how she felt about that. And if she should ever marry in her own era, her husband might realise she wasn't untouched. Should she risk it?

'Hey, we've only known each other for a week.' He reached out to brush her hair behind one ear. 'Let's take it slowly, OK? If you don't want your grandparents to know, I'll stay away, but I'd prefer to meet them and not sneak around. We can tell them how we met and that we're just friends.'

'I suppose. Very well, come over for the evening meal tomorrow and I'll introduce you.' Perhaps it would be good to get Mia's perspective on this dilemma. Estrid had always been able to talk to her grandmother about everything.

*

'You really like this man, don't you?'

Mia had seen through their claim of friendship almost immediately, but luckily, she hadn't said anything until Törn had left.

Estrid hung her head. 'Yes. Was it that obvious?'

'Oh, sweetheart, of course it was. You didn't take your eyes off him the whole time he was here.' Mia chuckled.

The two of them were sitting on the veranda while her grandfather had gone out fishing. It was his way of relaxing. Estrid sighed. 'I don't know what to do. Please, tell me!'

'I can't make that decision for you, but perhaps you ought to come clean and let Törn know the truth before you take things further. It's not fair to keep him in the dark. I could see that he's being very patient with you, and he's clearly guessed you're not like other girls. But unless you confess where you're from, he'll never understand your dilemma. Not really.'

'That's true. Thank you. You've been a great help.'

They didn't discuss the matter again, but before Mia and Haakon left to go back to the city, Mia surreptitiously handed Estrid a small box. 'Keep these by your bedside,' she whispered. 'And if you do decide to sleep with Törn, make sure he wears one of them, otherwise say no.'

'Oh, th-thank you.' Estrid was supremely embarrassed, but grateful all the same.

When Törn came over the following evening, she was determined to give him all the facts. After they'd eaten the takeaway pizzas he'd brought, she sat him down on the veranda.

'Törn, there is something I have to tell you. It might affect the way you see me and . . . well, you need to know. But you must swear an oath to keep it a secret. Can you do that?'

His eyebrows rose. 'Sure. Whatever it is, your secret is safe with me.'

'Swear on your honour,' she demanded.

Looking slightly bemused, he humoured her. 'I swear on my honour. You have my oath I won't tell a soul.'

She launched into her confession, talking as fast as she could in order to get it out of the way. His eyes grew round, his expression serious, and his mouth fell open. When she'd finished, he whispered, 'No way! You're having me on.'

'Er, what? I'm telling the truth. I could prove it to you, but I don't think you're ready to meet my parents yet.' And she wasn't sure the time-travel device would work on him, unless they were truly together as a couple. That's how it usually worked, in her family's experience.

She gave him a moment to gather his thoughts. He was clearly struggling, opening and closing his mouth several times as if he wasn't sure how to phrase what he wanted to say. Finally, he just shook his head. 'I don't believe it. It's too fantastical. There's no such thing as time travel.'

He stood up to pace in front of her, but she stayed seated. It was a lot to take in and if she hadn't grown up with this knowledge, she would have felt the same.

Stopping in front of her, he took her hands and pulled her up and into his arms, frowning down at her. 'If you don't want to sleep with me, you have only to say so. I don't force women into bed and I'm happy to just spend time with you.'

Estrid shook her head. 'I do want to sleep with you. I merely wanted to explain to you why it is a difficult decision for me. In a couple of weeks, I have to go back to my time. Then my father will continue his efforts to marry me to someone he wants an alliance with. Whoever my future husband is will presumably realise that I'm not untouched. You men can tell, right?'

'Um . . . not always.' He searched her gaze with his. 'You are really serious? And you can prove it?'

'Yes, but like I said, I don't think you'd want to go there yet.

I mean, if you wanted to marry me, I'd take you, but my father isn't going to appreciate me bringing home a man who has no intention of staying with me for the rest of my life.'

He stared at her for a while longer, then captured her lips in a fierce kiss, his arms wrapping around her to pull her close. After plundering her mouth thoroughly, he leaned his forehead on hers. 'I do, actually.'

'What?' Her head was swimming with lust and Estrid wasn't sure what they were talking about.

'I want to stay with you for the rest of our lives. I want to marry you. I want to go to the past with you. I want *you*, any way I can have you.' He kissed her again, as if he couldn't help himself. 'I'm crazy about you, and I've never felt this way before, ever.'

'Oh!'

He smiled. 'Do you think I'd survive in your time? What would I do there?'

'I don't know. Do you have enough silver to buy a farm?'

'Silver? Is that what you pay with?'

'Mm-hm. The more, the better. If you really wanted to come with me, you could do what Uncle Ivar did – he sold almost everything he owned here and bought silver to melt into ingots and armbands and brought it with him.' Estrid was still dizzy, but told herself not to get too excited. Törn might change his mind, although there was one other point she wanted to make. 'If you come with me, the people in your club would never find you.'

He grinned and pulled her in for a bear hug. 'You're right! That's genius.' He let go of her and started pacing again. 'Right, I need to think about this. It's all a bit sudden, but it feels right. Like it was meant to be.'

'The Norns,' Estrid muttered.

'What was that?'

'They weave the strands of fate. They must have meant for us to meet.'

'Hmm.' He didn't look as though he believed that, but when he came over to kiss her once more, she forgot about it. There was only the sensation of his strong arms around her, his soft lips on hers. She wanted to stay like that for ever.

To her surprise, however, he suddenly let go of her again and fell to one knee in front of her. 'Estrid – oh, God, I must be mad because I don't even know your surname – but Estrid, baby, will you do me the honour of being my wife? Marry me, please?'

It was her turn to gape like a fish, then she laughed and pulled him to his feet. 'Of course I will. But you might need to speak to my father first and you'll have to pay him a bride-price.'

'Bride-price. Right. Sure. Whatever you say.' Törn's expression was dazed, and he put his hands either side of her face. 'So no sleeping together until we're married, I take it.'

'I didn't say that. I consider us betrothed now, so that means we could perhaps bend the rules a little . . .'

He kissed her again, a hot, fierce melding of mouths that had them both breathless in moments. 'You're killing me,' he whispered, as his mouth blazed a trail down her neck, nibbling on the soft skin. 'I want you so much, Estrid.'

'Then take me upstairs. My grandmother left me a box with . . . those things that stop me having a child.'

Törn laughed and groaned at the same time. 'Oh my God,' he muttered. 'Your grandmother doesn't trust me to buy those myself? Then how am I ever going to convince your father I'm worthy of you?'

'Never mind them. Come.' Estrid pulled him towards the staircase and up to her bedroom under the eaves. 'Teach me what to do, Törn. I want to learn everything.'

*

'You're absolutely sure about this?' Haakon was staring intently at Törn, his expression worried. 'The Vikings did have divorce, but I don't think it was very common.'

Törn smiled. 'Relax. As long as we're allowed to marry, there isn't going to be a divorce. I swear, this is what I want. I'll do whatever it takes to be with Estrid for ever, and to tell you the truth, it's going to be a relief to get away from here. I've written a letter of resignation to the club, sold everything I own except my motorcycle . . .' That was staying in Mia and Haakon's shed as he couldn't bear to part with it, and they'd promised to look after it until he and Estrid came to visit. 'I've bought as much silver as I could lay my hands on, and I'm ready to face her father's wrath. If he wants me to fight him to prove my worth, I'll do it.'

He'd even started learning Old Norse, and Estrid was pleased that she could teach him something and not just the other way round.

'It's time to go,' she said, hugging her grandparents goodbye. 'Thank you for everything and we hope to see you next summer, if all goes well.'

Truth to tell, she was a bit nervous, but she knew in her heart she was doing the right thing, and if her parents didn't accept Törn, she'd return with him to his time.

Their journey to the past was as unpleasant as time travel always was, leaving them dizzy and nauseous, but it passed swiftly. Estrid knew that her parents would be at Haukr's place waiting for her, as that was what they had agreed before she left for the future. With determination, she took Törn's hand and headed out of the forest and up the slope to the longhouse.

'Are you ready?' She smiled at him and he smiled back.

Bending to give her a quick kiss, he nodded. 'Ready as I'll ever be, *ást mín*. Did I say that right?'

She laughed. 'Yes, you did.'

They entered the hall hand in hand, and found everyone seated for the evening meal. A hush fell on the assembled company as they walked the length of the room towards the dais, where her parents were sitting with their hosts. Their eyes widened at the sight of her and Törn, and her mother exclaimed, 'Estrid! What have you done now?'

'Nothing. Yet,' she lied. 'Mother, Father, this is Henrik Törn Arvidsson and he has something to ask you.' His father's name had been Arvid, and they'd decided it was best if he used the patronymic as was the Viking custom.

Törn bowed to them and said in his best Old Norse. 'It is a pleasure to meet you. I would like to marry your daughter, please.'

There were gasps from people all around, and Estrid saw Haukr try to hide a grin while his wife smacked him on the arm. There were definite snickers from Cadoc, Bryn, Gytha and Estrid's brothers and sister, but she ignored them, fixing her gaze on her parents.

'I'm sorry, I haven't had time to teach him much more than that, but Mother, you can converse with him in Swedish. Please consider his request or I will be going to live in . . . with him permanently.' She caught herself just in time as not everyone in this hall knew about time travel.

'Who is he?' That was her father's question as he tried to stare intimidatingly at Törn.

Estrid was pleased to see that her betrothed kept calm and held her father's gaze with one of his own. It was probably a good thing that his tattoos were covered by the shirt and tunic she'd made for him, and he already had long hair so he didn't look too out of place. Plus, he was a big, intimidating man.

'I told you. Can we eat first, then discuss this later?'

Hrafn hesitated, then gave a curt nod. 'We will definitely be discussing this, daughter.'

His tone should have made her scared, but it didn't. He'd never frightened her, and she knew he'd give in eventually. He merely had to mull things over first.

'Excellent. Come, Törn, I want to introduce you to my siblings.'

In the end, it was Estrid's mother who smoothed things over. She'd had a quiet chat with Törn and managed to convince Hrafn of his sincerity.

'Let's give the man a chance. He deserves it for being brave enough to come here, if nothing else.'

'Very well.' Hrafn capitulated. 'But I think it might be a good idea for the two of you to live with us for the first year so that Törn can learn all he needs to know before he has his own domains.'

When this was translated for him, Törn agreed. 'That sounds sensible. Are you happy with that, baby?' he asked Estrid.

'Very.' She squeezed his hand, which she hadn't let go of for an instant since they arrived. 'As long as we can be together, that's all that matters.'

'Good, that's settled then.' Törn bowed to her parents. 'Thank you for accepting me into your family. I am honoured and I will take good care of your daughter.'

He sent Estrid a secret look that promised so much more and she knew she had finally found the right man for her. She would never feel left out ever again.

Time Travel Discussion Points

What if you were able to time-travel for real – what would be some of the things you'd need to think about?

Here are some suggestions from a recent talk I gave together with my author friend Anna Belfrage*:

- First of all, you'd need to know roughly where you were going – what time period and place, so hopefully you have a reliable time-travel device.
- You'd have to research the clothing so that you can wear authentic garments. The worst thing you could do would be to turn up in twenty-first-century clothes as that would put you under suspicion right from the start. Explaining the workings of a zipper or elastic material to a Viking, for example, would not be easy!
- Make sure you have enough gold and/or silver with you to pay for food and accommodation, and perhaps even to use as bribery.
- Find out which language was spoken at the time you think you'll end up in and try to learn some of it if possible.

- Keep a low profile and do your best to blend in – no loudly voiced modern opinions on feminism and so on, as that could result in you being killed.
- Don't show off your knowledge in any way, especially not if you are female.
- Try to accept the mindset of the time even if it goes against everything you know and believe – you won't be able to change anything immediately.
- Be prepared for lower standards of hygiene – you'll be lucky if you even get a bath now and then.
- Get as many vaccinations as you can before leaving the modern world so that you can survive illnesses in the past with ease.
- And don't time-travel if you're ill yourself! A mere twenty-first-century cold might kill people in the past as the germs will be different.
- Be prepared to live a very simple life with a monotonous diet and no modern amenities – no indoor toilets, no showers, no electricity, etc.
- Also be prepared to work VERY hard!
- Don't drink anything that hasn't been boiled.
- Accept that there will be violence on a scale we are not used to – it was a case of survival of the fittest in every way.
- Do NOT try to change history!
- Remember – there will be no chocolate, tea or coffee if you end up before the eighteenth century! Can you handle it?

(*You can find more information about Anna at www.annabelfrage.com)

Time is no barrier for a love that is destined to be.

She couldn't be sure that she had travelled through time . . . but deep down she just knew. And her only way back had just disappeared.

Available now from

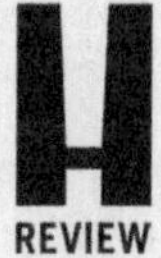

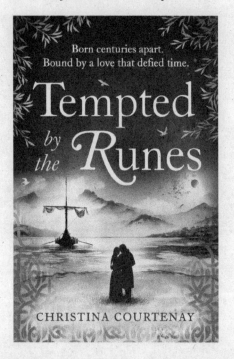

He travelled through time to capture her heart.

Ivar steps back in time determined to follow his destiny, and find the woman who has called to his heart . . .

Available now from

And don't miss Christina Courtenay's sweepingly romantic standalones!

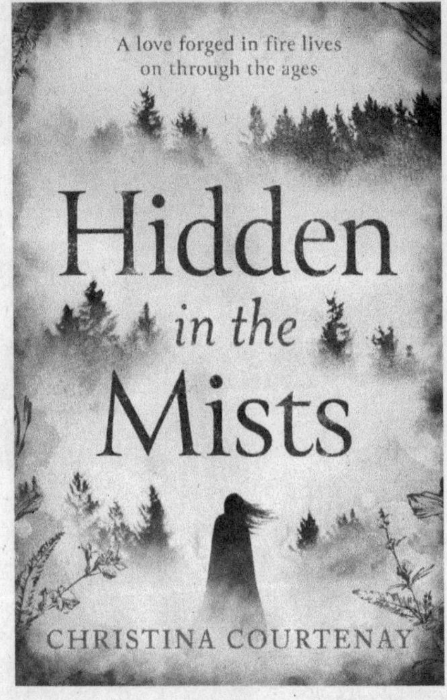

A love forged in fire lives on through the ages . . .

Available now from

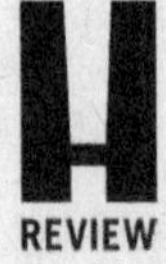